"[A] history mystery in fine Victorian style! Anna Lee Huber's spirited debut mixes classic country-house mystery with a liberal dash of historical romance."

—*New York Times* bestselling author Julia Spencer-Fleming

"Riveting. . . . Huber deftly weaves together an original premise, an enigmatic heroine, and a compelling Highland setting."

—*New York Times* bestselling author Deanna Raybourn

"[A] fascinating heroine. . . . A thoroughly enjoyable read!"

—*USA Today* bestselling author Victoria Thompson

"Romance, suspense, mystery . . . add up to a fine read."

—*Kirkus Reviews*

"Gripping. . . . Fans of C. S. Harris's Regency mysteries will be pleased."

—*Publishers Weekly*

"[Huber] designs her heroine as a woman who straddles the line between eighteenth-century behavior and twenty-first-century independence."

—New York Journal of Books

"[A] must read. . . . One of those rare books that will both shock and please readers."

—Fresh Fiction

"Anyone who enjoys historical mysteries, atmospheric settings, and strong female investigators should have Huber on their automatic buy list."

—Criminal Element

"One of the best historical mysteries that I have read this year."

—Cozy Mystery Book Reviews

A DECEPTIVE COMPOSITION

ANNA LEE HUBER

BERKLEY PRIME CRIME
New York

BERKLEY PRIME CRIME
Published by Berkley
An imprint of Penguin Random House LLC
penguinrandomhouse.com

Library of Congress Cataloging-in-Publication Data

Names: Huber, Anna Lee, author.
Title: A deceptive composition / Anna Lee Huber.
Description: First edition. | New York: Berkley Prime Crime, 2024. |
Series: A Lady Darby mystery
Identifiers: LCCN 2023058345 (print) | LCCN 2023058346 (ebook) |
ISBN 9780593639412 (trade paperback) | ISBN 9780593639429 (ebook)
Subjects: LCGFT: Detective and mystery fiction. | Novels.
Classification: LCC PS3608.U238 D43 2024 (print) |
LCC PS3608.U238 (ebook) | DDC 813/.6—dc23/eng/20240109
LC record available at https://lccn.loc.gov/2023058345
LC ebook record available at https://lccn.loc.gov/2023058346

First Edition: June 2024

Printed in the United States of America
1st Printing

For my cousin Kim.
A dear friend and one of my earliest playmates.
Your grace and resilience amaze me.

A Deceptive Composition

CHAPTER I

Everything that deceives may be said to enchant.

—PLATO

OCTOBER 1832

WARWICKSHIRE, ENGLAND

Come see who I found wandering the corridors."

I looked up from the sheet music at the sound of my father-in-law's voice, my fingers trailing to a stop along the pianoforte keys. I couldn't help but smile at the sight of Lord Gage ambling toward me, still favoring his recently injured right leg, with the warm and wriggling bundle of my daughter cradled in his arms.

"Wandering, was she?" I countered in amusement. Given the fact that she was all of nearly seven months old and unable to crawl yet, the idea of her wandering anywhere was absurd. It seemed far more likely he'd liberated her from her nanny's care in the nursery.

"Well . . . I could tell she was thinking it. If only she'd been able to work out the mechanics of this thing called walking first." Lord Gage grinned down at Emma, and she squealed happily in response before returning her gaze to the object which had captured her attention.

Truth be told, it was the same object that had caught *my* attention when I'd first entered the drawing room at Bevington Park upon our arrival two months prior. The Broadwood grand pianoforte had gleamed in the sunlight streaming through the tall western-facing windows, practically beckoning to be played. One might have been forgiven for believing that the manor's owner was an accomplished pianist, such was the pride of place the instrument held, but I knew this to be untrue. In fact, the next day when I'd sat upon the bench, I'd suspected I was the first person to do so since the pianoforte had been delivered and tuned. The instrument was purely part of the chamber's aesthetic, for Lord Gage decorated his homes for effect rather than to suit his comfort and taste. But given the enjoyment I'd received from playing the magnificent instrument, this was one matter in which it would be disingenuous for me to complain.

I ran my fingers lightly over the keys, repeating the last phrase of music I'd played from one of Schubert's impromptus. My husband, Sebastian Gage, had gifted me the sheet music of the set of impromptus for my birthday that spring, but I'd had little time to practice them in earnest until our arrival in Warwickshire. Some of the pieces were beyond my ability, and I would never be able to play them with great skill, but I had become determined to master the others. Or at least to do a credible job in performing them for my own pleasure.

Emma cooed in response, tipping forward in her grandfather's arms and reaching toward me. I sat her on my lap and predictably she lurched toward the keys, slamming her open palms down with relish as the pianoforte issued a series of discordant notes. There was nothing for it but to smile and hold fast to her little body lest she tumble forward in her unrestrained efforts.

"A veritable prodigy," Lord Gage proclaimed even as he winced at one particularly strident chord.

Though I'd been given over two months to grow accustomed to it, it was still difficult sometimes to reconcile the affectionate man before me with the father-in-law I had known. And if it was difficult for me, it must be doubly so for my husband, who had only known his father as cold, contemptuous, and impossible to please. Not that that side of Lord Gage had vanished entirely. He was still hard and critical, especially when crossed, but at least he was making an effort to build a relationship with us based on mutual respect and trust rather than merely obligation and duty. He might never hold as much esteem or devotion for his son or me as he did his granddaughter, but that was something we were both willing to accept. Particularly given the fact that Lord Gage was Emma's only living grandparent.

"What's this I hear?" Gage declared as he strode into the room. His golden hair was rumpled, and his sun-bronzed cheeks flushed from his morning ride. "Our daughter is giving her first recital and I wasn't invited."

Emma offered him a toothless grin, her golden curls—so like her father's—escaping from the sides of her cap. A trail of drool dribbled from her bottom lip and I managed to catch it before it fell to the ivory keys.

"Oh, this is just the prelude," I replied.

Gage flinched as Emma brought her hands down with more strength than I'd anticipated, producing several resounding crashes. Her father struggled to maintain his grin. "Oh, yes?"

Lord Gage chuckled. "Which direction did you ride today? Toward the lake?"

"Aye, and down through the pastures near Weethley."

I listened absentmindedly as the men discussed the estate—which my husband would one day inherit from his father. Lord Gage had been granted his barony and this property by the king a little over two years prior for his services during the late war with Napoléon and his more recent efforts on the sovereign and his friends' behalf as a gentleman inquiry agent. As such, Gage had spent little time here since then, and he had much to learn.

Truth be told, when we'd first arrived in late August, I'd been a little overawed. I hadn't expected a hovel, but neither had I anticipated this prime bit of real estate. Clearly it spoke to the immensity of either the king's affection for, or gratitude to, my father-in-law. Perhaps both.

Something that immediately raised questions in the cynical side of my brain. What exactly had Lord Gage done to inspire such gratitude? What delicate matter had he investigated or orchestrated to the sovereign's satisfaction? After all, I was better acquainted than most with the secrets the wealthy, titled, and powerful might hide.

But I also acknowledged that my father-in-law's friendship with King William IV was long-standing. Lord Gage had served under his command on the HMS *Pegasus* when the king was still a younger son—never expected to inherit the Crown from his older brother—and he'd remained a faithful friend through all the years that followed. He would, though, be the first to admit that their friendship had only lasted because he had proved to be useful to the king and his friends. Even so, this estate was quite the reward for such efforts.

Of course, I had no idea what state it had been in when Lord Gage had been granted it, or to what expense he'd had to go to in order to restore and refurbish it. Many of the furnishings and interiors were new, but that might have been less from need and more from my father-in-law's desire that his home be all that was fashionable and au courant.

Regardless, upon seeing the size of the estate, Gage had begun to feel more keenly the responsibility he held to it. One day, he would not only be in charge of the manor, but also all the land and workings, and the people who labored upon it. Their care and management—and to a great extent their future prosperity—would rest on his shoulders. Of course, that day might be decades from now. But then again, it might be next week. The attacks made on Lord Gage in August had awakened us all to the realization that our loved ones' tomorrows were never guaranteed.

"Have you given any greater thought to the dower house?" Lord Gage asked.

Gage's eyes lifted to meet mine. "I have."

Deciding our ears had suffered enough punishment, and sensing Gage wished for me to take part in this conversation as much as I wanted to, I pushed to my feet. Emma immediately protested.

Gage set aside his riding gloves and crop and reached for her. "Now, what's all this fussing?" He lifted her high into the air, transforming her cries into laughter as he let his arms drop as if he might let her fall. He repeated this several times as we made our way over to the pair of rosewood sofas positioned near the hearth. A blanket lay folded over one arm and I spread it over the portion of open rug farthest from the crackling fire. Gage set Emma down with a pillow propped behind her lest she topple backward and Lord Gage produced one of her ragdolls from his coat pocket, handing it to her.

There were those who might say children had no place in the grand public rooms of such a stately home. That their proper domain lay in the nursery, and only the nursery. But I was not of that mind-set, and to my shock and somewhat utter disbelief, neither was Lord Gage. I had anticipated numerous arguments over the subject upon our arrival, but as often as not, *he* was the one removing his granddaughter from the nursery or brushing aside the messes babies inevitably made as inconsequential.

Of course, he might have felt differently if he'd been the one forced to clean spit-up from the Aubusson rug or spittle from the silk cushions. The maids and housekeeper might rightly have resented Emma for causing them extra work, but her big blue eyes and happy grins had charmed them as surely as her grandfather.

Gage turned to me with a contented smile as he settled onto the sofa beside me while his father leaned forward to jabber with Emma. My husband smelled of wind, sun, and horse, but it was something I'd grown accustomed to since our arrival in Warwickshire. He'd begun taking daily rides across the various parts of the estate, both for his own enjoyment and to better acquaint himself with the property. Upon occasion, I'd also suspected he was escaping his father, but given their contentious relationship in the past, those instances were far fewer than I'd anticipated. Sometimes I even joined him.

The country suited my husband. I'd noticed this before, but now it was driven home even further. With his charm and good looks, he might thrive among the civilized society in Mayfair, but he also needed space and fresh air to exert himself. If I'd thought him arresting before, his artlessly windswept locks and sun-bronzed skin now made him irresistible, particularly when he seemed perfectly at ease in his surroundings as I'd never seen him before. A fact that made me realize he'd done an astonishingly good job of hiding his enjoyment of the countryside from everyone—including me—until now.

Undoubtedly his reconciliation with his father had a great deal to do with his newfound sense of peace. But I could also tell that he liked it here in this pretty corner of Warwickshire. He liked it a great deal. Which softened me to the possibility my father-in-law soon broached.

"The dower house, then?" Lord Gage declared, sinking deeper into the aubergine damask cushions of his chair and adjusting his charcoal frock coat. "As you've already seen, it needs some work. But the bulk of the house is in excellent condition, and any changes you wish can be done to your specifications. I suspect we can find a foreman to begin the work almost as soon as you say the word."

Though he didn't say so, I could tell how earnestly my father-in-law wanted us to accept his offer. It was written in the glimmer of his gray eyes and the stiffness of his posture.

What he'd said was true. Overall, the dower house was in good condition, despite sitting vacant for a number of years. Situated in a forested glade, tucked out of sight on the opposite side of the estate, it was perhaps a mile-and-a-half's distance from Bevington Hall itself but still situated within the park. As a dower house, it was intended to be the abode of the current lord's predecessor's widow—usually his mother—but that did not mean it couldn't be put to other uses. As Lord Gage's title was newly created, and his mother was deceased, there was no one to occupy it in the traditional sense, so he had offered it to us.

"Sebastian told me you've been considering purchasing a country house of your own," Lord Gage added.

I turned to Gage, somewhat surprised he'd discussed the matter with his father.

"Why go to the bother and expense when there's already a good home here for you? One to which you can retreat whenever you wish." He spread his hands. "And after all, this entire estate *will* be yours one day. Why not set down your roots here now?"

Just three months' prior, merely the notion of such a thing would have been unthinkable, but now it was at least worth considering. It did seem rather silly to search for our own country house when his father owned an estate of such size and grandeur with a separate home ready-made for us. Truth be told, Bevington Park was more than large enough to accommodate a family ten times our size, but the chief argument against our settling here was my fear that proximity might breed contempt.

Just because Gage and his father had reconciled, and for the most part managed to rub along rather well together, did not mean this would last. If the past was any indicator, Lord Gage would exert his stubborn high-handedness at some point, or Gage and I would fail to behave in a manner his father deemed proper. Disagreements were inevitable but might be mitigated with at least a modicum of distance.

"I concede those are all valid points," I admitted.

"Thank you, Kiera," Lord Gage replied with a pleased curl to his lips before I could finish.

"*But . . .*" I stressed. "It's not a decision to be made hastily." I reached over to clasp Gage's hand. "However, it is something we certainly need to consider."

"What more is there to discuss?" Lord Gage retorted, exhibiting his more typical impatience when we refused to do as he wished. "I recognize you have your inheritance from your mother and your stipend from me to do whatever you wish with," he appealed to his son. "But why throw away your money on another property when you spend so much of the year in London and Edinburgh anyway? Not to mention the inquiries you undertake on my and your own behalf."

"All further valid points," Gage agreed. As a gentleman inquiry agent like his father, with me assisting him in this capacity, we often found ourselves visiting far-flung places on the isle of Britain, and even on one memorable occasion in Ireland. The time spent at our country estate would probably be minimal. My husband arched his eyebrows in warning. "But pressuring us will not get you the answer you want any faster."

Lord Gage turned to the side, exhaling in obvious frustration. "Yes, yes," he admitted. Something he would never have done before his brush with death. His gaze dipped to where Emma played on the floor, babbling to Rosie, her ragdoll. "I'm sure you know my reasons for wanting you here."

We did. Both the good and the bad. For despite his evident affection for Emma, and his increasingly more apparent fondness for us, he also wanted us close so that he could keep us under his thumb, so to speak. It was simply his nature, and something I never foresaw entirely changing.

"But the decision is yours, and I will say no more on it unless you have questions," he finished.

I lifted my gaze to the landscape hung over the mantel of the fireplace while Gage asked his father his intentions for the dilapidated folly crumbling at the far edge of the lake. The painting depicted Bevington Park some years prior, having been commissioned by a previous owner. Though I hadn't yet been able to definitively identify the artist from the style and brushstrokes, I was fairly certain it was an early Gainsborough, for it bore many of his hallmarks, yet I still remained unconvinced. The estate records might have been able to tell us the name of the painter, but Lord Gage's new steward had been unable to locate the invoice or listing in the account registers. The young man had grumbled at the state of many of the records, making me suspect his predecessor had been rather lax in his duties.

I was about to ask whether the landscape might be removed from the wall so that I could examine the back for any clues or markings when a rap on the drawing room door preceded the entry of the butler. Bowcott was rather merrier than I'd anticipated one of Lord Gage's staff to be. His eyes twinkled and crinkled at the corners as if privately amused. Even when confronted with his lordship's contempt, he remained unruffled.

"You asked to be notified when the post arrived, sir," he intoned, holding out a silver tray on which sat three neat piles.

Lord Gage retrieved the stack indicated and Bowcott pivoted to grin down at Emma as he made his way around her to deliver the letters meant for me and Gage. Then he inquired if we wished for tea.

"Not at the moment," I told him. "Thank you, Bowcott."

"Of course, my lady." He bowed at the waist before retreating.

"I have been waiting to hear from Melbourne on a matter," Lord Gage explained distractedly as he shuffled through his stack of correspondence.

I didn't pry further. It was obvious how vexing he'd found it during his recuperation from his gunshot wound and near poisoning not to be able to resume his life in London these past few months. Letters were his only way to keep in touch with the powerful men who so often relied upon him.

A swift glance through my own missives revealed letters from my sister, Alana; Lorna, my friend and Gage's cousin's wife; and Eleanor, the new Lady Marsdale, though I suspected her rascal of a husband had also slipped in some sort of irreverent note, as usual. Thoughts of Eleanor brought to mind her brother, Lord Henry Kerr, who also happened to be Gage's half brother—the product of Lord Gage's brief affair with the Duchess of Bowmont, Henry and Eleanor's mother.

Gage's discovery of Henry's relation to him, and his father's machinations to keep the matter from him, had been the main source of contention between father and son over the past year, a wound that was still healing. Henry had remained with us for most of the summer, even assisting to apprehend Lord Gage's attackers. But he had returned to the estate of his acknowledged father—the Duke of Bowmont—at the end of August to assist with some matters troubling the large brood with whom he'd been raised. Henry had hoped to pay us a visit here before the end of the year, but it was nearly November and we'd heard little from him.

I leaned over, curious whether Gage had received a missive from his brother.

Realizing my intent, he offered me a tight smile. "Not today."

I nodded, returning to my own correspondence. It was then that I noticed the taut silence issuing from my father-in-law. Peering up at his face, I noted the brackets of strain about his mouth and the intensity of his gaze as he stared down at one of the unopened letters in his hand. It was obvious something about it had unsettled him. His complexion even appeared paler.

Then, as I watched, his cheeks flushed and his fingers flexed around the missive, crumpling it almost into a ball as he turned his head to the side to look at the fire. My stomach dipped at this display of suppressed fury, but I couldn't let it pass without saying something. Not when Lord Gage looked up at that moment and caught me watching him.

"What is it?" I murmured.

Gage stilled, glancing at me before turning to his father.

Lord Gage's mouth twisted. "As tediously observant as always, I see," he groused, but I didn't take offense. Not when it was clear he was only venting his discomfort at having been studied in an unguarded moment.

"Who is it from?" I pressed softly. My eyes dipped to the letter still clasped between his fingers.

He stared me down for another moment before transferring his gaze to his son. I thought he might refuse to answer, but then his eyes lowered to the missive as his fingers loosened their grip. "Amelia Killigrew."

Gage and I exchanged a look.

"Who's Amelia Killigrew?" he asked for us both.

Silence stretched again, broken only by the tick of the ormolu clock on the side table and Emma's grunts and babbles.

"My aunt," Lord Gage finally replied. His eyes when they lifted to meet ours shimmered with repressed emotions. "Her maiden name was Roscarrock."

I straightened in realization. For Roscarrock was Lord Gage's mother's maiden name. He had long described them as smugglers and rogues, but two months prior he had elaborated upon this report. Not only were they smugglers and rogues in truth, but Lord Gage had been arrested at the tender age of eleven for taking part in their free trading. The magistrate overseeing his case had given him three options—go to prison, pay a hefty fine, or purchase a commission in the Royal Navy. His father had washed his hands of him, but his Grandfather Roscarrock had chosen the latter. So off Lord Gage went to begin what would prove to be a long and illustrious career in the navy, in return never speaking to his Roscarrock relatives ever again.

Or so he'd claimed.

CHAPTER 2

I thought you had no communication with them," I voiced in confusion.

"I don't," Lord Gage snapped, the sound loud in the still room. Loud enough to startle Emma, whose lip quivered for a moment as if she might burst into tears, before she settled again with her doll.

"Have they *tried* to communicate with you?" Gage asked, trying a different tack.

"Some years ago, yes. But not since . . ." His father broke off, turning away and leaving his thought unvoiced. "Not for some time."

I tilted my head, curious what he was originally going to say.

He glanced down at the letter in thinly veiled disgust. "I'm not sure why they're writing me now."

"You could open the letter and find out," I coaxed, supplying the obvious answer.

Lord Gage scowled.

I knew he was ashamed of his past. His relationship with his sons—and me—had taken a large leap forward when he'd willingly shared it with us. I suspected it was the first time he'd spoken of it to anyone in decades. His fear of his past being revealed and destroying his reputation was genuine, and that dread was not unfounded. The upper echelon of British society was notoriously fickle. A person could be feted one day and then utterly shunned the next. But Lord Gage had confided in us, nonetheless, trusting us to keep his secret.

However, just because he'd taken us into his confidence did not mean he'd confronted any of the darker emotions associated with that incident. The guilt of knowing his friend had been shot and killed by the same customs officers who had arrested him. The pain of his father's rejection. The anger at his grandfather and the Roscarrocks for exposing him to that life and not preventing him from coming to near ruin at such a young age. The shame of his having committed such a crime. In many ways, he was just as ashamed, angry, hurt, and guilt-ridden as he'd been at eleven; and those emotions had colored his life in ways he didn't realize.

For his own sake, his past needed to be dealt with, and his relatives—at least, those still living—faced. Otherwise, that past would continue to haunt him for the rest of his days, however long that might be. The trouble was convincing my father-in-law of it.

"You must be at least a little curious what the letter says," I prodded.

Lord Gage arched his chin. "Not in the slightest."

I realized I should have anticipated just such a response from the stubborn man, no matter the evidence to the contrary.

"Surely you're not intending to just toss it into the fire?" Gage queried with a furrowed brow.

I sat forward in alarm as my father-in-law dangled the

missive between two fingers before him as if contemplating exactly that. "You can't do that."

Lord Gage arched a single eyebrow in sardonic challenge.

"What if it's important?"

He scoffed. "I doubt it."

"At least let me read it."

His second eyebrow joined the first.

"Or Gage." Perhaps that was more amenable.

Gage set aside his own letters. "She's right, sir. We should at least discover what it says." He held out his hand, urging his father to give it to him.

Lord Gage glowered at it for a moment before heaving an aggrieved sigh. "If it will silence you both, I will read it." He broke the seal with rather more force than necessary, crinkling the paper as he unfolded it. "Though, as I've said, I'm certain it's a waste of time."

I sat back in relief, trying not to stare as he began perusing the contents. Deep scores appeared between his eyes, etching his brow. His square jaw hardened, and his gaze bored into the paper like he was wielding a chisel. When he finished, lowering it to his lap to gaze at the rug before him, I'd barely digested two sentences from my sister's letter.

I didn't speak, though I was dying to ask him what it said. Clearly its contents had not been a waste of time. Not if the somewhat stunned expression on his face was anything to judge by. Stunned and agitated.

"What is it?" Gage prodded this time.

"My Uncle Branok . . ." his father began haltingly.

I glanced at Gage, recalling that Branok had been one of the names of his Cornish ancestors he'd jestingly suggested we name our child when I was still expecting Emma.

"He became head of the family when my grandfather passed some years ago," Lord Gage finished explaining, proving he was well informed of at least some aspects of his Roscarrock relatives' lives. "He died almost a week ago."

My first thought was that this was sad, but it didn't quite explain his reaction. However, he wasn't finished.

"They . . ." He gestured with the letter. "Aunt Amelia—his sister, not his wife. She . . . and I suppose some of the others . . ." He fumbled his words. Something I'd never expected to witness my stern, collected father-in-law do. Inhaling a deep breath, he plowed onward. "She believes he was murdered." His visage turned forbidding. "And she wants us to investigate."

My eyes widened in surprise. Even after having investigated over a dozen murders, I still never expected it. I didn't know whether that was a virtue or a failing on my part.

"May I?" Gage asked, not waiting for his father's permission before rising to take the missive from his somewhat reluctant grasp.

He sat down beside me so that I might peruse the letter with him. It wasn't long. Perhaps a dozen lines in a small, spidery script.

"She does more than ask," Gage said. "She essentially *begs* us to come. Clearly, she's aware of our presence here with you." There was a question in his voice.

"It's been reported in some of the newspapers," I replied. In supplements to their articles about Lord Gage's attack in Yorkshire and our subsequent inquiry to apprehend his assailants. It had been foolish to think the shocking incident wouldn't find its way into print, especially when it involved not only a man as powerful as Lord Gage, but also his charming son and scandalous daughter-in-law. Our exploits often ended up in the broadsheets and newspapers, among the society pages if not the front page.

Gage nodded at this explanation. "Though she gives few

details about her brother's death and why she believes it to be murder."

Lord Gage made a rather rude noise beneath his breath as he pushed to his feet. "Because if it was murder, it was likely deserved. Probably a rival smuggler or some other disreputable undertaking."

Gage and I exchanged a speaking glance as his father turned to pace before the hearth, drawing Emma's interest. But Lord Gage was too caught up in his own unsettled thoughts to even notice his granddaughter's cooing.

"Do you know for a fact that they're still smuggling?" Gage broached carefully. "Perhaps they stopped after . . ." He broke off before saying the rest, knowing his father would know what he referred to.

"They never stopped," Lord Gage bit out crisply. "At least, I know they hadn't stopped as late as 1815," he conceded. "But I haven't kept abreast of it since then."

It was somewhat disheartening to hear the Roscarrocks had continued the practice even after a boy had been killed and another arrested, but then I didn't know how difficult it was to extricate oneself from such a business. Presumably there were a number of people involved in a smuggling operation—some of them less tolerant than others. Lord Gage's grandfather might not have been able to stop even if he'd wished to.

"From what I understand, the lower tariffs and new coastguard service have effectively curtailed smuggling along much of the coast," Gage said. "So perhaps those activities are now in the past."

Lord Gage halted in his pacing to pin his son with an incredulous look. "You don't know the Roscarrocks. If anyone was to find a way, it's them." He flicked his gaze up and down over Gage's appearance. "Where do you think you get your dogged perseverance from?" He turned away, muttering under his breath. "Where do you think I get mine?"

Emma's eyes followed him as he moved to stand before one of the tall windows flanking either side of the hearth, his hands clasped behind his back. It was the posture I imagined he'd adopted at the helm of one of his ships when he was a captain in the Royal Navy, though now he was surveying his gardens rather than the rolling sea. Ostensibly anyway. It was more likely he wasn't seeing anything, his thoughts lying so deep in the past that he didn't even notice his granddaughter fussing. Normally, he would have run to soothe her, but now he seemed unconscious of it.

Gage's brow creased in concern, and I pressed my hand to his where it rested in his lap, urging him to go to his father while I collected Emma.

"What is all this commotion?" I murmured to her as I lifted her and Rosie, tickling her chin with the ragdoll. She giggled as I crossed to tug on the bell-pull. It was almost time for Emma's morning nap, and Mrs. Mackay would undoubtedly be anticipating my summons.

"Why do you think Great-Aunt Amelia is so desperate for our help then?" Gage asked his father. "Do you think perhaps the authorities aren't taking the matter of Great-Uncle Branok's death seriously *because* of the family's history with smuggling? Could the authorities be involved?"

This was an angle I hadn't yet considered, but it was worth questioning. After all, a preventive officer had shot Lord Gage's friend all those years ago. Might another have shot Branok Roscarrock, either with or without provocation?

If that was what Amelia suspected, it made sense she hadn't mentioned it in her letter. After all, she'd acknowledged her nephew's continued estrangement from the family and pleaded that he not make it his excuse for refusing to come to their aid.

As such, she must be aware that any remark about customs officers was certain to dredge up unhappy memories and harden his heart toward them.

I didn't hear Lord Gage's response—if he even made one—for Mrs. Mackay arrived to collect Emma. "I saw that yawn," she whispered in her Scottish brogue as she retreated, prattling as ever to the child. "Off to dreamland wi' ye."

"I take it you wish to refuse?" I heard Gage ask as I crossed the room to join them.

Lord Gage turned his head sharply to glare at his son. "I cannot go back there."

I found it interesting to note that he'd said *cannot*, not *will not*.

"Even though this is what we do?" Gage responded. "Help people who have found themselves in situations where their loved ones have been harmed and may not receive justice. Even though they are still family—by blood, if not bonds of affection?"

Lord Gage's mouth screwed up in distaste. "You have a rather mawkish view of our roles as inquiry agents."

But neither Gage nor I took offense, recognizing this as an effort to distract us. Amelia's letter had dredged up all sorts of sentiments Lord Gage didn't want to confront, so he'd opted to lash out at us instead. To attempt to turn the focus to us rather than himself. It didn't work.

"Why are you so reluctant to return?" I posited.

Lord Gage turned to look at me as if I'd grown two heads.

"I mean, other than because of what happened there almost fifty years ago," I clarified. "But that's a long time. Half a century."

His glare turned glacial, but facts were facts. He would turn sixty before the end of the year.

"Surely most of the people involved in that incident are

dead," I explained gently. "That, or they were too young at the time to remember much." I searched his features, trying to understand. "Or has something happened since?"

He turned away, directing his frosty gaze at the robin flitting from branch to branch of the shrub outside the window. "How would something else have happened? As I already told you, I haven't been in touch with them. Isn't their getting me arrested enough?"

I looked helplessly at Gage, uncertain what else to say. Fortunately, he'd grasped something I had not.

"I suppose Great-Uncle Branok was a key part of the smuggling operation." He crossed his arms over his chest, leaning his shoulder against the wall where one of the long, copper-colored damask drapes hung alongside the window.

Lord Gage gave a short grunt in response. "As eldest son and heir, he was always in the thick of it."

Gage's eyes shifted to meet mine, perhaps to check if I now apprehended what he did. His reluctance to return to investigate was as much about the victim as the place.

"I used to admire him," Lord Gage continued unexpectedly. "My father had no use for me, but Uncle Branok did. Called me clever." His lips curled almost into a snarl. "I was too young and foolish to grasp until it was too late that his interest was purely for selfish reasons."

I wondered if that were true. Or if the ending had cast a shadow over everything that had come before.

"Then perhaps you believe that, if he was murdered, he got what he deserved," Gage said, keeping his voice even and his expression neutral, as he often did to set a suspect or witness at ease. "That perhaps it was long overdue. And you're reluctant to stir up a possible hornets' nest for the sake of such a man."

Lord Gage plainly didn't like hearing this. "Don't use those interrogation tactics on me, boy," he growled. "Who do you think taught them to you?"

"That doesn't make what I said any less true," Gage countered, still refusing to be riled.

His father's contemptuous gaze flicked to me and then back again. "I take it the two of you think we should go haring off to Cornwall simply because my aunt cried foul."

"I think it should be considered." Gage shuffled his feet, turning to narrow his eyes out at the bright autumn sunlight. "And . . . I admit to a certain curiosity about my Roscarrock relatives. I have so few cousins, you know." Just three still living on his mother's side. "And I only met your parents once, when I was too young to remember. It would be . . . interesting to meet the Roscarrocks," he finished, choosing his words with care.

"They're not worth knowing," Lord Gage answered flatly.

"Even so."

He stared at his son's profile for a moment, perhaps waiting for him to elaborate, but when he didn't, Lord Gage turned to me. "And what's your excuse?"

I knew he wouldn't welcome my concern for his and Gage's well-being. My belief that Lord Gage needed to face his demons, so to speak. And Gage should at least be allowed to form his own opinion about his paternal grandmother's family. So instead, I focused on Amelia's plea.

"If a family member from which you've been estranged for almost fifty years is both desperate and courageous enough to write to you for help, then I think the request should at least be considered." My eyes met and held Gage's. "After all, your son received a similar request last summer from his maternal grandfather, the late Lord Tavistock. A request that, had we ignored, might have resulted in dire consequences." It also might have resulted in Gage never reconciling with his grandfather—with his entire Trevelyan family—or laying to rest some of the ghosts from his past.

"I suppose you're speaking of when my rapscallion nephew, Alfie, went missing and was found to be hiding at his lover's cottage," Lord Gage retorted, evidently unimpressed with this comparison.

"For good reason," I replied hotly.

"You'll recall, if Kiera hadn't found him and interfered with the killer's plans, Alfie would now be dead, along with his brother," Gage added quietly, the pain of that memory still reflected in his pale blue eyes. "And Alfie is no longer a rapscallion."

For one, he'd married that lover, whom I now considered one of my dearest friends.

The hard glint in Lord Gage's eye did not soften, but for once, he held his tongue rather than voice whatever acerbic remark sat at its tip.

I took the letter from Gage, skimming it once more with a frown. "I wish Great-Aunt Amelia had provided more details. We could write to ask for them, but a week has already passed, and you both know how time is of the essence in a murder investigation." I could only imagine they'd already buried the body, making the retrieval of any clues from the remains now impossible. Not that I would have relished examining a corpse in such an advanced state of decomposition.

When my father arranged my first marriage to the late anatomist Sir Anthony Darby, I hadn't known I would be regularly forced to stomach the assessment of weeks' old corpses. Sir Anthony had hidden well his intentions to compel me to sketch illustrations of his dissections for a definitive anatomical textbook he was writing. One that the parsimonious and vainglorious man did not wish to share credit for with a male collaborator. My skills as a portrait artist had made me the ideal target for his machinations, as well as my quiet, withdrawn nature and marked awkwardness among society. I sometimes berated myself for not having suspected ulterior motives during his courtship when he once asked me to draw his hand in detail, but the truth was, I had been completely oblivious to the oddity of the request until much later.

In any case, I had survived the three years of our marriage, and the subsequent scandal that had erupted after his death and the discovery of my involvement with his work. But it had taken me a long time to recover and enjoy life again. Gage had been a large part of that, as well as our collaboration as inquiry agents. Helping people who needed it, obtaining justice for those who had been murdered, putting the knowledge I had reluctantly accrued from Sir Anthony to good use had given my life and struggles purpose and fulfillment. And now that we had Emma, that added another dimension to my happiness.

"Yes, if we request more information, it could be another week before we receive a response, allowing that much longer for any evidence or witnesses to vanish," Gage agreed, eyeing his father.

Lord Gage huffed in aggravation, charging across the room toward the sideboard. "You do realize this could be a spurious claim. That Uncle Branok might not have been murdered at all." He removed the stopper from the decanter of brandy to pour himself a drink. I viewed his decision to indulge in spirits at—I glanced at the clock—half past ten in the morning as an indication of just how agitated he was.

"But what if he was?"

At his son's stark pronouncement, Lord Gage paused with the glass touching his lips, seeming to gather himself before tipping it back to take a healthy swallow. He set down the glass and turned to press both fists to the surface of the table. By the strain of the superfine fabric of his frock coat across his back and shoulders, I could tell just how rigidly he was holding himself even if I could no longer see his face. "Aye, there's the rub," he proclaimed in a voice so low I almost didn't hear it.

"I don't know how else to ascertain the truth than to travel there and find out for ourselves," Gage told him.

His father heaved a long, aggrieved sigh. "I see you are both determined to go."

Gage moved to my side, draping an arm around my waist. "You needn't accompany us." He turned to me, and I could see the sparkle of mischief in his eyes. "We could investigate the matter. If you would but write us a letter of introduction . . ."

"No, no." He finally turned to face us. "When something goes wrong—as it inevitably will—I'll not have it on my conscience that I sent you there on your own. Especially not if you're determined to take my granddaughter with you."

Given the fact I was still nursing Emma, we had no other choice. Unless I stayed behind. And I was not about to do that.

Lord Gage's expression turned forbidding. "You don't know the world you're about to step into. You don't understand the people. The Cornish are a breed unto themselves."

I found this to be a rather surprising statement coming from my father-in-law, whom I'd always viewed as eminently logical. But his view of the Roscarrocks, and the Cornish in general, was also skewed by some fifty years of anger and resentment. Given that, I supposed it made sense he would endow them with a rather ominous guise. Though that didn't halt the feeling that a cold wind had just blown across the back of my neck.

"But I suppose you'll see soon enough," he declared gruffly before drinking the rest of his brandy and striding across the room toward the bell-pull. "We'll leave before dawn. It will take three days to reach the border of Cornwall. I'll write to my steward at Liftondown and have the house prepared for us so that we can break our journey there the third night. It also wouldn't be remiss to have the place ready to retreat to should matters turn unpleasant and require our hasty departure."

Before either Gage or I could get a word in edgewise, Bowcott appeared and Lord Gage began to issue orders to his butler.

I turned to find Gage's expression somewhat guarded. I realized then that Liftondown must be Lord Gage's childhood home. The estate along the border between Devon and Cornwall he had inherited upon his brother's death. Lord Gage's father had been naught but a minor baronet, and Lord Gage naught but a second child. But Sir Henry Gage had died, followed by his eldest son, who had never married, leaving his second son, Stephen, the heir. However, by that time, Lord Gage already had his barony and its seat in Warwickshire, so he'd hired a competent steward to mind Liftondown and had the house shut up.

Gage had never been there, so I knew his curiosity about the place must exceed my own, but perhaps also his wariness. After all, his father had spent much of the first eleven years of his life there, and from the little we'd gleaned from his remarks about that time, it hadn't been happy. Perhaps he feared those shadows would still cling to its corridors.

Whatever the case, there was no turning back. Not when Lord Gage was now fully engaged in setting our departure into motion. I only hoped we wouldn't come to regret it.

CHAPTER 3

That's so sad," my maid, Bree, declared with a shake of her head. "That his lordship never had a chance to reconcile wi' his uncle," she clarified in her Scottish brogue when we all turned to look at her.

Having spent much of the day hurrying to pack and prepare for our departure, her appearance wasn't as neat as usual. Several strawberry blond curls had escaped from their pins to rest against the back of her neck, and there was a streak of dirt on the sleeve of her sprig green dress. But despite the busy day, she seemed as lively as ever that evening as Gage and I gathered in our bedchamber with our small staff. There hadn't been time to confer earlier in the day, but we knew an explanation was called for, particularly given the somewhat unorthodox nature of their roles and our relationships with them.

Anderley, Gage's valet—who was a dark foil for Gage's own golden good looks—stood with his arms crossed over his chest. "It seems unlikely that would have happened anyway."

Clearly, he'd heard gossip from at least one member of Lord Gage's staff, likely his punctilious valet, Lembus, for we'd not spoken to them before of Gage's father's past or his estrangement from the Roscarrocks. Even now, Gage was choosing his words with care.

"Aye, but the possibility was still open to him," Bree countered mournfully. "Noo it's not."

"She's right," Mrs. Mackay, our daughter's Scottish nanny, supplied. Her hands were clasped before her matronly frame, her silver hair a halo to her features. "'Tis always sad when the opportunity to mend one's differences—nay matter hoo small— closes forever. 'Tis something to be lamented."

A furrow formed in Anderley's brow, and I wondered if he was thinking of someone other than Lord Gage. Perhaps even someone from his family back in Italy. But Gage spoke before I could give the matter further consideration.

"We're going to need all of your help with this investigation." His pale blue gaze swept somberly over everyone present, including Emma slumbering in my arms. "My father warned us that the Cornish are an insular lot. They're not going to share what they know easily. *Not* that we haven't dealt with such people before."

It seemed to me, more often than not, we were confronted with such people.

"But this time, it's different." Gage frowned. "Familial relations can be an odd beast. Estranged family, in particular. I'm honestly not certain what we're walking into."

These words and the grim tone of his voice made my chest stir with apprehension, and I could tell the others had been similarly affected.

"So I want us all to be especially prudent and watchful, without seeming so." Gage rested his hands on his hips and turned to stare unseeing at the fire burning in the hearth.

Firelight flickered over his features, emphasizing the strong line of his jaw. "At least until we have a better understanding of what we're dealing with."

"Do you anticipate violence?" Anderley asked, being the first to dare to speak.

"No," Gage replied, though his tone was far from assured. "Not directly," he added, turning back to face us. "But . . . their history leaves room for doubt."

We all glanced at each other, perhaps wondering if we should be making the journey there at all. But if one of us was to go, then all of us would. After all, there was strength in numbers. And five—or six, if one counted Lord Gage—working together could prevail far easier than one.

I looked down at my child, her face soft with sleep, and my heart squeezed with love for her, with the desperate need to protect her. But I knew that if Gage genuinely felt there was reason to fear for her safety, he would never take her to Cornwall. He was just being cautious. Though I had to wonder what had inspired this more subdued outlook. Was he now regretting convincing his father to go?

I asked my husband exactly that once the others departed, with Mrs. Mackay carrying Emma off to the nursery.

Gage didn't seem surprised I'd asked. "No." He straightened from his stance leaning against the fireplace mantel to look at me. "We *need* to go. Or rather, my father needs to. And knowing what we do, we can hardly abandon him to face this alone." He reached out to rub his hands up and down the iris blue silk of my dressing gown covering my upper arms.

"The note did request help from both of you," I pointed out.

"Yes, but despite the fact they're family and I am curious about them, they're all but strangers to me. Given that, Great-Aunt Amelia can't have expected her plea to have the same effect on me."

I tilted my head, scrutinizing his features. "Actually, I think it *was* directed at you."

He tensed at this pronouncement. "But why . . . ?"

"Because of your reputation." I lifted my hands to smooth them over the lapels of his burgundy banyan. "Because if she's kept abreast of you at all—as she seems to, through newspapers and such—then she knows you're not as stubborn and close-minded as your father. That if anyone has any hope of convincing him to journey to Roscarrock House, it's you."

He seemed troubled by this deduction.

"Does *that* make you question your counsel?"

He frowned. "No. Well . . . question it? Yes," he admitted. "But not regret it."

"Because you can't imagine disregarding their letter," I inferred, knowing my husband well. He was nothing if not dutiful and honorable.

He nodded. "Considering we would have found ourselves back at this conclusion no matter how long we analyzed it, I suppose it's foolish to begin doing so now."

My eyes dipped to the strong muscles in his neck. "Not foolish, no." For I was doing exactly that. Wondering if my initial enthusiasm had been rather rash.

After all, Cornwall was a great distance from *anywhere*. It stretched out past the far southwestern edge of England like a lady demurely lifting her skirts to dip her toes into the Atlantic Ocean. Or like a claw scrabbling at the vast, unforgiving sea. It depended on one's fancy. Either way, if something should go wrong, we would be a very long way from any friends in London or even Alfie and Lorna in Dartmoor.

I worried my eagerness to see my father-in-law reconciled with his mother's family had clouded my judgment. That my desire to fix what might, indeed, be unfixable had blinded me. After all, Lord Gage *did* know the Roscarrocks better than I did. Perhaps what I viewed as his prejudice borne of festering shame and anger was actually more clear-sighted than I realized.

Gage's head dipped, trying to recapture my gaze. "Are *you* regretting it?"

"I'm regretting my failure to question my impartiality sooner."

He frowned in confusion. "About the Roscarrocks?"

"Yes." I fidgeted with his lapels. "For a woman who has never met them, I seem to have formed a rather more positive opinion of their innate goodness than your father's recollections would seem to illustrate."

"Recollections which, as we've established, are nearly fifty years old."

"Yes, but that doesn't mean they're inaccurate."

"Kiera." He waited until I looked up at him. "You have every reason to question my father's judgment when it comes to his perception of other people's characters. Just look at the way he misjudged you, and Henry, and about a dozen other people I could name. He treated you *abominably* before we wed, and *after*." He clasped his arms around my waist, drawing me closer. "Truth be told, for a time, I feared you would decide marriage to me wasn't worth suffering his scorn. But then you proved to be made of sturdier stuff than I'd given you credit for."

"You are not your father, Sebastian," I reminded him with a shake of my head.

"No, I am not. And I would trust your judgment of a person—even one you've never met—over that of my father's any day." He arched his eyebrows. "*Especially* if he has a personal connection to them."

"He does often seem to hold a skewed perspective of those he possesses any sort of emotional bond with," I conceded.

Gage arched his neck back, considering me. "And if that should fail to convince you, I would remind you that the one person he does have a clear perception of is his granddaughter, whom he rightfully adores. Do you honestly think he would let us set foot near the Roscarrocks with Emma if he genuinely feared them and whatever we might discover there?"

"Not in a thousand years."

He leaned close again, so that our faces were but inches apart. "And neither would I."

That much I'd already realized.

"Then we're bound for Cornwall," I murmured, confirming the decision that had already been made. "Or rather, Devon, first." I searched Gage's eyes for any reaction to this reminder. "You've never been to Liftondown, have you?"

A glint of anxiety flickered in his pupils. "No. Though it's about a dozen miles from Langstone Manor, as the crow flies."

Langstone Manor was his maternal grandfather's estate at the edge of Dartmoor, where he'd spent much of his childhood.

"So close?" I replied in shock. And yet Gage's paternal grandparents had only visited him once, when he was too young to remember. I supposed his mother could have taken him to see them, but she'd so often been ill, which was the reason they lived at Langstone in the first place rather than nearer to Plymouth. His father might have made the effort, but he was at sea much of the year—sometimes fifty or more weeks—which meant that after travel from Plymouth and back, he would have, at most, twelve days with his wife and son, or perhaps as little as three. It would have fallen to Sir Henry Gage and his wife to make the effort to see their only grandchild, something one would have thought they would do even if they were estranged from their son. Apparently, Lord Gage came by his propensity to hold long grudges naturally, heedless of who they hurt in the process.

"If my mother's description of it is to be believed, it is a rather bleak place," Gage replied.

Which was saying something, as Langstone Manor had

been far from sumptuous, even if it had contained a rather wonderful art collection.

"Maybe we can visit Alfie and Lorna at Langstone when we're finished in Cornwall," I suggested, trying to cheer him. I hadn't failed to notice he was avoiding discussing his paternal grandparents' absence from his life, but what could I say? It was clear he didn't know how to feel about it. After all, how do you mourn someone you never really knew? Perhaps you merely mourn the space in your life they should have occupied, the void their absence left behind. Like an echo of pain rather than the ache itself.

"I would like that," Gage agreed. "Their son is, what? Eight or nine months old now? He and Emma can play together."

I smiled. "I'm not certain babies actually *play*, but they can certainly babble at each other." I hesitated before voicing my next thought. "Has Alfie written to you?"

"No, but you know he's a terrible correspondent."

This was true enough. "Well, Lorna's letter today intimated that their son Rory will have a natural playmate soon enough."

Gage's eyes dipped to my abdomen.

I laughed. "And no, that is not a hint that I'm ready to add another child to our nursery. Not yet." I draped my arms around his neck. "Not intentionally anyway."

"I see," Gage replied silkily, drawing me closer. "Then, considering the long journey before us, perhaps we should consider retiring."

My breathing hitched at the gleam in his eyes. I slid my fingers up into his hair. "Yes, a good night's rest is exactly what we need."

"Hmm. Rest, yes," he hummed in a deep baritone just before his lips pressed to mine.

And rest we did. Eventually.

CHAPTER 4

We arrived at Liftondown House during a thunderstorm. The golden days of late October had faded into a damp and dreary start to November, and after struggling onward for three days over muddy and rutted roads, we were glad of the respite. Even if our first sight of the manor was far from inspiring.

It was first revealed to us in a flash of lightning as we passed between a gap in the scraggly high hedges, which had edged the road for some miles. A stolid, two-story block of gray stone, it perched on a lonely rise on the treeless expanse of the down which gave it its name. There were no trees or landscaping to soften it. No gardens or fountains. Just mud and heath and wind-hurtled rain beating at its walls.

For a moment, I feared the carriages would become hopelessly mired in the dip in the drive before the rise, but they somehow managed to navigate it. The next day I would discover that it was because someone had taken care to spread hay, but this couldn't be seen in the dark, and so could not comfort me that at least *someone* had been doing their best to make the place habitable. Through the veil of rain, the house looked deserted save for the light flickering in one window. But as we drew nearer, that one light turned to two and then three, proving there was some sort of staff waiting for us.

Our carriage drew to a stop a short distance from the door, and we hustled across the hay-strewn threshold into the house. Inside, we found ourselves in a narrow rectangular entry hall where the flagstone floor had been scrubbed clean. Though it wouldn't remain that way for long. A man whom I presumed to be the butler took our outer garments and gestured us through a doorway on the right, where a lad of no more than sixteen was working to coax a fire to life.

"Everything has been made ready as you requested, my lord," the butler informed Lord Gage as he took his hat and then greatcoat. "But Jemmy will need a few minutes to make his way through the bedchambers to set light to the kindling already laid. Mrs. Pigeon is preparing a tea tray. Should I tell her to prepare a more substantial repast?"

I peeled back the blanket covering Emma's slumbering figure, relieved to discover we were in capable hands.

Lord Gage declined the offer. "We supped in Okehampton, but tea would be most welcome."

"Of course, my lord." He bowed at the waist before ushering Jemmy out before him and closing the door.

Much like the entry hall, the drawing room was neat but dreary. The furnishings were old and shabby, the pattern worn in the rug revealing that little had been moved or rearranged in decades. The hearth—constructed from the same flagstones as the entry floor—appeared original to the house, and the golden drapes were faded to a sallow yellow from the sun.

I sank down in the armchair closest to the fire. I suspected its upholstery had once been a salmon pink, though it now appeared some indeterminate shade of beige. Emma continued to slumber, her face turned toward me, so I kept her swaddled in her blankets against the chill of the room.

Gage stood behind me, gazing down at our daughter, probably glad to be able to stretch his long legs after being confined for so long in the coach. One might have assumed this was also the reason for Lord Gage's pacing before the front window, but as usual, I saw more than he would have wished. There was a restless, agitated quality to his gait. One that indicated emotional distress rather than physical.

I peered upward, curious if my husband had noticed this, and found him now observing his father guardedly. For all the inquisitiveness Gage felt about this foreign place, Lord Gage must be feeling its familiarity quite keenly. I could only imagine the memories attached to it—both happy and unwelcome— were crowding about him like ghosts, demanding his attention. What he needed was a productive way to engage them.

"I suspect this was your mother's chair," I murmured.

My father-in-law turned his head to look at me and then Emma. "Yes."

"What was she like?" I asked, careful to keep my eyes averted as I smoothed the fold of the blanket draped over my arm near Emma's head. She didn't even stir a muscle. Oh, what it must be like to sleep so deeply, placing absolute trust in the arms that swaddled you. When did we lose that unalloyed faith, that blissful confidence that our needs would be met?

He paused to consider the matter. "She was . . . beautiful."

When he didn't continue, I prodded. "Golden-haired, like you and Sebastian?"

"No," he huffed, turning to look up at a painting of a hunting scene so that all I could see was his profile. "No, that feature comes from my father. Just about the only feature I inherited from him other than his height. He was a dour, craggy-faced fellow. My brother was much the same." He fell silent, staring broodingly at the pack of dogs posed with the various game their owners had killed.

I opened my mouth to nudge him again when he continued of his own volition.

"No, my mother was as dark-haired as all the Roscarrocks. A lovely almost blue-black, like a chough's wing." His mouth twisted in scorn. "They'll try to tell you they've hair that color because they're descended from King Arthur as, according to local legend, he turned himself into a chough until the day when he should be needed again." He scoffed. "They'll ask you to believe all sorts of nonsensical things. But their hair color does resemble a chough's feathers."

"Was it your mother who told you that legend?" I asked, following a hunch.

His slow response was answer enough. "She was a storyteller. All of them are. A family of veritable droll tellers, the entire lot. I suppose it was one of the things that intrigued me most as a child."

That was understandable, particularly if his father was as cheerless as he claimed.

"How did she come to be married to your father?" I queried, wondering at the match. A beauty from a lively storytelling family of smugglers seemed like an odd fit for a dour, craggy-faced baronet.

I glanced at Gage as he moved to sit in the chair next to mine. But then again, many would say that he and I were an even odder union—the charming golden boy and the macabre scandalous artist.

"Her fiancé was killed at sea."

My heart clenched in empathy.

He sighed. "'Tis a way of life in Cornwall. But I believe it broke her heart. After that, she didn't want to live anywhere near the sea. So she wed my father." His mouth flattened grimly. "And lived to regret it the rest of her life."

This last statement was telling, but my attention was diverted by another thought. "She must have been frantic when you went away to sea to join the Royal Navy."

Out of the periphery of my vision I could see Gage turn his head toward me, but I was more interested in the surprise that registered in my father-in-law's eyes as he did the same. It was obvious he'd never considered such a thing before.

"Did she not tell you?"

"No." He frowned, lifting his hand to scrape it back through his gray hair. I could have sworn it was shaking. His gaze dipped to the floor. "She washed her hands of me after my hearing before the magistrate. They both did."

This begged for further comment, but there was a rap on the drawing room door preceding the entry of a woman of some indeterminate age between forty and sixty bearing a tray. "'Ere ye are, m'lord. Ye must be chilled to the bone from this teasy weather." She set it on the low table near the center of the room, revealing not only a welcome pot of tea but also a plate of scones. Their sweet scent tickled my nose, overpowering the smell of damp and drying wool. "Especially with a little'n in tow." She smiled warmly at Emma. "I'm Mrs. Pigeon, by the by. The fires should be burnin' cheerily in yer rooms by now, and yer personal staff 'ave already made their way up to ready 'em."

"Thank you," I told the garrulous housekeeper. She and Mrs. Mackay would make a formidable pair. "These scones smell wonderful."

She beamed. "Thank ye, m'lady. My mum's own recipe. Shall I pour since yer arms are full?"

"Excuse me," Lord Gage told us absently as he slipped from the room, effectively ending our conversation for the evening. I turned to Gage, curious if he would go after him, but he remained where he was. In any case, if Lord Gage's past behavior was any indication, he would not have welcomed his son's consideration, instead preferring to muse in solitude.

I smiled at Mrs. Pigeon before belatedly responding. "Yes, please."

I was awakened the next morning by the rays of sunshine streaming directly in my face through a slit in the curtains. They were rather weak beams, but determined nonetheless, and that thought cheered me. For sunlight meant an end to the unremitting rain and an easier journey west into Cornwall.

I slid from beneath the covers, intending to pull the drapes more tightly closed and return to the warmth of Gage's side, but the view outside arrested me. A veil of fog hovered over everything, alternately revealing and concealing details as it shifted, filtering it all through a distorted lens. Closest and most easily recognizable was the small garden bordering the house. Much of it appeared overgrown save a small kitchen garden near the southeast corner. To the west, the stolid, gray bulk of a stable and carriage house materialized, its age evident in the worn stones and the droop of the roof. Beyond that stretched the grassy down, its stalks bent over, weighed down by the previous days' rain. But by far the most mysterious was the formation at the crest of a hill to the east.

My logical mind told me it must be a grove of tall trees, but obscured by the mist it appeared altogether strange and unworldly. There were few, if any, lower branches along the straight trunks, so that all of the twigs and greenery clustered at the very top. We hadn't been able to see it through the dark and driving rain the evening before, and to our eyes, Liftondown House had seemed the most substantial object for miles around. However, that copse of trees was significantly larger and positioned almost to loom over the manor below. I couldn't help but wonder which had sprung up first—the house or the trees?

Now too alert to return to slumber, I slipped into the adjoining chamber where our valises were being stored to don a simple walking dress. Then throwing a warm, woolen cape over my shoulders, I slipped down the back stairs to the rear entrance. I wouldn't venture far. Emma would wake soon, demanding to be nursed, and I didn't want to alarm anyone by my absence. But I also didn't want to miss my chance to stretch my legs before yet another long day confined to the carriage.

We had considered breaking our journey here longer, spending at least another day and night. Alas, too much time had already passed since Branok Roscarrock's death, and the more time we let slip by, the less chance we had of uncovering answers.

Given the early hour and the lingering fog, I expected to have the garden to myself. So the sight of my father-in-law made me stumble to a stop, allowing the door to slip from my grasp and close with a thud. He stood several steps ahead of me with his hands clasped behind his back, gazing out into the swirling mist as the hazy, orange halo of the sun struggled to burn through it. For a moment, I was uncertain what to do. His stance didn't invite company, nor did he speak, though he must have known I was there.

Maybe retreating would be best, but that reminded me of the way our relationship had begun. Before the events in Yorkshire in August, I'd done all I could to avoid the man and his barbarous tongue and cutting glares. I didn't want to return to such a fractious relationship. Especially not when we were heading into territory where he was going to need our support more than ever, whether he wished to admit it or not.

So instead, I strode forward to join him, wrapping my green cloak tighter around me against the damp chill. The mist condensed against my skin, both refreshing and slightly cloying.

Neither of us spoke as we stood side by side, observing the scrub and overgrown grass. Up close, it was evident the garden was in an even sorrier state than I'd first presumed. I might have remarked upon it, but I wanted him to speak first, to reveal what *he* was thinking. I knew prodding him would do little good. He would share what he wished to. Or what he was lulled into admitting in an unguarded moment.

My patience was rewarded.

"When my mother was alive, this garden was bursting with blooms, even late into the autumn and sometimes into winter. She wouldn't let anyone else tend her plants." Lord Gage's voice turned dry. "Which was good, because my father could barely afford the staff we had, let alone a full-time gardener for such a small plot of land. Of course, my brother Arthur was no better off, but I was still surprised to see it so sadly neglected when I came back for his funeral." I could hear the consternation in his tone. "I suppose I'd expected it to remain as it had always been, even without Mother to mind it."

I understood what he meant. "I remember returning to Blakelaw House for the first time after my father died and my brother had taken over the estate. Some months had passed." Nearly a year actually, for Sir Anthony had not allowed me to travel, not even for my father's funeral. I had only seen my family when they came to London, and even then our contact was limited. "But I still expected my father's study to be the same as he'd left it—neat and orderly and smelling of old leather and his pipe smoke." A smile tugged at the corners of my mouth. "My brother never could keep a room tidy, and no servant worth their salt would dare touch the papers on their employer's desk."

I sobered as the longing to see my father again suddenly welled up within me. "I think it's easier for our hearts to go on believing they're simply carrying on somewhere else, even if we know better."

We stood companionably in silence, listening to the distinctive call of a stonechat—a loud cheep followed by what sounded like two stones being clacked together. However, my thoughts were not on heath birds.

"What did you mean when you said your mother lived to regret marrying your father?" I ventured to ask, knowing full well he wouldn't like it. Though I felt there was a chance he might answer me without thinking.

Unfortunately, he wasn't so lost to the past that he didn't realize what I was doing. True to form, he turned to pin me with his stare, though this one was more muted with long suffering and grief than pure scorn. "Do you never tire of being impertinent?"

I turned away, unwilling to admit I didn't always understand where that line was. "Not when there's a question to be asked. Not when there's an answer that needs to be given," I replied instead.

A bird flew through the scattering haze, drawing our attention, and I thought for a moment that Lord Gage didn't intend to respond. Then he exhaled a small huff. "Merely that my father was not an easy man to live with." We watched as the same bird and another arched overhead. "And . . . despite her safety and security, the caged bird does not always sing."

Deep sorrow tugged at my heart at this imagery. Sorrow not only for Margaret Roscarrock Gage, but also for Lord Gage himself, for he could just as easily have been speaking of himself. He'd admitted that as a boy he'd spent so much time with his mother's family in Cornwall in order to escape his father—who'd had little use for his second son—and because the Roscarrocks were so much more adventurous and interesting.

Yes, it was those adventures, initially viewed as great larks, which had eventually gotten him into so much trouble. Yet for all of his disparagement of them now, it was the skills and traits he'd developed during his time with the Roscarrocks that had served him so well in the Royal Navy. Everyone said that the Cornish made the best seamen. Probably because they couldn't escape the sea. They lived it and breathed it from the cradle. And deny it or not, he was half-Cornish.

He arched his chin, almost as if scenting something. "We should be on our way. Before the weather shifts again." Then he turned with a swirl of his many-caped greatcoat, not waiting to see if I would follow.

I remained a moment longer, breathing in the morning mist. It was but thirty miles to Roscarrock House, but we'd been warned that each mile we traveled deeper into Cornwall, the less well maintained the roads became. There was no doubt it would be a jarring and uncomfortable ride. Emma was already out of sorts from the previous three days' travel, and I didn't expect she would be eager to find herself back in the confines of the carriage again, being jostled about.

Inhaling deeply, I braced myself for what was to come, both along the way and once we arrived. For it was clear, I was going to have to maintain a level head. If I'd learned anything over the course of our investigations, it was that even the most stoic of individuals could be overwhelmed and blinded by emotion. And stoic was not how I would describe my husband or his father.

CHAPTER 5

The edifice that emerged from the green hills bordering the sea wasn't the most impressive I'd ever seen, but it was quite possibly the most welcoming. Especially after hours of rattling over the most abominable roads with a cranky, fussing infant. And if we *weren't* rattling—and jolting, and jouncing—then we were struggling through mud so thick we'd been forced to get out and walk while the men pushed the carriages out of the mire. My father-in-law had cautioned us, but even his dire predictions had not gone far enough.

Sometime after we'd reached the edge of Bodmin Moor, I'd ordered Gage and his father out of the traveling chaise and told them to ride their horses. An order, I noticed, they were quick to accept. Such a long ride on horseback might aggravate Lord Gage's leg, but I was beyond caring at that point. Not when their withdrawal allowed me to have Mrs. Mackay and my maid Bree moved into the lead carriage with me so that the three of us might work together to comfort Emma.

Any normal lady might have simply passed the squalling child off to their nanny to contend with, as Lord Gage had been quick to point out, but I was no normal lady. I couldn't simply close my ears to her cries. Besides which, she needed to nurse, an activity she refused to do, to my growing frustration, worry, and discomfort.

Not that I could blame her. The jarring and lurching were also making *me* queasy. I'd not eaten a bite of the dinner laid before us at the last coaching inn. My husband and his father were wise enough not to remark upon it, or my surly mood.

Now that a stone-faced manor house slid into view, its slate roof mottled here and there with chartreuse moss, I felt a stirring of hope. Surely, we'd reached the edge of the isle of Britain and would drive over the cliffs into the sea if we didn't stop soon. Surely this must be Roscarrock House.

At the thought, a part appeared between the lush green headlands beyond the manor, allowing our first glimpse of the ocean. Its deep blue water sparkled in the rays of the sun as it sank toward its horizon in an almost periwinkle sky. I must have straightened or given some indication of my relief, for Mrs. Mackay and Bree both turned to follow my gaze out the window, exhaling breaths of their own.

"Finally," Bree muttered under her breath, breaking the long-suffering silence that had fallen between us, broken only by Emma's grunts, cries, and wails, and the croons and pleas of whoever's turn it was to attempt to soothe her. It was clear Bree hadn't meant to utter this aloud, for her eyes darted to mine. "'Tis only, I thought the roads to the Highlands were rough, but this . . . this . . ."

I held up a weary hand. "Say no more."

I peered resignedly at my seven-month-old daughter, who had burrowed into Mrs. Mackay's shoulder, part of her ragdoll Rosie stuffed into her mouth as she furiously sucked and gnawed on it, making little grunting noises. Her cheeks were red and her blond curls damp with sweat. I knew I should take her so that I could introduce her to the Roscarrocks, but Mrs. Mackay had somehow mollified Emma enough so that at least she wasn't howling. I feared if we transferred her to me, she would begin wailing again.

Deducing my thoughts, Mrs. Mackay spoke softly. "I'll care for the bairn while ye greet Lord Gage's family. Change her and wash her doon with a warm cloth. Then hopefully she'll settle to ye." She adjusted Emma's position against her shoulder. "Dinna fash. She'll sort herself quick once we've stopped movin'. Though 'twill likely be another few days before this tooth pops through."

It had been a not-so-pleasant surprise that morning to discover my daughter was also cutting her first tooth, for it only compounded Emma's, and consequently *all* of our, discomfort on this journey.

"Ye just breathe in that fresh sea air and try to relax," Mrs. Mackay advised. "The calmer *you* are, the easier she'll cooperate."

I recognized the wisdom of this and inhaled the salty breeze already seeping through the joints of the carriage deep into my lungs.

Bree shifted to the bench beside me, reaching up to fuss with the tendrils of hair which had escaped from my blue watered-silk capote to curl about my face.

"I fear I'm beyond repair," I told her, lifting the muddy hem of my once-smart king's blue carriage dress of figured gros de Tours. "I fear we all are," I added with a glance at their own hems and half-boots. I imagined the men were in an even worse state. Even Lord Gage's fastidious valet Lembus, who had remained in the second carriage rather than ride on horseback with his employer, Gage, and Anderley, must be soiled to some extent from the men's efforts to free the carriages from the mud.

"Aye, weel, they're a foolhardy lot if they dinna expect us to appear a little worse for wear," Bree declared with one last adjustment to my bonnet. "'Specially since they wanted us to make haste."

I couldn't argue with that. Not when I was harboring the same thought.

The carriage turned down a drive flanked by tall hedges on one side and barns and outbuildings on the other. It drew to a stop just shy of a small gap where the topiaries met the stone wall forming the north edifice of the main house. Gage soon appeared in the carriage doorway, lowering the step. He offered me his hand to help me out, and then turned as if to retrieve Emma.

I pressed my hand to his arm, halting him. "Leave her," I stated, and then softened my tone at his surprise. "For now."

He glanced between me and Emma, whose scrunched features revealed she was going to begin wailing again soon. A flicker of sympathy passed over his face and he nodded before closing the door and rapping on the side to indicate that the coachman could carry on toward the servants' entrance and stables.

We stepped back as they moved forward, nearly colliding with a man of wiry stature emerging from the gap in the hedges. He wore no hat, allowing the wind to comb through his gray hair threaded with the remnants of what once must have been a head full of blue-black hair. I guessed that he was approximately the same age as my father-in-law, though the years had not been so kind.

He took us in with one mildly hostile glance while a darkhaired man whom I suspected was his son observed us impassively over his shoulder, and then turned to sneer at Lord Gage. "The prodigal grandson returns."

The younger man seemed startled by the venom in his father's voice, but he didn't object.

"Bevil," Lord Gage replied with equal rancor.

Bevil shifted a step closer, nearly standing nose to nose with him. "Well, don't expect me to kill the fatted calf." His gaze dipped to rake over him. "Truth be told, I didn't believe you'd dare show yer face 'ere. Not after what 'appened. Not after what ye did durin' the war."

I slid a look sideways at Lord Gage, curious what that meant.

He arched a single eyebrow, one corner of his lip curling contemptuously. "If you'll recall, we *weren't* at war then. That was personal."

Bevil's eyes narrowed. "Ye nearly ruined us!"

"I don't believe *I* was the one breaking the law."

"Boys, boys!" a rasping voice scolded. It belonged to an older woman emerging through the hedges. She must have been nearing seventy, and although her back was still straight and her pale eyes sharp, she needed the assistance of a woman closer to my age to walk. A young woman whose dark eyes sparkled with open curiosity.

"Why must ye always bicker. Ye 'aven't seen each other in nigh on fifty years, and yet still you're squabblin'." The older woman gave a long-suffering sigh. "I suspect ye 'aven't even introduced yourselves, nor your kin."

Bevil continued to scowl, but Lord Gage stepped forward to take the older woman's hand, his demeanor softening. "Aunt Amelia. It's good to see you still looking so fresh and spry."

Her lips curled into a smile as she removed her hand from his grasp to pat his cheek. "Aye, ye always were the charmer." Her voice turned wistful. "Just like your mother."

"I received your letter," Lord Gage said, breaking the somber silence that had followed that statement.

"Aye," Great-Aunt Amelia spoke on an exhale. "Or else ye wouldn't be here, now, would ye?" Her expression turned shrewd. "Or do I 'ave yer son and daughter-in-law to thank for finally persuadin' ye to put the past in the past?"

Gage and I stepped forward as cued.

"My son, Sebastian," Lord Gage declared as Gage bowed over his great-aunt's hand.

"I'm pleased to meet you," he told her sincerely. I could see that my husband's good looks were having their usual effect.

"Oh, my. And don't you turn heads. I suppose this is what your father looked like twenty or thirty years ago." Her gaze slid sideways toward her nephew. "And what, with the devil he had inside 'im when he was young, he likely woulda trampled 'alf the hearts in the county."

Lord Gage frowned.

But rather than be deterred, Great-Aunt Amelia merely waggled her eyebrows at him.

"My wife, Kiera," Gage interjected, drawing me forward.

"I see," she murmured, scrutinizing me closely. "Lady Darby," she said, using my courtesy title from my late husband. "I have been looking forward to meeting *you*."

"Please, call me Mrs. Gage. Or Kiera, if you prefer. I suppose we *are* family."

I didn't explain that I despised still being addressed by the title my marriage to Sir Anthony had bestowed on me. That the courtesy society showed me by addressing me as such because my first husband outranked my second was not truly a courtesy at all, but a terrible reminder of all I'd suffered at Sir Anthony's hands.

"And your daughter?" Amelia asked.

"I'm afraid is a trifle fussy after such a long journey," I informed them apologetically.

"Oh, yes," the younger woman exclaimed in empathy. "The local roads are *terrible*! And to have traveled all this way so quickly." She smiled in commiseration. "But she will settle soon enough now that you've arrived."

I hoped so. I was already fighting against the urge to loosen my stays to relieve at least some of the pressure in my chest. Of course, I said none of this out loud, but I could tell that she understood. Probably because she was a mother herself.

"I'm Dolly," she said, nodding toward the dark-haired fellow. "Tristram's wife."

"And Tristram is my grandson," Amelia explained, making nearly everything plain as she then gestured toward the man who had antagonized Lord Gage. "My son Bevil's son."

"And you are Lord Gage's mother's sister?" I asked in clarification. "So Great-Uncle Branok was your brother?"

"Aye." A deep weariness seemed to cloak her, sharpening the lines of her face and bowing her shoulders. "But please, come inside, and I can better explain." Like her kin, she glottalized some of her words, turning the *T*s in the word *better* to mere breaks of sound.

Dolly and Tristram helped to guide her back toward the house, and Gage and I slowly followed, with Lord Gage and his cousin Bevil falling into step behind us. Neither man offered the other further antagonism, but I could practically feel the hostility bristling between them.

Once through the gap in the hedges, Great-Aunt Amelia's slow progress afforded me plenty of time to scrutinize our surroundings. We found ourselves in a walled garden—one that, by all appearances, was very old and likely medieval in origin. There were two levels, and we were currently on the raised terrace, which boasted a number of topiaries and beech trees as well as a pair of square gate piers denoting what must have traditionally been the main approach to the house on foot. Though it was already November, I could see that the lower garden still enjoyed a number of colorful blooms, which would not have survived so late in the season elsewhere.

The main block of the manor stood to our right, faced with bands of granite ashlar and squared rubble and slate. Building it thusly would have been an intricate process and the effect was quite pleasing, even if the remainder of the edifice was quite plain. Square, single-sash windows marched across the façade with a small Doric porch covering the entry. The flush panel door with a fanlight was painted white, as were the two columns flanking it.

We passed through this door and into a simple entry hall with flagstone floors and a set of stairs leading to the level above. A man who I supposed was their butler, though he was dressed far more humbly than any man I had ever seen in such a position, waited to take our outer garments while our hosts preceded us into a room on the right. Gage and I glanced down at the mud still splattering our lower extremities, some of which had even splashed as high as his thighs.

"Don't worry," a woman with sharp features entering from the rear of the house informed us. "It's not like we 'aven't seen the like every day of our lives." When still I must have looked uncertain, she threaded my arm through her own. "We expected ye to be dappered after such a journey. A cup of tea will soon set ye to rights, and then we'll let ye settle into your rooms."

I allowed myself to be propelled into what appeared to be the drawing room. Its windows looked out upon the pleasing aspect of both gardens. The furnishings were unexpectedly of a recent design, the upholstery in a shade of puce that was all the rage just twenty years ago. Though I feared it wouldn't remain looking neat and new if I sat upon it for long.

"Ah, there ye are, Joan," Great-Aunt Amelia declared as she settled deeper into an armchair situated near the hearth. I could smell the earthy scent of peat. "As ye can see, my nephew Stephen has arrived along with his son Sebastian and daughter-in-law Kiera." Her gaze shifted to me. "Joan is Bevil's wife."

I nodded to the woman who had directed me to a birchwood

settee with scrolled arms, doing my best to keep my stained hem from touching the silk as I perched at its edge.

"Welcome to Roscarrock," Joan told me as she sat opposite, next to her mother-in-law. "I believe I just met your daughter." She clucked her tongue in pity. "Teething, is she? Well, I've directed your nursemaid to the small bedchamber next to your own. I was afraid Tristram's children would be too rowdy for her in the main nursery."

"Thank you."

She waved her hand, dismissing any further comment on the matter before turning to Gage and his father, who had exercised their prerogative as men to remain standing. I suspected the long day's ride on horseback had made them both sore. I couldn't help scrutinizing Lord Gage's features for signs that his recently injured leg was paining him while Joan spoke. "I'll show ye to your rooms dreckly."

"You've met all of us who live 'ere in the main house, then," Great-Aunt Amelia stated, before I could question what *dreckly* meant. It sounded like a distortion of *directly*, but since Joan made no move to rise, I suspected it meant something more like *soon*. "That is, for the time bein'," Amelia continued. "My daughter and other grandchildren and their families live nearby, so you'll meet them in due time. But for now . . ." She glanced around at her family. "'Tis essentially us."

I considered this statement and the five new family members ranged before us as the tea tray was brought in. Though Bevil had held his tongue since his mother's scolding, I could tell he was still no happier about our presence. He stood near a window, turned partially away as if to avoid the sight of us as he scowled out at the sunken garden on the south side of the house. His wife Joan seemed a trifle more welcoming, or at least resigned to our presence as she slid forward to begin pouring tea for everyone. Their son Tristram slumped in a chair near the door through which we'd entered, observing us all with a pensive stare. His was the demeanor I most struggled to decipher, unable to tell if he was masking his dislike or reserving judgment. His wife Dolly, on the other hand, was the most outwardly accepting. However, even her pleasant smiles were edged with stiffness. Perhaps because she worried the rest of the family would not approve of her friendliness.

Whatever the case, it did not escape my notice that the most receptive was also the most recent addition to the Roscarrock family. Or rather, the Killigrews. I waited until the maid had left the room to voice the insight that had just occurred to me. "Then Great-Uncle Branok was the last of the Roscarrocks?"

They all turned to look at me. Even Joan paused midpour.

"That is, you all must have a different surname if Amelia was born a Roscarrock." When none of them spoke, I added uncertainly. "Unless I'm mistaken?"

"Nay. You're correct," Amelia responded. "I married James Killigrew. God, rest 'is soul." She clarified all of this while looking at Lord Gage, perhaps because she'd expected him to have already explained. "But there is still one Roscarrock yet in Cornwall. Branok's grandson, Meryasek."

I couldn't stop myself from looking at my husband. A glint of amusement flickered in his eyes at the shared memory of his suggesting this for our child's name. At the time, it had been a sort of game. But now that I was meeting the people who had either inspired or shared in the heritage of those sobriquets it seemed far less humorous. A realization Gage seemed to share as the mirth faded from his face.

"But Mery prefers to live in one of the cottages on the other side of the estate," Amelia continued as Joan rose to pass teacups to several of the men. "Or at least, he has 'til now." She frowned, her fingers fretting the fringe of her shawl. "Since the estate is all now his, sooner or later I suppose he'll wish to move back to the main house."

"Or more likely, he'll go on doin' whatever he pleases," Tristram grumbled. "'Specially without Great-Uncle Branok to keep him in check."

"Aye, well," Amelia said as she exhaled resignedly. "He just might surprise us."

"Then you 'ave more faith in 'im than I do." Bevil turned his head to scoff over his shoulder.

Though I had only known the family for a quarter of an hour, it was becoming evident that it was on Bevil's shoulders that much of the responsibility for the estate now rested. And yet he didn't own a square meter of it. It all belonged to his uncle's grandson—his second cousin. That couldn't be an easy thing to swallow. Particularly if Meryasek was as neglectful as they seemed to indicate.

"I take it Mery isn't married?" Gage asked.

"Nay." Tristram gave a gasp of derisive laughter. "And I pity the woman who agrees to be his wife."

"Tristram," his mother scolded, perhaps feeling this went too far.

Even Dolly looked slightly chagrined at her husband's remark.

Joan arched her chin as she passed me a cup of tea. "Mery may have sowed more than his fair share of wild oats, but I trust that he'll recognize he must stop his youthful indiscretions now and focus on his duty to the family."

And by duty, it was clear she meant producing an heir.

No one contradicted her. At least, not verbally. However, based on their facial expressions alone, the rest of the family did not share her confidence.

I sipped my tea, glancing surreptitiously at Lord Gage. He'd said very little since entering the house. I knew this couldn't be easy for him, and the rigidity of his posture bore that out. His expression was tightly closed off, much like his son's when he didn't know how to feel about something or how to mask his emotions. If anything, he seemed dazed from being here after so much time had passed. His gaze kept darting around the room and straying toward the window overlooking the terrace garden, as if cataloging both the new and familiar and struggling to reconcile it with his memory.

He was certainly not his normal self, and I suddenly felt an acute sense of protectiveness toward him. He seemed in many ways defenseless, and so I sought to keep the conversation and their attention focused on me while he acclimated himself. Gage seemed to sense this as well, aiding me in my efforts. That, or his natural curiosity spurred him to do so unconsciously.

"You said there was one Roscarrock yet in Cornwall," Gage pointed out, passing his empty cup back to Joan and declining another. "Are there Roscarrocks elsewhere?"

Amelia cast another sidelong look at Lord Gage. "I see my nephew upheld his vow to all but forget us." Her voice rasped like sandpaper. "There 'ave been Roscarrocks in this very spot . . ." She tapped the arm of the chair in emphasis. "Since the Norman conquest. We've owned this land unbroken for generations. My father . . ." She gestured toward the wall behind me, and I turned to discover a portrait hanging above the sideboard. A very credible portrait of a gentleman at the upper end of his prime.

"Meryasek Roscarrock, for whom Mery is named," she explained as I set my teacup aside and began to rise to my feet.

"May I?" I asked somewhat belatedly, for in my interest I was already rounding the settee.

Great-Aunt Amelia nodded.

My gaze strayed briefly to Lord Gage, who stared resolutely out the window at the front garden. No wonder he was uncomfortable. His grandfather—the man who had gotten him entangled with smuggling and, after he'd been arrested, had sent him to sea—was even now glaring down at them. Though, in truth, his likeness was far more beneficent. A few more degrees, lift to the outer edges of the mouth, and he would actually be smiling.

"'Tis painted by John Opie," Amelia declared with pride.

The Cornish Wonder.

"I thought I recognized his technique," I replied, leaning closer to study the work of the man Sir Joshua Reynolds had once praised. Opie had been the self-taught son of a carpenter and possessed a brilliant eye. I'd studied a number of his portraits over the years. He'd been remarkably prolific during his short lifetime, capturing many members of the nobility and royalty on canvas, and also apparently my husband's great-grandfather. This must be one of his earlier works, painted before he traveled to London, before he became so highly sought after.

"My father was an only child," Amelia continued, settling into her chair as if she was about to begin a long story. "But he produced four children, the first of whom was Branok. Now, Branok had but one son, Casworan. And a meaner, more ill-tempered man you'll never meet. He'd kick a dog as soon as look at it."

I snuck a glance at Lord Gage to see if his expression confirmed this, but either he wasn't attending to her story or Casworan's ill humor hadn't yet made itself known before he'd received his commission in the Royal Navy.

Amelia shook her head. "Casworan lived just long enough to beget Mery before gettin' 'imself killed in a tavern brawl, mourned by no one. And that makes Mery the last of Branok's line."

I nodded, following what she was saying.

"Father's second child was my sister Margaret. From whom you descend," she told Gage. Her clipped words suggested a grief that had never healed. "Next came my brother Swithun, who immigrated to Pennsylvania just before the colonies re-volted. Managed to survive and produce quite a healthy number of offspring." She cackled. "Probably just to spite Branok."

This caused a flicker of amusement to pass over Lord Gage's features, telling me he was listening to what was being said more than it seemed.

"And Father's last child?" Amelia sighed contentedly. "That would be me. I've two children, four grandchildren, and six great-grandchildren with one more on the way."

I smiled. "Something to be proud of."

"Aye." Her shoulders slumped inward, and the sparkle that had lit her gray eyes was now gone. "Now, ye know why I've asked ye here. I know time is passin' and ye must have many questions. But I'm not as young as I once was, and my heart . . ." She broke off, pressing her hand to her chest as she took several shallow breaths. "My heart is weaker than I'd like."

Joan hastened to her side, but Amelia stayed her with a touch of her hand and a smile that was meant to reassure.

"Tomorrow will be soon enough," she told the rest of us be-fore allowing Joan to help her to her feet. "I'll explain everythin' then."

I couldn't help but feel concerned as I watched her shuffle from the room with her daughter-in-law's help. Her breathing was labored and the vibrancy which had seemed to color her had been all but extinguished. Maybe this could be attributed to fatigue, but her comment about her heart and the worry scoring the brows of her family members made me suspect it was far more serious.

"I've matters to see to," Bevil proclaimed gruffly, striding through a second doorway which connected to an adjacent chamber. A short time later, we could hear another door open and then close.

A deep frown marred Lord Gage's features, making it clear

he was suspicious of what exactly those matters were, and whether they had anything to do with smuggling. I doubted his cousin would be so bold, regardless of their antagonism toward each other, but then I had only just met them.

Gage moved forward to engage Tristram in conversation, and I soon found Dolly hovering next to me.

"I can show ye to your room, if ye like?" she offered with a tight smile. "I'm sure you're anxious to tend to your daughter."

I was. Rather desperately so. I'd been struggling to ignore my growing discomfort. "Thank you."

Gage's eye caught mine as she ushered me from the drawing room and I knew he would wait to join me until after Emma nursed so that she didn't become distracted by his presence, as she was wont to do.

"Your mother-in-law said you have children," I remarked as we began to climb the stairs.

Dolly's pretty face brightened. "Aye. Two boys, aged eight and seven, and a four-year-old girl." She tucked a stray strand of honey blond hair behind her ear. "I'm glad Mother thought to put your daughter in a different bedchamber." She laughed somewhat apologetically. "I'm afraid my boys can be quite unruly at times, and their sister tends to follow suit."

"It seems little boys are often that way."

"Perhaps. But these boys certainly have Roscarrock blood flowin' through their veins, I can tell ye."

I didn't know what to say to this, especially after Great-Aunt Amelia's observations about her nephew Casworan and everyone's comments about Mery. It was almost as if they were saying too much Roscarrock blood was a thing to be avoided. Or perhaps they were simply attempting to excuse their poor behavior because of it. Nevertheless, I tended to believe that a person's character had less to do with their lineage and more with their upbringing and choices.

"Cousin Stephen," Dolly began tentatively. "He's not what I expected."

I could only imagine what she'd been told about my father-in-law. Particularly if Bevil was doing the talking. I doubted her mother-in-law's or husband's opinions of Lord Gage were rose-colored either, considering they had no firsthand knowledge of him.

"I suppose Gage and I aren't what you expected either," I observed casually. After all, they would only have had the newspaper reports to judge by.

The red suffusing Dolly's cheeks was answer enough.

"Things here seem . . . unsettled," I ventured after searching for the right word, hoping to draw her out by ignoring her embarrassment.

She eagerly leapt at the change of subject. "Great-Uncle Branok's death has troubled us all, of course. And Nanna's suspicions about how it 'appened."

I was quick to note she'd said they were Great-Aunt Amelia's suspicions, not everyone's. Did the others think differently?

"And we're all a bit anxious about whether Mery will abide by his granfer's wishes and keep Father—and Tristram after him—as his steward."

"Bevil worked as his uncle's steward?" I supposed that clarified some matters.

Dolly nodded, pausing as we reached the top of the stairs. "Great-Uncle Branok believed 'twas best to keep the position in the family, so he offered it to his nephew Bevil. He's served as steward here since Branok inherited the estate. And Branok promised the position to Tristram upon Bevil's retirement or death." We rounded the corner into a corridor as she continued. "Branok's will stipulated that Mery should keep the arrangement, but . . ." She shrugged one shoulder.

"That doesn't mean he will," I finished for her.

Her brown eyes were shadowed with worry. "So ye see, that's why we're all a bit . . . unsettled," she concluded, borrowing my word.

I nodded. "I do see."

She inhaled a shaky breath and turned to look down the corridor to the right. "Your daughter's nursery is through the door straight on, and your own bedchamber lies to the right of it at the corner."

I thanked her and tried to offer her some encouragement. "We'll do what we can."

She offered me a weak smile. One that was not brimming with confidence. It plagued my thoughts as I hastened to Emma.

CHAPTER 6

Gage found me thirty minutes later contentedly rocking our daughter in a chair which had been moved into the spare bedchamber along with a cradle. I was feeling relieved and far more comfortable than I had in days. Not only had Emma nursed, but we also weren't being rattled about in a carriage, and we didn't have to anticipate the same mistreatment on the morrow. As such, the rocking which had lulled my daughter to sleep was close to doing the same to me, especially as the last traces of sunlight streaming through the windows softened and waned.

Gage smiled down at us, his pale blue eyes warm with affection. Without speaking, he gestured to the bell-pull, and I nodded for him to summon Mrs. Mackay. True to her word, the nanny had worked her wonders on Emma, soothing her enough that she would settle down to feed. Her cheeks were now pale pink rather than fiery red and her golden curls sprang about her head without her cap, drying from the gentle washing they'd received.

I slowed my rocking and then stopped, hoping Emma would remain asleep. When she didn't stir, Gage gently lifted her from my arms and laid her in the cradle. She snuffled and we both stilled until we were certain she'd fallen back into slumber. I closed my eyes, murmuring a prayer of gratitude.

Gage pointed to Rosie, our daughter's ragdoll discarded on the table nearby. It was twisted hopelessly out of shape and sodden from Emma's slobber. I shook my head, trusting Mrs. Mackay had packed the extra ragdolls Bree had made our daughter so that this Rosie could be washed while Emma was none the wiser. Then he helped me rise from the chair. I groaned lightly as I stood, feeling twinges in my back from the four days confined to a traveling coach.

Hobbling forward, we made our way to the door, turning left to enter our bedchamber as Mrs. Mackay came bustling down the corridor on the right. A second set of stairs must lie in that direction. She nodded to us, and we disappeared into the corner bedchamber.

The walls, like those downstairs, were whitewashed stone and bare except for a small, oval mirror and a single shelf boasting a dancing figurine and a small bud vase absent of flowers. An old but well-cared-for set of walnut furniture filled the space, including a canopied bed, clothespress, and dressing table. The scent of the wood polish that had been used to bring it to a shine still hung in the air. Ivory drapes adorned the windows and bed, and an ivory counterpane embroidered with tiny yellow flowers marching across it in eight intersecting lines covered the feather mattress. The most colorful item in the room was a handwoven rug in deep red which lay across the dark wooden floor beside the bed.

While tending to Emma, I'd heard muffled voices coming from the room as Bree and Anderley unpacked and arranged our things, and I could see the evidence of their earlier presence.

My hairbrush and a few bottles were neatly arranged along the dressing table, as were Gage's shaving implements. A nightdress and wrapper were draped across the left side of the bed while a cornflower blue morning dress hung on the outside of the wardrobe to air out. I spied Gage's nightshirt and dressing gown arranged over the back of a ladder-back chair in the corner. However, our maid and valet had since retreated, presumably to locate their own accommodations for the duration of our stay.

"Where's your father?" I asked as he closed the door, curious if Lord Gage's assigned bedchamber was nearby.

Gage paused to light a brace of candles to combat the darkness before moving toward the edge of the bed to sink down. "He said he needed to stretch his legs."

My eyes widened, for this presumably meant he'd ventured outside. Following Bevil?

"Is that wise?" I asked.

Gage shrugged one shoulder. "Maybe not, but who am I to argue." His lips twisted. "I'm not my father's keeper."

The bitterness of this comment surprised me, and then I recalled that while I'd been contending with a squalling infant inside an enclosed carriage all day, he had ridden twenty or more miles with mainly his father for company.

I sat beside him. "I take it today's travel was no more enjoyable for you than it was for me."

Rather than answer—perhaps because it was self-explanatory—he asked a question of his own. "Did Emma cry the entire journey?"

I heaved a weary sigh. "Just about."

His brow furrowed in empathy. "Poor darling. And poor you."

"And poor Mrs. Mackay and Bree. None of us could comfort her."

He grimaced. "I take it, then, that you're not looking forward to the journey back to civilization?"

I grimaced in turn. "Why don't we trade. I'll ride on horse-back with your father, and you can travel in the carriage with Emma."

He chuckled. "Fair enough. We'll both have to suffer from a fair amount of grumbling."

"Was his leg paining him?"

He nodded. "I caught him rubbing it a few times. Though I don't know how severely." He kneaded his hands up and down over the tight riding breeches encasing his thighs, telling me he was suffering from a few twinges himself. Even with all the riding he'd been doing in recent months at his father's War-wickshire estate, he wasn't accustomed to the length he'd spent in the saddle today.

"Can I help?"

He followed my gaze to his hands, telling me he hadn't been entirely conscious of what he was doing. As his eyes met mine, the air began to thicken between us. "Not now. But . . ." His gaze dipped to my lips. "Later."

I swallowed, feeling a pulse of anticipation despite my fatigue. "What did you think of them?" I asked, trying to divert my thoughts away from his powerful thighs and how attractive he looked even splattered with mud, his jaw shadowed with stubble. "The Roscarrocks. Or rather, the Killigrews," I clarified. "Did Tristram tell you anything of interest after I left?"

"They . . ." he narrowed his eyes, compressing his lips as if searching for the right words ". . . were not what I expected."

"Dolly said much the same thing about us," I replied, reaching down to untie my kid leather half-boots.

"I suppose that was inevitable, given the fact we were forming our opinions of each other based purely on speculation and hearsay." He leaned back against his hands. "But Tristam seems like a decent chap. Though he clearly doesn't think much of Mery."

"None of them do."

"I'm curious to meet him."

I carefully extricated one foot and then the other from my boots, trying not to dislodge any of the dried mud. "If something happened to Mery, I suppose that would mean the estate would pass to one of Swithun's heirs," I ruminated.

"Most likely."

In Britain, inheritance usually passed to the heirs of the body following the male line, making Margaret and Amelia's children ineligible. Even though the Roscarrocks boasted no titles, and so were not bound by the hereditary laws of the peerage, it was doubtful they possessed any sort of patent stating otherwise.

I lifted my skirts to begin unrolling one stocking and then the other. "Then I suppose if Great-Uncle Branok *was* murdered, it removes inheritance as a potential motive for the Killigrews. Though it gives a fairly strong one to Mery."

"Maybe," Gage hedged.

I looked up at him to find him eyeing my legs. "You don't think it gives Mery a motive?"

"Oh, undoubtedly. A point that the Killigrews made certain we were aware of."

I allowed my skirts to fall back into place. "You think they did so on purpose?"

"Maybe."

I scowled at him.

"It's merely interesting to note." He sat forward. "How long do you think it would take to contact Swithun or his heirs and wrinkle out who would inherit the Roscarrock estate? And who's to say Swithun or his progeny would even *want* to travel to England to take possession? It's a long journey. Either way, it would take months, if not *years*, before any changes could be made."

"I suppose I follow your reasoning," I conceded, reaching up to loosen his cravat from around his neck. "But wouldn't that give them more motive to kill *Mery* than Great-Uncle Branok? After all, Branok was nearing eighty, while Mery must be less than half that."

His lips curled into a resigned smile. "It's simply a supposition, Kiera. Let's not get ahead of ourselves. We don't even know if Great-Aunt Amelia's suspicions are correct."

"Suspicions Dolly seemed to indicate the rest of the family didn't share," I informed him just as there was a rap on the door.

Gage looked as if he wanted to ask me to explain further, but instead he called out for whoever was knocking to enter.

The door opened to reveal Bree carrying a stack of towels while Anderley followed close behind with an ewer full of water. They both looked tired, but I noticed they'd at least had the opportunity to change out of their muddy traveling attire.

"Is Emma settled?" my maid asked as she set the towels beside the washstand.

"Yes. Hopefully for most of the night," I said. "What of you? Are your accommodations satisfactory?" I glanced at Gage. "Albeit a bit more cozy than usual."

Roscarrock House was by no means small, but it also wasn't a massive manor like those owned by many of the members of the nobility we often socialized with and undertook inquiries on behalf of. I estimated it boasted perhaps eight bedrooms, though with so many family members already living here, that limited the number of guest chambers available. Being medieval in origin, there was no floor below ground for the servants, nor had a third floor been added above where their quarters might be housed. As such, I suspected a servant wing had been constructed adjacent to the main residence.

"Aye, I'm to share wi' Dolly Killigrew's maid. She seems friendly enough." Bree cast a teasing look at the valet. "Anderley's no' so lucky."

His face constricted as he set the ewer beside the washbasin. "They believed they were doing me a kindness by allowing me to share with Lembus."

I grimaced, knowing how little Anderley liked Lord Gage's valet. Truth be told, Lembus was a pompous little toad, so I didn't blame him.

"If we had a dressing room, I'd suggest you make a pallet there," Gage told him.

Anderley clasped his hands behind his back. "Apparently, Lord Gage's *superior* room possesses a small adjoining chamber." It was clear by his supercilious tones that he was imitating the other valet. "So perhaps he'll tire of *me* and decide to sleep there." The sparkle in his eyes told me that he intended to help persuade Lembus to that conclusion.

I shook my head, struggling to withhold my amusement, for I knew from past experience just how persistent Anderley could be.

"As long as I don't have to hear about it from my father," Gage warned with a chuckle. "Now, give me the lay of the land."

Anderley nodded, producing a hastily drawn map from the inner pocket of his frock coat, which he unfolded on top of the dressing table. We all gathered around it as he pulled the brace of candles closer and began to explain.

"The main house forms a sort of rectangle with a courtyard more or less at its center. However, the western edge is merely a thick curtain wall with an arched opening leading to another outer courtyard enclosed on three sides." He pointed at the southwestern corner of the house. "The servants' wing adjoins the manor here, and the coach house here." At the northwest corner. "Abutting the house to the south are the gardens, and beyond that a number of fields. While to the north, opposite the main drive are several barns, outbuildings, and granaries, as well as a handful of cottages."

"What of this?" Gage asked, indicating a large oval southwest of the house, beyond the servants' wing.

"That's a pond. A drainage channel runs west away from it toward Port Quin, eventually turning into a small stream. The channel is dry now, but I suspect the pond spills over into it rather quickly during heavy rains."

Based on the look the two men shared, I could tell they each held suspicions about this convenient feature and what else it might be put to use for.

Gage's hand swept over the map along the scraggly sketched coast from Port Quin nearly to Port Isaac. "And all of this is more or less Roscarrock property?"

"Yes, as well as a sizable portion farther inland."

"You managed to uncover all of this just since our arrival?" I remarked in astonishment.

Anderley's lips curved into a furtive smile, leaving me to wonder how much of this was discovered by reconnaissance and how much by charming the information out of others.

"He had a bit o' help," Bree leaned over to whisper in a teasing tone. But rather than be annoyed by her interference as he might have in the past, he simply smiled wider.

I chose not to remark upon it, but the romance that had blossomed and then withered, only to blossom again between our personal servants was definitely near full bloom. Though it was difficult at times, I'd largely followed my husband's advice not to pry into their personal lives. Not unless they volunteered the information themselves. But there had been indications that Bree had finally decided to encourage Anderley's renewed overtures. Bright eyes and secretive little smiles and moments when she responded to my summons looking a little more breathless and rumpled than usual.

I turned to my husband, curious if he'd noticed their covert exchange, but he was leaning over the table, studying the map again.

"Great-Aunt Amelia has promised to explain her suspicions to us in the morning, and then we'll wish to see the place where Great-Uncle Branok's body was found." Gage looked up at his valet. "In the meantime, I need you both to keep your eyes and ears open," he informed them. "The family may be inclined to secrecy, but I'm hopeful their staff won't be so circumspect."

"They havena shared what troubles 'em aboot Branok Roscarrock's death, then?" Bree asked, having read between the lines. Her eyes darted between us, seeking clarification.

"No." Gage's brow furrowed. "Truth be told, they were more interested in discussing just about anyone else."

"I noted that as well," I said, tucking a few stray strands of my chestnut brown hair behind my ear. "Branok is the reason we're here. Yet none of them seemed in a great hurry to speak of him. Or his death."

A loud creak echoed through the chamber, reminding me of the sound of someone stepping on a loose floorboard. However, the noise didn't come from the direction of the door or the corridor beyond, but along the outer wall to my left. I glanced toward it distractedly.

"Despite the fact he's now cold in the ground, he evidently still holds some degree of power in this house," Gage remarked. "Or rather, his influence does."

As if in answer, another creak rent the air, this one deeper, almost like a groan. All of us turned in the direction of the offending noise this time. The candlelight behind us cast our shadows large against the wall.

"I don't believe I saw shutters on any of the windows. At least, not on this side of the house. Did you?" I asked, seeking an explanation for the noise. One that would lower the hairs that had stood up on the back of my neck.

"I didn't notice any," my husband replied, sounding more puzzled than concerned.

However, Bree was obviously unsettled, even going so far as to latch on to Anderley's arm as she murmured some sort of plea to one of the saints.

"It's an old house, *mia cara*," he assured her. "They make strange noises."

This was the first time I'd heard Anderley use a term of endearment from his Italian heritage, and it temporarily diverted my attention. Long enough for Gage to stride across the room and brush aside the drapes. "Easily medieval in origin," he confirmed as he leaned forward to examine the window casing. "Father told me the first farmhouse here was built during the twelfth century."

"Then I suppose it would be odder if the place *didn't* creak and moan," I supplied, trying to make light of the matter.

"Aye," Bree agreed, though she sounded unconvinced.

"Regardless, it's been a long four days," I added. "So perhaps we should all get some rest."

The men agreed, but Bree continued to stare at the window even as Gage allowed the drapes to fall back into place, her fingers gripping the crucifix which I knew lay beneath the bodice of her high-necked sprig green gown.

"Can this wait until morning to soak?" I prodded her, lifting the mud-streaked hem of my carriage dress. My bare toes poked out beneath.

She nodded hesitantly at first and then with more confidence. "Aye. 'Tis better if it dries completely. Wi' any luck, I'll be able to brush most o' it off. But I'll take your boots noo," she informed me, spotting them next to the bed.

Anderley instructed Gage likewise before helping him to remove his riding boots, which like all the best-quality attire had been crafted to mold to the owner's foot.

As the door closed behind our personal servants, our boots in hand, I presented my back to Gage so that he could begin unfastening my garments. Normally, Bree would have undressed me, but given our close quarters and everyone's need for sleep, this was the best alternative. Besides, my husband had played lady's maid for me plenty of times before. It was a skill at which he rather excelled.

"We don't need to worry that Miss McEvoy will allow her imagination to run away with her, do we?" he asked as his fingers moved nimbly down the buttons.

I knew to what he referred. Bree did tend to believe in the supernatural more easily than my pragmatic husband or his valet. She was Scottish, after all. As I was half-Scottish. But that didn't mean either of us were unbound by reason.

"No. I trust her to keep a good head on her shoulders." I turned my head so that I could see him out of the corner of my eye. "Though I'll remind you that even *you* have experienced things you can't explain."

His grunt didn't precisely signal agreement. "Perhaps. But an old house settling isn't one of them."

"Give her some grace. It's been a tiring day. And she didn't choose to travel here. We did."

He spun me around to face him, my gown and pair of stays gaping open at the back. "True." He heaved a long sigh, bending forward so that his forehead touched mine. "It has been a tiring day."

"Hmmm," I hummed as I began to unbutton his deep blue waistcoat and then his fine lawn shirt. "And it's made you a bit cranky."

He straightened. "Cranky?"

"Grumpy."

"Grumpy?"

A smile played at the corner of my lips. "Cross."

"Now, see here," he protested as I whirled away, dashing toward the other side of the bed, where he snatched me up as I gave a shriek of laughter. I covered my mouth, mindful of Emma sleeping next door.

He tumbled me across the bed before following me down. "I'll show you cross," he vowed, before pressing his lips to my neck. I moaned in pleasure as his mouth found the spot behind my ear that never failed to send licks of heat through me.

However, the second groan didn't come from me, but once again the window.

Gage broke off his courteous attentions to glare at it. "If it's going to do that all night, I truly will become cross."

I plunged my fingers into his golden hair, turning his gaze back to meet mine as I trailed my foot up his leg. "Then I'll simply have to distract you."

I didn't have to make the suggestion twice.

CHAPTER 7

B ranok always knew his death would be unnatural," Great-Aunt Amelia declared the next morning, seated at the end of the long table in the dining room. Her gnarled fingers gripped the mug before her, steam still rising from the tea as she stared into its depths, almost as if she felt it held all the answers. "Even as a young man," she elaborated before lifting her gaze to meet Gage's and then mine. "He dreamed of it, ye see. Dreamed of 'is murder. 'Twas a shadow that followed 'im all his life."

Lord Gage scoffed in his chair across the table, his arms crossed over his chest. "If he did, I would suggest that says more about his conscience than the means of his demise."

Amelia turned to glare at him until Gage prodded her to continue. "Branok dreamed he would be pushed off a cliff?"

She shook her head. "Not the exact method, ye mind. Or rather, it changed from dream to dream. But the result 'twas the same." She turned her head to look out the window at the gardens. A vine still bursting with purple clematis flowers trailed along its edge, the petals fluttering softly in the breeze. "Death unnatural," she pronounced solemnly just as a cloud scuttled across the sun, casting the house and gardens in shade.

"And that's why you believe your brother was murdered?" Gage asked, seeking clarification. Though his demeanor was polite and his manner confiding, I could sense the barely restrained impatience humming beneath his skin and tightening his brow.

"Partly," Great-Aunt Amelia conceded as the sun emerged from the clouds again, bathing the floor beneath the windows in light. Its wood, like the length of the table, was worn and scarred in places, marred with the patina of time. "But I also know Branok was murdered because it's impossible that he could 'ave fallen. He knew those cliffs." She stabbed the table with her finger in emphasis. "Knew 'em like the backs of his 'ands. And respected 'em! He knew where 'e could step close to the edge and where 'e couldn't. When the wind were too blustery and when it weren't. There's no way 'twas an accident."

Gage looked toward the other family members present, but they seemed content to let Amelia do the telling. If Dolly had been there, she might have revealed more than the others' pensive expressions implied, but she had been called away to settle a dispute between her children.

"There wasn't any evidence of a rockslide in the place he went over," Bevil supplied gruffly, perhaps feeling compelled to contribute something to the conversation.

Then the cliff hadn't suddenly given way beneath him, but that wasn't the only natural cause that might have precipitated his fall.

"What of his heart?" I queried, watching as Amelia pressed her hand over her chest. "You told us you suffer from a weak heart. Might Branok have suffered from the same?"

"Nay," she refuted. "He was fit as a fiddle 'til the day he died."

"Yes, but issues of the heart are not so easily diagnosed. He might not have experienced any symptoms—or no alarming ones, at any rate—until the attack occurred."

Amelia shook her head. "Nay. I'll not believe it."

But just because she didn't want to believe it didn't make it untrue. I looked at the others again, but their expressions still remained unmoved, revealing nothing of their thoughts on the matter.

"What of his state of mind?" Gage ventured delicately. "Was he agitated or perturbed in any way?"

A deep frown scored Bevil's features even as Great-Aunt Amelia began to shake her head in protest. "He weren't mad, if that's what you're implying." Her gaze cut sourly toward Lord Gage, as if his son's question was his fault.

"I'm not trying to imply anything," Gage replied. "Merely attempting to understand whether his thoughts might have been disordered enough that he turned careless. Had he fought with anyone recently, for instance?" His gaze shifted to appeal to Tristram. "His grandson Meryasek, for instance." Who had still not appeared at the main house to be introduced to us.

Tristram turned to his father, who answered for them. "Not that any of us recall." Bevil's scowl deepened. "'Least, no more than usual. He was always after Mery to take more of an interest."

"Who found the body?" Lord Gage asked almost dispassionately. This might have been a welcome change from his perpetual air of restrained hostility, if not for the fact he was speaking of his uncle's human remains. In this instance, *some* emotion—even antagonism—would have been preferable to none.

A muscle ticked in Bevil's jaw. "*I* did." He shrugged toward his son. "And Tristram and Mery came up a few minutes later." He dipped his gaze to glower at the remnants of his breakfast. "We all went searchin' after he didn't show up for supper."

"Why did you go searching for him?" Gage had sat forward

incrementally as he asked this question, so I knew he'd caught the scent of something. And when Bevil didn't answer immediately, I began to believe he was right.

"Because Branok never missed supper," Amelia interjected. "Not if he could 'elp it."

Whether this was true or not, I couldn't say, but it was clear they were hiding something. Or, at the very least, they weren't sharing all. Joan had even begun to fidget with the trim on her sleeve, bunching and rolling the lace between her fingers.

But Gage didn't press, perhaps realizing, as I did, that we would get nothing from them now. It was best to let them believe their behavior had gone unnoticed until we had more information.

If Lord Gage had also noted this, he seemed to be of a similar mind, for he began to push to his feet. "Then you can show us precisely where his death occurred?"

Bevil remained seated for a moment longer before agreeing. "Aye."

Tristram seemed of a mind to come, too, for he joined the rest of us in departing the long southern-facing chamber, leaving Joan and Amelia at the table scattered with breakfast dishes the staff had yet to clear away. After ascertaining the place was best approached on foot, I donned my freshly cleaned and polished kid leather half-boots and pulled on a warm forest green woolen pelisse over my cornflower blue morning dress.

"'Tis a bit of a nip and a scramble," Bevil warned me when I met the men in the entry hall.

"I shall manage," I assured him.

He eyed me doubtfully, but then shrugged. "Suit yourself."

With that, he led us out the door and across the main drive to a smaller lane between a number of the barns and outbuildings. We passed a few grooms and farmhands about their tasks. Most ignored us, though one younger lad leading a horse was so curious he only narrowly avoided stepping in a large pile of horse droppings.

At the far edge of the farm buildings, a line of small cottages hugged the lane. I suspected they were abodes for the farm-workers and perhaps even their families. The sight of laundry fluttering on a line stretched between the houses seemed to confirm this.

At the end of the lane, we struck out across the fields, skirting the edge of one bordered by rowan trees. These trees led us to a narrow strip of wilder, uncultivated land which gradually widened into a bell as we neared the coast. Though I couldn't yet see it, I could hear the rumble of the waves as they rolled up onto the shore and crashed against the rocks. The air was pungent with the scent of brine and the lushness of sunbaked gorse and wild fennel. I had to lift my skirts, lest they become tangled in the scrub.

Then the vegetation began to thin, and I spied a deep scar in the rock face leading into a little cove. The tide foamed against the rocks as it rushed in and then retreated. But rather than enter it, Bevil abruptly led us away to the left and up toward the cliffs overlooking the tiny inlet. The climb to the top was steep and bordered by a thicket of brush and brambles, but once I reached the top, panting, I could see for what seemed like miles down the coast in either direction.

"To the west is Varley Head," Bevil informed us, I supposed to give us a sense of our location. He turned to nod behind us. "To the east, Lobber Point, and beyond that, Port Isaac." I noticed his breathing wasn't labored, nor had he broken a sweat.

Lord Gage, on the other hand, was definitely favoring the leg in which he'd been shot some months earlier. Something Bevil's bushy eyebrows eloquently communicated his derision of without saying a word when his cousin was the last to reach the summit.

"Uncle Branok 'ad to have fallen from here," he told them, pointing toward a spot far below. "We found 'im there."

One by one, we inched closer to peer over the side of the cliff, the wind snatching at our hats. The drop was substantial. Certainly far enough to kill a person. Especially as the sand and shingle beach was punctuated with craggy rocks lapped by the tide. It was on its way out, but at high tide the water probably came all the way up to the cliff face.

"It's fortunate the body wasn't swept out to sea," Gage remarked.

"Aye," Bevil agreed. "Another few hours and we might not 'ave found him."

Tristram stood with his hands locked at his sides, a troubled look on his face, possibly reliving the memory. It would not have been a pleasant one.

Branok's body would have been battered and broken, with numerous fractures and contusions. The incoming tide might have washed away some of the blood and evidence, but not all. Not if it hadn't yet carried away the body. It would have been a horrific death, but hopefully a swift one. I found myself praying he'd not suffered long. That he'd struck his head so hard on the way down that he died instantaneously. Anything else was too terrible to contemplate, but the question needed to be asked.

"He was . . . expired?" I choked out.

Out of the corner of my eye, I saw Bevil turn to look at me. "Aye."

I nodded, swallowing. "No sign he regained consciousness after . . ." I broke off, leaving the question unfinished, though I trusted he knew what I meant.

It took him a bit longer to respond this time. "Nay."

I nodded again. "Good."

His delay in answering might have meant he was lying, sparing my sensibilities, but I chose to believe him, nonetheless.

Gage had been pacing left and right, attempting to examine everything from slightly different angles. "How on earth did you retrieve his body?"

"When the tide is low enough, you can make your way 'round to it from that little cove we passed, but ye 'ave to be wary." He glanced at his son, who continued to stand immobile. "We 'ad a devil of a time gettin' to him and carryin' him back as the tide was rushin' back in."

Tristram's gaze lifted to his father, and the wariness I'd expected to see stamped there had been replaced by flushed cheeks and snapping eyes I could only surmise was anger. But at what exactly? Having been forced to risk his own life to retrieve his great-uncle's corpse? Depending on how harrowing the experience had been, I supposed it was possible, but I couldn't help but wonder if there was something more.

"Is the tide far enough out for us to go there now?" Gage asked, weighing his father's fitness out of the corner of his eye.

Bevil scrutinized the wash of the waves and the movement of the water farther out to sea. "Aye. Should be safe enough."

Knowing well how my father-in-law's stubbornness might drive him to push himself beyond his physical ability and injure himself, I reached out to grasp Lord Gage's arm. "Lend me your assistance descending this hill, will you?"

He didn't respond, but he also didn't push me away, allowing the others to go ahead of us. My husband's gaze met mine briefly, letting me know he was aware of exactly what I was doing. I only hoped his father hadn't seen the gleam of gratitude in his son's eye.

We started out slowly, stepping with care through the steepest part of the rise. Only after the angle decreased to one more manageable did Lord Gage speak. "So this is what I am now? An invalid forced to remain back with the ladies." His voice was brittle and bitter, and I knew he was thinking of the look his cousin Bevil had directed at him when he'd been the last to reach the summit.

"Another lady might take offense at that," I replied. "She might feel slighted that you haven't professed yourself flattered and delighted to be chosen for such an honor."

He arched a single eyebrow mockingly. "Yet you are no such lady."

"True," I agreed blithely. "I know you too well."

"I feel there's an insult in there somewhere," he ventured after a moment of silence.

I laughed. "Only if you rank consequence over affection." I twinkled at him. "But then I've seen you crawling around on the floor making silly faces at your granddaughter."

A grin hovered at the edges of his mouth. "I refuse to be impugned for such a thing."

"As you shouldn't," I assured him. "Emma adores you."

"Yes, well, you know the sentiment is mutual."

We skirted to the right of a sharp bramble patch, by this point having lost sight of the others.

"Don't think I don't know what you're about," Lord Gage scolded. "You've completely taken the wind out of my sails. And a justifiable wind it was, too."

"How so?"

"Bevil thinks me soft," he growled.

"I should like to see how fast he climbs a hill after taking a gunshot to his rectus femoris," I protested. "Not very quickly, I wager. But tell me, what did you think of the place Bevil estimates your uncle fell from? Do you think he's accurate?"

"If he's being truthful about where they found his body . . ." He appeared to ponder the possibility that he hadn't, but then shook his head. "And I don't see why he wouldn't be. Then yes, that seems the most feasible spot that he tumbled from."

I gnawed on my lower lip, ruminating on what this meant.

"What?" Lord Gage jostled me when I didn't answer fast enough. "What is it?"

"It's only . . ." I hesitated, wondering if I should wait for Gage to join us before sharing my thoughts, but then I decided he'd undoubtedly already come to the same conclusion. "I don't see how Branok could have accidentally fallen from that cliff. Even if he'd been suffering from a heart attack or an apoplexy or . . . or a sudden attack of gastric fever, he would merely fall to the edge of the path and the brambles would catch him."

Lord Gage's brow furrowed as he considered this. "He would have had to jump or be *thrown* from the cliff to land where he did." The lines scoring his brow deepened. "Then his death couldn't have been an accident. It was deliberate on his part, or someone else's."

I waited a moment for this to sink in before continuing. My father-in-law might have his problems with the Roscarrocks. He might have avoided them for almost fifty years. But that didn't mean discovering that his once-beloved uncle had either been murdered or committed suicide was easy.

"Yet the physician and local constable both ruled his death an accident, and so the coroner's inquest followed suit. Why?"

"I suppose that's a question we'll have to put to them," Lord Gage answered as we reached the entrance to the cove.

But Gage, Bevil, and Tristram had apparently already gone ahead, having disappeared from our view around the nearest rocky outcropping. I frowned, not liking the idea that Gage was wading into a precarious position with just the aid of Bevil and Tristram. After all, those two men were both suspects in Branok's death.

Regrettably, there was no way either Lord Gage or I could catch up to them now. Not after seeing how uneven the rugged shoreline was. It would be far too easy to twist an ankle or fall and bruise a hip. So we kept close to the opening, where a small waterfall cascaded down to the cove below. I ventured a bit farther out as the sea retreated with the tide, exploring the rock pools and inspecting the limpets and anemones clinging to the sides of the rocks, my gaze ever going back to the cliff face around which Gage and the others must return, but I didn't go far.

A caw drew my gaze upward as the distinctive blue-black body of a chough circled overhead twice before flying inland. I had opened my mouth to jest to Lord Gage that King Arthur had come to examine our worthiness when a young man appeared over the hill. His hair was windblown and the same blue-black shade as the chough's feathers. If I had believed in such things, I might have thought he was the chough turned into man, but I knew better. This was a Roscarrock. And there was only one left in Cornwall we'd yet to meet.

Mery stopped to stare down at me, and though there was nothing hostile in his demeanor, there was nothing welcoming either. Meanwhile, my father-in-law had followed my gaze to the figure in question and risen from the rock where he'd perched to come stand next to me. Mery's posture stiffened slightly at the sight of him, and then he approached, padding down the incline to the shingled sand.

"An' 'ere I thought ye were a mermaid," he drawled, revealing a West Country accent thicker than we'd heard from his other relatives. I suspected it was done on purpose.

"Surely, not," I replied uncertainly. There was something in his gaze that wasn't quite respectful.

He turned his head toward the sea and shrugged carelessly. In fact, everything about his appearance was rather careless: from his shaggy, windblown hair to the dark stubble shadowing his jaw to his loose, wrinkled clothing. Had I not known better, I might have believed him a vagabond.

"You're Stephen," he proclaimed, turning to glare at my

father-in-law, who arched his eyebrows disdainfully at being addressed as such. But rather than be chagrined, Mery only evinced amusement at having ruffled his consequential cousin's feathers. "Lord Gage," he corrected as if even this was a joke.

The look he fastened on me bordered on insolent. "And you must be the witch."

CHAPTER 8

I beg your pardon?" I replied icily.

He lifted his hands, laughter glinting in his eyes. "I meant no offense."

Of course he had.

"We like our witches, mages, and pellars here in Cornwall." He stepped back to prop one boot up on a rock, crossing his arms over his chest. "Once upon a time, ye would've been revered." Maybe so, but his stance and his half-lidded eyes made it clear that was not the case now.

However, I'd confronted more than my fair share of men like him. They wanted nothing more than to elicit a reaction, and I was not going to give him the satisfaction. My father-in-law, on the other hand, was on the verge of delivering him the blistering put-down he clearly desired. And while there was nothing more I would have liked than to hear Lord Gage defend me after so many years of enduring his scorn, it would merely play into Mery's hands.

So I gripped my father-in-law's bicep firmly with my hand and turned the conversation in a direction Mery almost certainly didn't wish it to go. "My condolences on the death of your grandfather."

Mery's features constricted, though I couldn't tell if it was sadness or anger he strove to control.

"As I understand it, he was like a father to you. I'm sure this must be a difficult time for you."

He turned to look out to sea again, his cocksure posture softening. "Why? Haven't ye heard?" he challenged. "I inherit everything."

"Yes, but that doesn't replace your grandfather," I said, able to recognize his bluster for what it was—a shield for his pain.

Lord Gage seemed to sense this as well, for he'd fallen silent, allowing me to do the talking. That was, until Mery made his next statement.

"Nay. 'Tis much better."

"Perhaps you helped matters along, then?" Lord Gage posited. "Pushed your grandfather over the cliff so you could claim your inheritance all the faster."

Mery's eyes glinted with mockery. "Ye are so far from the truth, ye might as well be in India." His contempt sharpened to a knife's point. "And I hope I'm around to witness it when ye realize it."

I didn't know what to make of this statement. "But you *were* there when Branok's body was found, weren't you?"

His gaze swung toward where three men could now be seen picking their way back across the craggy shore, hugging the rock face as the tide washed over their boots. I exhaled in relief at the sight of Gage's familiar silhouette in the middle, the hem of his four-caped greatcoat snapping about his legs.

"So they say."

I scrutinized Mery's hardened features. "That's not really an answer."

He shrugged.

I thought Lord Gage might press him further, but he merely eyed the younger man with disfavor. Perhaps, like his son, he preferred to gather more information before pressuring a suspect. After all, we had very little facts to go on, and if it proved Branok had committed suicide, then there was no murderer to apprehend.

Even so, Mery bore watching, for like many of the others, he knew more than he was saying, and as somewhat of an outsider to the rest of the family, his loyalty was less certain. The others might be swift to blame him because he was guilty. But they might also be swift to blame him because they feared he knew too much, and they didn't trust him to keep quiet. What better way to cast aspersions on his honor and forthrightness than to make him a suspect.

"I see you've met Mery," Bevil remarked once he'd drawn close enough for us to hear him. His sharp gaze riveted on the younger man. "Ye haven't been borin' 'em with your granfer's tall tales, have ye?"

Mery scowled fiercely, refusing to answer and making me suspect this statement held some hidden meaning.

Gage's color was high, but he appeared none the worse for the trek except for some damp near the bottom of his greatcoat as he passed Bevil to offer Mery his hand. "Sebastian Gage."

Mery seemed surprised by the gesture but accepted his hand readily enough. "Meryasek Roscarrock."

Gage nodded, turning to survey our surroundings. "This is quite the estate you've inherited. Wild, but beautiful." He turned back to the man no more than five years his junior. "Though I'm sorry for your loss."

Rather than toss back a glib remark as before, Mery simply dipped his head in acceptance.

If Gage found his behavior questionable, he didn't indicate it, instead returning to the matter at hand. "Who was the physician or surgeon who examined the body?"

"That'd be Tom Wolcott." Bevil paused before adding, "My niece's husband."

I frowned. And yet the nature of the death had caused him no concern? But then, perhaps he'd only examined the injuries after Branok had been brought to him. Perhaps he hadn't seen the cliff he'd gone over.

"Tristram can take ye to him," Bevil offered.

"Was the parish constable or magistrate called to the scene?" Lord Gage interjected.

Bevil's jaw clenched. "Aye, and the constable deemed it an accident. 'Twas only later that we questioned it."

"That *you* questioned it or Great-Aunt Amelia?" My query was directed at Bevil, but I was watching Tristram and Mery just as closely.

"'Tis true. Mother voiced more doubts than the rest of us," Bevil conceded begrudgingly. His gaze fastened on Lord Gage. "If it'd been up to me, I wouldn't have contacted ye with naught but speculation. But as you can see, Mother has a mind of her own."

Gage shifted his feet, propping one booted heel on a rock much like Mery had done a short time ago, though his stance was artless whereas Mery's had been posturing. "Then you saw no reason at the time to question the inquest's verdict?"

"Nay." Bevil exchanged a look with Tristram. "That is . . ."

"The parish constable is no friend to the Roscarrocks," Mery explained, staring broodingly through the overgrown fringe of his hair. "An' he made sure the rulin' was death by misadventure."

Lord Gage asked, "Who's the constable?"

Bevil once again seemed hesitant to speak, but for what turned out to be a very different reason. "Cuttance."

Lord Gage stiffened. "The old preventive officer? He's still alive?"

"His son."

I turned to Gage, curious if he knew what had unsettled his father. And then I remembered. My father-in-law had been apprehended as a boy by a preventive officer. Apprehended after his friend was shot and killed by the same man. The elder Cuttance must be that official.

"Then the younger Mr. Cuttance bears a grudge?" Gage clarified.

"He would say not," Tristram began.

Mery scoffed.

"But it's obvious from the number of times he's shown up on our doorstep with one complaint or another, or insisted on makin' a search of the property, that he does."

Bevil nodded toward the path up the hill we'd taken to the cliff Branok had most likely fallen from. "Patrols our coastline more than the others as well."

"You can't blame him for that," Lord Gage charged. "You *are* smugglers."

All three Cornish men scowled.

"*Were* smugglers," Bevil retorted. "We haven't been free traders for more than twenty years."

Lord Gage's mouth curled in a sneer. "You expect us to believe that?"

"I don't care if ye do or ye don't." Bevil squared his shoulders to face him, clenching his hands at his side. "Though ye should know the truth of it. You decimated our ships in '02. And don't think we didn't know it was *you* who targeted our vessels so ruthlessly."

"I hoped you would."

I stepped between the men before they could come to blows. "Gentlemen, please. To the matter at hand," I scolded, before turning to appeal to our Cornish relatives. "Are you suggesting that this Mr. Cuttance might have been patrolling your coastline the evening Branok died? That Mr. Cuttance might have been the last person to see Branok alive?" The remainder went unspoken, for I wasn't quite ready to accuse a man I'd never met—an officer of the parish—of murder.

"It crossed my mind," Bevil replied, being equally circumspect.

I pressed two fingers to my temple, for this complicated matters. Cuttance was the man to whom we would have to apply for more information, and he could just as easily deny or mislead us. We could apply to the local magistrate, but not every justice of the peace was as invested in the day-to-day running of their parish. If he trusted Cuttance, then he might know very little of the details of Branok's death, and our attempt to go over the constable's head could simply make matters more contentious.

"We should speak to him as well, then," Gage declared, for there was no other option.

Bevil glanced at his son. "If ye go before midday, ye should still catch him at 'ome."

Gage peered up at the sun. "Then I suppose we shouldn't waste any time."

He offered me his arm, turning our steps back in the direction we'd come. Once again, Bevil and Tristram led the way, while Lord Gage followed and Mery trailed along at the rear.

I peered over my shoulder before whispering. "Do you know what happened in '02?"

A furrow formed between Gage's eyebrows. "The Peace of Amiens."

The temporary cessation of war between Britain and Napoleonic France. The uneasy truce had lasted for a little over a year before hostilities resumed, but during the fifteen months when peace had reigned, many of the Royal Navy's warships would have been recalled home or reassigned to other duties.

I studied Gage's troubled features out of the corner of my eye. "I gather you didn't see your father more often during that time." Gage would have been five years old—old enough to remember. And by that time, he and his mother would have already moved from Plymouth to Langstone Manor at the edge of Dartmoor to live with his maternal grandfather.

"No." He inhaled a ragged breath. "Apparently, he and his ship were reallocated to fight a different battle."

One that also happened to be personal to him. Stopping the rampant amount of smuggling that was taking place along Britain's coast. While Britain's naval power had been focused on its enemies, namely France, I imagined there hadn't been enough resources left to combat the free trading problem. But with the fighting ceased, even temporarily, and the Royal Navy's ships returned to its territorial waters, it could heighten patrols and squash the smuggling problem once and for all. Or, at least, severely cripple it.

Given his history with the area, it made sense for Lord Gage to have been assigned to patrol the waters off Cornwall's northwest coast. Or perhaps he'd requested it. I could well imagine him doing so. I couldn't even say I blamed him. But Bevil's remarks seemed to indicate that perhaps his cousin had gone above and beyond duty into the realm of personal vendetta.

I could tell that my husband wondered, as I did, whether this vendetta had so preoccupied his father that he hadn't taken the full amount of leave he was due. It was one thing to accept that war had kept his father away for fifty weeks out of the year. It was quite another to know his father had chosen to pursue revenge, even in the guise of fealty, rather than spend time with his wife and only child.

We returned to a flurry of activity at the manor. Staff bustled through the rooms and about the gardens, moving furniture, airing linens, and trimming hedges. Even Great-Aunt Amelia and Dolly were at work in the dining room arranging flowers in about a dozen vases and ewers.

"What is all this?" I asked in bewilderment. Through the windows I could see tables being created from long boards and trestles.

"There's so many family members and neighbors to introduce ye to, we decided 'twould be easier to bring them all to *you*," Amelia replied as she clipped the ends of a pair of camellias.

I realized then that they intended to host some sort of dinner party or soiree, and by all appearances they intended it to be a grand one. I glanced at Gage and his father helplessly. "Oh, but we wouldn't dream of putting you to all this trouble. Especially not so soon after Branok's death."

"'Tis no trouble. We Cornish love a good party. Branok, chief among them. So there's no fear he'd disapprove."

"'Twould probably enjoy the notion of our thumbing our noses at convention," Joan added as she entered the door at the far end of the room, which I'd learned that morning led to the kitchens in the servants' wing. The way the tiny hairs curled about her head as if she'd walked through a cloud of steam made me suspect food preparations had already begun in earnest. Knowing that, we could hardly ask them to cancel the party now.

"Did ye see what ye needed to see?" Great-Aunt Amelia's voice was thick with meaning. She was asking if we were ready to accept that her suspicions about Branok's death were justified. That it hadn't been an accident.

Rather than confirm this, Lord Gage instead elected to demur. "We have more questions."

But Amelia was shrewder than that. Her lips curled in

satisfaction as she continued her cutting and arranging. "Then 'ave Tristram take ye wherever ye need to go to ask them."

As this was exactly what we intended to do, none of us responded as we filed from the room. I noted that Dolly had remained silent through this exchange, but she looked up as I passed to offer me an encouraging smile. I hoped we'd have time to talk later when I returned.

Bree was waiting for me in my bedchamber, evidently having already been informed of our intent, for my sage green riding habit with gold epaulette trim was draped across the bed. "Is it murder, then?" she asked as I set aside my pelisse and bonnet and turned to allow her to begin unfastening the buttons of my morning dress.

"It's certainly suspicious," I told her. "And difficult to imagine Branok tumbling over the cliff by accident." I hesitated to conjure the other possibility that had crossed our minds, perhaps because in some ways it was worse. "But that doesn't mean it's murder."

Bree tugged harder at the edges of my gown than usual. "Suicide, ye mean?" She mumbled a swift prayer. I knew, as a Roman Catholic, this would unsettle her more than me, for I liked to think the Lord might still be merciful to those who had committed such an extreme act. "But why?" she gasped, and I knew she was asking about his motivation rather than why we suspected it.

"I don't know," I admitted. "Certainly, the picture his family paints of him doesn't suggest a man likely to take his own life. But maybe he was keeping something from them. Something that would explain his taking such an uncharacteristic and desperate measure."

"Like what? That he was sick?"

"It's possible. If he were in a lot of pain, if he felt there was no hope, he might have decided he couldn't endure it anymore and that the only way to find relief was in death."

Bree whisked my gown over my head. "But why not seek oblivion in a bottle? Whisky or laudanum or the like. Why throw himself over a cliff? Seems a foolish way to escape further pain."

I had to concede she was right. An overdose of medication or even a gunshot to the head seemed a more foolproof method. But we didn't *know* Branok Roscarrock. We didn't know his loves, his hopes, his fears. Lord Gage's impression of him was fifty years old, and while we might have thought to gain a clearer picture of him from the rest of his family, he seemed in some ways to be an enigma to them as well. That, or they were withholding information. Something we'd already suspected.

"Perhaps there's something about that cliff that was meaningful to him," I suggested after fastening my riding boots, standing to slide my arms into the frilled white habit shirt Bree held out for me. "Or maybe it was a spontaneous decision. One born of some extreme pain." I exhaled in frustration as I fastened the four buttons at the front of the shirt. "I'm afraid without more information, it's all purely speculation." But something else to question Dr. Wolcott about.

"What of the goings-on here?" I asked as Bree helped me into a second petticoat and then my riding skirt. "Anything to report?"

"No' unless ye count this *cèilidh* they're plannin' for this evenin'. The whole house is bein' turned inside oot because o' it."

"It seems quite sudden."

"Aye, though the staff seem to be takin' it in stride. Mayhap they're used to such chaos." She brushed a piece of lint from the gigot sleeve of the jacket before holding it up for me to slip on. "I'll offer to help where I can. If I wriggle my way into their good graces, perhaps they'll share somethin' pertinent to our inquiry."

Even though she'd phrased it in such a mercenary manner, I knew Bree would have offered to help regardless. At her core, she had a kind heart.

Once my sugar-loaf hat with chinstrap was firmly in place, I took up my long whip and paused to check my appearance in the mirror. My skin glowed healthily from the morning's exertions and my eyes were bright with inquisitiveness. "Tell Mrs. Mackay I'll return to tend to Emma before her midday nap."

CHAPTER 9

The hamlet of Trelights, comprised of little more than two or three dozen stone rubble cottages with rag slate roofs and a dissenters' chapel, lay a short distance to the south across rolling fields and down narrow lanes lined with hedges. Villagers had to venture two miles north to Port Isaac for most businesses, including a pub. However, Dr. Wolcott lived in a home that was slightly larger than those around it, boasting what appeared to be a newer addition to the original cottage, as well as a square outbuilding dug into the side of a mounded hill.

The physician was younger than I'd expected—probably only a year or two my senior—and possessed a lean physique with a strong profile, and a shock of yellow hair. He didn't seem surprised by our appearance on his doorstep, and we soon learned why as he shook Tristram's hand. "Heard there's to be quite the doings at the manor tonight in honor of your guests."

"Aye. Seems word is spreadin' fast," Tristram agreed.

A young woman with blue-black hair and dainty features

peered around the corner as we were ushered inside, her hands resting over her rounded stomach. "Well, it's not every day we get to meet new relations *and* enjoy the Roscarrocks' hospitality." She eyed us all curiously as Tristram introduced us.

"My wife, Anne," Tom Wolcott contributed as Tristram finished, though the hand he'd placed on her back had already made their relationship plain. "We can talk in my study," he told us, evidently already aware of the reason for our visit.

I approached Mrs. Wolcott, allowing the men to go before me. "Congratulations."

She glanced down at her abdomen self-consciously. "Oh, thank ye, my lady."

"Your first?"

"Aye." She laughed lightly. "How could ye tell?"

"My daughter is seven months old, so not long ago, I was in very much the same condition."

"Ah. I look forward to meetin' her."

"Anne," Dr. Wolcott turned to say, his eyes soft with affection. "Perhaps some tea for our guests. Will you tell Mrs. Durdle?"

"Aye," she told him before dipping a brief curtsy. "Excuse me."

I followed the men into Dr. Wolcott's study, relieved when the physician didn't object. At times, medical men proved to be the most stringent opponents, both because I was a lady and because of my scandalous involvement with my first husband's work with anatomy. Either Dr. Wolcott was more open-minded about such things or he wisely recognized that if my husband and father-in-law didn't object to my presence, then it wasn't his place to do so.

Unlike most gentlemen's studies, I found the room to be rather inviting. Perhaps because, in many senses, it resembled more of a sitting room. The white walls were covered in colorful watercolors of plants and flowers, and the drapes had been pulled back to allow sunlight to spill into the room. A comfortable settee and two armchairs were arranged near the hearth, while a small desk and cabinet sat at the other end of the chamber. Though physicians most often made house calls, I wondered if Dr. Wolcott also sometimes consulted with patients here.

He gestured for us to be seated, before choosing one of the armchairs for himself. "Now, I surmise you're here about Branok. Nanna Killigrew has been very vocal about her belief that his death was murder." He spread his hands wide. "But I don't know what else I can tell you."

"You examined the body?" Gage prompted.

Dr. Wolcott dipped his head. "Aye. There were a number of lacerations and contusions, as well as broken bones. All injuries you would expect from such a fall. Nothing to raise undo concern." His brow furrowed lightly, and I could tell something was niggling at him.

"Except what?" I prodded.

He glanced at Tristram before continuing. "The only wound that gave me even a moment's hesitation was found in the middle of the back." He gestured behind him. "Just below the fourth rib. There was a laceration, a puncture, about three quarters of an inch in depth. But the rocks where he fell are sharp, and all sorts of debris washes up from shipwrecks and the like. Given the wound's shallow depth and rough edges, any number of things could have caused it during his fall." He leaned forward slightly, as if to convince us. "It wasn't the cause of his death."

"What was?" Lord Gage's voice was pitched low, making me suspect he wasn't entirely unaffected by the evidence of his uncle's injuries.

"Severe trauma to the back of the head."

"Then he would not have remained conscious for long?" I

asked, wanting to ease my mind that Branok had not suffered much beyond the initial fall.

Dr. Wolcott's eyes glinted with something akin to regret, perhaps at causing me distress. "I suspect he was dead or, at the very least, insensible before he reached the bottom."

Tristram pushed to his feet, striding toward the window, where he stood rigidly, looking out at the front garden. This was obviously not easy for him to hear either.

"The trauma he suffered to the back of his head," Gage began, keeping a watchful eye on both his father and Tristram, as well as the doctor. "Is there any way to be certain it was caused by the fall and not, say, a blunt object swung at Branok from behind." The implication being that the blow had then propelled Branok over the cliff.

Dr. Wolcott shook his head. "There were so many injuries caused by the fall, particularly to the head. There's really no way to determine if one was delivered by a blow rather than the impacts of the fall. Not when they would have happened almost simultaneously. At least, not that I'm aware of."

It was true. The wounds from the fall would have almost certainly obscured any evidence of a strike. Thus, there was no way to conclusively confirm or refute the possibility.

Lord Gage scowled. "Did you mention this at the coroner's inquest?"

Dr. Wolcott straightened, frowning defensively. "No, because it's not my place to do so. I present the evidence, as I find it. It's up to the constable and the jury to interpret it."

He was correct. The parish constable should have been the one to examine the site of Branok's death and note that an accidental fall was questionable. He was the one who should have investigated the potential that a blow had been struck before the fall. So why hadn't he?

"Did you perform an autopsy?" I asked deferentially, not wishing the physician to take further affront and refuse to answer any more of our questions. "Were you able to tell if something natural might have provoked his fall?"

"I did not," he replied. "It seemed unnecessary. And at the time, Nanna Killigrew seemed distressed by the notion. It was only later that she became suspicious."

I found this statement to be interesting. I wondered what had made Amelia change her mind. Did she suspect someone in particular? Perhaps someone from her own family? That might explain her failure to make a bald accusation. Maybe she wanted to be sure before she took such a drastic step, and that's why she'd asked for our help. Though not entirely impartial, we were more objective than most, including their own parish constable.

I glanced at Lord Gage, where he sat scowling down at the wooden floor. Or at least, Gage and I were fairly objective. I didn't think anyone would classify my father-in-law as impartial. Not about the Roscarrocks.

"What of Branok's health otherwise?" I queried. "Did he suffer from heart problems like his sister?"

This provoked a reflexive grin from Dr. Wolcott I didn't at first understand. "I take it you are unacquainted with Branok Roscarrock, my lady. The only way he would have solicited a physician's advice is if he were on his deathbed, and perhaps not even then."

Tristram grunted as if in agreement.

"But he was nearing eighty years old, so it seems likely he suffered from a number of complaints. Though he didn't share them with me."

The tea tray was brought in then by a short, pleasant-faced woman of about forty, so all talk of death and autopsies ceased. I'd not had the opportunity to ask Dr. Wolcott about Branok's mental state, but then I supposed he'd already answered it. If

Branok were in pain or struggling otherwise, he would not have shared it with his great-grandniece's husband. There was a chance Dr. Wolcott might have observed something in the older man's demeanor, but I decided he was far more prone to share it with me if I asked him privately, either later at the party or another time.

So instead, I agreed to the physician's request that I pour, and set about preparing everyone's tea.

If Dr. Wolcott was all that was gracious and accommodating, Mr. Cuttance was the exact opposite. We managed to track down the parish constable and preventive officer on the western edge of Port Isaac.

Having left Trelights by following the narrow tracks that served as roads, we traveled north toward the sea—its expanse an endless deep blue horizon beneath billowy, white clouds. Though they and the ocean all but disappeared as the lane descended a steep hill where roadside hedges and overarching trees bursting with autumn colors swallowed riders in their cool shade, only to spit them out almost in the heart of the warren of terraced buildings that formed the seaside village of Port Isaac. The white and natural stone structures were constructed right up to the harbor's edge, where boats rested off-kilter on the sand as the tide was out.

Our horse's hooves clattered over the cobblestones as Tristram led us toward a junction with a street leading east, but we stopped short before a handsome edifice that bore a sign telling us this was the Golden Lion. "That's him," Tristram said over his shoulder, nodding toward a man who had strolled out of the tavern and paused to adjust his trousers around his rounded gut. "Officer Cuttance," Tristram called to get his attention.

Cuttance checked his footsteps, lazily scrutinizing us before swaggering in our direction. "Well, young Killigrew, what 'ave we 'ere." His gaze sharpened as he inspected first my father-in-law and then my husband. "This wouldn't be Stephen Gage return to Roscarrock, and his son, by the looks of it."

"That's Lord Gage to you," my father-in-law replied as he dismounted.

"Aye, I'd 'eard," Cuttance replied without correcting his error. He scratched idly at the bristles dusting his jaw, nodding once to a passing villager who eyed us all with curiosity. "Though that don't change who ye are." He leaned forward. "Or what you've done."

I felt my ire rising as the odious man baited my father-in-law, and decided then and there that I wouldn't be dismounting. As a lady, it was my prerogative, and I fully intended to exercise it. Gage had turned to help me do just that, but one glimpse of the tight moue of my mouth and he lowered his arms.

"I'm afraid we're less concerned with such inconsequential ancient history," I pronounced, arching my chin, "than the events a fortnight past."

Cuttance's beady eyes narrowed up at me. "Aye, I know why yer here. Branok. But the jury at the coroner's inquest ruled his death to be by accident or misadventure. So I don't know what ye hoped to achieve by muckin' in matters that ain't yer business. Ye've no authority here." He grimaced. "But I do."

"I wonder if your magistrate would say the same." Lord Gage turned to Tristram. "Who is that again?"

Cuttance's face reddened. "And I wonder what yer friends in London would make of your smugglin' history should the papers catch wind of it."

I struggled not to react, knowing Lord Gage feared just such a disclosure being made public. Even Gage seemed unsettled by the threat, stepping forward to decry, "Now, see here—"

But his father cut him off. "There's no need for that, Sebastian." Neither his voice nor his face betrayed the smallest hint of agitation. "Mr. Cuttance knows his family has as much to lose from such a revelation as I do," he continued, his words coolly clipped. "Perhaps more." He tilted his head, his scrutiny of the man as slicing as I recalled it being on our first meeting. "I must wonder if you have the same arrangement your father did."

Tristram's horse suddenly snorted in protest, tossing his head. While Tristram acted swiftly to soothe the gelding before he could harm anyone on the narrow thoroughfare, I spared a moment to ponder what had triggered the steed's behavior in the first place. It was true, it might have been something as simple as the pressing crowd and tight space, or even a sting from an insect, but it was clear from the glance Lord Gage darted Tristram's way that my father-in-law suspected something else.

Cuttance, meanwhile, appeared apoplectic. A reaction that seemed extreme given the circumstances, but then, his demeanor had been abrasive and antagonistic from the start. Unmeritedly so, if the cause of his contention lay fifty years in the past.

Unless the reason for his hostility was not Lord Gage, but the Roscarrocks. That might have explained why he barked at Tristram in parting rather than Lord Gage. "I'll only warn ye once, Killigrew. Keep your family in line, or I'll be forced to do it for ye." Then he stomped off, shouldering his way past a pair of men who had lingered to watch our exchange.

"That could have gone better," Gage quipped dryly.

Lord Gage grunted. "Having known his father, I can't say I didn't expect just such a welcome." He turned his penetrating gaze on Tristram. "But I suspect Uncle Branok believed he had his uses."

Tristram scowled. "Well, I'm not Branok, and he certainly didn't take me into his confidence. If you've got somethin' specific ye want to ask, you're better off speakin' to my father or

Mery," he snapped, remounting his horse, and turning its head back in the direction we'd come.

Gage and his father exchanged a speaking glance before following suit.

The source of Tristam's frustration seemed evident to me. After all, he and his family lived and worked on an estate he didn't own, at the sufferance of first his great-uncle and now his cousin. Having witnessed his father endure the same fate his entire life, he must have no delusions what this meant. Perhaps if a relative had provided him with a small annuity or inheritance, or had bought him a commission in the army or Royal Navy, he might have been able to forge a different life with better prospects for his wife and three children. But the Roscarrocks seemed to prefer to keep the family's power and wealth concentrated in the hands of the heir. Unless someone forced their hand, as in the situation with Lord Gage.

Given all this, I couldn't help but feel empathy for Tristram. For his circumstances and for Mr. Cuttance's blustering threats. Threats that only heightened my suspicion of the constable.

As far as I could tell, the most glaring reason for Cuttance to oppose our investigation of Branok's death was because there was something he feared we would uncover. Something he wanted to keep from being known. Unfortunately, that could be a number of things. Perhaps he'd bungled the inquiry? Perhaps he'd taken a bribe from someone? Or maybe he'd murdered Branok himself? Until we knew more, we were merely guessing.

Only one thing was for sure. We wouldn't be getting any assistance from the man. We could contact the local magistrate, but given the little evidence of foul play we'd gathered so far, that seemed premature. After all, just because circumstances seemed to indicate the fall was unlikely to have been accidental did not prove it was murder.

Regrettably, I feared that even if a murder *had* occurred, it was already too late to prove it. That the evidence we needed had been washed away by the tide or decomposed with the body. Unless something unexpected came to light, I wasn't sure what more could be done.

CHAPTER 10

Good heavens," I murmured from my position near the window, peering down at the garden path below. "I thought tonight's dinner party was for relatives and neighbors, but it looks as if they've invited everyone for ten square miles." Laughter drifted on the evening breeze, as well as the music of a violin striking up a jaunty tune.

"Aye, Cora warned me 'tis a large family," Bree replied, joining me in my perusal of the guests below.

A large family, perhaps, but not of Roscarrocks. Not if Mery was the last of them.

"Much like in the Highlands, everyone here seems to be related to everyone else, in one way or another," Bree added. "Tends to happen when ye live so far from the rest of civilization."

I supposed that made sense. After all, more than half of my brother-in-law's staff at Gairloch Castle in the Highlands were related to each other. This proved to be both a boon and a bane to my sister in her management of the household, for while they all looked out for each other, they could also hold fierce grudges. I suspected the same could be said of the people below. The question was, had one of those grudges gotten Branok killed?

I heaved a weary sigh. Gage and I had already spent much of the afternoon riding about the countryside searching for anyone who might have witnessed anything the day Branok died, but no one admitted to seeing him or anyone else strolling toward the coast path that day. Not after midday that day, in any case, when several of the staff members at Roscarrock House reported they'd last seen Branok to Lord Gage. They'd brought a dish in while he was seated at the dining table, or they'd observed him standing at the side entrance, seeming to be absorbed in watching the antics of a pair of warblers. But none of them could then tell us where he'd gone.

This left a gap of nearly six or seven hours between the time Branok was last seen and when his body had been found. During some of those hours, Branok might have already been dead, but how many? Dr. Wolcott might have been able to tell based on rigor mortis and such, but I'd forgotten to ask him.

However, that would still not tell us whether Branok was murdered, or if he'd thrown himself off that cliff, or if some previously unconsidered circumstances had conspired to cause his death. I'd spent much of my time nursing Emma that evening while contemplating ways an accident still might have occurred. What if he'd tripped over a rock and it had thrown him forward? Or what if he'd been so lost in thought he'd not paid attention to where he was going? Having seen the place from which he'd tumbled, neither of these struck me as likely scenarios. There had been no large rocks to trip over, and the gorse and bracken lining the path was so jagged and prickly, he would surely have been recalled to his senses before he passed the point of no return.

And wasn't all of this terribly morbid to be ruminating over while tending to my sweet daughter?

I rested my head against the window frame, wishing I might have spent the evening rocking Emma in my arms instead of dressing for a party. Considering my awkwardness and failure to grasp social cues that no one else ever seemed to miss, soirees and gatherings were already difficult enough for me even in the best of times, but when I was fatigued and irritable after a long day, they could prove downright disastrous.

"Come, m'lady," Bree said, her voice soft as if she sensed my distress. "Let's finish yer hair."

I allowed her to coax me to sit on the bench set before the dressing table. I scrutinized my appearance in the oval looking glass as she carefully wielded the hot tongs to curl the hairs at my temples. The gauze muslin evening gown Bree had chosen for me was perfect—fine enough for a London ballroom, but not so fine that I would be out of place at this country gathering. We'd been informed there would be dancing, and the full skirts and green gauze ribbons allowed for such movement. The cheery green-and-pink running pattern of the pelerines on the bodice also did much to highlight what little color I had in my cheeks. Of course, my lapis-lazuli blue eyes were as brilliant as always, but there was little that could dim them.

"You mentioned Cora," I murmured, knowing Bree preferred to prattle as she worked. "Is that Dolly Killigrew's maid?"

"Aye. And she's a font of information, I tell ye. Thinks Mrs. Killigrew's expectin' again, though her mistress doesna want to admit it."

I eyed Bree curiously, wondering if this was meant to be an oblique poke at me. It was true, my courses had yet to return since giving birth and I was fatigued. But I was breastfeeding, and I'd also just traveled hundreds of miles and spent an entire day fruitlessly searching for answers to a question that was beginning to seem unanswerable. Given all of this, it seemed premature to assume anything in that regard, though Gage was as attentive as always.

"What else did she tell you?" I prodded, toying with the amethyst pendant draped around my neck.

"That two months ago, Mr. Roscarrock dismissed a third of the staff."

My gaze flew to hers in the reflection of the mirror, finding her eyebrows arched significantly. "Really?"

"Aye. Cora said they've all had to take on tasks they shouldna, but they dare not complain, lest they find themselves dismissed, too."

I pondered this information as Bree began to curl the hair on the other side of my head. "Perhaps the Roscarrocks are not as wealthy as they wish to seem." If so, did that mean they'd been telling the truth when Bevil claimed they were no longer involved with smuggling? Or rather, were they living beyond their means? And what was this evening's party—at no small expense—meant to prove?

I waited until Bree had finished curling the section of hair closest to my skin and allowed it to fall gently back against my face, the tendrils still warm from the tongs, before speaking. "Let us know if you note any other signs of financial strain."

"I can already tell ye the staff have been grousin' aboot a leak in the roof over the servants' quarters. They say the slate has been repaired several times, but what it needs is to be stripped and replaced."

At a hefty cost, I imagined. But was the Roscarrocks' reluctance to do so because it merely inconvenienced their staff and not them? Or was it because they didn't have the money to make the repairs? Either way, I couldn't imagine any of the staff members were happy about this party when the funds could have been put to better use.

I considered all of this as Bree finished my hair and then moistened a towelette with my favorite floral-scented perfume to dab it across my neck and decolletage to help mask any lingering odor of scorched hair and the day's exertions. The noise from the party outside was growing louder and I could only hope it didn't wake Emma sleeping in the room next door. I had seen the tip of her first tooth protruding from her gums earlier, and she was still fretful from it working its way through. Sliding my feet into my dancing slippers, I crossed to the window once more, intending to shut it. However, the old wooden frame appeared swollen, making it difficult.

"Bree, lend me a hand."

She dropped the pile of discarded garments she'd been gathering on the end of the bed and moved to my side, but even with our combined strength we couldn't force it. Leaning closer, she examined the frame. "There's a splinter o' loose wood here. Lower the window slowly while I push it in."

I followed her directions, taking care not to pinch her fingers. Once past the obstruction, it slid shut, sealing out at least some of the merry music and voices. Curious about the sturdiness of the frame, I glided my hand over the trim where the wood had begun to splinter internally, scrutinizing its integrity. But my interest was soon diverted by a marking on the plaster of the wall adjacent to it.

"What is this?" I asked, trailing my fingers over the circular ridged pattern. It appeared almost artistic in design, but then why was it hidden here, next to a window where the drapes would cover it?

"Ye mean, you've never seen one before," Bree responded in some disbelief. "'Tis a witch mark."

I straightened, removing my hand. "A witch mark?"

"Aye. They used to put them by every door and window, and

even the hearth, to ward off witches. Ye see the pattern. 'Tis like a labyrinth the witches get trapped in and canna escape."

I peered closer, noting she was right. There was an opening to the ridged design near the window, but if one followed its path, it circled around and around itself, leading to the center, like the hedge maze at Gairloch Castle.

"Ye can still see them in lots o' older buildings. Houses and cottages, manor homes, churches," Bree explained. "That is, if they havena been plastered or papered over."

"And you've seen them before?"

"They were used in Scotland, too." She turned toward the other window, which was already shut. "My parents' cottage has 'em. So did Langstone Manor."

Gage's cousin's estate on Dartmoor. Given the age of that manor, this did not surprise me.

"Here's another," she said, pointing at the wall in approximately the same place next to the other window behind the drapes.

I moved closer to see that she was correct. "Then they're no cause for alarm?"

"Nay. Simply evidence that someone in the past believed in witches and feared 'em enough to try to keep 'em oot o' their home."

I thought of the strange noises we'd heard the previous evening coming from the area around the window. From the pucker between Bree's brows, I could tell she was thinking of them as well. But I did not believe in witches. At least, not the type who had supernatural powers and could steal into houses unseen.

After all, hadn't I been called a witch enough times to prove what an archaic, ignorant, intolerant term it was? In this enlightened age, calling a woman a witch was nothing more than slander.

I frowned, recalling how Mery had called me a witch, though he'd tried to imply it wasn't an insult. Just as those who called my eyes witch bright attempted to laugh it off as merely a jest. Mery had claimed that witches were welcomed here in Cornwall, but these witch marks would appear to contradict this. He'd also used another word I'd thought it better not to ask him to explain.

"Bree, do you know what a pellar is?"

She eyed me curiously. "From what I can gather, they're like witches, but also no'. They heal wi' herbs and folk remedies, and work charms and such. But they're also somehoo like a justice o' the peace or a magistrate, and also somehoo like a priest." She shook her head in a mixture of bafflement and disbelief. "I overheard two o' the women who were hired to help wi' the dinner preparations discussin' the matter while they peeled potatoes and cut onions. The cook didna look happy wi' 'em, but seein' hoo she was already run off her feet, she couldna afford to offend 'em by shushin' 'em. She told me no' to mind their quibblin'," Bree finished, reaching out to adjust the fall of the sleeve of my gown.

"But why? Pellars don't sound particularly ominous."

"Because the women seemed convinced that if a pellar were aboot, the matter o' Mr. Roscarrock's death would already be solved. Though they seemed to disagree on what sort o' justice the pellar would deem was merited. One woman claimed it was sinful to wish ill o' anyone, while the other thinks Mr. Roscarrock got what he deserved."

I suddenly felt cross. It was easy, and perhaps tempting, to believe that a person with supernatural powers could discern the truth with a wave of their hand. However, the world did not work that way. It took hard work to put the pieces together to uncover the truth and unmask a killer.

"How did *you* hear about pellars?" asked Bree.

"Mery Roscarrock mentioned them in passing."

Bree's expression darkened. "The staff are no' fond o' that one."

I arched my eyebrows, urging her to explain.

"He's a brooder. Sour and temperamental. And a scoundrel." Bree gathered up the pile of clothes on the bed again. "There may be nay more legitimate Roscarrocks, but rumor has it there are plenty o' illegitimate ones."

I didn't have a response to this, and a burst of muted laughter coming through the now-closed window reminded me it was long past time I made an appearance. So I donned my warm plum pelisse trimmed with ermine and made my way toward the stairs. Five children ranging in age from about one and a half to seven years old lined the rail to stare over the banister at the guests gathered below. Knowing Dolly and Tristram had only three children, I surmised two of them must belong to guests. I smiled at them all and their nursemaid before lifting the skirts of my gown to descend.

I spied Gage's golden head among those gathered in the entry and, as if sensing my scrutiny, he lifted his gaze to meet mine. A soft smile of pleasure lit his face, warming me to my toes. But before I could take even two steps in his direction, Great-Aunt Amelia latched on to me with a remarkably strong grip for someone her age.

"Kiera, there ye are. I've some people for ye to meet."

Her use of the word *some* was a bit misleading, for the number of people she introduced me to was well over two score. She propelled me through the house and out into the gardens, gleefully presenting me to everyone we passed as both Lady Darby and Mrs. Gage. True to Bree's report, everyone *did* seem to be related to nearly everyone else, but I lost track of the names and degrees of separation in the thicket of family trees that formed their community. Blearily, I wondered if they would all have to be interviewed about Branok. It would take days. No, weeks to complete the task.

The very thought was daunting, and while I tried not to reveal my bewilderment and dismay, I feared I wasn't entirely successful. Not if my father-in-law's commiserating smile was anything to judge by. I had thought to be the one offering him consolation, for I knew tonight would not be easy for him, but he appeared to be holding up rather well under the strain.

"If it's any solace, none of them expect you to remember their names," he leaned down to murmur when I found myself standing next to him at the periphery of the gathering. The whirlwind that proved to be Great-Aunt Amelia had spun itself out, and now she was seated in a comfortable cane-back chair being plied with sustenance by well-meaning family members. "They'll not hold your reputation against you either, seeing as how many of them believe the gentle folks in London to be far too soft." He exhaled a long breath. "Here, death—and everything that goes with it—is simply a part of life."

This was the first time I'd heard him say anything remotely complimentary about this land of his ancestors, and I couldn't help but study him out of the corner of my eye. His shoulders were tight, and he was undoubtedly far from relaxed, but either by force of will or desire, a genial smile curled his lips rather than the contemptuous sneer he'd adopted much of the time since our arrival. He was also right. I hadn't detected any disgust or enmity when Amelia had disclosed my past—in both subtle and not-so-subtle ways—to those she'd introduced me to, only curiosity.

"I suppose Emma is asleep?" Lord Gage said, softening my heart toward him even further. "She would be enthralled to see the garden like this."

I had to agree. Lanterns had been strung throughout the garden from trees and poles, lighting up the night, and placed down the center of the tables draped in white cloths. A profusion of camellias, hydrangeas, tibouchina, and myrtle filled vases and porcelain pitchers, lending their sweet fragrance to the evening air. The last vestiges of sunset were fading in the west over the sea, while stars filled the canvas of the sky overhead. Three firepits crackled and popped merrily at the periphery of the gathering, spaced evenly to provide both additional light and warmth, as well as a place to roast nuts, cheese, and various other tidbits, of which there were plenty.

The long table inside the dining room practically yawned with food, both familiar and unfamiliar. Pilchards, lobsters, oysters, mussels, potatoes prepared three ways, asparagus, fruits, and cheeses nestled alongside local specialties like pasties, saffron buns, and young nettle tips. Bree had already warned me about the stargazy pie. The Cornish delicacy sounded fanciful enough, but was made from six types of local fish and decorated with fish heads and tails which emerged from the crust like live fish leaping out of the waves. Some sort of heroic tale explained the origin of the dish, but even had I known it, I wasn't sure I would have found the pie any more appealing.

"I'll concede one thing," Lord Gage remarked, his eyes fastened on the fiddlers in the corner playing a lively reel. "My relatives certainly know how to enjoy themselves."

A makeshift dance floor had been created, and several couples twirled across its expanse while others clapped in enjoyment.

"They remind me of my mother's family," I told him, feeling a sudden pang of longing for Uncle Andrew and Aunt Sarah, for cousin Jock and all the others. Then a welcome pulse of amusement superseded my melancholy as a fellow dancing with a large pilchard spun into view. "Including him."

Lord Gage actually chuckled. "There's always one in every family."

With his face lit with good humor and his silver eyes twinkling with merriment, I was reminded of what a good-looking man my father-in-law was still purported to be, and how much his son resembled him. From the strong jawline and cleft in his chin to the sculpted cheekbones and the twist of curls at his forehead—though Lord Gage's hair was no longer blond but gray. This was how my husband would look in twenty-five years' time.

Like everyone here, he was dressed to impress. Though, truth be told, much like his son, Lord Gage rarely appeared anything but impeccable. Tonight, he was not wearing his usual dark evening attire, but a more colorful frock coat and trousers, like the other gentlemen present. His coat was a lovely pigeon blue which gave his gray eyes almost a crystalline quality.

I was about to tease him about his informality, considering the fact he'd required Gage and I to dress for dinner every night at Bevington Park. A tradition strictly maintained by much of society, but one that Gage and I sometimes eschewed when it was just the two of us dining together. But I noted a woman approaching us, hesitantly at first, and then with more assurance.

"Stephen," she murmured in a pleasing alto. "Stephen, is that really you?"

Lord Gage stiffened, and I thought for a moment he was going to deliver her a set-down for speaking to him so familiarly. Then I realized it was not outrage but astonishment that he felt.

"Tamsyn?" he replied, almost in wonderment.

She smiled in answer, drawing a smirk from him and a crack of laughter.

"By God, it's good to see you."

CHAPTER 11

Witnessing my father-in-law's delighted reaction, I couldn't help but scrutinize the woman he'd called Tamsyn more closely. I guessed she was of a similar age to him and possessed a very fine pair of sloe brown eyes ringed with thick lashes. In fact, at one time she must have been a real beauty, though time had worn some of that away. A number of her teeth were missing and there was an unevenness to her jawline that made me suspect part of the bone had deteriorated. It must have been painful to eat, which accounted for the extreme slimness of her frame. But for all that, there was also a heartiness to her, a time-worn resilience, like granite.

"I'd not thought to see you here," he declared, taking hold of her hand and bowing his head with the same exquisite grace he showed the ladies who fawned over him in London. "But I suppose the Grenvilles *are* Roscarrock kin."

"Strained though that be at times," she replied.

This comment seemed to dampen some of Lord Gage's delight.

"However, I'm a Kellynack now."

His eyebrows arched. "You wed Ethan, then?"

"I did. God rest his soul." She turned to me, offering her hand. "We haven't been introduced. Tamsyn Grenville Kellynack."

Prodded by this statement, Lord Gage stepped in to perform the remainder of the niceties. "My daughter-in-law," he explained before arching his neck to peer over the heads of those nearby. "My son is around here somewhere."

"Pleased to meet you," I told her.

"Likewise."

"Mrs. Kellynack is a cousin some degrees removed, and an old friend," Lord Gage clarified. The warmth with which he infused the word *friend* made me suspect this wasn't just a passing remark.

"Aye, a friend too old to put up with this Mrs. Kellynack nonsense," she teased. "Tamsyn I've always been, and Tamsyn I'll always be. The same to you, Mrs. Gage."

I smiled. "Then you must call me Kiera."

"Oh," she crooned. "Now, aren't you lovely. And I suspect your son is as meddlesomely 'ansome as *you* always were," she told Lord Gage.

"Meddlesome?" he protested.

She planted her hands on her hips before elaborating for me. "There wasn't a girl from age three to age sixteen who wasn't fawnin' over the boy, and he didn't pay them any mind."

"I noticed *you*," he replied with flattering intensity.

"Only because of Jago."

A heavy silence fell, ending their friendly and flirtatious banter, and I could only surmise it was because of her mention of Jago. Although Lord Gage had never told me his name, from the grim set of his mouth, I suspected Jago must be the friend who was killed by the revenue men so long ago. Yet, thus far, no one had dared to speak his name. No one but Tamsyn.

"You've been away too long, Stephen." She shook her head sadly. "Jago wouldn't have wanted that."

"But maybe his mother would."

"Auntie Pasca? Nay. She's naught a bitter bone in her body."

"She's still alive?" Lord Gage seemed alarmed to learn this.

"Aye. Ye should pay her a visit."

I could tell it was on the tip of his tongue to refuse when the sound of raised voices drew everyone's attention toward a man who was climbing wobbly up onto a chair with the help of his no-more-stable friends. Obviously, they had been imbibing freely from the spirits provided.

"Oi!" the man shouted, slurring his words. "Let's 'ave a toast to ole Branok." He raised his glass, sloshing half of it over the side onto his laughing companions. "'Is 'ospitality be as generous in life as it were in death."

I glanced at Lord Gage, wondering if this was meant to be an insult to Mery and the Killigrews while the man tittered before continuing.

"Almost as generous as 'is supply o' brandy, Holland, an' good Irish whiskey."

"Here, here!" his friends echoed as, almost to a man, every other head swiveled to look at us, as if belatedly realizing not everyone among them was so accepting of the implication. Lord Gage's expression had turned thunderous, but he held his tongue. Perhaps recognizing it would do no good to object when most, if not all, those present were perfectly content to partake of the spirits and possibly other goods that had been smuggled in to avoid paying the tariffs the government imposed on such imports.

In any case, the man on the chair was soon yanked down by

a woman half his size, who latched onto his ear. "Cam, ye great dobeck! Shut your gob."

"Cam *is* an idiot," Tamsyn said to Lord Gage. "Always has been."

"Maybe so," Lord Gage answered in a deceptively calm voice. "But that doesn't mean the Roscarrocks have stopped their free trading."

Tamsyn clamped her lips together, seeming to struggle with how to respond. And *that*, in and of itself, spoke volumes. "I'm not privy to such information," she finally said. "But I will say, we're never for want of fine spirits in these parts."

"Did you know Branok well?" I asked, deciding this was my opening.

Her dark eyes shifted to me. "Better than most, but still not as well as some."

I was about to ask her what that meant when she elaborated.

"I don't think anyone truly knew Branok. His actions, at times, were inscrutable." She huffed. "Perhaps even to himself. What I *do* know is that I wouldn't trust him. Not even if I was drownin' and he rowed toward me with the only boat in the sea."

I didn't know how to respond to this or the deep well of hostility which seemed to underscore her words, but it seemed to strike a chord with Lord Gage. Perhaps because it confirmed what he already wanted to believe about his uncle and all of the Roscarrocks.

Which only made matters all the more awkward when Bevil suddenly appeared at our side. "Tamsyn," he greeted her stiffly. "How fares your brother? Heard his leg's been givin' 'im trouble again."

"Aye," Tamysn confirmed, her voice tight but cordial. "Dr. Wolcott says there's naught left to do but amputate, but Gil would still rather contend with the pain than the loss of 'is limb."

Bevil nodded. "Gil was always tough."

Tamsyn made no verbal response to this, but from the fierce light in her eyes I could tell there was more to the matter than either was saying. Some hidden undercurrent that made me hesitate to ask what had happened to Gil. But Lord Gage still had other matters on his mind.

"Quite the selection of spirits," he bit out in his typical acerbic tones.

Bevil's jaw hardened. "Aye. Branok always was particular about his liquor. Would've mortgaged the estate if that's what he had to do to get it." He turned away to growl in an undertone. When he caught sight of me watching him, he nodded his head toward the house. "Ye should try the Punch."

I offered him a smile. "I will."

He clomped off before I could attempt to converse more, and I felt a stirring of empathy for him. Clearly, I wasn't the only one who felt awkward in social situations or who made abrupt statements to try to cover that fact. I spied his wife Joan standing near the side of the house, sneaking glances at him as he circulated among the guests. I wondered if she felt the need to monitor him as my older sister, Alana, always had me, ready to step in to smooth over any gauche remark I might make.

Dolly waved her hand, beckoning me to join her a short distance away. Lord Gage and Tamsyn had their heads bent toward each other in conversation, so I excused myself to cross the short distance to Tristram's grinning wife. She looked fetching in a gown and pelisse of pale blue, her blond curls swept up high on her head. I couldn't help but search her features and figure for any indication that what her maid had shared with Bree was true, but if so, I could discern no obvious physical evidence that she was with child again. Even I knew better than to ask.

"Here ye are," Dolly exclaimed, drawing me closer. "I've some ladies to introduce ye to."

I realized then that she had been standing with a trio of women all of a similar age to us. They smiled in welcome as Dolly presented them each in turn.

"Anne, you've already met."

"Yes," I replied, nodding at Dr. Wolcott's pretty dark-haired wife. "Lovely to see you again."

"Likewise."

"And this is my sister-in-law, Morgan Knill." Dolly gestured to a woman with thick ash-blond hair and the same sharp features as her mother Joan.

Morgan nodded demurely, also much like her mother.

"Her husband is somewhere about." Dolly made a brief show of searching for him before leaning in to murmur. "He's a dissenter, but we don't 'old that against 'im."

Morgan continued to smile good-naturedly even as Dolly giggled. Given the fact we were in Cornwall, I suspected by *dissenter*, she meant Methodist, and wondered if the Knills attended the chapel we'd seen in Trelights earlier that day. Word was there were many of John Wesley's followers in Cornwall because he'd preached here numerous times in the latter half of the previous century.

"And this is Imogen Trewhella."

The final woman was by far the tallest and possessed soft brown hair clipped short, which accented her high cheekbones.

"Her 'usband Ervan is Tristram's first cousin," Dolly explained as I briefly clasped Imogen's proffered hand.

"Then you're all Great-Aunt Amelia's granddaughters or married to one of her grandsons?" I clarified, wanting to understand their relation.

"That's correct." Imogen flashed an impish grin. "We're the Merry Wives of Roscarrock."

"No one calls us that," Morgan countered dampeningly.

"Dolly does."

"'Tis true," Dolly chimed in to say.

Morgan arched a single eyebrow. "No one *else* does."

But this distinction didn't seem to bother Dolly, who ignored her, gesturing to me with a flourish. "And of course, *this* is Kiera Gage." She dimpled. "She's one of us now."

"It's nice to meet you," I told them all sincerely.

A tiny pleat formed between Morgan's brows. "Yes, but . . . shouldn't we be addressin' you as Lady Darby?"

"Please, don't," I hastened to assure her, before telling them all, "Kiera will do."

Dolly rocked back on her heels. "Like I said, one of us. And she has the most adorable little girl with golden curls." She peered over her shoulder in the direction of the house. "Looks just like her da'."

We all followed her gaze toward where my husband stood speaking with a pair of men Amelia had introduced me to not a quarter of an hour earlier, yet I'd already forgotten their names. When Gage looked up to find us all watching him, he smiled uncertainly, as if he wasn't accustomed to receiving admiring glances—if not outright stares—from women everywhere he went.

"I'd heard the rumors about young Stephen . . . now Lord Gage," Imogen clarified for Morgan. "But I'm not sure I believed them until now."

"Aye, ye can certainly see the resemblance between Mr. Gage and his father," Anne ventured.

Dolly reached up to finger the cameo necklace draped around her neck. "Nanna says that if Mr. Gage 'ad the Roscarrock hair, he'd look like 'er father did when he was young."

"Perhaps," Morgan conceded. "But Nanna says the same about Mery, and I don't see much of a resemblance between him and Mr. Gage."

Dolly and Imogen grimaced in agreement.

"I doubt Mr. Gage spends half his day lathered and the rest lazin' in bed either," Imogen scoffed to the others, agreement, though Anne's was tempered.

"None of you like him, do you?" I asked, seeming to confirm it when no one leapt at the chance to be the first to answer.

"'Tis hard to like someone who has always been so disagreeable," Dolly finally said.

Having known my fair share of such people, I nodded. "I suppose I can understand that."

"But I don't think he knows any other way to be," Anne protested, directing her gaze somewhere at the vicinity of our feet. "We've all heard how 'orrible his father was, and 'ow his mother simply *abandoned* him here." Her words had grown more impassioned as she spoke, but now they softened again as she rested her hands protectively on her rounded stomach. "And I . . . I don't believe Branok was much kinder."

Given the cruelty they'd ascribed to Mery's father, Caswaran, I'd wondered whether he'd learned any of it from his own father, Branok. I supposed this was at least partially an answer.

"Maybe not, but *we've* all tried in turn to be kind to 'im." Morgan draped an arm around Anne's shoulders. "You've a good heart, but ye can't blame us for not likin' the man. Not when he treats us as he does."

"I suppose. But he's not *all* bad," Anne insisted. "Frankly, what I think he needs is a good wife."

Imogen scoffed. "If anyone will have 'im."

"Don't be daft," Morgan protested. "Of course they'll have 'im. He owns this entire estate now, doesn't he? 'Tis more likely, he'll find himself trapped into marriage. Or facing an angry father's pistol." She arched her eyebrows. "So I'd be mindful of who takes any sudden interest in 'im. Because whoever he weds will become mistress of Roscarrock."

Dolly, in particular, appeared pained by this idea, and I couldn't blame her. After all, her family lived here at Mery's sufferance. Any bride Mery took might not be able to force them from the property, but she could make life very unpleasant for them.

"Mery knows that," Anne assured them, and then flushed. "He said that's why he only bothers with barmaids and the like."

"Aye, but if he was sufficiently lathered, would he know the difference?" Imogen pointed out. "He certainly didn't know the difference when he punched that baronet last year."

"That was just a bar fight," Anne said.

Imogen shrugged as if to say she didn't see the distinction.

"Is Mery prone to violence?" I asked, trying to glean as much useful information from this conversation as I could.

"Aren't all men?" Imogen surprised me by being the one to reply. "At least, under the right circumstances," she added, softening the cynicism of her response.

"I suppose you're thinkin' of Branok's death," Morgan said, removing any hope of further subterfuge.

"Mery *was* the person with the most to gain," I replied evenly.

"Aye, and we all know Nanna asked ye 'ere because she doesn't believe her brother's death was an accident. 'Cept, it wasn't any of us." She glanced at the other women. "None of the immediate family anyway."

"How can you be certain?"

Morgan arched her chin. "Because that wouldn't be our way."

This seemed a rather ingenuous statement from a woman who had otherwise not exhibited the least amount of naïveté.

"Besides, Mery didn't want to inherit. Not yet anyway." Anne seemed certain of this. "He preferred things the way they were."

"Without responsibilities," Imogen muttered dryly.

This time Anne didn't flinch from the unflattering implication about her cousin. "Aye."

"Then, if not a family member, who *do* you believe harmed Branok?" I pressed. "Or don't you believe he was murdered at all?"

Dolly's cheeks flushed under my regard. "Mr. Cuttance has never liked Branok. At least, that's what Tristram says."

I wondered if Tristram had also told her about our interaction with the parish constable that morning. If so, she might just as easily be telling me what she thought I wanted to hear rather than her honest suspicions.

"I'd take a look at the Grenvilles," Morgan said softly.

I turned to her in surprise. "The Grenvilles?"

"Aye, they've long 'eld a grudge against the Roscarrocks."

I glanced in the direction where Lord Gage and Tamsyn had stood, but they were no longer there. "Because of Jago? Because he died while transporting smuggled cargo on behalf of the Roscarrocks?"

"Partly. There's also the matter of Gilbert Grenville's leg," Morgan added.

Tamsyn's brother? Bevil had just asked her about his lower limb.

"They blame the Roscarrocks for that as well?" I asked.

The four women exchanged looks before Dolly spoke. "It happened years ago. Gil was helpin' the Roscarrocks with some work on the estate."

"He broke his leg," Imogen chimed in to add. "'Twas never set right."

"This was before my Tom took over the practice," Anne interjected.

Imogen nodded. "It never healed correctly. Pains him awful, I 'eard."

"And since it 'appened while aidin' the Roscarrocks, there

are some Grenvilles who blame Branok," Morgan summarized, smoothing back the tendrils that had escaped her tightly bound hair.

"And you think they might have killed him for it all these years later?" I asked as the latest reel ended to a smattering of applause.

Her only response was a shrug.

Anne turned aside, fiddling with her necklace. I suspected she must be aware of her husband's recommendation that the leg be amputated. But since she chose not to share this information with the others, I decided to follow her example. After all, just because Tamsyn had informed Lord Gage and Bevil didn't mean the Grenville family wanted it aired to everyone else.

It was clear, at least to me, that the trouble with Gilbert Grenville's leg wasn't simply a break that hadn't knit properly. Not if amputation was now the physician's counsel. There must be more to it.

In any case, all of this information about the Grenvilles and Mr. Cuttance was purely supposition and hearsay. None of which proved guilt. Not on its own. We needed something more concrete.

"What of the evening Branok's body was found?" I asked, addressing Dolly specifically. "Did you notice anything odd when he was brought back to the house?"

Her eyes widened at the question, and I realized it was perhaps too blunt, too macabre for such a setting, but I blundered forward anyway when she didn't respond.

"What of the rest of you?" I asked. "Were you notified that evening? Perhaps even summoned here. Or were you told the next day?"

"He . . . wasn't brought here," Dolly stammered, finding her voice.

I frowned. "What do you mean?"

Dolly looked to Imogen and Morgan as if for confirmation. "Branok's body wasn't brought here to the house." She nodded to Anne. "He was taken straight to Dr. Wolcott's."

I supposed this wasn't unheard of, even though under normal circumstances the body would be taken to the closest residence. Especially if there was any chance of rendering the injured person aid. Then the physician or surgeon would be summoned *there* to examine them. Yet Branok's body had been transported several miles farther inland, likely by cart, to Dr. Wolcott's home in Trelights instead.

"Did *you* see anything?" I asked Anne, wondering how late it had been and if she'd retired or if the commotion of their arrival with Branok's broken body had perhaps woken her.

"I . . . I saw Uncle Bevil, Tristram, and Mery arrive. Heard 'em talkin' to Tom. But . . ." She shook her head again. "I didn't see anything else."

"You didn't see the body?"

"Nay." She clutched the Indian shawl draped around her shoulders tighter. "Tom said he didn't want me distressed. Forbade me to even go near the icehouse."

Which was the structure built into the side of the hill behind their cottage I'd noticed earlier that day, I presumed. "Is that where Branok's body was stored? Until he was laid out in his coffin for the vigil before his funeral, that is."

Once again, the women exchanged wary glances. "He was never brought back to the house," Dolly explained.

This was definitely a surprise. I supposed the notion that he'd somehow survived his fall and might yet wake must have seemed ridiculous. But even under the most strained circumstances I'd found that the bereaved often clung to tradition just as tenaciously as a ward against superstition as well as a final good-bye.

For four days, the body would be watched over day and

night, in either an opened or closed coffin, if necessary. Friends and family members would congregate to share their grief in the parlor where the vigil was held, where the flowers would be continuously refreshed in order to mask the odor of the decaying body. Then the coffin would process to the church and later the graveyard, where it would be lowered into its final resting place.

Most genteel women did not take part in the procession or attend the funeral and internment. It was generally frowned upon. So the four-day vigil over the body was usually their last chance to say their farewells. But this was Cornwall. Perhaps they didn't follow the same strict protocols.

I glanced at Morgan. I also knew that dissenters often held a different view of the matter than the Church of England, and so rather than being prohibited, women were often encouraged to attend their loved ones' funerals. But given the fact Branok had been Anglican, I doubted Morgan would have pushed herself forward in such a manner unless the other women were doing so.

"Then there was no vigil?" I replied, seeking confirmation.

Imogen crossed her arms over her chest almost defensively. "The men believed it would be too distressing."

"'Tis probably true," Morgan countered. "The sight of a dead body in such a state would undoubtedly give one nightmares." She seemed to realize too late that I had witnessed bodies in far more gruesome conditions, and flushed to the roots of her ash-blond hair.

Not wanting to draw more attention to the fact than necessary, I ignored it. Though the truth was, many of those corpses *had* given me nightmares.

"In any case, the funeral was held just two days later," Dolly supplied. "It was decided that would be best."

Decided by whom? I couldn't help but wonder. The same men who had found Branok's body? The same men with motives to want him dead?

"'Twas difficult to argue they weren't right," Anne contributed in a small voice.

And the trouble was, she was correct. Ostensibly, their decisions not to follow tradition seemed justified. Branok's body had obviously been discovered in a mangled state. There would have been no illusions that he would revive. So transporting him directly to Dr. Wolcott's and keeping him there in order to avoid upsetting the ladies seemed a prudent choice, as did hastening his funeral and burial.

But these seemingly sensible decisions could also be indicators of subterfuge. Perhaps they'd worried the women would notice something the others had not, so they'd elected to prevent even the possibility. Or perhaps they'd feared Dr. Wolcott would discover evidence he might have initially overlooked, so they'd rushed the burial. After all, the only men who could attest that the death had happened the way it did were those same three men who had found Branok's body. Even Dr. Wolcott would have been making his assessments based on the information they'd provided.

I wasn't prepared to call them all liars, or even to believe them to be, but I was still ill at ease. Something about their actions was out of kilter, and the fact I couldn't pinpoint what troubled me about them disturbed me more than I liked.

CHAPTER 12

"Come," Dolly urged with a grin as she weaved her arm through mine and towed me toward the house. "The crowder will only play another reel or two, and then Rabby James has agreed to weave a tale or two for us all. We want to 'ave our food and good seats before he begins."

Ever since Lord Gage had mentioned that his family were all able droll tellers, I'd become curious exactly what this meant, so I eagerly followed the other ladies into the dining room to fill a plate and collect a mug of cider. We returned to discover that Tristram and the other husbands had secured us seats at a table near the center of the gathering. Gage was there as well, laughing and enjoying himself among his newfound relations. I was happy for him, but I also couldn't repress a twinge of worry for his father.

The last I'd seen, he hadn't been relishing the company other than Tamsyn. But then again, he hadn't seemed to hate it either.

A surreptitious glance about the garden showed him standing at the edges of the gathering once again, speaking to a few older men.

I'd just taken my seat when the fiddler ended his tune with a flourish and another man holding a fiddle took center stage in the middle of all the tables rather than on the dancing floor. To a casual observer, he was rather unassuming, standing just a few inches taller than five feet, with a head full of silver-threaded brown hair and weather-beaten clothes. But there was a twinkle in his eye and a graceful theatricality to his movements that indicated he had the charisma of a true showman. And from the moment he first drew his bow across his fiddle strings, he held us all in his thrall.

"Aye-ye! Who's ready for a lusty tale?"

A holler went up from a few of those gathered, and soon we were being treated to the amusing ballad "Richard of Taunton Dean" and his clumsy courtship of a parson's daughter. It also wasn't long before he had us all joining him in singing the rather catchy chorus. A series of other songs followed—"Ann Tremel-lan" and "The Streams of Lovely Nancy"—interspersed with tales of mermaids and giants, of black ships that brought bad luck, and of witches and the wind charms sailors paid them to enchant to capture the wind. One legend even told of the land of Lyonesse, which allegedly lay just off the tip of Land's End, having been consumed by a great storm. Purportedly the great underwater city's bells would ring again if ever another calamitous storm was on its way.

It was evident that many of the people there had heard these tales and ballads several times over, yet they seemed just as entertained as if they were hearing them for the first time. There was no doubt they were an active audience—laughing, clapping, stomping, singing, and even at times good-naturedly heckling the droll teller. I couldn't recall an evening when I'd enjoyed myself more.

The gathering was even so informal that many couples were seated as we were, with Gage straddling the bench and me leaning back against his chest with his arms around me, conserving warmth as the temperature that autumn evening dipped closer to freezing. The freely flowing Punch and cider, as well as various other liquors, also helped insulate everyone from the cold and lighten spirits.

"Aye-now. I've one more tale to tell," Rabby James declared after taking a long drink from his glass. "And this one's not so well known."

"How 'bout the tale of the women who saved Padstow from the Spaniards with naught but their red petticoats and a 'obby 'oss," one man slurred, spoiling much of the denouement.

"Nay. This one's even better," Rabby replied amiably. He leaned forward slightly, his eyes alight. "For it involves treasure."

This certainly captured everyone's attention, and the assembly hushed each other as Rabby began his tale.

"Many, many years ago, but not so very long 'tis beyond remembrance, a great ship was caught in a tempest. The wind raged and 'owled, ripping the sails to shreds. And the sea heaved and it roared, knocking the great ship about like it was naught more than a biskan, a fingerstall." He lifted his finger in illustration, and I realized he must have meant a thimble. "The ship was blown off course, hurled toward a shoal littered with razor-sharp rocks that looked to the sailors like the devil's teeth. But their captain was canny and strong. And though it took the strength of seven men, they steered the ship away from those jaws of death.

"'Owever, the writhin' sea refused to be denied, and even the captain's cunning could not save them from what he didn't know. For not far away lay a shallow sandbar. One which the great ship 'ad no hope of avoiding. It was soon driven to ground with such a shuddering force that it tore the main mast from its mooring."

Rabby turned slowly in a circle as if to ensure all were listening. "Now, the people in the village nearby had watched the ship's floundering with concern."

There were a few dry chuckles from the audience.

"And bein' the good and brave Cornish men and women they were, they set out across the treacherous sea to do everythin' they could to help the stranded and drowning sailors." Rabby paused, arching his eyebrows. "They only asked that they be allowed a token of the cargo in return."

Even I caught the meaning of this wry jest. These villagers were wreckers. People who descended on shipwrecks all along the coast of England and picked them clean of every valuable, whether they had the legal right to do so. It was a controversial topic, particularly when there were allegations that the ships had been lured to their doom for that very purpose. Those in shipping and industry and the government would argue that these people were thieves and murderers, and a public nuisance.

I turned to look at those seated around me. But I suspected Cornish men and women would tell a different tale. After all, these wreckers did often risk life and limb to save the survivors, and they were also often the ones forced to clean up after and bury the dead who washed ashore. And the plunder *had* landed on their veritable doorstep. For those miners, fishermen, and laborers who made little in wages, wreckage must seem like a blessing and a boon to their mean subsistence. And for coastal landowners like the Roscarrocks, I could only assume they clung tenaciously to their ancient rights of wreck.

"But what the villagers didn't know," Rabby continued as his voice gained intensity, "was that this was no ordinary vessel. It belonged to the King of Portugal. And the barrels and crates weren't filled with merely silk, brandy, olive oil, cork, and figs, but actual treasure. Gold and silver and copper and precious gems. The very sight of it made the villagers near crazed, and the Portuguese sailors they had been attempting to save turned mad with the fervor to keep it from them, even as the waves continued to pound and batter the ship. It was as if they had all been infected by some sort of fever. One that burned hot through their veins, too powerful to resist."

Like everyone else, I found myself now leaning forward, hardly daring to breathe as I waited to hear what happened next. And Rabby, as a gifted storyteller, knew exactly how to draw out the moment and keep us on tenterhooks.

"'Twasn't enough they were fighting the unforgiving sea and shifting sands, they were fightin' each other." Rabby shook his grizzled head. "Dozens, perhaps 'undreds, died that day from the pitiless waves, the rush of backwater as the sand was swept from beneath their feet, and the steel blades of their opponents. Those that did escape scattered to the wind with their treasures, only to be pursued by their neighbors as well as the Portuguese sailors. For the fever made anyone who even heard of the gold and silver and jewels covetous. Friends skirmished with friends, and then the local gentry joined the battle, demanding their cut. All while the foreigners petitioned the government to confiscate and return their property."

Rabby turned a slow circle again, sweeping his gaze over everyone listening with bated breath. "In all the land, there was but one soul who had not been infected. One soul whose heart remained pure. One slip of a girl whose chief desire was not for the gold." Rabby's gaze rested on me for a few beats longer than seemed natural, and I perked up, wondering if it had been done with intention. "Though possess it, she realized, she must if she was to purge the land of this sickness. It had already killed her father and her brother, leavin' her alone but for her sole companion, a mangy mongrel she loved more than anything else in the world. Fed him better, too."

Some of those listening chuckled, but my heart clenched, beginning to suspect what was to come.

"This slip of a girl lived her life all but ignored and overlooked by those around her. In fact, the dog was more recognized than her, as he'd stolen cuts of meat and assorted pieces of shoe leather in the past. But she preferred it this way, and to her ends, this worked in her favor, as she went about unnoticed, gathering information and making her plans. Then one by one," Rabby tiptoed toward one young woman and then another, snatching something from each of their plates in illustration. "She stole into the homes, shops, manors, and caves where the pieces of treasure were kept and carried them away to a location known only to her. There she concealed them, with the village none the wiser as to who'd taken them."

He whirled about suddenly, his eyes seeming to search the edges of the gathering for someone in particular. "All went according to plan until the night the final object was obtained. The mongrel the girl had been so careful to secure before venturin' forth each evening chewed through the rope that restrained him and followed her to the home of the butcher, who had hidden a salver of pure gold." He shook his head. "The treasure had grown jealous, you see. For the girl did not love it like all the others did. So it vowed to take the one thing she *did* love.

"The girl got away safely, but when the butcher woke to find the thievin' mongrel in his 'ouse, he snatched up his pistol. Hearin' the gunshot and her dog's whimper, the slip of a girl raced back to the butcher's 'ouse, droppin' the plate to the ground as she fell to her knees to wrap her arms around the dyin' animal."

Rabby's visage swam before me as tears filled my eyes, and

from the sound of sniffles and soft sobbing around me, I knew I wasn't the only one affected by the sad tale. One big bear of a man standing beyond the droll teller even swiped his arm across his eyes. Gage's arms tightened around me, either offering comfort or seeking it. Perhaps both.

"And as the mongrel took his final breath, so did the girl, her heart havin' broken clean in two." Rabby shook his head. "But with this one selfless act of pure love, all the treasure's power was undone. The villagers' eyes were opened, their shame complete. So they buried the girl beside her beloved dog and erected a cairn to her honor along the sea cliffs to remind them of the dangers of greed.

"As for the gold plate?" He nodded his head toward the west. "'Twas given to the church. You can still see it at St. Endellion's. And the rest of the treasure?" His eyebrows arched. "The girl took that secret to her grave, and to this day, 'tis never been found." He lifted his fiddle to his shoulder, turning to gaze over his shoulder where I could see Lord Gage standing next to Bevil. "But some say on a windy night, near Pentire Point, you can still hear her mourning her beloved hound. And if your heart is true, and ye listen carefully, she just might whisper the location of the treasure to ye." With this, he set his bow to the strings and began to play a doleful tune.

The mournful song threatened to make me start blubbering. I pushed away the remnants of my second glass of Holland-soaked Punch, wondering if it had been stronger than I'd realized. Gage rubbed his hands up and down my arms, but when I tilted my head back to peer at him, it was to discover his half-lidded eyes were trained across the crowd. I followed his gaze toward his father, who still stood at the edge of the gathering. At first, I didn't know why this warranted his interest, but then I slowly became aware of what he must have already noticed. That we weren't the only ones watching Lord Gage.

In fact, several members of the Roscarrock family were scrutinizing him rather than Rabby. Bevil stood next to him, cutting his eyes periodically in his cousin's direction, while Amelia sat some feet away not bothering to conceal her sudden interest. A quick sweep of the guests showed Mery had also made an appearance, hovering near the steps leading down into the sunken garden, with his eyes fastened on Lord Gage. Even Tristram studied my father-in-law over the blond head of his wife. Though when he caught me watching him, he swiftly looked away. But if my father-in-law was aware of their interest, he gave no indication of it, continuing to observe the proceedings with the same lightly furrowed brow he'd worn from the beginning.

I turned to Gage, curious what—if anything—he proposed to do. Should we perceive this as a threat or was there some other explanation for the Roscarrocks' keen absorption with his father?

"Come," he urged, drawing me away from the table. Our fingers twined together as we ambled toward the dance floor, where we had a clearer view of Lord Gage. But the Roscarrocks seemed to have lost interest and my father-in-law started moving toward the house. The other fiddler—or crowder, as Dolly had called him—began tuning his instrument, suggesting the evening's dancing wasn't done.

Gage waylaid a servant, asking him to locate Anderley. Then he pulled me into his arms, twirling me across the lawn as the strains of a lively reel began. It wasn't long before I'd almost forgotten the tense moment. Dancing tended to require all of one's concentration, especially when you were being passed from one enthusiastic Cornishman to another.

It wasn't until Gage partnered with me for a second time that Anderley finally appeared. He stood scowling at the edge of the dance floor, all but tapping his foot in impatience. It wasn't like the valet to behave this way. It bordered on insolence.

When the reel ended, Gage led us over to Anderley, urging him a short distance away from the crowd so that he could address him in some privacy. "I'd begun to think that footman failed to deliver my message." When Anderley didn't bother to reply, but instead continued to stare tight-lipped at his employer, Gage's features took on a far more forbidding cast. "I need you to instruct Lembus to sleep in Lord Gage's dressing room tonight and here on out."

I turned to Gage in surprise.

"It's merely a precaution," he added for my benefit. "But a necessary one." He arched his eyebrows at Anderley. "Should Lembus argue, remind him of his duty. And should he argue still, send him to me."

Though Anderley didn't openly challenge Gage's instructions, it was evident how he felt about them.

"This is a boon for you, at least," I told the valet, trying to jolly him out of whatever melancholy he'd sunken into with the idea that he would no longer have to share his lodgings with the sour Lembus.

But Anderley merely turned his glower on me.

In the face of this, Gage's voice grew clipped and stern. "Your orders are clear. You're dismissed."

The valet barely sketched a bow before striding off.

"What just happened?" I asked in bewilderment, unsettled by Anderley's behavior.

However, if Gage was listening, he gave no indication of it, simply continuing to frown at his departing valet's back before walking away, muttering something to himself under his breath.

I was still ruminating on Anderley's contentiousness an hour later when I made my way back upstairs to my bedchamber. My feet were sore and my head ached from too much Holland-soaked Punch and spiced cider and too little sleep. Bree arrived soon after me, setting to work on my fastenings.

"Did something happen to upset Anderley tonight?" I asked, hoping Bree might be able to elucidate the cause to me. "When Gage spoke with him an hour ago, he was almost hostile, and completely unlike himself."

"I dinna want to talk aboot it," Bree replied tersely.

When she'd walked in, I'd been too distracted by my own fatigue to notice how she might be feeling, and then she'd turned me about to begin on my buttons. But apparently her mood wasn't much of an improvement over Anderley's.

"Oh, no. Did the two of you fight?" I ruminated, uncertain whether I'd actually meant to ask the question aloud.

"I said I dinna want to discuss it," Bree snapped, and then, as if realizing how brusque she was being, she added a more softly worded, "m'lady." But like a prick to my conscience, this only served to remind me I had no right to ask her to divulge her personal matters. Not if they didn't affect her work.

I knew it was her right not to share everything with me. After all, just because I was her employer didn't mean I had leave to pry into every aspect of her life. Gage had even warned me about doing just such a thing. But I couldn't help it. I cared for Bree and Anderley. I considered them more like friends or family than staff, a fact I knew would scandalize most people of my station. Just as I was aware that such a relationship was intrinsically unequal and weighted in my favor as their employer. But I cared for them nonetheless and worried for their happiness.

An uncomfortable silence fell between us as I stood stiffly, waiting for her to finish unfastening all the tiny little buttons down my back. I was debating whether to introduce a more mundane topic or remain quiet until she retired when she spoke in a determinedly even voice. "'Twas a lively party."

"Yes," I said. "Yes, it was."

I felt the last button give way and then she began to tug at my stays. "Those fiddlers certainly ken how to wield a bow."

"Did you hear the droll teller?"

"Aye!" she answered enthusiastically, but then hesitated. "At least, some o' his tales and ballads."

"The beginning or the end?"

"Beginning."

I nodded. Then I wouldn't bother to ask her whether she'd noticed anything amiss about the Roscarrocks' strange behavior. Though I did wonder what had pulled her away, and whether it accounted for her vexation. "Did you learn anything of interest?" I asked, hoping to distract myself from the desire to prod at the source of her discontent one more time.

She didn't answer immediately, instead waiting until she'd whisked my dress over my head and helped me to remove my stays. "Only that the amount o' Holland gin, brandy, and Irish whiskey . . ." She screwed up her face at this last, and I couldn't help but smile at her loyalty to Scottish single malt. "In their cellars is rather astounding."

"Someone made a comment about that, and it raised Lord Gage's suspicions. And his hackles," I added in full honesty.

"Aye, and well it should. For judgin' from the sheer volume and quality, I would wager they either smuggled it themselves or are fencin' it for someone else."

This was a possibility I hadn't considered. Maybe Bevil and the others had spoken true, at least in the strictest literal sense. They weren't smuggling, but rather brokering the sale of contraband brought ashore by other free traders. Either way, if they hadn't paid taxes on it, the act was illegal.

It also raised some interesting implications surrounding Branok's death. Perhaps he'd run afoul of these free traders and they'd killed him. The place of his demise could fit the scenario of a clandestine meeting gone wrong. But if this was the case, we would need proof, and I doubted Bevil, Mery, and the others would willingly share any details that might implicate themselves in such a criminal enterprise. If another gang of smugglers—be they rivals or conspirators—were the culprits, we would have to go about gathering evidence in a different way.

I raised the theory with Gage when he returned to our bed-chamber. I'd been lying in bed for some time, attempting to drift off to sleep despite the sounds of music and laughter still filtering through the window glass, but my mind was too full of information, and none of it was fitting together satisfactorily. It made me restless.

A feeling my husband seemed to share if his exasperated sigh as he sank down on the edge of the bed was any indication. He hadn't seemed surprised to discover I was awake. Nor did he refute the possibility I'd raised. On the contrary, he confessed his thoughts had run in a similar vein.

"It's perfectly obvious they're concealing something from us. They deny they're still smuggling, yet they host this soiree where spirits of obvious quality flow freely. I don't know whether to believe they're simply that reckless, or if I should feel that my intelligence has been insulted." Though I couldn't make out his features in the darkness, I could tell by the tone of his voice and the hunch of his shoulders that he was not only discouraged but exhausted.

What we both needed was a solid night's rest. However, there was one more issue that couldn't wait. It had knotted my stomach for the last hour and more. "Are you genuinely worried for your father's safety?"

He turned his head to look at me, and while I still couldn't see his face, perhaps he could see mine. "I don't want to be, but . . . I know you saw it, too. The strange way Bevil and

Amelia and some of the others were looking at him. Almost as if they expected something from him."

"That's exactly it," I agreed. "But what?"

"I don't know, and until we do, I'd rather Father not be left alone at the opposite end of the house."

"Which is why you sent Anderley for Lembus," I replied in understanding.

"Yes. Lembus may be a peevish fop, but he's undoubtedly loyal to my father and anxious to keep the prestige his position as his gentleman's gentleman gives him. He'll make sure Father's safe. Or send for us if he isn't."

I nodded, though he couldn't see it. It was the simplest solution, at least to ease our minds.

"As for Anderley . . ." Gage paused again, turning to me. "I'm fairly certain I know what's going on. So don't let it concern you. I'll take care of it."

It was on the tip of my tongue to ask him to explain, but I heard how tired he was. "Come to bed," I urged him, lifting my hand to him. "The rest will keep until morning."

My husband didn't require much convincing. He clasped my hand briefly before shedding his clothes and leaving them in a pile on the floor as he always did when Anderley wasn't there to tend to them. A fact which would have exasperated me had *I* been the one required to clean up after him. Then Gage crawled beneath the covers, settling his long, warm body alongside mine. I rolled over to rest my head against his shoulder, smoothing down his chest hair so that it didn't tickle my face.

"When do you need to tend to Emma?" he murmured as I inhaled the musk of his skin.

"Soon enough that I'm not sure it's worth falling asleep, but if I don't—"

"She'll sleep 'til dawn," he finished for me with a low chuckle before pressing a kiss to my forehead. "Tell Mrs. Mackay to bring her to you here."

"And shock her sensibilities with your immodesty," I jested, poking him lightly on his bare chest.

"I doubt Mrs. Mackay can be shocked. But I can put on a nightshirt if that's the problem."

"Did you bring one?"

"Of course."

I snorted, for there was no *of course* about it. He only slept in a nightshirt on the most frigid of nights.

"How unladylike," he teased.

Such a response called for a wry retort, but I couldn't summon the energy to form words, let alone lift my head to fix a proper glare on him. So instead I ignored it, allowing myself to be dragged down into the sweet oblivion of slumber that sleeping next to my husband only seemed to provide.

CHAPTER 13

We largely had the dining room to ourselves the following morning. Save for Tristram, who stepped in long enough to grab a piece of dry toast, the rest of the Roscarrocks and Killigrews remained in bed, apparently having drank and danced later into the night than their houseguests. They were also probably nursing aching heads. I knew I was suffering from a small megrim, and I could tell Gage was feeling at least some twinge of discomfort. Only Lord Gage appeared none the worse for the late night and imbibing, but perhaps he'd consumed less than the rest of us.

But despite our relative privacy and the numerous things we needed to discuss, by unspoken agreement we all remained silent on the subject of Branok's death. After all, the walls were thin, and there were servants moving in and out of the chamber and always listening, even if we were supposed to pretend they weren't. However, that did not stop me from making several observations.

While the family strove to hide it well, there were indications of financial strain everywhere. Chipped dishes, mended tablecloths, a cracked windowpane, a moldy smell in one corner of the parlor, cracked masonry in the courtyard. Taken one at a time, they might have been dismissed, but altogether they amounted to more.

Bree had already told me about the leaking roof over the servants' quarters and the fact a third of the staff had been dismissed. I could see evidence of that loss in staff in the gardens where the remnants of the party lay discarded and untended to. In a house with sufficient staff, some of them would already be awake and at work to tidy and clear away the mess.

Not wishing to dwell among the detritus of the previous evening, we strolled as a trio down into the lower garden and then out toward the pond. Trees ringed a portion of the water, stretching their branches still speckled with brilliant autumn leaves over the surface to be reflected back at the sky. Meanwhile, we could see the line of the ocean glittering in the morning sun between two folds of the coast. The highest point of the undulation to the south marked the cliff from which Branok had fallen to his death, though no one could have seen him from such a distance. Especially with all the brambles and vegetation crowding the crag.

We all stared wordlessly across the water, the chill breeze tugging at our garments. The sun at our backs cast our shadows across the ground and out onto the pond—my shorter one in a distinctive bonnet between their two tall straight figures. The wind was strong enough to carry with it the scent of the sea, but every once in a while, I would catch notes of grass and the more stagnant pond.

It was a beautiful place. There was no denying it. I didn't say so aloud out of deference to Lord Gage's feelings, even though one glance at his face showed me he was perfectly aware of the fact, and hard-pressed not to also feel it square in his chest on that lovely autumn morn. After all, he had spent much of his childhood here, where he had many happy memories. One bad recollection did not wipe away all the good simply because one wished it.

"I think it's time we take a sharper look at this smuggling business," Gage announced without preamble, I supposed deciding it was better to jump straight into the fire rather than dither around the edges. "And given your history here and everyone's awareness of your antipathy toward the enterprise, that makes me the man to undertake the investigation."

He turned to both of us with a sharp glint of determination in his pale blue eyes, as if he expected us to argue, but neither Lord Gage nor I disputed the point. He was right. Lord Gage would get nowhere with such queries and, as a gentlewoman, I acknowledged that the men involved in such an enterprise were unlikely to share any information with me. Though that wouldn't stop me from questioning some of the women who might know something.

"How do you propose to go about it?" Lord Gage queried, pivoting slightly so that most of his weight rested on his uninjured leg.

"I've written to an old friend who lives just south of here," Gage replied. "I'm hoping he'll be able to shed some light on the situation."

"Trelawny?"

If Gage was surprised his father knew this, he didn't show it. "Yes. Last I'd heard he was back in Cornwall for a visit with his family."

"Who's Trelawny?" I asked, wondering if I'd ever heard my husband mention him.

"Edward Trelawny." Shadows gathered in his eyes. "We met while fighting in the Greek War of Independence."

I understood his reticence to say more, knowing that chapter of his life aiding the Greeks in their fight for independence from the Ottoman Empire had been one of the darkest and most difficult. I also now recognized who this Trelawny figure was. He had been an intimate of Shelley and Lord Byron, and a novelist and adventurer in his own right. He'd also served with the Royal Navy for some time during the wars with Napoleonic France, making me wonder if Lord Gage was acquainted with him.

Gage clasped his hands behind his back. "I know it's only been a couple of days since our arrival, but I'm considering riding south to pay him a visit. Though it will take the better part of the day to reach Trelawny's home and return." There was a question in his eyes that I suspected had little to do with his seeking permission to go and more to do with his ensuring Emma and I were looked after in his absence.

Lord Gage nodded his head in understanding. "It would be helpful to have an outsider's perspective. Someone who is familiar with the personalities and the politics of the area." His gaze cut to me. "Meanwhile, Kiera and I will continue questioning people closer to Roscarrock."

"I'd like to speak to Dr. Wolcott again," I said. "One or two things have occurred to me since yesterday morning that I'd like to ask him." I glanced over my shoulder in the direction of the house. "And as I understand it, Bevil and Joan's daughter Morgan married a dissenter. A Methodist likely. I have to wonder how he felt about Branok and the Roscarrocks' nocturnal activities."

"But Methodism wouldn't keep him from supporting smuggling," Lord Gage countered. "At least, it didn't stop the Carters of Prussia Cove near Mount's Bay," he sneered. "The 'King of Prussia,' as they call John Carter, and his brothers were some of the most prominent free traders in all of Cornwall during the latter half of the last century. And *they* were Methodists." He turned away. "Though I did hear they banned cursing and crass discussion among their crews, and they seemed to pride themselves for their honesty." He scoffed as if he couldn't quite credit this.

"Morgan's husband still might be worth talking to," I replied, privately hoping Morgan was present when we did so. She seemed to know things the other wives did not, and I had to wonder whether that was because she was Bevil's daughter and therefore considered more trustworthy, or because she was simply more observant.

Lord Gage grunted in approval.

I noticed Gage was studying his father closely and I wondered why until he spoke. "You might also consider questioning the droll teller from last night. Our relatives seemed particularly interested in his last tale. The one about the treasure."

Lord Gage frowned. "They were probably worried they might be implicated."

Gage and I shared a look. Could that be all? Had they been worried Lord Gage would open an inquiry into a past wreck and their potential involvement with it?

But my husband's thoughts had gone one step further than mine. "Did *you* ever witness a wrecked ship?" he asked his father.

Lord Gage's scowl deepened, and it took him a moment to respond. "No. Though occasionally I heard my relatives talking about them."

"Did they ever mention one of them belonging to the King of Portugal?"

Lord Gage aimed a scornful glare at his son, but the disdain slowly died, being replaced with some emotion more akin to puzzlement.

"What is it?" I asked. "Have you thought of something?"

"No, I just . . ." he began, but then broke off, shaking his head vehemently. He paced several steps away, stopping to stare briefly toward the outbuildings in the distance, where a number of laborers and farmhands could be seen going about their daily tasks.

I looked to Gage for some clarification, but he could only shrug. We joined his father, where he stood examining some sort of stone rubble structure with a beehive-type corbeled roof built into the side of the banked ground behind the outer courtyard of the house.

"What is it?" I asked.

"A wellhouse," he explained absently. "Though from the looks of it, it might no longer be in use. It sits over a natural spring."

The sound of voices drew my attention toward the house. Just over the top edge of the embankment I could see Great-Aunt Amelia hobbling alongside her daughter-in-law Joan toward the stables and carriage house. Or perhaps they were bound for the barns and outbuildings beyond. Whatever the case, they didn't seem to be cognizant of our presence. Which wasn't to say there was anything suspicious about their movements. At least, not like Mery, who came skulking out of the door to the servants' quarters a few moments later and, skirting the pond, set off to the west toward Port Quin. He pulled his coat over his head, presumably to block out some of the bright sunlight.

My concentration returned to the two Killigrew women as they disappeared from sight. A number of questions still lingered about Amelia and her motives for sending for us. Particularly why she'd changed her mind about Branok's death after he'd already been buried. I couldn't help but feel she had more to say.

"Perhaps we should also speak to Amelia again," I suggested. "This time privately."

Gage began to nod, but his father cut him off.

"Leave Aunt Amelia to me," he murmured, never removing his gaze from the wellhouse.

We waited for him to elaborate, but when he didn't, Gage cleared his throat awkwardly. "I'll set off, then, before the morning is too advanced." He pulled me close to his side, leaning his head down to speak to me softly. "Should there be trouble while I'm gone, you can rely on Father or Anderley."

It was on the tip of my tongue to question that, especially after his valet's belligerent behavior the previous evening, but I could see in his eyes that he knew what I was thinking of and telling me to dismiss it.

"I would trust either of them with my life and yours," he added, clearly sensing I needed extra reassurance.

Out of the corner of my eye, I saw Lord Gage straighten, telling me he'd heard his son's pronouncement and was not unaffected by it.

"I'll be back by nightfall," he promised, pressing a kiss to my brow before turning to stride toward the house to collect his things for the journey.

I tried not to feel any sense of loss or foreboding at his departure, but the truth was I always suffered a pang of apprehension and longing when we separated, even for a short time. I wondered briefly at his decision not to take Anderley with him, but then realized Gage's protective nature was well established, particularly toward his family. I'd butted up against it often enough to know that he would view it as his solemn duty to ensure Emma and I, and even his father, were well guarded. In any case, there was no reason to believe he would be in any danger, and he would be carrying at least one pistol on his person on the chance there was trouble.

I turned to find Lord Gage watching me, perhaps expecting me to shed a tear or protest my husband's absence. Or maybe he thought I'd oppose the idea of being forced to investigate alone with him. While it was true he wasn't my first choice in a partner, over the past few months we'd managed to live together quite peaceably. I suspected it helped that I refused to be either cowed or intimidated by him. *And* that I was Emma's mother. Whatever the case, there was no reason we shouldn't be able to work together amicably.

"Why don't we begin with the droll teller," I suggested.

While Bree had helped me dress that morning, she'd informed me that Rabby James had been given a bed in the servants' quarters for the night. So it made sense to begin with the person closest to hand. However, when we asked after the fellow, we soon learned that he'd already moved on, tramping either south or east to his next destination, wherever that might be. I understood then that he wasn't simply a local storyteller, but a wandering minstrel, traveling the countryside to tell tales and play music for his living. If we took to the saddle, we might be able to catch him, but no one knew exactly in which direction he was headed. Given that, it seemed a foolhardy mission to go cantering up and down the dusty lanes searching for him when we weren't even sure he had anything relevant to tell us.

After checking on Emma, I set off with Lord Gage on horseback, riding toward the village of Trelights. The brilliant early morning sun was now tempered somewhat by clouds, and a glance to the west, far out over the sea, suggested rain might fall by the afternoon. I hoped that wouldn't impede Gage's journey.

Dr. Wolcott wasn't at home when we arrived, but Anne greeted us warmly and plied us with tea, promising her husband would return shortly. Lord Gage employed his renowned charm to good effect, and soon had Anne blushing and beaming with pleasure. Not that she wasn't already radiant from the child growing inside her.

"Kiera, 'ow fortunate ye are to live with two such kind and

amusing men," she declared. "Ye must spend all of your time smiling."

"Yes, it's difficult to keep my head out of the clouds," I replied in jest, though Lord Gage must have sensed some of the wryness behind my tone, for he turned to look at me. He would be perfectly aware that he'd rarely, if *ever*, practiced his charm on me.

Anne laughed, unaware I wasn't being anything but sincere.

"Since we have a moment," I said, leaning toward her to confide, "I did wonder if you might be able to help me with something that's been perplexing me."

"Of course." She blinked earnestly, seeming to derive as much pleasure from being asked for her assistance as Lord Gage's flattery. I supposed, being the youngest adult of her kin and the wife of a highly competent husband, she wasn't often asked for her help.

"Your cousin Morgan raised the concern yesterday evening of preventing Mery from being trapped into marriage since he's now inherited Roscarrock House. Which is understandable," I explained carefully. "But I did wonder . . . why *isn't* he already married?"

A tiny pucker formed between her brows.

"After all, he's been the heir for decades. Ever since his father's death. And I can't help but be curious why he wasn't *compelled* to wed," I finished almost apologetically.

Anne smiled sadly. "Great-Uncle Branok did *try* to force him to take a bride. One with a significant dowry. He even banished Mery from the main 'ouse and effectively cut him off." She gave a solemn chuckle, replacing our empty tea things on the tray. "But Mery proved to be even more stubborn and strong-willed than his granfer."

Lord Gage grunted. "And perversely, I suspect Branok was proud of that."

Anne looked up at him, the twinkle in her eye confirming this.

"A trait which must run in the family," I couldn't resist muttering as I took one last drink of my tea before passing the cup back to Anne.

My father-in-law turned to me sharply and I met his gaze evenly, daring him to deny that his past insistence that his sons do exactly as he directed and yet show strength by standing up to him was not also perverse.

This coaxed a covert smile to Anne's lips. "Aye. Even Mery exhibits such a perverse contradiction." Her mirth faded. "Says he doesn't trust women. I believe it's because his mother abandoned him when he was so young." She turned her head to the side, lowering her voice nearly to a whisper. "But he can't sleep—not truly anyway—without either bein' inebriated . . . or havin' a woman by his side."

I studied her smooth profile and the taut cords of her neck. It was clear that she'd not shared this information lightly. Just as it was clear, at least to me, that her cousin, at one time or another, had slept by *her* side. Whether this had occurred when they were just children or later when they were older, whether it had been chaste or not, was less obvious.

Before I could figure out how to prod deeper without exposing her to Lord Gage's ridicule, a cheerful whistle carried to us from outside the window along the walk. The front door opened to admit the whistler and, a few moments later, Tom Wolcott appeared in the entry to their drawing room.

"My lord, my lady," he said, nodding his head deferentially to us each in turn. His posture turned rigid and formal—a stark contrast to his previous relaxed cheer. "Had I known you intended to call, I would have remained at home."

He gripped a black medical bag in his hand, giving credence to his wife's assertion that he'd been called out to a patient in the village. Not that we'd doubted her.

"Of course we understand you have your charges to see to," Lord Gage demurred. "But if we might have a moment of your time, a few additional questions have occurred to us."

"I'm at your service." Dr. Wolcott stepped back to gesture down the corridor. "Why don't we step into my study."

Anne's face fell as, once again, her husband was evidently intent she not chance hearing any gruesome details of her great-uncle's demise. Though I wished I could protest on her behalf, I knew it wasn't my place. Nor was either man likely to listen to me. Furthermore, Anne might prove to be a distraction. One that would prevent Dr. Wolcott from being as candid as we needed him to be. So I merely offered her a commiserating smile and retraced my steps from the previous morning to the inviting study with colorful watercolors adorning the walls.

"Now, what did you wish to ask me?" Dr. Wolcott said to Lord Gage as they claimed the two armchairs while I perched on the middle of the settee. Only when my father-in-law directed his attention to me did the physician realize I was actually the one with questions.

"As I understand it, Branok's body was brought straight here rather than your being summoned to Roscarrock House."

He rested his elbows on the arms of the chair and clasped his hands before him. "That is true."

"When he arrived, could you tell how long he'd been deceased? Based on rigor mortis and such."

He seemed slightly taken aback. "I . . . I'm afraid his body was so severely damaged from the fall . . . Many of his bones were shattered and his muscles . . ." He broke off, clearing his throat. "I didn't trust that a corpse in such a dreadful state would present the typical stages of decomposition." Something of my disbelief and skepticism must have shown on my face, for he cleared his throat again. "*However*, based on insect activity and the damage to the pocket watch found on his person, I strongly suspect he was deceased no less than three hours when he was found."

It took me a moment to properly gather a response, still struggling as I was with the doctor's decision not to note the level of rigor mortis in Branok's corpse. I found it difficult to believe that the body had been so damaged that such an assessment would prove useless. As such, I couldn't help but wonder if Dr. Wolcott had not, in fact, consciously elected to ignore it, but instead had simply *failed* to do so, and now he was making excuses.

He *was* a relatively young physician, and I doubted he'd seen many cases of traumatic death. If it was merely a matter of inexperience, then I found I could overlook such an error. His surprise at my even broaching the subject seemed to indicate such.

But it could also be attributed to something quite different. Something far less forgivable. If so, he wouldn't be the first medical man to underestimate me and the extent of my knowledge. And he probably wouldn't be the last to whom I would deliver a comeuppance, whether I'd intended to or not.

"You said he was found with his pocket watch?" Lord Gage queried, redirecting the conversation as I considered whether to prod deeper into Dr. Wolcott's pretext.

Dr. Wolcott jumped at this. "Yes. Though I can't state definitively whether it stopped immediately after his fall or continued to work for some time following."

"I assume the watch was returned to Bevil or Mery."

"Yes, but . . ." He flushed. "I believe it was buried with Branok."

Of course it was.

I nearly sighed aloud, and then turned to my father-in-law to see if he also found Dr. Wolcott's behavior suspicious, but his expression revealed nothing but a keen interest in what he was saying.

"Who made the decision to keep Branok's body in your

icehouse rather than lay him out in the parlor at Roscarrock House?" I inquired, ignoring Lord Gage's startled look. "And who decided to hold the funeral two days earlier than usual?"

Dr. Wolcott frowned, now growing angry rather than annoyed by my pointed questions, but I'd expected just such a shift in his demeanor. "Bevil and I did," he answered defensively. "As I've explained numerous times now, the body was in a terrible state. The . . ." He stumbled over his words briefly. "The bowels had even burst, and the smell . . ." He cringed. "It was only going to get worse. There was no way he could have survived the fall. And no way he could be given the usual vigil and procession." His pale eyes dared me to suggest otherwise.

I didn't attempt to do so. Not when his explanation sounded perfectly reasonable. And yet, I still felt something wasn't quite right. For while everything the doctor had said seemed entirely rational and truthful, his behavior suggested otherwise.

Lord Gage and I excused ourselves a short time later, collecting our horses from Dr. Wolcott's man-of-all-work.

"When did you learn about Branok's lack of a vigil?" my father-in-law asked me after the servant had stridden away.

"Yesterday evening." I searched his shadowed eyes. "That troubles you."

It was a statement rather than a question, but he answered, nonetheless. "Yes." He frowned. "Though I'm not certain why."

I glanced discreetly toward the window overlooking the drive, spying Dr. Wolcott watching us. "Because despite your family's seeming straightforwardness, no one is being fully honest with us."

With the use of the mounting block, I hoisted myself into Figg's saddle. Lord Gage stepped forward to help me adjust my foot in the stirrup as I held up the train of my charcoal gray riding habit with velvet collar and cuffs. But rather than release me immediately, he waited for my gaze to meet his.

"I warned you."

There was no gloating in his voice, no satisfaction. Only weary resignation.

"I know," I conceded.

He nodded once and stepped back to mount his own steed.

CHAPTER 14

The cottage where Morgan Knill lived with her husband Anthony lay a short distance to the east. Anne had told us how to find it. We'd just passed through the gate pillars overgrown with clinging ivy and started down the drive when we spied Morgan and her two children emerging from the trees. They all held baskets filled with plums and apples—large red ones and a smaller golden variety. At the sight of us, Morgan shooed the boy of about age ten and the girl aged six on toward the house and paused to greet us, propping her basket on her hip.

"Good morn," she declared, shielding her face from the sun with her other hand. "What brings ye this way?"

"Good morning," Lord Gage replied. "We hoped we might have a word with you and your husband." He glanced around him. "Is he about?"

"I'm afraid you've missed 'im," she said, not sounding all that sad that we had. "Not two hours ago, he set out for St. Austell with the last of this year's harvest bound for the market. He probably won't return until Tuesday." Three days hence.

"I see," Lord Gage murmured, turning to me, for it had been my idea to speak to the Knills.

"Is there somethin' I can help ye with?" Morgan asked, shifting the load of her basket to her other hip and brushing strands of ash-blond hair back from her forehead. Whether it was actually heavy or not, it made me anxious to conclude our discussion, so she needn't stand there hefting her burden any longer than necessary.

"We simply wanted to speak to you about Branok's death and find out if either of you had anything to share you might not have wished to state in front of the others." I added the last for Morgan's benefit, since I'd already talked to her about the matter the previous evening. There was little point in prodding her about the dissenter issue without her husband present. Not when we couldn't gauge his reaction.

Judging from Morgan's steady stare, she wasn't fooled. "Nay. I've told ye all I know. And Mr. Knill knows even less. He and Branok largely avoided each other. 'Twas easiest that way."

"They quarreled?"

She shifted her basket again, peering over her shoulder toward her children still making their way up the drive toward the cottage in the far distance. "They didn't see each other often enough to quarrel." She shrugged. "They simply agreed to differ. And the easiest way to keep that agreement was to avoid each other."

Despite her determined aplomb, this sounded to me like a potential motive for murder. Particularly if their differences were contentious.

"You're welcome to ask 'im about it yourself on Wednesday," she muttered in sudden impatience, turning to follow her offspring. "Now, if you'll excuse me, I really must go."

She didn't wait for our reply, but hurried on down the drive, leaving us staring resignedly at her back. There was nothing for it but for us to turn and go, once again feeling thwarted. A sensation that was only enhanced by the chough perched on one of the gate pillars as we passed back between them. His distinctive call sounded like mockery. *Chee-ow. Chee-ow. Chee-ow.*

"What did Mrs. Knill tell you yesterday?" Lord Gage asked me after we'd ridden several minutes in silence but for the clop of our horses' hooves against the dirt road. I waited until we'd navigated around a particularly muddy stretch beneath the shade of a copse of beech trees before replying.

"That it couldn't have been any of them—the immediate family, that is—that killed Branok. That it wouldn't be their way."

He scoffed, just as I'd expected him to.

"She told me to look into the Grenvilles." I studied him out of the corner of my eye, curious to see his reaction. "That they've long held a grudge against the Roscarrocks."

He scowled at the road ahead of us. "For good reason, if they have."

"Not just because of Jago," I persisted, knowing that was what he was referring to.

He met my gaze.

"She mentioned Gilbert's leg. That it had been injured years ago while helping the Roscarrocks with some sort of work on the estate."

His expression darkened. "Smuggling."

My eyebrows arched in query more than surprise. Of course, that would be his first assumption.

"Tamsyn told me." He narrowed his eyes at the tangled hedges bordering the road. "Apparently it was crushed and never set properly."

That was what the Merry Wives had told me, though they hadn't mentioned smuggling. I didn't know whether that was because they hadn't known that was the cause or if they had obfuscated.

"Then the Grenvilles do hold a grudge." I frowned. "But did Tamsyn say if there was more?"

My father-in-law looked to me in question.

"It's simply . . . there seemed to be more the others weren't telling me. Or perhaps it was just Morgan who gave me that impression." I exhaled in frustration. "I sensed there might be yet another reason for the Grenvilles to dislike the Roscarrocks."

"Tamsyn didn't say anything. But we could ask her," he offered, not sounding the least opposed to the idea.

It was strange to hear him call a woman by her given name even though she'd invited us to do so. Normally Lord Gage was quite formal, insisting on proper titles. Even as his daughter-in-law, I had been addressed as Lady Darby or Mrs. Gage until quite recently. It had not been difficult to deduce why he was such a stickler to protocol, though I was certain he would have been horrified to realize his motives were so transparent. Because despite everything he'd achieved, deep inside he struggled not to think of himself as the mere second son of a minor baronet once arrested for smuggling. That insecurity drove him to hold fast to those things that were tangible evidence of his success—his title, his position, his reputation, and his wealth.

Incidentally, this insecurity also put him at odds with his son because Gage *didn't* measure his success by any of those things. They were useful tools, but not achievements in and of themselves. Though, to be fair, he'd had a much different upbringing than his father.

However, here was Lord Gage, willingly shedding his carefully cultivated image and pretense for a woman he hadn't seen in nearly fifty years.

"The two of you were close," I prodded lightly, knowing that if I showed too much interest he would refuse to respond.

"Jago and I were close, and Tamsyn was his cousin. She seemed to always be under foot, insisting we include her."

"And did you?"

"Sometimes. Sometimes not." He turned to watch a squirrel scamper up a series of exposed roots revealed in the road embankment to our right. "As we grew older, it got harder to deter her. Especially when she was taller and faster than us for a time."

I was attuned to his tone, listening for the things I knew he wouldn't readily admit. Or at least, that I didn't expect him to.

"It was a long time ago, but when I think back, I do believe I thought I'd marry her one day."

My head snapped around in surprise.

"Oh, not anytime soon. I was only eleven. Nor was I smitten with her or any of that claptrap. It simply seemed the way it must happen." He shrugged and then turned to look at me, a sharp gleam in his eyes. "Is that what you wanted to hear? You and your cursed all-seeing eyes." His upper lip curled in annoyance. "I could tell exactly what you were thinking last night when you watched us together."

I wasn't about to apologize for being observant. Particularly when it proved so invaluable to our inquiries in the past. Instead, I elected to tweak his nose a bit. "It was good to see her, I imagine."

The sardonic glare he fastened on me was so exasperated that I was hard-pressed not to giggle. That urge became almost unbearable when he began to mutter to himself. Something about upstart women and the downfall of humanity. I stared straight ahead and let him mumble and grumble, knowing his real struggle was with himself and all the emotions these memories from his boyhood brought forth, not me. He'd spent so much of his life fighting and suppressing and denying his past and how he felt about it. It was foolish to think he would submit easily to it now that he was being confronted with the people and places he'd avoided for so long.

"Did Tamsyn believe the same?" I asked, deciding I wasn't finished badgering him.

The withering look he cast my way was answer enough. "I don't know," he bit out. "It's not as if I asked her." Then his irritation suddenly faded. "But I know she took Jago's death hard."

My heart clenched as his face turned pale and stony.

"I saw her." His throat worked as he swallowed. "On the day I was released from custody and escorted to Plymouth to take up my commission. She was standing outside the jail." His expression was stark. "She loved Jago. He was more like a brother than a cousin. And she looked like her heart had been pulled clean from her chest."

I didn't question this assessment. I could only imagine what it would be like to lose my brother or sister, or even one of my beloved cousins, in such a tragic way. But I also wondered if Tamsyn's grief had also been compounded by the loss of her friend. Lord Gage might not have died, but he'd been lost to her just as surely.

If Branok had been the one responsible for placing Jago and Lord Gage in the position to be shot and arrested, I could understand Tamsyn's desire for vengeance. Though would she truly have waited almost fifty years to exact it?

Unless she'd just found out.

The road passed over a rise, and then the hedges began to fall away, affording us a view of the Roscarrocks' golden fields and green meadows stretching out toward the cliffs and the sea. The clouds we had seen gathering over the ocean earlier that morning now all but choked out the sunlight struggling to pierce through the cover. The breeze tugged at the veil of my hat draped down my back and sent autumn leaves scuttling down the path. However, I gauged there was no need to urge our horses into a canter. We should still return before the rain began to fall. Allowing me time to prod my father-in-law about one more matter.

"You told us what happened the evening Jago was killed and you were apprehended for smuggling, but you didn't go into much detail," I prompted gently, knowing this was a sore subject for him.

"There was no need to," he bit out.

"Perhaps not then, but . . . I can't help but wonder if it might be pertinent now."

He turned to glower at me.

"At least we then might understand better all the factors involved. Such as where exactly you were when the preventive officers caught up with you? Who directed you to transport the goods? Did you submit when you were challenged or were you attempting to escape?"

"Does it matter?"

"It might."

He fell silent, as if indicating the matter was closed. It was true. I couldn't compel him to speak. But the more I thought about it, the more significant it seemed to become. After all, Gage and I knew only the barest details of the matter. Knowing the rest might not enable us to solve the riddle of Branok's death, but it might help us better understand the undercurrents that ran between the Roscarrocks and all their extended family, including the Grenvilles. It might help us to know what unspoken secrets and hostile glances and strange reactions were relevant to our inquiry and which were not.

I decided to raise the subject with Gage when he returned. Perhaps together we might be able to persuade his father to tell us more.

In any case, I was soon distracted by a figure striding down the road toward us. From such a distance, I couldn't discern more than the fact it was a female, but Lord Gage seemed to recognize her quickly. That, in turn, told me who she was. I wondered if her ears were burning.

"Just the people I was lookin' for," Tamsyn pronounced as she drew near enough for us to hear. She had been walking fast, mostly uphill, but she didn't appear winded.

Lord Gage dismounted, and I began to follow suit, but she waved me back in my saddle.

"I know 'ow awkward it is to get in and out of those side-saddles, 'specially without a convenient mountin' block nearby. What I 'ave to say won't take long."

"Has something happened?" Lord Gage asked in concern.

"Nothin' more than that you've been invited to tea. Both of ye. And yer son." Her eyes scrutinized Lord Gage closely. "By my Auntie Pasca."

Jago's mother.

"You told her I was here?" my father-in-law protested, his back stiffening.

"'Course she knows yer 'ere! Everyone's been talkin' about it." Tamsyn arched her eyebrows. "And if ye don't accept her invitation, she'll be terribly offended."

Lord Gage's face reflected a confusing jumble of emotions, all of them raw. I found myself wanting to shield him from them, but I knew I couldn't. That I shouldn't. Because while it was evident that facing Jago's mother was the last thing he wanted to do, it was also clear that it was what he needed most. So before he found his tongue, I answered for him.

"Of course we'll come."

They both turned to me, but while Lord Gage's astonishment thawed into a renewed desire to throttle me, Tamsyn's gaze glinted with the recognition of a co-conspirator.

"Good. Monday afternoon," she stated with finality, relaying the rest of the details.

I thought then that she intended to continue on her way, but apparently, she had more to impart, and these words were a great deal more difficult to say. Her hands fidgeted with the dagged trim of her pelisse, and her eyes kept straying in every direction except our faces.

"The second thing I've come to tell ye is not so easily said, but I know you'd prefer to have the truth, whatever it might cost ye."

I glanced at Lord Gage, unsure whether we should be alarmed.

"But before I do." She exhaled, finally lifting her gaze to meet mine and then Lord Gage's. "You're aware that a vigil was not 'eld for Branok. Nor the usual funeral trappings."

"Yes," I answered hesitantly.

She nodded. "Then you're also aware that the only people to see 'is body were Bevil, Meryasek, and Tristram, as well as Dr. Wolcott."

I began to ascertain the direction she was leading us. "Yes."

She paused, almost as if waiting for us to say it. "Have you wondered if they might be lyin'?"

"About the manner of his death and the nature of his injuries?" Lord Gage asked as we shared a speaking glance. It was clear that, while he might trust Tamsyn, he hadn't completely forgotten the importance of keeping our suspicions close to the vest as inquiry agents.

"That and . . . about the fact he died at all."

CHAPTER 15

B oth Lord Gage and I blinked at Tamsyn in shock.

"Are you saying . . . ?" Lord Gage began, but he seemed unable to finish the statement.

Tamsyn's mouth pursed as she seemed to give careful consideration to her next words. "I believe I saw 'im. This morn, out near the cliffs at Doyden Point." She turned to peer in that direction. "'Twas from a distance, so I can't be certain, but . . ." She broke off, searching Lord Gage's face. "I think ye know I wouldn't 'ave brought the matter to ye if I wasn't confident that was in truth Branok Roscarrock I saw. Alive and well."

His face flushed with anger and outrage, and his hands clenched into fists at his side as he turned to pace away. "If he is alive. If Branok is playing us for a fool . . . Why, I'll kill him myself!"

"But why? Why would he do such a thing?" I protested, not ready to believe it all so quickly. Yes, the lack of a vigil and the odd funeral arrangements raised some doubts, but they could just as easily be explained. And while only four men had seen Branok's corpse, and they were all related to the man, would they truly all lie about it?

"It's Branok," Lord Gage snapped. "He wouldn't need a reason to do such a thing beyond the desire to cause mischief and get a bit of revenge before he does pass on." He narrowed his eyes. "He's probably been planning this for some time."

"Then Amelia must also be part of it," I pointed out. "After all, she sent the letter asking us to come." It was my turn to pause and consider. "Unless she doesn't know, and her sending for us was an unforeseen complication."

Despite his angry remarks, he seemed to be struggling with what to make of this as much as I was. After all, we only had the word of Tamsyn that Branok was alive, and she'd only seen him from a distance.

"How far away was he?" I asked her.

"About one hundred and fifty yards."

Too far then to see his face. "What made you so certain it was him?"

Lord Gage frowned at me, but Tamsyn seemed to expect my questions. "Because of the way he moved. And the shifty way he kept glancin' about. 'Twas clear he didn't wish to be seen."

But there were any number of reasons a person might move about furtively, and they had nothing to do with having feigned their own death.

My skepticism must have been evident, for she nodded. "I know it's 'ard to believe. But aren't there people ye know well enough that you'd recognize them at such a distance?"

I had to concede she was right. Gage, for instance. I felt I would know him anywhere. And my brother and sister, and even my brother-in-law. But these were the closest people to me in the world. Had Tamsyn honestly known Branok *that* well? And if she had, what did that say about their relationship?

"You'll 'ave to decide for yourself. I simply thought I should warn ye of what I'd seen. Because if Branok *is* alive . . ."

She didn't finish the statement. She didn't need to. The implications made me flush hot and then cold. For nothing good could come from such a deception. Nothing good at all.

"Thank you," I replied.

She nodded and glanced over her shoulder toward the darkening sky in the west. "Now, I'm sure ye have your daughter to tend to, and we all need to be gettin' out of this rain."

"Allow me to escort you home," Lord Gage offered. "Kiera knows the way back to the manor."

Tamsyn touched his arm lightly. "No need for that. Ye know 'tisn't far." She strode off before he could object further. "But think on what I've said," she called back to us.

While Lord Gage remounted, I watched her go, her brown aventurine skirts swishing back and forth as she hurried down the lane. For the life of me, I couldn't decide whether she'd truly seen Branok. Clearly, she believed she had, for I could see no purpose in her lying about such a thing. Not when the truth was bound to be revealed sooner or later. Though it muddied the waters in the meantime, and distracted us—at least temporarily—from the facts of the matter. Could that be motive enough?

I frowned, unhappy with this development. And at the cold drop of rain that landed on my cheek as I peered up at the sky.

"We'd best hurry," Lord Gage said as the rain began to fall in earnest. We urged our horses into a canter.

At the manor, we dismounted swiftly, allowing the grooms to see to our steeds, and hurried through the outer courtyard into the inner one. I hadn't approached the house from this direction before, and while the rain hampered my view, I could see that the courtyard was shaped more or less like a rectangle with a small projection toward the stable corner. A number of tables and benches sat beneath a shallow, sloped roof, while much of the rest of the space was interspersed with crates and pots filled with seasonal flowers. During the chill of late autumn through early spring, I imagined it was a welcome spot to sit sheltered from the blustery winds on a sunny day. Two sets of stairs led up to the upper story from the courtyard. The first seemed to connect with a small tower adjoining the servants' quarters, while the second aimed toward the bedchambers along the northern block.

"That will take you to Emma fastest," Lord Gage directed me. "Turn right down the long corridor after you enter, and it'll guide you straight to your bedchamber door."

"But what of you?" I countered, realizing he didn't intend to follow.

His expression was grim and determined. "*I'm* going to have a word with my cousins."

I halted him with a hand to his arm. "Is that wise? Perhaps you should wait for your son."

He scowled fiercely. "I'll thank you to remember this is my mother's family, Kiera. *I'm* not the one who came stumbling in here blindly. I know what they're capable of. I'll not be made a fool of any longer."

He shook off my grip and charged into the house. I hesitated for a moment, uncertain whether to follow him, but it was past time to feed Emma and my responsibility to her must come first. If my father-in-law wanted to rage at someone and set the entire household at sixes and sevens without more proof than what Tamsyn had told us, I couldn't stop him.

Lifting my skirts, I padded up the stairs, mindful of any slickness because of the rain, and entered the door at the top on the left. A few steps took me to a junction with another door to my left, a door a short distance straight ahead, and a long corridor to my right, just as Lord Gage had described. This must have been the route I'd seen Mrs. Mackay take two days prior when she was returning to mind Emma.

I heard faint voices through a door in the middle of the corridor on the left, one of which sounded like Dolly, while a series of playful shrieks emerged from the chamber on the right, indicating the nursery. Otherwise, the corridor was silent and dark. I paused long enough at my bedchamber to remove my jaunty hat and gloves before rapping on the door of Emma's nursery and entering.

Mrs. Mackay was jouncing Emma up and down near the window as she gnawed on one of her ragdolls. "There she is," she told her. "I told ye your mam was on her way."

I smiled at Emma, already unbuttoning the coat of my riding habit as I moved to take her from her nanny. "How is my sweet girl this morning?"

Emma grinned back, revealing her first tooth, and reached for me, allowing her ragdoll to tumble from her grasp.

"Happy as a lark," Mrs. Mackay replied as I rubbed my face against Emma's downy blond curls and kissed her brow. "We went oot to see the flowers while the sun was still shinin'."

"Did you?" I cooed. "I'm sure you liked that," I told Emma.

Sinking into the rocking chair, I settled Emma so that she could begin nursing and draped a blanket over my shoulder in hopes she would become less distracted when I turned to address Mrs. Mackay. "Any developments here?"

She paused in her bustling about the room, tidying what little mess there was, and brushed a few stray silver hairs back from her forehead. "None. Other than some keen interest in where Mr. Gage rode off to this morn." Her eyebrows arched in emphasis.

"Who was interested in that?"

"A number o' the servants, though Miss McEvoy believes some o' 'em were askin' for their employers."

I nodded, for I trusted Bree's discernment. In general, she

was a good judge of people and often formed connections for me between the upstairs and downstairs before I realized it.

"There was also a bit o' a stramash between Mr. Killigrew and Mr. Roscarrock."

I looked up in surprise. "Bevil and Mery?" I asked, seeking clarification.

She nodded.

Emma grunted in disapproval, and I lowered my voice. "Did they come to blows?"

"Nearly."

I remembered seeing Mery slip out of the entrance to the servants' wing earlier that morning. "When was this? What was said?"

"Several hours ago. Before Mr. Gage left. We were in the garden, and he came to say good-bye to the bairn."

I suspected he'd also been issuing instructions to Mrs. Mackay for both Emma's and my safety while he was away, but I did not question her about them.

"From what I could gather, Mr. Roscarrock had threatened Mr. Killigrew in some way, and Mr. Killigrew challenged him in return."

"Did you hear what the threat was?"

Mrs. Mackay shook her head. "Nay. But Miss McEvoy might ken more."

"Are Mr. Roscarrock or Mr. Killigrew or his son here now?" I wondered who, if anyone, my father-in-law might have found to confront.

"Last I ken, all the Killigrews were in residence, though Mr. Roscarrock stomped off a fair bit ago."

He'd likely gone off to his cottage, which we'd yet to visit. I glanced toward the window where rain was now streaming down the glass panes. And apparently I wouldn't be visiting this day either. I peered down at Emma, resting contently in my arms. Nor would I be taking her on any excursions. Our trip to the cove would have to wait for more auspicious weather.

When Emma fell asleep, I laid her in her cradle and returned to my bedchamber to ring for Bree. There was no sound of raised voices or slamming doors, so presumably Lord Gage had found no one to vent his fury toward or his tirade had already ended. I held a brief flicker of hope that perhaps good sense had prevailed, and he'd decided to wait to confront his relatives about Tamsyn's claims until he was in a calmer frame of mind, and we possessed more information, but Bree quickly dampened that spark.

"Did one o' the Grenvilles truly tell you they'd seen Branok Roscarrock alive and well?" she demanded to know the moment she closed the door.

I sighed, sinking down on the edge of the bed. "Who did his lordship challenge?"

"Bevil."

I crossed my arms over my chest. Of course, it would be the cousin with whom matters were already so contentious.

"But many o' the others were there as well."

"Mery, too?"

Bree urged me to my feet, stripping my coat from my shoulders. "Nay. He departed after his row wi' Bevil earlier."

"Mrs. Mackay told me about that. Did you hear the threat Mery made?"

"Nay. 'Twas all verra vague." She brushed at the dampness still clinging to the woolen fabric before draping it over the bench. "Clearly they didna want anyone else to guess what they were talkin' aboot, but what else could it be but a threat to Bevil's position workin' for him?" Bree had begun to unbutton my skirt and then straightened with a gasp. "Unless it's to do wi' keepin' the secret that Branok's still alive."

I grasped the bedpost to steady myself. "I suppose that's a possibility, though we've no proof that what Tamsyn said was true. The man she saw was almost one hundred and fifty yards away, and she never saw his face."

This seemed to dampen Bree's enthusiasm. "Weel, his lordship evidently believes her."

"Yes, because he *wants* to," I pointed out. "He wants to believe the worst of his mother's family."

Bree considered this as she finished removing my garments. "Aye," she finally concurred. "So he's no' the most impartial investigator."

"That's putting it mildly," I agreed, sitting down to remove my half-boots while Bree pulled my dress of white challis printed with small bouquets and boasting epaulettes on the sleeves from the wardrobe. My shoulders slumped as I thought of how contemptuous and scornful Lord Gage could be. "I suppose he accused them of all sorts of terrible things."

Bree's stricken expression was answer enough.

I wondered if they would even wish for us to continue investigating. Not that such disapproval had ever stopped us before. Once set on the course of an inquiry, we felt it our duty to see it through, whether the initial complainants wanted us to uncover the truth or not. Though they *could* evict us from Roscarrock House, leaving us to seek shelter elsewhere. I doubted Lord Gage had given that possibility any thought. Or perhaps, believing Branok alive, he was ready to depart.

Of course this had to happen on the day Gage rode south to uncover more information about smuggling and wouldn't return until nightfall. That is, if the rain didn't hinder him.

"Where did Mery sleep last night? Do you know?" I asked as my thoughts returned to Mery and Bevil's argument.

Bree held out a pair of stays. "The master chamber."

Which, I supposed, by all rights was now his even if he'd not claimed it yet. So his skulking out of the servants' quarters had nothing to do with the previous evenings' sleeping arrangements. Unless . . .

"Was he alone?"

Bree's silence was telling, and I turned so that I could see her face, forcing her to release the ribbons of my stays which she'd been adjusting. She seemed torn. "I dinna ken. No' for certain. But . . . Cora wasna in her bed when I retired last night. And . . ." She struggled to continue meeting my gaze. "And she wasna in it when I woke either."

"I see," I replied, understanding her conundrum. Cora was Dolly's maid, and I had sensed how much Bree liked her. "Perhaps you simply slept soundly. Did her bed appear to have been disturbed?"

"Maybe?" she answered honestly. "'Twas made, o' course. But it didna appear *exactly* the same. And I *was* verra tired by the time I laid my head doon last night."

It had been extremely late, I recalled. But she'd also been angry and out of sorts over whatever had occurred between her and Anderley.

"You didn't drift off to sleep right away, did you?" I searched her freckled features. "Your mind was busy."

She nodded reluctantly, and more than anything I wanted to pry again, to ask her to confide in me. But I knew better. If she wished to explain, she would. I had to respect her privacy.

However, that didn't stop me from expressing my concern. "Are things better this morning?"

She bent over to pick up my boots, answering obliquely. "By degrees."

I watched as she set the boots by the door and then allowed myself to be turned around again so that she could resume dressing me. It was obvious that whatever had happened to upset Bree had not been fixed. Not genuinely. And that made me wonder about Anderley.

Presumably Gage had spoken to him today and he was somewhere about, ready to assist, if necessary, but I'd not seen him. Not since his shocking behavior the evening prior. I wanted to ask Bree if she knew where he was, but decided against it, forcing my mind back to Cora.

"So Cora may or may not have slept in her bed. Which means she might have slept with Mery, though we have no proof of that. She could just as easily have slept somewhere else."

Bree tugged more sharply on my garments than necessary, making me hesitate over this remark. Did Bree think Cora had slept with Anderley? I suppose he did have a room to himself now that Lembus had been directed to sleep in Lord Gage's dressing room, but I struggled to believe Anderley would be capable of such a thing. Though, to be fair, I'd also never expected to witness Anderley behaving so insolently toward us as he did the previous evening.

This caused a sharp conflict within me, one that I felt in the pit of my stomach. I didn't like doubting Anderley this way. I'd grown fond of him since my marriage to Gage, and I'd come to rely on him and all the members of our staff who had joined us in our investigative endeavors. Some months ago in Scotland, Anderley and I had formed a bond over art, as well as our mutual affection for Gage—whose life Anderley had saved more than once—and Bree. I knew Anderley loved her. I'd seen it in his eyes, in his words, in the way he'd fallen to pieces when she'd almost died.

But I could also see that he was growing impatient with her insistence that they take matters slowly. His relationship with Gage had also been strained by Gage's half brother Henry's recent involvement with our inquiries, taking the role Anderley had so often occupied. Now that Henry was no longer with us, it didn't mean those feelings of displacement had disappeared. Perhaps Anderley was harboring more anger and resentment than we realized. Gage had assured me just last night that there was no cause for concern about his valet. I wished I could believe him.

Resolving to push the matter from my mind for the moment, I returned to the issue of Cora. "Didn't you tell me she warned you about Mery?" I asked Bree.

"Aye. Said he was a scoundrel wi' any number o' sideslips dandlin' on their mam's knees. But . . ." She paused, as if not liking what she had to say next. "It could be a matter o' her protestin' too much."

I realized she was referring to the line in Shakespeare's *Hamlet*. "Can you talk to her? Ferret out what you can?" I hated to ask it of her, especially after her reaction earlier had raised the specter of Anderley's possible involvement. But there was no one else to whom I could give the task. Cora would grow suspicious if I began asking questions, and Mrs. Mackay was busy with Emma much of the time. We'd already established why I couldn't ask Anderley, the natural second choice, which left Bree.

"Aye," she answered quietly. "I'll do my best."

"I know," I assured her. "You always do."

But rather than be cheered by this compliment, she merely seemed more dejected. I couldn't say that I blamed her.

CHAPTER 16

I had nearly given up on Gage returning that evening. It had been a tense afternoon with most of us confined to the house because of the rain. All except Lord Gage and Bevil, that is, who had both taken themselves off somewhere—presumably separately—in a fit of pique. This left me with the unenviable task of trying to mitigate the awkwardness that had followed the heated accusations and arguments flung by both sides.

Not being known for my charm or social skills, I keenly felt their lack, struggling along as best I could. Fortunately, when I brought Emma down to the drawing room after her nap, her adorable grins and playful exclamations made up for any number of my deficiencies. She even managed to smooth away the frown lines I'd begun to believe would permanently score my father-in-law's face when I brought her down for one more visit after dinner.

Lord Gage had returned to Roscarrock House just in time to join us at the table, though his hair was still damp. I wasn't certain traipsing about in the rain all afternoon had been the best thing for him. It was evident when he rose from the table that his leg was aggravating him. But I kept my concern to myself, knowing he'd not thank me for it.

It didn't take much discernment to guess he'd been searching for Branok. I could think of few things that would drive him so stubbornly out into this weather. It was also clear his mother's family was perfectly aware of this fact as well. They eyed him with either reticence or open hostility. Had he not elected to retire early, I would have taken him aside to suggest he do so. I would have done the same myself if I'd not been worried for Gage.

The clock ticked ever closer to ten, and I'd begun to convince myself he must have taken a room somewhere for the night to escape the weather, when a commotion in the passage leading from the back parlor alerted me to his arrival. I abandoned the yarn I'd been winding for Amelia and hastened to greet him.

"What an abysmal journey you must have had," I exclaimed at the sight of him, wet and bedraggled, dripping all over the rug as he struggled out of his greatcoat. He was soaked and almost certainly chilled, but I exhaled in relief to find him whole and hearty and safely returned.

"I almost stopped for the night near Wadebridge," he replied before turning to Joan, who had followed me from the room. "I do beg your pardon, madam. I'll change out of these wet things just as soon as I may."

"I've sent for your valet, and I'll have a warm hip bath sent up to you when the water is heated," she told him.

"Thank you," he said as I began to hurry him up the stairs, anxious to see him made comfortable and to hear whether his journey had been worthwhile. There was also much for me to impart to him.

Once inside our room, I helped him out of his frock coat and brushed away his icy fingers to begin on the intricate draping of his cravat. He smiled down at me. "Perhaps I should hire you as my valet. No offense to Anderley, but you're far prettier to look at."

I offered him a coy little grin in response. "I suspect I would make you late for everything."

"Why is that?" he asked as his damp hair dripped onto the linen.

I arched a single eyebrow, allowing him to deduce what I meant.

"Ahhh," he answered, his pale gaze growing decidedly warmer. He reached up to clutch my upper arms, crushing the puffed sleeves as he drew me closer. "Yes, you would."

We were unceremoniously interrupted by a rap on the door, one that was too tentative to be Anderley. I backed away from Gage, lest I shock the Roscarrocks' staff before calling for them to enter.

A footman entered carrying the hip bath and a stack of towels while a pair of maids followed behind carrying buckets of water. I directed the footman to set the bath by the hearth while the maids set the buckets on the floor and swiftly departed. The footman then dumped the water from each of the buckets into the tub as swirls of steam rose toward the ceiling, before squaring his shoulders to face my husband.

"We couldn't find Mr. Anderley. But if it pleases ye, sir, I could attend ye."

A sinking feeling filled my stomach as a frown creased Gage's face. Even so, he dismissed the young man with a light voice. "That won't be necessary."

I stood holding Gage's soiled cravat between my fingers as the footman shut the door firmly. "I wonder where Anderley is?" I ventured, uncertain whether I wished to draw Gage's attention to it at the moment and risk upsetting him. He had been very angry with his valet the prior evening.

But Gage appeared relatively untroubled. "Undoubtedly off investigating one thing or another," he replied as he sat to remove his riding boots, demonstrating his apparent trust in Anderley. Trust that I prayed he still deserved.

I watched for a moment as Gage struggled with his Hoby boots. He usually required Anderley's assistance to remove them, particularly after a hard day's ride, and I pondered whether we should recall the footman to help when the first boot loosened, sliding from his foot.

"Was all your discomfort at least worth it?" I asked, draping his cravat over the back of the chair.

"Trelawny wasn't there," he said, and I might have responded with commiseration if not for the glint in his eyes. "But his family was. And they had plenty to say." He set the boot to the side before beginning to tug at the second. "Father was correct. Despite all the government's efforts, the smuggling has never truly stopped. Oh, the Martello towers they built to protect the coast during the war with Napoléon helped, and the large number of smuggling vessels captured and sunk by the Royal Navy during the Peace of Amiens certainly hindered the free traders. And the recent reorganization of the preventive services has undoubtedly proved a more effective deterrent. But the smugglers have simply altered their methods in order to circumvent all that."

"Including the Roscarrocks?"

He grunted as the second boot came free. "If the reports the Trelawnys' have heard are to be believed." He leaned forward, resting his elbows on his knees as he wiggled his toes. "Rather than risk their own vessels, they now charter French ships because the revenue cutters can't impede them as long as they remain outside territorial waters. The smugglers send agents over on the mail packet to France, and various other countries, to secure their contraband of brandy or silk or sugar or tobacco—whatever products prove profitable to avoid paying tariffs for—and then hire a ship and crew. Once completed, the agents sail back to England with the vessel, commanding them where to either sink the goods in tubs offshore to be collected later by locals in smaller fishing boats, or directly meet the locals who take the contraband off the ship into their boats."

I moved a step closer. "And this is what the Roscarrocks do?"

Gage spread his hands wide. "According to the Trelawnys."

I considered all this. "If that's true, then Bevil lied outright to your father."

"That, or he's indulging in obfuscation."

I turned to him in question.

"They're not Roscarrock ships or crews. Maybe the agent isn't even a Roscarrock. In fact, he probably isn't. If the enterprise is of any significant size—and it must be to make such an undertaking profitable—then they may be only one of several families involved."

"And if that's true, if practically the entire community is involved, then that makes it all the more difficult to convince any of them to share what they know." I felt like we were back in Yorkshire, confronted with the silent collusion of an entire village yet again.

Gage nodded dourly, bending to remove his stockings. "Though I may have a plan to circumvent that."

Before I could ask what this meant, he shifted topics. "But what of here? Were you and Father able to uncover anything?"

"Were we," I muttered with a wry laugh, drawing his gaze. I quickly recapitulated the days' discoveries, including Dr. Wolcott's failure to note rigor mortis and the fact that Morgan had let slip that her dissenter husband and Branok had avoided each other. Gage seemed to think little of the fact Bevil and Mery had exchanged heated words, but I had saved the biggest revelation for last.

"We met Tamsyn Grenville Kellynack on our way back to the manor. Did you have a chance to meet her last night?" I queried, recalling that Gage hadn't been a part of our conversation in the garden.

He stood, stretching his arms over his head as he squinted his eyes as if trying to remember. "A woman about my father's age with dark eyes and dark hair going to gray? Yes, we were introduced."

"Well, she was Jago's cousin. Your father's friend who was killed. And apparently she was also quite close to your father."

If Gage read anything more into these words than their surface meaning, he didn't indicate it, instead unfastening his waistcoat and discarding it on the floor before starting on the buttons of his fine white lawn shirt.

"We've been invited to tea on Monday, incidentally. By Jago's mother."

This succeeded in capturing his interest. His eyes flared wide, correctly interpreting how fraught the visit might prove to be for both parties. "Then I'm glad I didn't postpone my journey to see Trelawny until then," he remarked, resuming his disrobing.

"Tamsyn also informed us of something a bit more . . . alarming." I licked my suddenly dry lips, uncertain why I hesitated. "She claimed she saw Branok along the coast near Doyden Point."

"The day he died?" Gage asked, lifting his shirt over his head.

"No. This morning."

Gage's fingers slipped, nearly dropping the shirt into the hip bath. "This morning?" he repeated incredulously.

"Yes." My gaze dipped momentarily to the musculature of his chest before returning to his face as his shock dissolved into skepticism. "Claimed?"

"She admits he was at least one hundred and fifty yards away, too far to make out his features, but she insists she recognized him from the way he moved."

"Did Father believe her?"

I arched a single eyebrow. "What do you think?"

Gage turned away with a softly muttered curse, scraping a hand back through his damp hair.

"He insisted on confronting Bevil and the others, who denied it, and then went traipsing off in the rain. Presumably to search for his uncle. Leaving *me* to try to soothe a lot of frazzled tempers."

Gage's gaze softened with empathy.

I crossed my arms over my chest, feeling suddenly exposed. "As you know, that is not my strong suit."

He pulled me toward him, and I allowed myself to melt into his embrace. "Has Father returned?"

I nodded against his bare shoulder. "Just in time for dinner. Though he retired early."

"Leaving you alone again." He bowed his head; his exhaled breath stirred the hairs at my temple. "I wish I'd been here."

"I do, too," I admitted. "Perhaps you would have been able to talk some sense into him."

His voice turned wry. "I doubt it, but at least I would have been here to lend you support."

I pressed closer. "Then you don't believe Tamsyn?"

He lifted his head to look down at me, but rather than answer, he turned the question back on me. "Do you?"

I retreated a step so that I could see his face more fully. "It seems improbable."

"But it's troubling none the same."

"I can see no good reason why Tamsyn would lie." I frowned. Unless it was to widen the rift between Lord Gage and his mother's family. But I didn't share this out loud. "She must simply be mistaken. But if she isn't . . ."

Gage's brow furrowed, echoing the same confusion and apprehension I felt.

"Why would they lure us here with such a pretense? What could they hope to gain?"

If they'd wished to reconcile with Gage's father, this certainly wasn't the way to do it. It would cause an even bigger breach than before.

"I don't know," he admitted, lifting his hand to cradle my cheek. "Mrs. Kellynack simply must be mistaken."

Having felt the iciness of his fingers, I grasped his hand between mine. "Enough of this. It can wait. Get in that hip bath before the water cools completely."

A teasing smile hovered on his lips, which I was surprised hadn't turned blue. "Aye, m'lady."

I turned away to search the clothespress for the nightshirt he'd claimed Anderley had packed him, only to have him draw me closer, pressing a kiss to my lips.

When he pulled back, it was to gaze down at me with earnest eyes. "We'll sort it out. Together. Like always," he assured me.

My heart swelled with love for him. "Of course we will."

A glimmer of mischief lit his eyes. "And if I should require additional warming?"

Some impish impulse overtook me as I began again to turn away. "I shall ring for more water." I grinned as he pulled me back once more.

"That's not the answer I was hoping for."

"It isn't?"

He arched his eyebrows at my coy remark.

Pressing my hands to the bristles dusting his jaw, I allowed him to see my full affection for him in the depths of my eyes. "I shall always be here for you."

I paused, noting that my words had affected him as deeply as I'd hoped. Perhaps too deeply for this moment. "Now . . ." I whispered, pausing for dramatic effect. "Get in the bath."

He smiled, and this time he obeyed.

CHAPTER 17

We attended church the following morning at St. Endellion, where the Roscarrocks had worshiped for centuries. Tombs and memorials to the family lined the north aisle and the churchyard, and even a pew bench end boasted the Roscarrock family arms. It was a lovely old church, rich in history and ornamentation. One that had been dedicated to St. Endelienta, who, as Amelia explained, had been King Arthur's goddaughter.

Apparently, St. Endelienta had been very fond of cows, for Arthur killed the person who slayed her favorite bovine, even after Endelienta had brought the cow back to life. Then when *she* died, the cow brought her to the very spot where the church was built. I had long ago learned not to bother questioning the logic or validity of tales about medieval saints.

The droll teller had claimed that the salver of pure gold from his final tale—the only part of the Portuguese treasure that had ever been recovered—could still be seen at St. Endellion. While it was true there was a gold plate propped on a shelf along the north aisle, there was no evidence it had actually come from a shipwreck or Portugal, for that matter. Half the churches in England probably boasted a similar artifact.

Seated at the front as I was, flanked by my husband and father-in-law, I had little opportunity to observe anyone else during the service. But when we departed, I couldn't help but note that Anderley was not among those filling the pews with Bree and the staff from Roscarrock House. Mrs. Mackay had remained home with Emma, in fear she was developing a bit of ague.

If Gage noticed his valet's absence, he didn't show it, and it was hardly the time for me to mention it. Not when we were being greeted by many of the same people we'd been introduced to at the party the Roscarrocks had hosted, including the Grenvilles. If Lord Gage had revealed that it was Tamsyn who'd told him she'd seen Branok alive and well, the Roscarrocks surprisingly bore her no grudge. Which made me suspect my father-in-law had at least been circumspect in that regard. Even so, his interactions with everyone, including Tamsyn, were decidedly stilted.

Gage and I had hoped to speak with him on the carriage ride to and from the church, but Tristram had claimed the seat next to him so as not to overcrowd the Killigrews' conveyance. We intended to make a second attempt before dinner, but by the time I'd attended to Emma, the family was already sitting down at the long table in the dining room. Only Mery was absent, but he'd also not joined us for the morning service.

The meal began with our making small talk about things such as the weather. Amelia shared that November was known as the "black month" in Cornish. *Miz-dui*, she called it. And that the sun we'd enjoyed during our first days here was unlikely to last. "Though we would welcome it, if it did continue to shine," she added, turning toward the window where the sun beamed down on the ground, still damp from the lingering morning showers.

"Just so long as the ground doesn't freeze before Martinmas," Dolly chimed in to say.

"Aye." Noticing my curiosity, Amelia's eyes twinkled. "There's an old sayin'. 'If Martinmas ice can bear a duck, the winter will be all mire and muck.'"

I smiled at the rhyme.

"'Tis just another way to say 'an early winter is a surly winter,'" Bevil groused between spoons of his potato and leek soup.

"Then I hope for your sakes the winter is late," I remarked. For I couldn't imagine Bevil being surlier than he already was. He clumped about the house, scowling and sending suspicious or outright hostile looks our way, particularly toward Lord Gage. Even now, he periodically darted an antagonistic glare at his cousin across the table.

"Every season 'as its time and place," Amelia reminded us. "We need the winter just as we need the summer. Everything in balance. Like the ebb and flow of the tide." She sank back, scrutinizing us with her pale eyes. "Everyone remembers 1816. The year without a summer. But I recall a winter when I was a child when it was so warm and mild, ye couldn't believe 'twas January and not July. Oh, but the storms that year! They were somethin' fierce." She shook her head sadly, her raspy voice losing some of its strength. "We lost a lot of good men to the sea that year."

My gaze naturally gravitated toward Lord Gage, wondering if he was thinking, as I was, of his mother and her lost first love. His concentration seemed devoted to the food before him, but the tiny furrow in his brow suggested he was also attending to our conversation. Had I been alone with Amelia, I might have asked her about her sister and her first betrothed, but doing so now, in front of the family with Lord Gage looking on, seemed too intrusive.

Gage bantered with Amelia and utilized his charm to draw more stories about the history of the family and the area from her and some of the others. Even Joan, Dolly, and Tristram shared a few anecdotes from their lives. Only Bevil remained silent, supplying grunts when the others required his participation. That is, until someone weaved a story involving one of the Grenvilles.

He waited until the laughter had subsided before remarking to Lord Gage in a biting tone, "I know who it was that convinced ye Branok is still alive."

Lord Gage lifted his gray eyes, narrowing them to slits at the tone of his cousin's voice.

"'Twas Tamsyn, wasn't it? Even now, you'd believe any ole rubbish she tells ye."

Lord Gage arched his chin. "You're one to spout morals. Her hands are far cleaner than yours."

"The Grenvilles' 'ands have never been clean. You know that as well as I do." Bevil pushed to his feet, throwing down his napkin. "And as for Tamsyn. Fifty years changes a person. You don't know 'alf of what she has or hasn't done." His gaze raked over his cousin in disgust. "Though I suppose I shouldn't be surprised you'd take her side over ours. You always did prefer pretense." He turned to leave the room as Lord Gage also rose to his feet.

"That's rich coming from a man who has surrounded himself with trappings that aren't even his."

My eyes widened at the cruelty of the remark even as Bevil's footsteps faltered, and he aimed a look filled with pure malice at my father-in-law.

"Boys," Amelia gasped much too late.

Neither of them listened. Bevil continued on into the interior of the house, while Lord Gage strode toward the adjoining room and the door leading out into the gardens. We heard a slam and then soon saw him striding by the windows in the direction of the pond and the cliffs beyond. I could only presume he was tramping off to search for Branok again, stoking his anger and disgruntlement with every step.

Dinner ended on this discordant note, as Amelia clutched her hand to her weak heart, confessing her desire to rest, and Joan and Dolly escorted her from the room. Tristram made his excuses, trailing off in the direction of his father.

I turned to Gage uncertainly. Matters couldn't carry on like this. Everyone was getting more deeply hurt by each other with each passing day, and we were no closer to uncovering the truth about Branok's death than before. That was *if* there was any to find.

Gage crossed the room and leaned down to press a kiss to my brow. "I'll find him." He followed the same path as his father, not even breaking stride as he passed the windows.

I looked up as a maid entered. "I beg yer pardon," she exclaimed, stumbling to a stop. "I thought the family was finished."

"We are," I told her with a weak smile, pushing back from the table.

I climbed the stairs to Emma's chamber, needing the peace and comfort cradling her in my arms always brought me. But she was still napping, her face softly reposed and her normally fisted hands relaxed. I was tempted to reach out to run my fingers through her soft curls, but I was afraid it would wake her.

Mrs. Mackay arched her eyebrows in question from her seat near the window, clearly sensing my apprehension. I shook my head, trying to reassure her, and then slipped back out of the room. Once in the corridor, I hesitated. I stared at my bedchamber door, knowing I could take a nap myself. I could certainly use the extra sleep. Except the idea of lying alone with my thoughts was about as appealing as one of my father-in-law's snide remarks.

So instead, I found myself wandering through the rooms on the main floor of the house, all of which were empty. Strolling out into the garden I spied Dolly seated at a table positioned underneath the shade of a large beech tree. Sometime in the last quarter hour, Imogen must have decided to pay a call, for she perched next to Dolly, leaning toward her avidly as if to hear every word. I could only imagine Dolly was rehashing what had happened over dinner. Although when they caught sight of me, neither of them looked abashed, instead waving me over eagerly.

Half the tree's leaves had already fallen to the ground, their dampness squelching beneath my feet and releasing an earthy aroma as I approached.

"We figured we risked less of a chance of bein' overheard out here," Dolly explained, passing me a towel. "But you'll need this. It should absorb most of the moisture."

I set the towel down on the rain-soaked wooden bench and sat on top of it, hoping she was right. "You were expecting me, then?" I asked, as they'd had the forethought to bring an extra linen.

Imogen grinned. "Sooner or later." Sunlight dappled her features as it shined through the remaining leaves, adding highlights to her short brown hair, which fell in waves about her face. "Now," she coaxed. "Tell us everything. Did Tamsyn Kellynack truly claim she'd seen Branok alive?"

I turned to Dolly, who blushed lightly, evidently having relayed at least this bit of gossip from dinner. "From a distance. Though, to be fair, she wasn't absolutely certain it was him."

Imogen made a rude noise at the back of her throat. "To be fair, she wouldn't 'ave told ye if she wasn't sure unless she wanted to cause trouble."

My cheeks stung even though I knew the rebuke wasn't aimed at me. "I did wonder."

"I told ye Kiera wouldn't be insensible to her guile," Dolly said.

But Imogen seemed to want further assurance. "So you doubt her claim?"

"Of course I do," I said. "Identifying someone from such a distance is hardly proof. The veracity is questionable enough that her even making it has to draw *some* scrutiny."

Imogen sat back, seeming content with this response; however, I wasn't finished.

"But why would Tamsyn want to cause trouble?" I asked, repeating her words before turning to Dolly. "And what did Bevil mean when he said the Grenvilles' hands aren't clean?"

The two women looked at each other, clearly debating what to share. I'd hoped they'd be honest with me, or at least corroborate what I'd already learned from other sources, but there was no guarantee they would be so forthcoming. After all, just because I liked them didn't mean they would place their trust in me over what they might believe was in their family's best interest. I couldn't even say I would blame them.

Dolly was the first to speak. "The Roscarrocks and Grenvilles 'ave long been partners in many . . . endeavors," she finally settled on before glancing at Imogen again. "Includin' smugglin'."

I nodded, keeping my expression even. For one, I already knew about the connection between the two and their smuggling operations. This was merely further confirmation. For another, I didn't want to discourage their willingness to share by responding with too much passion.

"But despite that, or perhaps *because* of it, they've also had their share of disputes."

"To hear the family histories," Imogen chimed in. "It seems

to be mostly tit-for-tat sorts of things. They stole our sheep, so we'll steal theirs."

"He blackened my brother's eye, so I'll blacken his," Dolly contributed.

"They didn't give us our fair share of the bounty, so we'll report them to the preventives, and likewise." Imogen waved her hand in a circle. "You apprehend what we're saying."

I nodded again, strongly suspecting I wouldn't be receiving such an unbiased recitation from anyone but these two women who had not been born into the Roscarrock family, but rather married one of their kin.

"But . . . there are a few instances when matters 'ave grown rather . . . contentious."

Dolly's dark eyes were dismayed. "They've set fire to each other's property and exchanged musket balls and bullets." She shook her head sadly. "A young lad was even killed several decades ago as the result of some disagreement."

I wondered if the young lad was Jago. If so, this was the first I'd heard of his death involving any sort of conflict between the Roscarrocks and the Grenvilles. What little Lord Gage had shared with us about the incident seemed to imply that Jago had been killed by the local preventive officer, Mr. Cuttance Senior, in the pursuit of his duty, catching smugglers and confiscating contraband. Was Dolly speaking of another young lad, or was there more to the story? More than perhaps Lord Gage even knew?

"Normally these sorts of clashes—even the violent ones—have been naturally resolved," Imogen explained. "Often because they needed to band together to confront some common enemy."

Dolly crossed her arms over her lavender pelisse. "The Roscarrocks and Grenvilles might feel a natural enmity toward each other at times, but they're not goin' to stand by and let some outsider threaten the other."

I understood, for Scotland's clans had exhibited a similar mind-set for hundreds of years. That is until the Acts of Union and the resulting Jacobite rebellions had finally succeeded in provoking divisions between many clans that superseded their previous cultural loyalties.

"But there's been no natural resolution to their latest dispute?" I deduced.

A leaf fluttered to the table between us, and Imogen picked it up, twirling it between her fingers. "Nay. This time . . . this time the fallin' out feels more permanent."

Dolly's features were pensive as she stared down at the wooden grains of the table.

"Their most recent dispute," I murmured as the scent of the sea teased my nostrils, drawing my gaze toward the ocean beyond the rising hills. "Does it involve Gilbert Grenville's leg?"

When neither woman answered, I turned to find them studying me warily.

"How did ye know?" Imogen asked.

"It seemed a logical guess, as Morgan already admitted the injury occurred while he was assisting the Roscarrocks." Since they had both been privy to the conversation, this should not be a shock.

"Well, it's even worse than she told ye," Dolly confessed, only to have Imogen shoot her a quelling glare. Dolly shook off the hand Imogen had placed on her arm. "Kiera needs to hear the full truth, not just what Morgan sanctions us to tell her."

Imogen seemed less certain of this than Dolly, but she stopped trying to silence her.

"They left him. Where he damaged his leg," she clarified without being specific. I suspected that was because the location would make it obvious that they'd been retrieving smuggled goods. "Whether this is because they thought he was embroiderin' his injury or because they believed someone else would go back for him depends on who ye talk to, but they all left him." She shifted uncomfortably. "In a place he couldn't be left indefinitely."

Because of the tides? Had they left him to possibly drown?

"How did he make it out?" I asked.

"Of his own volition."

On a leg that had been crushed? I winced, knowing that must have been excruciatingly painful.

Dolly's answering grimace told me I was probably correct. "That's why the doctor said his leg would never heal right. That if he'd immobilized it immediately, the bones could have been set, but additional movement had caused damage that couldn't be repaired."

"And so, the Grenvilles blame the Roscarrocks," I surmised, though she hadn't been clear exactly *which* Roscarrocks had done it, nor did this statement properly articulate the gravity of the circumstances.

"Aye," Dolly said.

I turned to gaze out over the sunken garden and the pond beyond. A pair of geese floated on its surface.

Knowing that the Roscarrocks had left her brother for dead, even unwittingly, must make Tamsyn furious. It must make all the Grenvilles furious. Furious enough to want revenge. The question was whether they'd taken it. Had they confronted Branok? Had one of them pushed him from the cliff?

Tamsyn's claims that she'd seen Branok alive could just be a ploy. A way to insinuate doubts into our investigation. After all, if Branok was actually alive and well, just performing some sort of cruel trick, then the Grenvilles couldn't have killed him.

"Then neither of you believe Branok could still be alive?" I asked them pointedly, wanting to be given straight answers for once.

"Nay," Imogen stated emphatically as Dolly shook her head. "I may not have seen Branok's body, but Tristram did, and my husband would never lie about such a thing."

It was clear Dolly believed this, but that didn't mean I did. After all, Tristram was under the thumb of Branok, Mery, and his father Bevil. In fact, Branok controlled the livelihoods of all three men and their families. If he ordered them to do something, how hard would it be to deny him? Would they dare?

I turned away again. The trouble with this case was that nothing was straightforward. Nothing was uncomplicated. And it all hinged on a single truth we had yet to find a definitive answer to. Had Branok Roscarrock been murdered?

Suddenly, I craved nothing so much as solitude. I needed somewhere to untangle my thoughts, to unravel all the kinks and lay the threads of this investigation out in a nice, neat line. And I couldn't do that while others were looking on.

So I excused myself from Dolly's and Imogen's company, ignoring their uncertain glances, and set off in the direction of the pond. Circling its perimeter, I recalled that Anderley had mentioned that a dry creek bed led off to the west. After a few moments searching, I found it, for with the past twenty-four hours of rain, it was no longer absolutely dry. Mindful of the soggy ground at its center, I strolled alongside it, observing how the boggy trail turned to a slow trickle and then an actual stream. The sky overhead was a brilliant periwinkle blue and the clouds that remained were no more threatening than the down on a thistle.

With each step, I felt my mood lifting, if not my general state of perplexity. A trio of seabirds flew overhead, their calls echoing over the wavering grasses. The gentle ripple of the stream soon found itself competing in my ears with the rolling tide of the ocean crashing against the rocky shore, alerting me to my proximity to the sea before I saw it.

This, then, must be Port Quin, I realized, spying the small number of cottages clustered near the inlet that cut between two grassy forelands. Which was also where Mery's cottage was located. Slowing my steps, I examined the options before me, curious which belonged to Branok's grandson. The buildings were all crafted of stone and slate, between which sprouted wild fennel, gorse flowers, and a few late-blooming primroses. A number of pilchard sheds dotted the harbor, where the fish would be pressed, salted, and readied for shipment. Two men rolled one of the barrels they were packed in from one of the cellars toward a cart.

It wasn't a large village, and most of the cottages huddled close together, save one. It was set farthest back from the shore and boasted no garden and very little embellishments of any kind. Not even a crude wooden bench to encourage neighbors to sit and chat for a spell or from which to remove your muddy shoes before entering the house. It seemed to me a bachelor's abode, and as such, I suspected it was Mery's.

I began to sidle toward it, but then hesitated about twenty feet from its door, wondering if it was wise to approach. I had been curious where the Roscarrock heir who no one seemed to like—except Anne—lived, but now that I'd seen it, I wondered if it might be best to pass by. After all, Mery had a reputation as a rogue. One who might view my presence in his cabin as an invitation, no matter my protests, and I hadn't thought to bring along my reticule with its Hewson percussion pistol tucked inside.

On the other hand, Mery's cottage was the perfect location, near to the manor but far enough away for privacy, where Branok might have concealed himself. I wondered if Lord Gage had thought to look here. Though I had strong doubts about

Tamsyn's claims—ones bordering on disbelief—there was still the slim chance she'd been correct. If so, it would behoove us to search Mery's cottage before they realized we'd thought of it.

I lifted my foot to do just that when the door suddenly opened and Mery, himself, stepped out.

CHAPTER 18

It was not an auspicious reception. In fact, Mery glared at me as if I'd committed some grave infraction. He was dressed as carelessly as all the other times I'd seen him, almost as if he'd just rolled out of bed after sleeping in his clothes.

"What do *you* want?" he demanded, closing the door to his cottage firmly before striding toward me. "Don't tell me Amelia has sent ye to do her fetchin'."

"No, I was just . . . out for a walk," I replied with as much aplomb as I could muster. "It wasn't until I saw these cottages that I realized this must be where you lived."

"Aye, well, now you've seen." He grasped my arm, walking me back in the direction I'd come.

"There's no need for such behavior," I protested, pulling against his grip. "I'm not refusing to leave." Finally managing to extricate myself, I rubbed my upper arm.

"Don't scowl at me like that," he countered. "I didn't hurt

ye." His hazel eyes scrutinized me sharply before he turned away. "I'd have to be a timdoodle to risk angerin' a witch."

Angered by his disrespect, I narrowed my eyes and hissed, "Too late."

His frown transformed into a rather spiteful grin. "Ye admit it, then? You're a witch?"

I ignored him, remembering how Mery had baited us in the cove, hoping to provoke a reaction. He was the type of fellow who loved to stir the pot, deflecting attention away from himself. No wonder his relatives didn't like him.

"Ah, don't stop talkin' now. Not when ye were just gettin' interestin'."

But I refused to be roused further, answering instead in a carefully neutral voice, "If I'm a witch, I guess that means those witch marks by the windows in the house didn't work." I'd not yet checked any other windows than the two in my bedchamber, but after what Bree had shared about them, it was a safe bet they were inscribed on the walls in more than just my room.

"Aye, but *those* are to keep out the evil, not the good."

I turned to him in surprise. That he'd spoken of the witch marks as if they were genuine and not just some ancient superstition, and that he'd so breezily classified me as good.

His ground-eating strides continued several steps before he noticed my pace had slackened. He shook the shaggy blue-black strands out of his eyes as he turned to look back at me. "Am I wrong?" he taunted. "Are ye here with ill intentions?"

"An interesting question," I replied, surprising him in turn. I watched him carefully as I closed the gap between us. "I suppose it depends on what your family's objective was in inviting us here. If it was to uncover whether your grandfather was murdered, then our intentions are in alignment. *But . . .*"

A muscle twitched at the corner of his eye.

"If it was for some other reason, then . . ." I shrugged one shoulder, allowing him to finish the thought.

Mery glowered. "*I* didn't invite ye here. Nor did I ask ye to investigate." He turned to continue stalking toward the manor. "Just because the Killigrews and I are related doesn't mean we have the same objective. Or that we're *ever* in alignment."

"True." I hastened to catch up with him, eager to capitalize on the opening he'd offered. "We've yet to hear your version of events, so why don't you share it with me."

"Why? I already know you've been askin' questions about me."

Thanks to his cousin Anne, no doubt.

His voice fairly dripped with cynicism, so I opted for brutal honesty. "Naturally. You're your grandfather's heir. So if he was killed, suspicion has to fall on you."

"I did not murder my granfer," he growled.

"Then help us figure out who—*if anyone*—did."

He didn't respond immediately, but rather appeared to be considering my request. Which was far more promising than the swift refusal I'd anticipated. So I resolved to be patient, to let him come to his own conclusion. Whether it would be to our benefit or not, I didn't know, but he did relent enough to offer me his arm to help me traverse a particularly slippery section of the trail alongside the stream. Once we reached surer footing and I'd released his arm, he bowed his head, his brow furrowing. "I believe it's the latter."

I blinked in surprise. "That no one killed him?"

"Aye."

"Then, how do you explain—"

He exhaled audibly, cutting off my question. Whatever he was about to say pained him in some way. "Great-Aunt Amelia doesn't want to admit it, but . . ." He glanced at me fleetingly, before returning his gaze to the path before us. "Granfer 'ad heart problems. Much like her. He . . . knew they were gettin' worse."

I spoke slowly, deliberating over my words. "And you think he might have . . . fallen over the cliff?"

His lips pressed together so tightly they showed white. "I think 'twas accidental," he finally said. "That he had a massive attack and lost his balance. Though he shouldn't 'ave been there alone in the first place," he finished angrily.

It struck me that, of all the versions of events we'd heard thus far, this seemed the most realistic. Perhaps we'd overestimated the strength of those brambles from stopping someone from falling. "So Amelia sending for us was . . . what?"

"A wild-goose chase."

He offered no placating words, but then, he'd not been the one to send for us. This, I supposed, explained his absence and reticence in talking to us, as well as his hostility. Rather than have to lie and pretend he agreed with the others, it was easier just to avoid us.

The stream had thinned to a trickle, and I could see the pond ringed with trees and the manor beyond it. My time with Mery was almost at an end, and I didn't know if I would ever have the chance to speak with him alone again, so I pressed for clarity.

"Then Branok isn't still alive?"

Mery's shoulders tensed as he tossed a glower at me. "I 'eard Tamsyn Kellynack has been makin' such ridiculous claims. Nay. I saw . . . his body." Each word felt forced from his throat. "He's dead."

This proclamation had the ring of finality, and I let it stand as such.

In any case, we'd been spotted. Tristram stood next to the table where Dolly and Imogen still sat, watching as his father strode around the edge of the pond toward us. The mayflies must have been swarming, for Bevil waved his hand in front of his face as if to brush something away. However, his eyes remained trained steadily on us.

"Aye, an' here comes the inquisition," Mery muttered under his breath. "Don't say I didn't warn ye."

"What is there to question us about?" I asked, but he only cast me a wary look out of the corner of his eye.

"Good afternoon, Kiera," Bevil said in greeting. "Went for a stroll, did ye?" His gaze slid toward his uncle's grandson. "I hope Meryasek wasn't botherin' ye."

"Not at all! We happened upon each other, and he kindly lent me his escort." This was embellishing a bit, perhaps. A fact that Mery seemed to find amusing if the sudden quirk of his lips was any indication. But something about Bevil's insinuation that Mery was up to no good, despite all evidence to the contrary, irked me.

"Aye, sure," Bevil grunted as if this was doubtful, falling in step with us. "Did ye see our dolphin, then?"

"No. I didn't make it that far." I turned to him eagerly, for this was the first I'd heard of the creature. "Is there truly one?"

He nodded, scratching his chin. "We see 'im from time to time. Sometimes brings a friend."

The prospect of seeing a dolphin delighted me.

"Though he 'asn't been seen in some weeks," Bevil cautioned, glancing toward Mery, who kept his eyes averted. "Did ye enjoy a pleasant stroll?"

This seemed like a searching remark, one that was directed as much at Mery as me. Mery's loose-limbed frame now seemed tense and guarded, which put me on my guard as well.

"Aye. We discussed witches," Mery remarked, his eyes glittering in challenge when he cast me a swift look. One that warned me not to mention his opinions regarding his grandfather's fate.

"Witches?" Bevil repeated.

"I noticed the witch marks by the windows in Roscarrock House and mentioned them to Mery," I elaborated, hoping to keep the conversation directed away from my status as a possible witch.

"I see. Aye, those are ancient. Naught to be concerned with now."

"Don't tell Great-Aunt Amelia that," Mery retorted, earning him a scowl from Bevil.

"Amelia believes in witches?" I asked.

"Nay, but her mother did," Bevil replied reluctantly.

Who would have been Lord Gage's grandmother. I put aside this information to be contemplated later.

We walked on in silence, though it was far from a comfortable one. We rounded the largest grouping of oak trees near the pond and had neared the outer garden gate before Bevil clumsily tried to break it.

"Anything else ye discussed?" he interjected, trying and failing to sound disinterested. I couldn't help but feel there was something he was fishing for, and I began to understand Mery's passing mention of inquisitions.

"Just casual remarks," I said with a shrug before attempting to turn the question back on Bevil. "Why? Was there something we should have talked about?"

From his alarmed expression and fumbling tone, plainly he'd not been expecting this. "Nay. Just . . ." He scratched the back of his head. "Just makin' conversation."

I felt a pulse of guilt for making him embarrassed, wondering if perhaps I'd misconstrued his intentions. Hadn't I noticed the other night at the party how awkward he was in company? Perhaps he genuinely had been trying to make conversation with us and had simply gone about it ineptly. I had found myself in enough similar situations to recognize the signs and was chagrined I'd not realized it before. Instead, I'd assumed the worst.

Anxious to make up for it, I smiled up at him contritely. "There are so many seemingly disparate details to this investigation, I feared perhaps I'd forgotten to ask something. Though that does remind me, did either of you notice whether Branok's watch was underwater when you found him?"

"Watch?" Bevil asked, turning to Mery, whose expression also flickered with confusion.

"Yes. His pocket watch?" When still neither of them spoke, I found their bewilderment odd, but continued to prod. "Dr. Wolcott mentioned it had been damaged in the fall. That it stopped approximately three hours before you found the body."

"Oh, aye," Bevil agreed, glancing at Mery again, who kept his thoughts to himself. "It was damp, but I don't recall if it was underwater." When Mery added nothing to these claims, Bevil asked me, "Why did ye want to know?"

"I was just curious how far the tides had come in, and when, in particular, they might have reached the watch."

He nodded, though he still didn't look like he understood.

But Mery did. "To help tell you when he died."

"Or at least give us a more accurate indication," I conceded, but my suspicions were aroused, and I couldn't leave it at that. Not when there was an easy way to test them. "Perhaps if we could examine it." I looked to them hopefully.

Bevil began rubbing the back of his neck again. "I believe 'twas all burned or thrown out. Along with his clothes. None of it was salvageable, and it seemed best to be rid of it."

"Oh," I replied simply, turning to Mery to see if he would add anything, but he kept his eyes trained forward. Even when he held the garden gate open for me, he kept his gaze carefully averted. For good reason.

Because they were lying! Dr. Wolcott had said he'd given them the watch to be buried with Branok, yet neither of them remembered this? I found this impossible to believe. Which meant that Dr. Wolcott had almost certainly *also* lied. But why? It didn't make any sense.

Something I reiterated to Gage and his father when we found ourselves with a few moments alone before the evening repast. We had been informed this would consist of lighter fare, as the main meal of the day had occurred following church, but we still felt compelled to dress for it. Lord Gage and I hovered near the warmth of the fireplace in the small sitting room adjoining his bedchamber, eager to ward off the chill that had settled in with the passing rain, while Lembus finished arranging Gage's cravat.

It had taken all of my forbearance not to demand to know why his father's valet was helping him to dress and not his own manservant. A forbearance I could tell, from the sharp-eyed looks my father-in-law continued to send his son's way, he was not going to continue long. For once, I was glad of Lord Gage's critical nature. Because my husband certainly didn't seem concerned with Anderley's continued absence or in explaining why.

"Clearly, Dr. Wolcott is hiding something," Lord Gage pronounced. "Though whether that's his having a hand in Branok's death or merely his incompetence in failing to note rigor mortis remains to be seen."

"Perhaps," I acknowledged, knowing it was a distinct possibility, and yet still feeling oddly unsatisfied with that conclusion. The trouble was that every time I felt we'd uncovered a reasonable explanation for Branok's death and the circumstances surrounding it, someone had to do or say something to complicate matters. If Bevil and Mery had not seemed so baffled by my mention of the pocket watch, and had they and Dr. Wolcott not made contradictory statements as to its current location, I might have been ready to dismiss the entire inquiry and declare Branok's death an accident, for we had no concrete evidence to the contrary. But now I was forced once again to reexamine every statement and discovery.

"What of this feud between the Roscarrocks and Grenvilles that Dolly and Imogen mentioned?" I crossed my arms over my pink watered-silk bodice, determined to have an answer from my father-in-law. "It seems to be long-standing, but you didn't mention anything about it."

"Because it seemed inconsequential," he replied with maddening apathy.

My eyebrows arched high. "Even after Tamsyn made her accusations?"

His jaw tightened as if refusing to even deign to give an answer to this query.

"Come, Father," Gage interjected as Lembus finished. "You know it's a legitimate question."

Lord Gage transferred his glower to his son before speaking to Lembus. "You may leave us." He waited until the door clicked shut before speaking again. "What I *think* is a legitimate question regards the competency of your valet, Sebastian. I heard what happened at the party, and Mr. Anderley has been conspicuously absent since. Yet, as I understand it, he's still in your employ."

Annoyance tugged downward at the corners of Gage's lips. "All will be revealed in time. You needn't concern yourself."

This piqued my curiosity, but I knew better than to press the matter until we were alone. Especially knowing Lord Gage was using it as a diversion tactic. Something Gage stressed.

"*You* are straying from the point. You've gone haring off, yon and hither, risking your health and injury searching for Branok based purely on the word of a woman who may have ulterior motives to make such a claim."

Lord Gage plainly didn't appreciate being scolded by his

own son and drew himself up to his full height to retort. But not only was Gage an inch or two taller, he wasn't finished.

"A few months ago, you nearly died not once, but three times," Gage's voice cracked. "And I do not care to repeat the experience." He inhaled a ragged breath. "But if my plea isn't enough, then I beg you to at least think of Emma. She would not understand if you were no longer here."

This effectively took the wind from Lord Gage's sails, for his chest deflated and his brow furrowed with something akin to regret.

"Will you at least consider our feelings before you go charging off into the rain or start leaning precariously over cliff-sides?"

I turned to my husband in alarm. Was that where he'd found his father that afternoon? Dangling over a cliff?

"I was searching for a cave," he protested.

Gage's pale eyes lost none of their intensity or appeal.

His father's jaw worked. "But yes. I shall take more caution."

Gage nodded once, clasping his hands behind his back. "And this feud?"

He sighed. "Yes, of course, I was aware of it. Though, obviously, not the events that have taken place over the last fifty years."

"Did Tamsyn explain the full extent of what happened to her brother?" I asked.

"That they left him stranded at the base of a cliff with the tide coming in?" My father-in-law's voice was tight with censure. "Yes."

"Then you understand why she might crave revenge, one way or another?"

His eyes flashed. "That doesn't mean she took it."

"No. However, it *does* mean her words should bear greater scrutiny. After all, she isn't unbiased."

"Perhaps." Lord Gage crossed the room to examine his appearance in the old mirror hanging on the wall to the left of the door. He adjusted the diamond stickpin nestled in the folds of his cravat. The hard glint in his eyes matched the gem's brilliance. "But I still find myself more inclined to trust Tamsyn than any of the members of my family. For good reason."

Gage and I exchanged a speaking glance, both uncertain whether his father was capable of viewing anything with impartiality when it came to the Roscarrocks and their kin.

"Have you spoken with Great-Aunt Amelia?" Gage queried.

His father's movements faltered as he straightened the lapels of his black evening coat, telling me that in his obsession with locating Branok alive he'd forgotten. "No. But I will."

My silk skirts rustled as I moved closer to him, knowing that he wouldn't like what I had to say next. "Dolly also mentioned that a boy was killed several decades ago because of a disagreement between the families." My father-in-law's eyes riveted on me in the reflection of the mirror. "Could she have meant Jago?"

He turned away abruptly, but not before I saw the fierce frown that creased his handsome features.

"*Was* there some sort of quarrel that precipitated the events that led to you being arrested and Jago being shot?" I turned to Gage for support as his father kept his back to us. "What exactly happened that night and the days leading up to it? You've never gone into detail."

It was the same question I'd asked on the road yesterday. The same question he'd brushed aside as inconsequential. But I was beginning to believe those details might be more important than any of us realized.

When still Lord Gage didn't speak, Gage prodded gently. "Father?"

"Not . . ." He rounded on us, raising his voice and a gesticulating hand, but turned only so that we could see his profile. His hand fell to his side, slapping his leg as he struggled for composure. "Not now," he stated in a more even voice once he had himself in hand.

We stared at him for a few moments before Gage replied, "Of course."

"They will be waiting for us," Lord Gage declared after inhaling a calming breath. He turned to offer me his arm.

I accepted it, willing to make peace, acknowledging he was right. Now was not the best time to broach such a topic. Particularly given his emotional reaction. But his continued resolve not to discuss it only made me more intent to find out why.

CHAPTER 19

The Grenvilles lived but a few miles to the southwest, where their farmland adjoined the Roscarrocks'. It had been thus for centuries, my father-in-law explained as we rode past fields now lying dormant after the recent harvest. The crops grown had changed, as had the acreage devoted to livestock, but not the boundaries or the surnames of the owners. But this didn't mean that the two families were equals. The Roscarrocks' estate had always been larger, and its portion of coast longer. And they had never let the Grenvilles forget it.

Yet there was one thing in which it was clear the Grenvilles had surpassed the Roscarrocks, and that was offspring bearing the Grenville name. At almost every cottage we passed once we'd entered Grenville land, someone lifted a hand in greeting as Lord Gage explained either who they were or whom they were likely the descendants of. In nearly every instance, the surname was Grenville. Perhaps if Branok's brother hadn't elected to immigrate, the discrepancy would not have been so great, but as it was, the difference could not be denied. Especially now that Mery was the only true Roscarrock left. In a country which valued the continuation of the male line almost above all else, this was no small distinction.

We carried on past the drive which led to the main house where Tamsyn lived with her brother Gil, instead veering down a narrower track which led to a cozy little cottage overlooking the cliffs and the sea beyond. As we drew nearer, Lord Gage grew silent, which only accentuated how much he'd been chattering before. If anything, my father-in-law's conversation was known for its sparsity and bluntness, not its loquaciousness. This, more than his stiff posture or stilted demeanor, revealed exactly how nervous he was about facing his friend Jago's mother after so many decades of avoiding her.

Despite November's chill, a small garden bursting with pink, yellow, and white blooms surrounded the cottage. Some of them were not native to England's shores, and their unusual blossoms and leaves livened up what would otherwise have been another drab stone house. Someone who lived here evidently loved horticulture.

We began to dismount from our steeds as the door opened and a woman about Gage's age with sandy brown hair appeared in the doorway. She smiled in welcome, her hands clasped before her, as we secured our horses' reins to the fencepost nearby lest they decide the exotic blooms looked like tasty treats.

"Ye must be Lord Gage," she murmured softly to my father-in-law before ushering us inside. "And Mr. and Mrs. Gage. Welcome to our home. I'm Pasca's granddaughter."

"Lily, is that our guests I hear ye speakin' to," a voice called from the next room. "Well, quit dawdlin' and bring them through."

"Yes, Gran!" Lily called back. Her eyes twinkled. "As ye can hear, she's impatient to see ye."

Given the ease and good humor Lily displayed, I decided that must mean Tamsyn had spoken true. That Pasca didn't blame my father-in-law for the death of her son. But a glance at Lord Gage showed that he was still apprehensive about this meeting. It wasn't easy to face the most painful memories of your past, and being forced to confront those people who had been part of it, even along the periphery, had a curious way of making you feel it all the more deeply. I knew this from experience.

Lily led us into a parlor at the back of the cottage. It wasn't grand by any means, not compared to the drawing room at Roscarrock House and certainly not the one at Bevington Park—Lord Gage's Warwickshire estate—but the view from its windows surpassed both. They perfectly framed an idyllic slice of coast with its green rolling hills, golden sand, deep cerulean water, and brilliant blue sky.

So arresting was the vantage that for a moment the woman seated before it was all but lost to my notice. But then she wasn't paying me the least bit of mind. Not when she had the fifty-nine-year-old visage of her long-lost son's friend and a younger version of those same features to gaze at.

Given my father-in-law's age and the fact Jago had been of comparable maturity, Pasca must have been nearing four score years of life. The lines and grooves of her face showed this, as did the gray hair neatly restrained at the back of her head. She sat very composed on a horsehair settee with her hands resting in her lap. Their joints were swollen, suggesting arthritis, but if she was in pain, she didn't show it.

However, her most striking feature was her eyes. Not only were they clear, exhibiting none of the cloudiness older people sometimes suffered from, but also a brilliant shade of almost turquoise, such as I'd never seen before. Gage's eyes were pale blue, but their color was that of a winter sky the morning after a snowstorm, and almost crystalline in quality. Pasca's eyes were at once more vivid in hue and more mellow in aspect. Soothing rather than piercing. My fingers itched to capture them and her entire face on canvas, wondering what mixture of pigments would accurately replicate the color.

Turning from Pasca, I realized that Lord Gage had come to a stop in the middle of the room, almost as if his legs would carry him no farther. His gaze remained fixed on Pasca, his expression lost and uncertain, offering us a glimpse of the boy he'd once been. The one who had been hurt, ashamed, frightened, and grieving the loss of his dearest friend.

I began to go to him, unable to bear him standing there alone, staring down his bleak past. But then Pasca patted the seat next to hers, and like a child compelled, Lord Gage strode woodenly forward to do as he was told. Gage and I sat in the two cane-back chairs across from them as they studied each other, each of them swimming in their memories. We might not have even been there for all the notice that they paid us.

Eventually, Lord Gage gathered his tattered composure. "Good afternoon, Mrs. Grenville."

Pasca's mouth curled into a sad smile, her eyes glittering with tears. "Ah, Stephen." She rested her hand on his. "I'm glad you've finally come."

He seemed slightly abashed by this remark, though I didn't think she had meant it in scolding. "I thought it would be easier for you not to see me."

She shook her head. "'Twasn't your fault. I knew that. Just as I knew 'ow much it hurt ye to lose Jago." She exhaled in mild reproof. "And then they sent ye away, so ye had no one to grieve with. No one who truly knew him anyway." She patted his hand. "I'm sorry for that."

Lord Gage's throat worked as he swallowed. "It was only right that I should go when I had lived and Jago had not," he murmured in a voice of such desolation that it plucked the heart from my chest.

"Is that what ye think?" Pasca asked. "*Nay*, Stephen. 'Tisn't true." Her face crumpled. "And had I known that's what ye were thinkin' for even a second in all these years, I woulda walked all the way to Plymouth or London or wherever ye were myself to tell ye. Woulda forced my way onto one of your navy ships, too." She nodded in emphasis.

A hint of humor lurked in Lord Gage's voice though his face betrayed nothing. "I would like to have seen that."

"Woulda made it, too." She narrowed her eyes playfully. "Or don't ye know where Jago got his impishness?"

Mirth pulled briefly at his lips, and Pasca smiled, revealing gaps where some of her teeth should have been, but it slowly faded. "Ye were *both* failed by men who should've known better. Sendin' boys out to do their dirty work." She scoffed derisively. "And then standin' back to watch as ye were forced to pay for their crimes." Lowering her gaze to her lap, she smoothed her hands over the faded chintz of her skirt, collecting herself before she spoke again. "Though, to be fair, I know yer granfer did what he could for ye."

The manner in which Lord Gage's face constricted made it clear that he didn't believe this, but Pasca didn't see it.

"And he never shied away from the facts of what 'appened to Jago. He would look in on me almost as much as my own kin and speak to me of my son. And you." She looked up at him then. "He would tell me where ye were and what ye were doin'. He was always quite proud of ye."

To Pasca, Lord Gage must have appeared untroubled by these revelations for she said nothing further, but I could see the consternation flickering in his eyes.

She patted his hand again. "Now, introduce me to your family."

. Lily seemed to take this as her cue to bring in the tea tray and begin pouring for everyone.

"I presume this is your son," Pasca said, turning to Gage. She cackled. "Gil was right. Ethan Kellynack never woulda had a chance with Tamsyn had ye been around. But then your fine boy wouldn't be here, would he?" Pasca continued with a sorrowful shake of her head. "Tamsyn was never able to have children, ye see. The poor girl." Her face softened as she looked at Gage. "I suspect your wife must've been a good woman. And beautiful."

"Yes," Lord Gage confirmed, his eyes locking with his son's. "A very good woman."

I felt a lump form in my throat at the mutual regard the two men shared and the underlying truth such a simple statement made. Their contentious past only made it more poignant.

"And this, then, is your daughter-in-law," Pasca guessed, her kindly gaze revealing nothing of her knowledge or lack thereof of my reputation. "But I also hear ye have a granddaughter." The quirk of her mouth suggested she already knew how smitten Lord Gage was with Emma. Or perhaps it was the affection all grandparents shared for their grandchildren.

Either way, they spent much of the remainder of our time with Pasca discussing their offspring, both grandchildren and great-grandchildren. Lord Gage even mentioned his other son Henry, though for good reason he didn't go into great detail about his antecedents. When they broached the subject of Jago again, it was less fraught, and they were able to share memories and even a few laughs over various things he'd done or said. Each retelling revealed a different side of my father-in-law that neither I nor Gage had ever seen. It was enlightening, reassuring, and also somehow heartbreaking to know that he had once been just another energetic, mischievous boy. One eager to please and belong, anxious to find his place. It broke my heart anew to realize how his life here had ended.

While his time with Pasca was healing, I could tell that it had also dredged some terrible things to the surface, namely his consciousness of all he'd lost. It was etched in the deepening lines of his face as we rode back to Roscarrock. As such, I wasn't surprised when he excused himself upon our arrival and set off in the direction of the cliffs. Clearly, he had much to reconcile with.

At first, this didn't concern me greatly, my thoughts being consumed with Emma. But once her belly was filled and I was seated on the floor, playing with her, a sudden wave of anxiety washed over me. I brushed it aside, focusing on my daughter and her giggles as I made her ragdoll dance. However, the worry returned and intensified when Lord Gage did not appear for dinner.

We waited a quarter of an hour for him to appear, but when it was discovered that he wasn't even in the house, Amelia ordered that the dishes be brought to the table. By this point, my appetite had all but deserted me, and I more or less picked at my food as the meal lingered and the shadows deepened toward twilight. Gage's inclination to eat wasn't much stronger, nor his interest in the conversation other than whether anyone had seen his father after he strode away from the stables upon our return from Auntie Pasca's cottage.

When the last course of nuts and cheeses was set before us, Gage pushed back from the table. "I'm going to search for him."

"I'll help," Tristram offered immediately.

"Aye," Bevil grunted in agreement, swiping his napkin over his mouth before rising.

"You'll wait here?" He leaned down to ask me.

I nodded, grasping his hand as he turned to leave. "Be careful."

He squeezed my fingers in reassurance before following Bevil and Tristram from the room. In short order, we heard one of the outer doors open and shut as they set off into the night.

I turned back to the table to find all three women watching me.

Dolly offered me an encouraging smile. "They'll find 'im."

"I'm sure they will," Joan contributed. "Wasn't his leg injured some months back? Perhaps it merely gave out from all his exertions."

"Yes, I suspect you're right," I said.

But Amelia seemed less convinced. Her gaze shifted toward the windows where the drapes had yet to be drawn against the encroaching night. Wisps of gray hair fluttered along her hairline in a stray draft. I was about to ask her what she was thinking when someone in the doorway spoke.

"M'lady."

Such was my distraction that it took me a moment to realize the maid was speaking to me. "Yes?"

The girl flushed under my regard. "Mrs. Mackay is askin' for ye?"

"Thank you," I said, pushing stiffly to my feet. "Please excuse me," I told the Killigrew women and hastened up to Emma's nursery.

However, alarmingly, Mrs. Mackay was waiting for me outside the door without my daughter. She held up her hands as if to halt my flow of words before they began. "Emma is restin' peacefully," she assured me. "I didna mean to alarm ye." She nodded toward the door to my bedchamber, which opened. "'Tis Miss McEvoy who asked me to send for ye."

I pressed a hand to my rib cage, exhaling in relief as the bedchamber door opened to reveal Bree waiting for me. "What is it?" I asked her.

She ushered me inside and Mrs. Mackay nodded stalwartly before returning to her charge. Bree closed the door softly. Her brown eyes were alive with concern. "Is it true that Lord Gage hasna returned?"

"Mr. Gage and the Killigrew men have just set off to look for him." I searched her features. "Why?"

"Did they go in the direction o' the cliffs?"

"I suspect." When she didn't speak immediately, but instead bit her lower lip as if uncertain whether to say more, I scowled and demanded. "Bree, what is it? Tell me."

"I dinna think that's the way he went," she admitted.

"What do you mean?" I was growing impatient with having to draw the truth from her.

She seemed to recognize this and squared her shoulders. "Because I saw him headin' off down a trail leadin' west. No' the one that leads to Port Quin, but another that leads in a more southwesterly direction."

Which was more or less the direction in which the Grenvilles' property lay. But perhaps Lord Gage wasn't going back to see Pasca but rather Tamsyn, and he hadn't wanted any witnesses.

I frowned. No, that didn't seem right. My father-in-law had never been the sort to confide in another person. He was more likely to brood and hide, preferring to lick his wounds in privacy. If I had learned anything about him over the past few months, it was that he would wish to go someplace he could be alone.

Though that didn't mean that the place couldn't also hold significance.

Having had an inspired thought, I whirled toward the wardrobe. "I need a walking dress and my stoutest boots."

"What do you intend to do?" she asked, brushing past me to gather these items.

"I think I know where he went."

Her eyes were wide as she turned to look at me, draping my smoke blue merino gown over the bed. "You're no' thinkin' of goin' alone?"

"If I must." I slipped my feet out of my slippers and turned to allow Bree to undo my buttons. "I hoped Anderley might go with me. Unless he accompanied Mr. Gage."

"He's no' here."

The terseness in Bree's voice alerted me to the fact I wasn't going to like her answer.

"What do you mean?"

"When I spied Lord Gage . . ." She broke off, hesitating for a moment before sighing resignedly. "'Twas because I was followin' Anderley."

"Where was he going?" I asked in genuine shock.

"I dinna ken. But he wasna alone. One o' the Roscarrock farmhands was wi' him."

I silently digested this information, not liking the picture that was forming. I'd grown fond of Anderley. I trusted him. Just as I knew that my husband and Bree did. But his recent behavior called that trustworthiness into question. And it was something I was no longer willing to ignore, no matter what Gage said, for it had hurt Bree and left us all in a difficult position.

Stifling my own anger and disappointment at Gage's valet, I urged Bree to work faster.

"I should come wi' ye," she stated as she finished fastening my walking dress.

"No. I need you to stay here with Emma and Mrs. Mackay. Should Lord Gage return before I do, heaven forbid, and require medical attention, I'm not sure I trust anyone but you to give it to him." Sliding my arms into my forest green pelisse, I opened a drawer in the clothespress to extract my reticule. "Don't worry." I pulled my Hewson percussion pistol from its depths. "I won't be unprotected." Checking to be sure the gun was loaded, I slid it into my pocket.

Bree was too sensible to argue when she knew there was no

hope of winning the argument, but that didn't stop her from scowling in disapproval.

"If Gage should return before I do, tell him what you told me and that I went to speak to Amelia about my intuition," I directed before hurrying from the room.

I was relieved to discover she'd not yet retired but sat knitting alongside Joan before the fire in the drawing room. Both women lowered their piecework as I entered the room. My attire must have made my intentions clear.

"Where was Jago killed and his lordship arrested?" I demanded without preamble. I trusted they knew what I meant. It had been one of the topics uppermost in our minds since our arrival, yet no one had dared to address it directly. When neither woman answered, I moved closer. "It was somewhere to the west, wasn't it?"

"Aye," Amelia replied, jolted from her stunned reverie. "Near Epphaven Cove. If ye continue west down the path from the garden, 'twill lead ye straight to it."

"Thank you," I said, already backing from the room.

CHAPTER 20

The moon was near full, casting such a bright, hallowed light over the garden that I almost didn't need the lantern I'd collected from a servant. An owl hooted in the boughs of one of the trees through which a gentle breeze blew, rustling the leaves still clinging to the branches. I picked my way through the grasses and out from the gap in the terraced garden wall, finding myself crossing a patchwork of open fields. The path skirted their divisions, so that to the left lay the dark, churned earth of a potato field and to the right the remnants of harvested barley stocks glimmering gold in the moonlight.

If not for the chill of the sea-scented air stinging my cheeks, and the uneasiness riding on my shoulders, I might have enjoyed myself, for it was a beautiful night. But I was all too conscious of my exposed position—so much so that I shuttered the lamp to douse some of its conspicuous brilliance—and fearful of what might have befallen Lord Gage. A dozen or more fantastical suppositions, each one more alarming, flitted through my brain.

Suppositions I persisted to squash, lest they spur me into a gen-uine panic, yet they continued to spring from my ponderings.

I had been walking for what I estimated to be about half an hour, maintaining my course west even as I passed numerous crossroads and trails, when I finally caught sight of the sea rip-pling and glittering in the light of the moon. It was naught but waves of light and shadow, a dance of silvery white and midnight blue, but mesmerizing all the same. And there, perched on a rock overlooking the sandy cove below, sat my father-in-law.

I stumbled to a stop upon my first glimpse of him, too grate-ful to do more than exhale in profound relief. After working so hard to repair the damage to their relationship and progressing so far over the past few months, the last thing I wanted to tell my husband was that his father was dead. Particularly knowing we had been the ones to convince him to come here. Now, I wouldn't have to. Though that didn't mean Lord Gage didn't have some explaining to do for causing us so much worry.

He turned his head as he heard me approach, his posture stiffening perhaps in dread. But once he realized it was only me, he relaxed. "Kiera," he murmured softly. "I hoped it was you."

This scattered all the thoughts in my head, for it was the last thing I'd expected him to say. This man who had been so cold and disdainful, if not outright cruel, when we first met. He'd openly opposed his son's marriage to me, requiring me to black-mail him just to attend. He'd lied and manipulated, and nearly destroyed all hope of a relationship with both his sons purely out of sheer stubbornness.

But he was not the same man he'd been three months ago. I wasn't even sure he was the same man he'd been last week. And Auntie Pasca's words had shaken him, forcing him to alter him-self again. Or at least alter his thinking about his past.

"I suppose you're going to scold me," he said, adopting a meek tone rather than the biting one I might have expected.

"You've caused us a great deal of distress," I told him. "Your son and cousins are, even now, out searching for you on the cliffs near Roscarrock House."

"But only you realized where I'd gone." There was a glint of something in his eyes, though I couldn't see it clearly in the darkness. A hint of what I suspected was approval. "You, who always see too much." It was the first time he'd said it without a whiff of scorn. "How did you know where this place was?"

"Amelia. But why didn't you tell us where you were going? Or at least return at a decent hour?"

Aggravation had crept into my voice, and his lips curled into that charming smile I'd seen him wield so often on others, but never me. "Would you believe I lost track of the time?"

I arched a single eyebrow to tell him exactly what I thought of that, even as I reluctantly felt his charm working on me.

His chuckle transformed into a forlorn sigh as he turned back toward the moonlit sea. "I thought not. Though it is at least *partially* true. I didn't mean to stay here so long, but . . ."

"You had a lot to think on," I finished for him when he couldn't seem to find the words.

He seemed relieved not to have to explain. "Yes."

He slid over so that I could join him on the rock. I had to admit it was a lovely vantage, if a trifle cold on this gusty November evening. I wondered how he wasn't shivering in his greatcoat after so many hours' stillness.

For a time, we sat in silence, listening to the snap of the wind and the gentle wash of the tide rolling in and out over the sand below. But eventually the subject had to be broached, and I realized I would have to be the one to do it.

"Tell me what troubled you so much about Pasca's words."

He didn't speak, but I noticed his hands opening and closing in mute frustration where they rested on his knees. Perhaps my question had been too general, the answer too difficult to voice.

"Did you really think she'd blame you for Jago's death?" I asked gently.

He swallowed. "Why not? I did."

Those two bleak words squeezed my heart like a fist. "Do you understand now how wrong that was? You were merely following orders."

"Yes, but . . ." He frowned. "I have always felt there was more."

"What do you mean?"

"That there is something else to it. Something I should remember." His voice grew frustrated. "But I can't." He pounded his leg. "I can't remember."

"Something that explains why you blame yourself?"

"Yes!"

I hesitated. "Something that explains your great anger with the Roscarrocks?"

He turned slowly to look at me. "Yes."

"And Pasca's words didn't help you remember?"

"No. But . . ." His gaze lowered to the pebble-strewn ground through which tufts of sea thrift sprouted. "I don't think it's to do with my grandfather." His face constricted in pain. "Or I don't want to believe it is." He removed his hat, scraping his hand back through his hair before replacing it.

"You seemed surprised he knew so much about where you were and what you were doing," I prodded. "At least enough to report to Pasca."

"I was. But Grandfather had friends in the Royal Navy. He must have obtained his information from them."

"Checking to see his grandson was well cared for."

He nodded absently before muttering, "It was more than my father ever did. Though he also never got me arrested and banished to the sea."

I could sense he was conflicted and waited for him to continue.

"Before Jago was shot, I thought my grandfather was the greatest man alive. He had time for me when, my being a second son, my father didn't. But grandfather didn't seem to care about any of that. He taught me how to swim and fish and shoot and ride. He showed me how to tie knots and bowl and cheat at cards." A smile flickered across his features only to be snuffed out. "And how to swindle and smuggle and countermand the authorities."

He hung his head low. "When I was arrested and forced to stand before that magistrate, I realized how wrong I'd been. How much better off I would have been left to my father's instruction and dubious affection." He straightened. "I decided then and there that, if I ever had a son, it would be better for me to be cold and exacting like my father than risk hurting him as my grandfather had harmed me." He shook his head dejectedly. "But I hurt Sebastian anyway."

So startling was this confession that I couldn't form a response. Neither Gage nor I had ever understood why his father treated him like he did, but with this revelation, much was made clear. I only wished Gage had been here to hear it.

"I can tell I've shocked you," he said after several moments of silence.

I ignored this question in order to ask a more important one. "Why have you never told Sebastian this?"

"Because I didn't quite understand it myself. Not until recently. Maybe not even until today."

"You need to tell him."

He turned to look at me, perhaps surprised by my insistence, and I stared back at him, refusing to break eye contact until he agreed.

"You should also know," I added more calmly, "there is a middle ground."

"Yes. Or rather, I do now. After seeing Sebastian with his own child. He has found the better way."

He sounded so forlorn that I reached over to touch his arm. "It's not too late to change. In fact, you've already done so."

His expression tightened as if repressing strong emotion. "That's true. But here . . . everything is harder. I fear . . . I am not my best self."

"Something neither of us fault you for," I assured him. "We know this has been difficult." I swallowed my pride before admitting something else. "And perhaps altogether unnecessary."

He eyed me with interest. "You don't believe Branok was murdered?"

"We've found no real evidence of it. Just a whole lot of muddied water," I groused.

He turned to gaze out over the sea, his thoughts concealed from me. I'd expected him to jump at the chance to mock me for my and Gage's insistence on investigating, but he didn't. Neither did he rush to agree or suggest we leave. Instead, he seemed to give the matter careful consideration. Which gave his next pronouncement all the greater weight.

"You're right. We've discovered nothing by way of proof. Though I've been hesitant to say so because I'm perfectly aware of my prejudice and my desire to depart this place. However, if you are making the proclamation." His gray eyes glittered in the light of the lantern sitting between us. "Perhaps I might now make the suggestion that we quit this godforsaken county."

I couldn't help but smile at the return of his sardonic sneer. "I wouldn't call it godforsaken. It's actually quite beautiful in its own wild and wistful way." I lifted my eyes to the stars now glittering overhead, their twinkling light showering like raindrops over the sea. It was a sight I was quite sure I would never forget. "But yes, it's time to go."

Lord Gage bowed his head and exhaled as if a great weight had suddenly been lifted from him, and I felt all the guiltier for not only bringing him here, but not noticing it before.

"Let's go tell the others."

He pushed slowly to his feet before offering me his hand to pull me to mine. I scrutinized his gait as we carefully traversed the rockier ground, looking for any indication he'd aggravated his wound from all his traipsing up and down the coastline, but he seemed to move with relative ease. Then we set off arm in arm back toward Roscarrock House for what I believed would be the last time.

However, as we drew nearer, we steadily became aware of some great commotion. At first, I thought it was to do with my absence, even jesting, "Oh dear. I'm afraid Sebastian must be quite cross with me for setting off alone."

"You let me handle Sebastian," Lord Gage said.

But by the time we reached the garden, it became evident that whatever had happened was much more serious. Candles seemed to light every window and we could hear raised voices and doors opening and shutting as people moved about in the grassy area where several of the tables from the party were still set up. Our approach went unnoticed until we were close enough to note that something rather large rested on one of the tables. Something large and wrapped in a sheet. It was on the tip of my tongue to call out, demanding to know what all the fuss was, when someone spotted us, pointing in our direction.

Bevil charged toward us like a raging bull. "You bleddy bastard!" he hollered, adding a few more curses, some of which I understood and some that I didn't.

I considered stepping in front of my father-in-law to block the man, for his intent was clear, but I doubted my interference would deter him. In fact, I thought it quite likely he'd pick me up and fling me aside.

He planted his cousin a facer before Lord Gage had gathered himself enough to drop the lantern and lift his hands to block another punch. "Ye killed him, didn't ye?" Bevil demanded. "'Twas what ye always wanted to do, and ye got your chance."

"Killed who?" Lord Gage retorted. "What are you hollering about?"

Bevil swung out with another fist, his wiry stature making him quick. But despite not being back to his full health, Lord Gage was stronger and returned this blow with a stinging one of his own to the other man's right cheek.

"Stop!" I shouted. "Stop this! What on earth is going on?" I inquired as my husband and Tristram raced forward to help restrain their fathers.

"I'll kill ye," Bevil vowed, lunging forward even as his son held fast to his shoulders.

Gage had less of a struggle to control his father, who, after all, hadn't started the fight. "Where were you?"

"At Epphaven Cove," Lord Gage replied.

"About thirty minutes' walk to the west-southwest," I informed him.

Questions flashed in his eyes, but they would have to wait.

"What happened?" My gaze flicked over his shoulder toward the object wrapped in a sheet. I thought I detected something staining one portion of the fabric. "Did someone truly die?"

A quick glance around told me that everyone was present save two people—Mery and Anderley. That last possibility made my heart stutter with fright.

Gage's eyes darted first to his father and then Bevil, before landing on me. "Branok Roscarrock."

CHAPTER 21

For one long moment, I thought I'd heard Gage incorrectly. "I don't understand." I looked about me, seeking an explanation from those gathered around us. "We already know Branok's dead."

Gage's eyes were as hard as granite as he glared at Branok's relatives, specifically Bevil and Tristram. "No, we were only led to believe he was dead. Now he truly is."

My eyes flared wide, struggling to grasp all of the ramifications of this revelation.

"Then Tamsyn was correct," Lord Gage snapped. "She *did* see him striding about near the cliffs."

"Aye, and *you* finally tracked him down and killed him," Bevil snarled, pulling against Tristram's grip.

I reared in startlement, but Lord Gage faced this accusation with far more composure, narrowing his eyes to slits. "I didn't. Though it's quite convenient for you to accuse me so that you can avoid answering any of the difficult questions we shall be asking of *you*. Such as, why did you *lie* about his death and lure us here in the first place?"

"'Twas all Branok's doing," Tristram replied only to have Bevil hush him. "Why? He's no longer alive to force us to do as we're told. So why should we keep quiet to save his skin."

"Shut yer gob," Bevil reiterated. "Or I'll shut it for ye."

Tristram glared daggers at his father but clamped his lips tight, turning away.

"I suppose that's the body," I asked now that I had myself more in hand.

"Yes," Gage answered me.

I began to cross the garden toward it. "Where is Mery?"

"Fetching a cart," he replied, confirming my suspicions.

"To transport him to Dr. Wolcott?"

"Yes."

"I'll go with him." My resolve hardened along with my countenance. "Dr. Wolcott already lied to us once. I'm not about to leave him alone with the body before I've had a chance to examine it."

Gage seemed relieved to hear it, but also ventured a more practical question. "What about Emma?"

"With any luck she'll sleep until morning, but Mrs. Mackay will know to use goat's milk if it becomes necessary."

Glancing over my shoulder, I discovered the others had followed us, crowding close to listen. I did my best to ignore them, adopting an air of brisk proficiency as I scrutinized what I could about the body through the sheet. I had been correct. There was a bloodstain corresponding to the upper-right portion of his chest, though not a large one. "Shot or stabbed?"

"Stabbed."

I nodded, beginning to pace around the body. "The weapon?"

"Not found."

I leaned closer to examine another stain near the top of the head, but straightened again at the harsh tone of Lord Gage's voice.

"I want to see him." His face was set in rigid lines, his gaze resolute. "To be sure."

He was right. Though I presumed Bevil and Tristram had already made the identification, that very act of naming this body had proved them unequivocally untrustworthy. We needed to be certain this time that Branok was truly dead, and neither Gage nor I could identify him. Only Lord Gage.

I opened my mouth to ask if he was sure he would still recognize him after nearly fifty years, but then let my lips fall shut. In spite of his animosity toward Branok, Lord Gage was bound to find viewing his uncle's lifeless body difficult enough without my belaboring the issue.

Slowly, I gripped the clean edge of the sheet and peeled it back from the face. There was no mistaking from Lord Gage's reaction that this time there were no tricks at play. That the man lying on the table before us with naught but a few wisps of gray hair clinging to his scalp was none other than Branok Roscarrock. Not when genuine pain flashed across my father-in-law's features followed by roiling anger. He nodded jerkily and turned away.

Hearing a hiccupped sob from one of the women present, I swiftly covered the body again, but not before noting that the stain I'd seen at the top of the sheet didn't seem to correspond to any injury on the head. It must have come from his surroundings.

"Where was he found?" I asked Gage.

"Out near Kellan Head, above Port Quin."

Approximately a mile then from Epphaven Cove. This was a far greater distance than it at first seemed, considering the twists and turns and changes in elevation along the coastal path, but still not far enough from where I'd located Lord Gage for my liking. Not that I believed my father-in-law had anything to do with his uncle's death. Not having just seen what state he'd been in. Unless his distress had also been the result of his having just murdered a man. Regardless, given his absence and proximity to where the body was found, he must be considered a suspect. His relatives certainly did so.

My anger flared hot, thinking of their deception. This all might have been avoided if they'd been truthful.

I tamped down my frustration, ordering my thoughts. "First things first," I informed Gage and anyone listening, for we could hardly keep from being heard. "Dr. Wolcott and I will examine the body. We should be able to determine the approximate time of death as well as more specifics about the weapon and the manner of attack." Though I suspected the culprit had already discarded the knife, likely hurling it into the sea.

"You . . . you're going to examine the body?" Dolly interrupted us to ask. Her eyes were wide with shock and possibly revulsion.

"It's what I do," I replied impassively, though I felt myself shrink a little bit inside. I'd faced such reactions many times, but it was never easy. Especially when they were from someone I considered a friend.

"I'll find out who last saw Branok alive," Gage said, his gaze shifting briefly over his shoulder to pin Bevil and Tristram. "And everyone's whereabouts since then."

I turned toward the rattle of approaching wheels. "And I'll speak with Mery."

"But you can't go with him alone," Gage protested, recognizing as I did that Mery still had the most to gain from his grandfather's death.

"I *would* suggest that Anderley accompany me, but apparently he's missing again," I muttered dryly.

Gage scowled in displeasure, but it never reached his eyes.

Which told me my husband was not being entirely forth-coming about his valet. Had there been time, I would have pressed him, but given our audience and Branok's corpse, I held my peace.

"Then you should take Miss McEvoy," he insisted.

Bree stepped forward from the crowd of servants and I instructed her to fetch her cloak.

Mery's appearance was as disheveled as ever, but his expression inscrutable as he swung the cart around, halting next to the table where Branok's body lay. Gage pulled me aside, leaning close to speak into my ear. "I trust you took protection with you when you went in search of my father." There was a hint of reproof in his voice, and the look I gave him in return let him know I didn't appreciate it.

"Of course," I retorted in clipped tones, even then fingering the pistol still secured in my pocket.

"Don't hesitate to use it."

What precisely he expected, I didn't know, but I doubted Mery or Dr. Wolcott would attempt anything. Not when everyone knew where we were and what we were doing. Even so, I would be keeping a close eye on them both.

In short order, the body was loaded toward the back of the cart while Bree clambered into the front, sitting as far away from the corpse as possible. Lord Gage stood off to the side, his arms crossed and his eyes brooding, as I was helped up onto the perch beside Mery. I trusted Gage would ask for his assistance in questioning the others. That was, if Lord Gage didn't naturally insinuate himself as I expected.

We set off, the cart jouncing over the uneven ground until we reached the relatively smoother lane. We hadn't even passed through the pillars marking the turn from the manor's drive onto the road proper before Mery cast a sidelong glance over his shoulder. "Gage didn't trust ye alone with me, I see."

The drawl of his voice was biting, but I refused to be riled. "Well, you did lie." I turned to scour his features. "Even as recent as yesterday."

He glowered at me, and for a moment I thought he meant not to answer. "Aye, well, I was hardly given a choice." So he intended to blame Branok, then. Just like his cousin.

I turned away. "There's always a choice." Even out of the corner of my eye I could tell he didn't like hearing this. "Sometimes the circumstances are just more difficult than others."

"Aye, well, if I didn't want to be cut off without a farthing and thrown off the estate, I 'ad to do as Granfer wished."

I didn't emphasize that these were hardly the direst of circumstances, especially for a strong, young man who might have benefited from being forced to become industrious rather than lying around like a wastrel. Not when there was another point to be made.

"But now that Branok's dead, that's no longer the case. Now *you* can do whatever you wish."

I heard Bree shift behind me, perhaps worried this comment had been too confrontational, but I was simply stating the truth. This was something Mery couldn't refute, and judging by the hard line of his jaw, he knew it.

"He was in your cottage yesterday, wasn't he?" I demanded, realizing now why Mery had hustled me away.

A muscle jumped in his cheek, telling me just how hard he was clenching his teeth, struggling to restrain himself. "I suppose there's no point in denyin' it."

I waited as he clicked his teeth and flicked the reins, directing the horses to turn down the road that would lead to Trelights. My thoughts drifted back over the remainder of our conversation and Bevil's interruption. "Bevil worried you would reveal something to me. That's why you warned me about his interrogation."

Mery didn't bother to confirm or refute this because it was obvious.

I ducked my head as something swooped lower over us—perhaps a bat—before flying on. "And I suspect your attempting to persuade me that Branok's alleged fall from that cliff was an accident was not part of his plan."

Mery's head snapped around to look at me.

"Not after he'd already gone to so much trouble to draw us here by faking his murder."

"Ye should've gone," he snarled.

"We were going to. Tomorrow."

He looked like he didn't quite believe me.

"After all, there was no proof of foul play. Because there *was no murder*," I emphasized. My voice turned grim. "Until now."

We crested a small rise, and the trees arching overhead and the hedges bordering the road parted enough for us to see the sky and all the stars still twinkling overhead. Its beauty seemed a cruel juxtaposition to the gruesomeness of the cargo we carried behind us. Fortunately, the cold air would slow its decomposition.

The first cottage along the road leading into the village came into view, alerting me we would soon arrive at Dr. Wolcott's, so I bent my mind toward the questions that were most pressing.

"When did you last see your grandfather?"

Mery wore no hat, and I could see in the light of the carriage lantern that the tips of his ears were cold as he scraped his hand through his unruly blue-black locks. "Shortly after ye left for the Grenvilles. He knew while ye were away it would be safer for 'im to venture out."

"Did you follow him?"

He shot me an angry look. "Nay. I took myself off to the Golden Lion in Port Isaac. Ran into your husband searchin' for his father on my way 'ome." His tone was heavy with insinuation, which I ignored. I wondered how reliable the locals would be in either confirming or denying his alibi. Mery might now be one of the largest local landowners, but if rumor was right, he wasn't very popular with the neighboring populace.

"Who knew that Branok was still alive? Obviously you, Bevil, and Tristram, as well as Dr. Wolcott. But who else?"

His mouth flattened as he slowed the horses to turn a sharp corner. The homes and shops lining the road sat dark and quiet, as if slumbering like their owners.

"Did Amelia?"

"Aye. But as for the rest, the other wives and such." He shrugged. "I don't know."

"What about Anne?"

He turned to me sharply even as he was steering the horses into another turn. "You'll have to ask her and Tom that, but I don't think so."

Another few feet, and he veered into the doctor's drive, careful not to overset our cargo.

"Why are we here, Meryasek?" I asked as the horse's harnesses jingled as we came to a stop. "In Cornwall," I specified, though I could tell by the look in his eyes that he already knew what I meant. "Why were we lured here?"

For a moment, he sat staring straight ahead and I thought he might actually be considering answering me. But then a light flared in one of the physician's windows, and Mery reached down to set the brake before clambering out of the carriage to approach the rear door to the cottage. I peered back at Bree, curious what she had made of our exchange.

"He kens," she whispered.

"Of course he does. Yet even in death, he allows his grandfather to compel his silence."

"Unless he has a reason to remain silent, too."

I watched Mery as he spoke to the servant who had answered

Dr. Wolcott's door, recognizing I would do well not to underestimate him. Mery might be a profligate and a rogue, but he clearly possessed intelligence, as well as a healthy sense of self-preservation. He would know when speaking up would be in his best interest and when it wouldn't. As such, I had to question the motives behind his reticence.

"Keep an eye on Mery and Mrs. Wolcott," I instructed Bree. "The cousins are close. But my question is, how close?"

Bree's gaze met mine, sparkling with disapproval.

"It may be entirely innocent," I cautioned. "But I need to know."

A few moments later, Dr. Wolcott came bustling out the door, still donning his greatcoat, and followed Mery toward the wagon. He stumbled to a halt at the sight of me perched on the seat. I could see the words forming on his lips—the refusal to allow me to participate—and I prepared my rebuttal. But then his shoulders slumped, and he simply shook his head in resignation.

While the men wrangled the body from the back of the cart, I climbed down, collecting one of the lanterns from the side of the wagon, and urged Bree to follow me. I spied the Wolcott's housekeeper standing in the doorway, observing proceedings, and crossed toward her to ask that my maid be allowed to wait inside.

"Of course, ma'am," she replied. "I'll put the kettle on, shall I?"

I thanked her before turning to follow the men toward the icehouse. There was no need to wonder what the housekeeper's reaction was to this. She made a choking-gasping sound so loud that I feared she'd swallowed her tongue. I trusted Bree to lend her aid should it be needed.

Quickening my steps, I hastened past the men to swing the wooden door wide to allow them to enter. Trailing them inside, I noted the table positioned near the center of the room, but closer to the door, so as to preserve its distance from the shelves at the back where food was stored. It being late autumn, there was no ice left, but come late December into January, I suspected the building would be well stocked. However, that didn't mean the room wasn't cold. Partially concealed underground as it was, and with the near-freezing temperatures outside, the shed was sufficiently chilled for our purposes.

The body having been laid on the table, I set the lantern down near the head and informed Mery he could go.

A mulish expression crossed his features. "What if I wanted to stay?"

"Trust me," I replied, removing my hat and fur-lined gloves and reaching for one of the aprons hung on a hook next to the door. "You don't want to."

Dr. Wolcott stood stiffly observing us, but upon seeing that I intended to begin with or without him, he reached for the other apron. Carefully, I peeled back the sheet, noting any stains and their corresponding position, and allowed the shroud to trail down over the edges of the table. When Branok's face was revealed, Mery abruptly turned away and strode from the shed, allowing the door to swing shut behind him with a thud. I paid but a fleeting thought to his reaction, wondering if it was one of guilt, shock, or grief, before narrowing my focus to the body before me.

CHAPTER 22

"Could you light the other lantern?" I requested, nodding toward where it hung on a hook near the door.

Dr. Wolcott slowly complied, allowing me a moment to observe the body without the doctor observing *me*.

Death could distort the appearance of an individual, having stolen their vitality, their animation . . . their soul. Yet there was no disguising the fact Branok Roscarrock had led a hard life. It was scoured across his face like the lines of a map. Wrinkles, scars, moles, and liver spots marked the skin revealed above his scraggly gray beard. I tried and failed to detect any resemblance to his relatives save for the line of the jaw and the cleft in his chin, but perhaps the relation would have been more obvious if I'd seen him alive.

His clothing was worn but well cared for, save the blood now soaked into the brown fabric of the coat. Unbuttoning it, I peeled it back to reveal that the white linen shirt over his left chest was even more saturated, however, not as extensively as I'd expected. The tear in the fabric was also not clean enough to convince me it was the entrance wound.

"Help me roll him onto his side," I told Dr. Wolcott as he rejoined me, having set the second lantern near the body's feet. The crossbeams helped illuminate the shadows which would have been created by just one.

I wedged my hands beneath the body near the hip and the shoulder blade, lifting upward as Dr. Wolcott reached across to pull. As the body shifted, I could see that the sheet underneath was more saturated than the front, though still not to the extent expected. This told me that Branok had lain dead for some time before he was found, his blood leaching into the ground. Leaning closer, I could also see that the fabric of his coat bore a telltale tear.

"He was stabbed from behind," I stated. "Straight through the heart, from the appearance of the angle. We'll be able to tell more definitively once the coat and shirt are removed."

Dirt and grime covered the fabric as well as his hair, likely collected from the place where he'd died. My gaze returned to the tear in the coat and then the smaller rent in the shirt as we lowered the body to its back again. "The blade must have been tremendously long."

"Aye," Dr. Wolcott agreed. "I'd say about nine inches. I've seen fillet knives of that length."

"Where have you seen them?"

"Most of the fishermen have them."

"Most?"

He looked up to meet my eye. "Aye. 'Tis a common knife in Cornwall."

Then finding such a blade would not necessarily lead us to the killer. "Perhaps there will be bruising from hilt marks."

Dr. Wolcott shook his head. "Not from a fillet knife."

I would have to trust his expertise in this, though I would be looking for bruising all the same. Particularly given his past deceptions.

I narrowed my eyes, contemplating the wound as a thought occurred to me. "Who did you tell about the puncture wound you allegedly found in the middle of Branok's back? The one you couldn't definitively state had happened in a fall." I'd tried and failed to keep the withering tone from my voice. "Or was that simply a lie made up on the spot for us?"

He flushed, telling me I'd hit upon the truth.

"Then I suppose it's a coincidence that this stab wound is just left of center." In any case, it seemed more pertinent that the wound went straight through the heart than that it slightly resembled a passing lie told by the physician. However, my aggravation having already been stirred, I couldn't resist layering on the scorn as I drawled, "Let's test for rigor mortis, shall we?"

I ignored his frown, directing my attention to Branok's face. The muscles around the eyes and mouth were constricted, as were those in the neck, as I felt gingerly along its length. His skin was cool to the touch, though not entirely devoid of warmth like the corpses Sir Anthony used to have delivered to his private anatomy theater in London.

"He's been dead for at least two to three hours," I ventured, moving to his arms and hands, as Dr. Wolcott followed suit with the opposite limb. They were also stiff, or in the process of becoming so. "Probably more like four to six," I added with a frown as I glanced about me for a clock. But, of course, there wouldn't be one inside an icehouse. "What time *is* it?"

"I glanced at my watch when I was summoned from bed, and it was just gone ten," he replied, still working the right arm.

"Then Branok must have been killed sometime between four and six o'clock."

We had departed for tea with Pasca Grenville at approximately a quarter to four, and Mery had said he'd last seen his grandfather at about the same time. Which meant that Mery might have been the last person to see him alive. He also might have followed Branok out to Kellan Head and killed him, but so might have any number of other people, including Bevil, Tristram, one of the Grenvilles, or even Dr. Wolcott.

I eyed the man across from me, attempting to read any nefarious intent in his features, but he seemed absorbed in his examination of the body.

Unfortunately, this broad window of time of death also didn't absolve my father-in-law of the possibility he might have had a hand in Branok's death. After all, we'd only stayed at Pasca's for about an hour. Which meant that by the time we returned to Roscarrock House, there was still approximately thirty minutes of time in which Lord Gage might have discovered his uncle's perfidy and killed him. If so, it must have been an impulsive action, for I could not imagine my father-in-law carrying around a nine-inch fillet knife for just such a purpose. But maybe Branok had been the one carrying the knife and it had been taken from him in a struggle. We would have to search the body for other bruises in addition to those caused by a hilt.

"I didn't want to lie to you, you know."

I looked up at Dr. Wolcott as he carefully lowered Branok's arm back to the table. His brow was tight, and his skin flushed despite the chill of the room. "Then why did you?"

He struggled to meet my gaze. "Because I felt like I had no choice."

I stared at him, waiting for him to continue.

He pressed his hands to the table next to the body, leaning into it so that the muscles in his neck and shoulders bunched. "Branok forced me to compromise my professional integrity. I was attending a woman who had gone into labor. The wife of one of his farmhands. Though that's not his only job," he muttered wryly. "The woman was near to delivering when Branok . . ."

he gestured angrily toward the corpse ". . . and his men burst into the room and insisted on storing their contraband there. I ordered them to depart, and they did, but only after leaving their goods behind." He turned his head to the side. "You must understand, my chief concern was for the mother and the safe delivery of her child."

"Of course."

"But when the preventive officers arrived to search the farmhand's cottage, they were told there was a woman laboring in the other room so that they wouldn't search it . . . and I said nothing." He closed his eyes. "Though I wish to God I had now. But there was the mother to consider, frightened and straining to bring her first child into the world. I couldn't subject her to another group of men trooping into the chamber, not to mention whatever foul air they might be bringing with them."

"Being a new mother myself, I can appreciate that," I conceded. "But why didn't you say anything later? I'm sure you could have gone to the preventives and explained."

The look he gave me was sharp with cynicism and incredulity. "Clearly, you've learned nothing from your time here, Mrs. Gage. Had I gone to the preventives, Branok's retaliation would have been swift and fierce. And no one would have stopped him." He laughed harshly. "In fact, the preventives might have helped him."

I wasn't altogether surprised to hear this, but that didn't make it any less unsettling. "So Branok used threats and intimidation to keep you in line."

His gaze lowered again. "Anne warned me. She told me what Branok was like. But I didn't listen. Or rather, I thought I was beyond compromise."

I tilted my head, unwilling to allow empathy over his predicament to cloud my judgment. "So everything you've told me until tonight was pure fabrication."

He flinched, looking up into my vexed glare. I arched a single eyebrow daring him to lie.

"Branok concocted the ruse about his falling to his death, and I was supposed to fill in the necessary details."

"Such as the watch being found under his body?"

Now I knew why Bevil and Mery had reacted so strangely when I'd asked them about it.

Dr. Wolcott grimaced. "Aye, well, that was a mistake. When you asked about his state of rigor mortis, I didn't know what to say. I didn't expect you to know . . ."

He broke off, but I understood what he meant. Despite my macabre reputation, he hadn't expected me to know so much about dead bodies or their decomposition.

"I had to account for my failure to note the body's rigor in estimating time of death," he continued after clearing his throat. "And a stopped watch was all I could think of, ridiculous as it was."

I could sense how ashamed he was, so I decided not to press him further about his medical claims. All of it had been fiction anyway. Branok's alleged fall. Finding his body. Bringing him here to be examined. The scrapes, bruises, and other punctures.

I paused, thinking back over the statements we'd collected.

"How did he pull it off?" I asked. "*Did* they come here that evening? Or is Anne and everyone else aware of the trick?"

Dr. Wolcott shook his head. "Anne doesn't know. Most don't. Easier to keep the secret that way." He turned to stare at Branok's boots, his lemon yellow hair catching the lantern light and seeming to almost glow. "Bevil, Tristram, and Mery wrapped a bundle of reeds in a blanket and transported it here in the cart. They didn't let anyone else see or touch it, except a glimpse from a distance. Branok counted on the horrifying nature of his alleged injuries to keep most people away."

"He also counted on his injuries convincing people why

observing the traditional vigil over his body would be unnecessary and a swift funeral and burial was best," I remarked wryly.

Branok's feigned death explained a number of inconsistencies with the statements and behavior of his relatives and neighbors, but his real death presented us with as many questions as it answered. Infuriatingly, we would have to begin our investigation all over again. The circumstances had changed and much of the evidence we'd gathered to this point was useless. Everyone we'd spoken to thus far had been either deliberately lying or operating under the same misapprehension we were.

I glared down at Branok's visage constricted in death, battling frustration. It was difficult to feel any compassion for the man and the fate that had befallen him after he'd manipulated everyone around him, including me, my husband, and Lord Gage. Yet murder was a tragedy, no matter the circumstances. I had to believe that, or I risked losing my humanity. At the very least, we needed to ascertain the truth. What happened then wasn't for us to decide, but at least the truth could point us in the right direction.

And that search for the truth began with conducting a thorough examination of the body.

I exhaled a long breath, releasing some of the tension knotting my muscles. "Shall we begin in earnest, then?" I asked, moving down toward Branok's feet so that I could start by removing his boots.

Dr. Wolcott didn't respond, and I could surmise from his uncomfortable expression what he was thinking. "You're truly going to stay?" he finally croaked.

"If you're protesting out of concern for my delicate constitution, I assure you, I've seen much worse, in much more advanced stages of decomposition," I told him as I studied the bottom of the first boot.

"Perhaps, but . . ." He made a sound between a groan and harrumph. "This is highly irregular!"

"Maybe for you," I reminded him, setting one boot down and reaching for the other. "But need I remind you that your past duplicity makes my presence doubly essential?" I flicked my gaze toward him. "How can we be certain you're not lying about your findings if I'm not here to corroborate them?"

He drew himself up in affront. "Then perhaps you would prefer that I depart, leaving you alone to complete this bleddy business."

"If you wish," I replied, refusing to be provoked by his threat or to feel abashed for stating the truth. "But given the fact that my father-in-law must also be considered a suspect, I thought it best that we both be present so that all parties are satisfied there is no tampering." I set the second boot next to the first and moved back up the body to his torso, facing Dr. Wolcott again. "However, if the idea of collaborating with a woman is too distasteful, I quite understand." I offered him a prim smile before returning my attention to the corpse.

Truthfully, if the man was going to continue to vex me, it might be best if he *did* abandon me to finish this examination alone. It would certainly prove less distracting, for I was used to scrutinizing human remains either alone or with only Gage for company. It was easier to concentrate that way. Easier to distance myself from what I was doing and the complicated mix of emotions and memories it aroused.

I lifted Branok's arm, debating whether the growing rigor would make it too difficult to remove the coat and shirt or if I should simply cut the garments off him. It was doubtful anyone would wish to keep them.

"I've scissors," Dr. Wolcott offered in a more conciliatory voice. And we set to work.

. . .

I stepped outside the icehouse door to discover a world blanketed in fog. At some point during the night, the mist had crept in from the coast and smothered the village in a damp haze. One that was as thick and muffling as the fog I'd experienced elsewhere in Britain, but in Cornwall it smelled of the sea.

I blinked my weary eyes, struggling to make out shapes as my mind still spun unpleasantly from the night's observations. There was also a familiar ache in my chest as I realized how long it had been since I'd held Emma. I wasn't used to being away from her so long, and after the night's efforts, I was particularly anxious to see her.

I rolled my shoulders to attempt to ease the stiffness in my muscles. Dr. Wolcott and I had examined every inch of Branok's body, determined not to miss the least bit of evidence it might yield. A full autopsy had proved unnecessary, but we'd combed through his hair and scrutinized his clothing and searched his pockets. All in an effort to uncover who had stabbed him, or at least to narrow down the details of when and how and what weapon was used.

Unfortunately, we'd discovered little more than what our initial inspection had already yielded. Branok had been killed by a long implement, likely a fisherman's fillet knife, roughly nine inches in length, at between four and six o'clock the previous afternoon. He'd been stabbed in the upper back, piercing or at least nicking the heart, and left to die somewhere near Kellan Head above Port Quin. This much was certain, and was precisely what Dr. Wolcott would report to the coroner's inquest when it convened within a few days' time. The jury would undeniably bring back a verdict of "murder by person or persons unknown." But the identity of the perpetrator was no clearer to me now than it had been before. With any luck, Gage might have uncovered some information that could further illuminate us, but for now, my thoughts were as obscured as the doctor's courtyard.

Dr. Wolcott joined me in my contemplation of the predawn mist, and a glance at his profile showed he was as bleary-eyed as I was. His shock of yellow hair stood up in tufts around his head and his jaw was dusted with pale stubble. I suspected I looked equally unkempt.

"We've answered much," he declared softly, though I couldn't tell if he was trying to reassure himself or me.

"Yes." I sighed. "Except the most critical question."

The only one anyone really cared about.

He scraped a hand over his jaw. "Aye."

His house was barely visible through the mist, the warm glow of a lantern set near the back door beckoning us toward it. But neither of us moved. We were both still held immobile by the night's events.

"Who do you think did it?" I ventured. When he was slow to respond—either because he was weighing his words or too fatigued to string them together—I prodded him. "Who has a motive? Other than you."

Dr. Wolcott squeezed the bridge of his nose. "I suppose I deserve to be a suspect. But I will tell you now, I didn't do it. I might have wished Branok to the devil a time or two," he grumbled under his breath. "But I didn't actually send him there." He straightened as if just having a thought. "And I have an alibi. Isn't that what they call it? I was summoned over to Trewetha a little around three to tend to a pair of sick children. Didn't return 'til after six," he finished resolutely, and I had to acknowledge that would remove him from suspicion. His claims would have to be verified, but I didn't expect to discover he'd lied.

"Then who?" I pressed.

His shoulders slumped again. "Any number of people could have done it. Branok wasn't exactly the most agreeable person.

He wanted everyone to hop to his tune whenever he wanted it played, and not a moment later."

"And if you didn't?"

His expression was grim, sensing I'd already deduced the answer. "He found a way to make ye do so in the future."

I turned to gaze out into the swirling mist, wondering if my father-in-law had, in fact, been the lucky one. After all, if he'd remained here, he would have eventually found himself under his uncle's thumb as well.

If I were to believe Dr. Wolcott, that meant that Branok's tyranny made nearly everyone a potential suspect. If so, we had dozens, if not hundreds, of people to question and consider. The enormity of the task threatened to overwhelm me. Until I recalled one critical thing.

"Yes, but most people believed Branok was already dead. Who didn't?" I queried. "Who other than you, Mery, Bevil, and Tristram? And Amelia," I added. "Mery already admitted that."

Dr. Wolcott shrugged.

"What about the constable who was supposed to investigate? Mr. Cuttance?"

He paused, considering this. "I don't know. You would have to ask Bevil. But . . ." His pale gaze turned suspicious. "He seemed perfectly happy to accept my findings without ever seeing the body."

This could mean the fellow was simply lazy. Or squeamish. But at the very least, his failure to do so was a dereliction of duty. No wonder he hadn't wanted us investigating.

Well, we were definitely going to be "mucking in his matters" now, as he'd so eloquently put it.

We had five suspects, then, but that didn't mean someone else hadn't uncovered the secret. Joan or Dolly or someone in Port Quin.

Then there were the Grenvilles. Tamsyn had told us she'd

seen Branok. She'd been certain of it, even from a distance. And she was right. Could she or any of her relatives have decided to take revenge for Gil's broken leg or any of the other grievances that family held against Branok and the Roscarrocks?

I pressed my hand to my head, feeling myself start to sway. Everything was such a muddle.

Dr. Wolcott grasped hold of my elbow. "There's nothing more to be done now," he told me solicitously. "So let's get you back to Roscarrock House."

I accepted his wisdom, allowing myself to be led toward his cottage. Perhaps everything would be clearer after I closed my eyes for a bit.

CHAPTER 23

Unfortunately, my respite would prove all too brief.

Once Mery and Bree had been roused from their places, dozing in the kitchen and parlor, we'd clambered back into the cart and set off toward Roscarrock House. Mery had thought to clean the back of the cart, and so Bree had urged me to sit with her wrapped in a warm blanket, lest I tumble from the perch in my fatigue. She'd assured me she'd keep a sharp eye on the rogue handling the ribbons, and so I allowed myself to be persuaded, soon nodding off with my head cushioned against Bree's shoulder.

I blinked open my bleary eyes again after just a quarter hour's rest as we reached the manor. The sun had yet to pierce the horizon, and what predawn light there was was obscured by the fog. However, the windows along the lower floor, as well as some above, still blazed with candlelight. I gazed up at them in confusion, still struggling to alertness as Bree led me along the path toward the door. Having handed the reins to a groomsman,

Mery followed us in equally wary silence. Everyone should have been abed.

At the threshold, we discovered why they were not. No one could have slept through the row currently taking place in the drawing room. A swift peek at the railing above revealed Amelia, Joan, and Dolly holding her youngest child—all in their nightclothes—staring down at the entrance to the drawing room. There was no sign of Mrs. Mackay or Emma, but if my daughter was still slumbering through this racket, it was nothing short of a miracle.

Her grandfather and Bevil were shouting at the top of their lungs, while Gage and Tristram once again tried to separate them. From the state of the room and the blood dripping from a cut next to Bevil's eye, some sort of physical altercation had also ensued. A continuation of the confrontation in the garden, I presumed.

None of the men appeared to have yet retired, though their coats had been discarded and their cravats loosened. Cut glasses littered several of the surfaces, half-filled with an amber liquid, and I could smell the malty aroma of either Irish whiskey or Holland genever. This had undoubtedly only added fuel to the fire blazing between the cousins. Fuel that I would have thought my husband would have been astute enough not to let them pour down their throats.

"You've been wanderin' the estate ever since ye arrived. Lookin' for somethin'," Bevil charged, his speech slurred. "Even afore Tamsyn told ye she'd seen Branok."

"You *followed* me?" Lord Gage retorted and then scoffed. "But of course you did. Had to make sure I didn't stumble onto your *deceit*."

"What were ye lookin' for? Did ye think to keep it for yerself, ye selfish bastard?" Bevil's eyes were wild, making his statements all the more confusing.

But Lord Gage seemed to all but ignore his allegations, caught up in his own agenda. "I was checking Grandfather's hidey holes," he spat back.

Bevil swayed on his feet, either from too much drink or his cousin's assertion.

Lord Gage plainly believed the latter, for his eyes glittered vengefully. "Didn't realize I knew where those were, did you? Or you didn't think I'd remember. Well, I do! And I found your bribe for Cuttance. Or rather, Branok's bribe, isn't it? Since it's all *his* money."

Bevil appeared momentarily at a loss for words. Long enough for me to exchange a surprised glance with my husband. By all appearances, he seemed as startled by this revelation as I was.

"I . . . I don't know what you're talkin' 'bout," Bevil finally stammered unconvincingly.

Even his son glowered at his denial. "There's no need to lie for 'im anymore, Father."

Bevil turned his glare on Tristram.

"He's right," Mery said, having followed me into the room. His gaze met Tristram's and held. "There's nothin' Granfer can do to us now."

What exactly this meant, I didn't know, but there appeared to be some sort of silent communication occurring between the two younger men. Something that went far beyond the surface meaning of their words.

"No, but there *is* something *we* can do if you don't cooperate," Lord Gage threatened.

Bevil's eyes narrowed to slits beneath his bushy brows. "I see 'ow it's gonna be. Yer gonna blame *us* for all your faults and mistakes. Just like always."

"And what's that supposed to mean?" he snarled back.

Bevil pointed an accusing finger at Lord Gage, staggering backward as he did. "*You* killed Branok."

"Gentlemen," Gage declared, raising his voice and stepping between them. "Why don't we cease the finger-pointing." He arched his eyebrows at Bevil, whose arm remained extended. "Until we have all the facts. Such as . . ." he swiveled toward me ". . . time of death?"

"Between four and six o'clock in the afternoon." I shook my head apologetically. "We couldn't narrow it down any further than that."

"Then he was killed before dinner?" Gage clarified.

"Yes."

"So I couldn't have done it," Lord Gage pronounced, arching his chin. "Not while I was at Pasca Grenville's."

Except, he could have. I'd already calculated he would have just barely had enough time. He'd certainly been agitated enough. But I didn't state any of this out loud. I didn't need to.

"Ye returned nearly an hour afore dinner," Bevil replied. "And took off toward the cliffs. If that's not suspicious, I don't know what is." He turned to scrutinize me mistrustfully. "And how do we know your daughter-in-law isn't obscurin' the facts for ye?"

"Because Dr. Wolcott and I examined the body together," I answered crisply, having already expected one of them to challenge my findings. "You're free to consult him if you believe I'm lying. After all, he's one of you, isn't he? He was part of the deception." It was all I could do not to storm from the room. "Though I'm starting to wonder why I bothered. Obviously, you all lured us here under false pretenses. So why should we stay to investigate now that you have a real mess on your hands?" I rubbed my hand over my forehead, feeling the weight of all the hours of sleep I'd missed during the night, and turned to look at Lord Gage. "Maybe we should simply leave today, as we planned."

"Nay! Please."

I pivoted to face Great-Aunt Amelia standing in the doorway leaning on Joan's arm.

"Please," she continued to plead. "I know ye have every right to be angry. We . . . we did lie to ye. But that was all Branok's doin'! And now that he's murdered . . ." Her eyes flickered over my features. "It *was* murder?"

"Yes." There was no doubt about that. He certainly hadn't stabbed *himself* in the back.

She exhaled, closing her eyes, and then nodded. "Now that he's been murdered, we truly *do* need your 'elp to find out who did this."

I was fully cognizant of why she was directing her appeal to me and not my husband or father-in-law. She'd not even glanced at them since entering the room. She thought that, of all three of us, I, as a woman and a mother, would be most easily persuaded. However, I found the tactic only made me more angry and more desirous to wash my hands of them, in spite of—or perhaps *because* of—the softening toward her I felt in my heart.

In her dressing gown with her wispy gray hair trailing down her back, she seemed to have aged before my eyes. The pluckiness I'd admired had all but vanished, leaving behind a worn and worried woman. But I steeled myself, knowing from personal experience that age was no barrier to duplicity.

"You may not like what we uncover," I reminded her, crossing my arms. After all, the majority of our suspects were standing in this very room.

Joan's hands briefly tightened where they gripped her mother-in-law's arm and her opposite shoulder. An involuntary reaction, I suspected, and perhaps a telling one.

"Aye," Amelia replied. "But we need the truth anyway." Her eyes drifted from person to person. "Or else we're liable to tear ourselves apart tryin' to uncover it."

This was an astute observation. One that told me she was not as confident as I'd expected that one of the people here had not done it. Which made my own suspicions all the greater.

"Then perhaps you might begin by confirming something for us. Who knew that Branok had feigned his death?" It was a challenge of sorts, to see if they would lie. "Everyone currently present? What of Joan?"

Joan began to shake her head, but then checked herself before nodding resignedly.

"What of Dolly?"

Everyone looked at Tristram.

"I didn't tell her." He scowled at his father. "You instructed me not to."

"Anyone else besides Dr. Wolcott?" I turned to include everyone in this request.

"What of Mr. Cuttance?" Gage asked.

I shared a look of solidarity with him, glad he'd already considered the constable.

"Care to amend your earlier statement?" Gage directed this question at Bevil.

"Nay," he bit back. "Cuttance is a fool. A greedy fool, but a fool all the same. Branok set aside money to bribe him, but in the end 'twasn't necessary. Cuttance was too lazy to investigate. Took us at our word." He grunted. "I think he was just 'appy to see the end of Branok."

The last had undoubtedly been added to point our suspicions in Mr. Cuttance's direction, but it was also probably true. I doubted there was much love lost between the man who served as constable and preventive officer and Branok, despite any bribes Branok had evidently been paying him.

It was clear that my husband had more information he'd gathered from these people, questioning them while I was examining Branok's corpse. I would be better off consulting with him before I pressed further. However, there was one question I wanted an answer to before we proceeded another step.

"*Why* did Branok feign his death?" I demanded. "Why were we lured here?"

My queries were met with silence, their gazes either dropping to the floor or silently darting to one another. Only Mery dared to meet my eye, but his face was carefully devoid of all emotion save a watchfulness that I'd begun to realize was almost habitual.

When a muted cry suddenly pierced the air—one that I immediately recognized as my daughter's—I knew I was not going to get the answer I wanted.

"We . . . we don't know," Amelia stammered.

I narrowed my eyes.

"Branok didn't tell us," Joan added.

But I didn't believe this for an instant, and I let them know it. I shook my head and made a sound of disgust as I strode from the room. Had I been in any state to travel, I would have taken Emma into our carriage and ordered our coachman to head toward Liftondown House. Only the fatigue that dragged at my every step as I climbed the stairs kept me from giving way to the impulse.

Somehow, I made it to Emma's nursery, settling into the chair to cradle and nurse her. As always, the act of caring for my sweet girl soothed me, and I found myself unable to keep my eyes open or even to lift my head. How I managed not to drop her or to eventually make it into my own bed, I'm not certain, but I suspected it was some combination of Gage, Bree, and Mrs. Mackay that maneuvered me there. The next time I woke, it was to find that five hours had passed, and that the nanny was bringing Emma to me because she needed me again.

I rolled to my side, tending to her while I struggled to clear the cobwebs from my mind. While I would have liked nothing more than to sleep for five *more* hours, I knew that was a luxury I couldn't afford. There was too much to do, and too many things to be confronted for me to simply lie about. In any case, now that my mind was churning again, it would never let me rest. Not when there were answers to be uncovered.

Though the morning must have been far advanced, the light piercing through the curtains was muted. Rain pattered against the roof, and I could just make out the faint rumble of thunder in the distance. I sighed. Not the most auspicious day to be out and about, but such things had never stopped us before.

However, I lingered under the covers, listening to Emma chatter and watching her explore the bedding. It wouldn't be long before she was crawling and pulling herself up. When Gage entered a short time later, it was to hear Emma squealing with laughter as I tickled her and pressed kisses to her chubby cheeks.

He stood at the end of the bed, smiling at us. "I have to say, I much prefer the sounds in here to those in the rest of this house."

I turned to look up at him, seeing the lines of fatigue pulling at the corners of his eyes and mouth. "Is everyone still arguing?"

"When they're even speaking to each other."

I offered him a grimace of commiseration before pushing up on my elbow to arrange my pillows so that I could lean back against them.

"Don't you want to go back to sleep?" he asked me.

"I want to," I admitted, settling into place and lifting Emma up into the vee formed by my bent legs and torso so that she could face me. "But I won't. Did *you* get any rest?"

He rounded the bed to sit next to us. "A few hours." He took hold of Emma's hand, pretending to nibble her fingers.

"Are they still claiming that luring us here was Branok's plan and they have no idea why?"

He offered me a cynical glance that said it all.

I thought back over all of the times I'd thought Tristram or Amelia or Mery were grieving or worried because Branok had been murdered and they didn't know who to suspect or what the future held. Yet now we knew all of that anxiety was directed toward something different. Toward their fear of being caught out. I wished I'd taken more time earlier to question the motivations behind their emotions.

But how could we possibly have known they were playing such a dirty trick? The very notion sounded beyond ludicrous, particularly with so many people involved. Even so, it had been carried out, and successfully. But we still didn't know why. Why concoct such an elaborate scheme? There had to be a reason— and an important one—to exert such an effort. And I didn't believe for one second that they were all blind to its purpose.

I huffed in aggravation. "I feel like refusing to investigate unless they fully cooperate. Except, your father *is* a suspect, one they'd probably most like to pin the matter on. And I don't trust Mr. Cuttance or whoever the magistrate is to be impartial." I brushed a stray curl from Emma's forehead, trailing my fingers over her cheek. "There's also Dolly and Imogen, and the other women to consider, as well as the children. I hate leaving them without answers." It would worry them. It must.

"What else were you and Dr. Wolcott able to discover other than when Branok was killed?" Gage asked.

I told him what little we'd learned from the body, and also relayed what Dr. Wolcott had told me about Branok's ploy, as well as the physician's alleged alibi. "We should verify it, but I don't think he's the killer."

"I agree," Gage admitted, absently rubbing his jaw as he contemplated all I'd told him. "And I think you're right about such a weapon being an odd choice for my father. He wouldn't choose a fisherman's knife."

"Not unless he took it from Branok, but then there should have been evidence of a struggle, and there wasn't. Whoever did this was either able to sneak up on him unawares or stabbed him after he'd turned his back on them."

"Which means they'd have to be someone he trusted."

I arched my eyebrows. "Someone he trusted, but discounted."

He paused to scrutinize my features. "You're thinking of Mery."

"Or Tristram." I tilted my head in thought. "Or Tamsyn. But I can't see him turning his back on your father or Bevil. Or Cuttance."

Emma began to protest our ignoring her, so I laid her on the bed between us to wiggle and roll.

"If Tamsyn, then why not also Amelia or Joan?" Gage posited. "Though a knife is usually a man's weapon."

"Usually," I repeated dryly.

He lifted his gaze to meet mine and I could tell the moment he recalled the knife-throwing woman I'd faced in Argyll.

"But you're right," I conceded. "I was initially thinking of Mery. He seems to have the most to gain from his grandfather's death. That hasn't changed. Plus, his whereabouts during the window when Branok was killed are rather ambiguous. He claims he last saw his grandfather leaving his cottage about the time we departed for Pasca Grenville's, and soon after he went to the Golden Lion in Port Isaac."

"We did meet him returning from there, reeking of smoke and spirits," Gage confirmed.

"Yes, but it's the work of ten minutes for him to accompany his grandfather out to that headland, kill him, and then carry on to Port Isaac. And we've only *Mery's* word as to when Branok actually left his cottage." I watched as Emma rolled over to her stomach and began sucking on her fist, still working on her tooth. "Unless someone else saw Branok after that?"

"No one claimed to have seen him yesterday," Gage said. "And only Bevil admitted to speaking to him the day before."

I began to pleat the hem of my shift. Whoever had helped me undress this morning had evidently decided not to bother having me swap the undergarment for a night rail. "Then Mery was likely the last to see him alive. Unless he's *not* the killer." I frowned, thinking back over our conversation in the cart the previous evening and his expression before I'd left the drawing room. "But he definitely knows something." I narrowed my eyes. "And he doesn't trust his relatives."

"What makes you say that?" Gage asked.

"He's guarded, watchful. Like he doesn't know precisely where or when the next blow is going to fall, but he knows it's coming."

I could see that Gage knew I was speaking from experience. That I, too, had learned to be guarded and watchful when I'd lived under Sir Anthony's roof, and it had taken some time for me to relax my vigilance.

"Not that his relatives actually resort to physical violence," I qualified.

"But the premise still stands," he finished for me, reaching for my hand.

"Yes."

Gage's expression was taut, so I squeezed his fingers hoping to reassure him and bring him firmly back to our present rather than worrying about my past. "Perhaps he expects them to accuse him."

"They did before, when it was only a faked death."

Though now I had to question why. Why had they pointed the finger so firmly at him? Had that been part of the plan? Or had the Killigrews been improvising? I supposed it must have occurred to them that we would see Mery as an obvious suspect, so perhaps they'd elected to play to what they believed would be our preconceived notions.

Whatever the truth, we would never have the full picture until we also understood why Branok had feigned his death and persuaded us to come here. If any of them were to tell us, I suspected it was Mery, and the others knew it. Or, at least, Bevil did.

Emma flopped over onto her back, kicking her legs and drawing a smile to my lips. I watched as Gage leaned over to blow kisses against her cheeks. He pulled one of her ragdolls from somewhere concealed on his person, and I couldn't help but feel my heart brim over with warmth at the picture they made.

Which made the ache I felt recalling what Mery's childhood had been like all the more pronounced. Lord Gage might not have been the kindest and most attentive of fathers, but he had loved his son. If I'd ever doubted it, everything he'd revealed to me the evening before had made that abundantly clear. And Gage's mother had adored him. Mery, on the other hand, had lost his father in a drunken brawl and been abandoned by his mother, leaving him to the dubious care of his grandfather and assorted other relatives.

"You know, Mery might be the rightful heir of Roscarrock, but he's far from in control."

Gage looked up, seeming to be struck by this thought as much as I was.

"And I'm not sure he'll have an easy time wresting it away from those who are."

He frowned. "For all the disparaging things they've had to say about him, one thing's clear. He's not ruthless enough."

I nodded. Which rather turned things on its head. "We need to find a way to speak to him when the others can't interfere. And I think I know how." I sat up. "But I need to speak to Bree."

"I'll find her for you," Gage said, planting one last kiss to

Emma's cheek. "I imagine she's waiting for your summons." He lightly grasped hold of my chestnut brown hair trailing over my shoulder, urging me closer so that he could kiss me as well. "Though I wish we could delay the day a little longer. With Emma giggling and you dressed only in your shift." His gaze took on a rakish gleam at this last remark, which drew a blush to my cheeks. Then his face fell as he sighed wearily. "But I know we have a murderer to catch."

I drew him back to me, planting another kiss on his lips. "With any luck, this will all be over soon."

His expression was resigned. "And I'll never ask my father to introduce me to any of his long-lost relatives ever again."

CHAPTER 24

Bree arrived shortly after Mrs. Mackay departed with Emma, and seeing the worry and fatigue shadowing her eyes and dragging down her shoulders, I couldn't stop myself from reaching for her hands. Even her normally bouncy strawberry blond curls fell listlessly around her face. "You must not have gotten any more sleep than I did."

She offered a weak smile. "Cora insisted on proddin' me wi' questions."

"Did she?"

"Aye," Bree replied, understanding why I found the interest shown by Dolly's maid to be notable.

"Was it the type of normal gossiping done by the staff or something more focused?" I asked as I sank down on the bench wrapped in my dressing gown and allowed her to begin picking out the snarls in my hair.

"Fairly typical. Though once she realized I wasna goin' to be as forthcomin' as she wished, she became more pointed in her queries."

"Pointed about what?" I caught Bree's eye in the reflection of the mirror. "Mery?"

I hadn't forgotten our suspicions that Cora might have warmed Mery's bed.

Bree's mouth quirked wryly. "She couldna seem to decide whether the blackguard killed his grandad or he's too tender-hearted to commit such an act."

I arched my eyebrows. I supposed that answered one of our questions. For it seemed doubtful she would have voiced her opinion with such vehemence or that it would have swung in such a wide arc if her emotions were not somehow engaged. I was simply glad for Bree's sake that this meant it was unlikely Cora was also involved with Anderley. Not that I'd seriously considered the possibility, no matter how uncharacteristically the valet was behaving.

"Did she ever settle on one verdict or the other?" I asked.

"If she did, it was after I'd already fallen asleep." A crease formed in her brow. "In any case, I wouldna trust her opinion. No' when I have better intelligence for ye."

"You overheard Anne speaking with Mery?" I deduced, swiveling to look directly in her eyes. It was the reason I'd been so anxious to speak with her. I'd been too tired to keep my eyes open during the cart ride home to ask her, and Mery might have overheard us.

"I didna catch the beginnin' of their conversation, but it was clear Mrs. Wolcott was shocked to discover Branok wasna already dead and buried. She was verra distraught by the deception and her husband's part in it. Mery kept tellin' her that it was all Branok's fault. That they'd had no choice. But she wasna havin' it. Told him Branok might've bullied 'em into doin' as he wished, but he couldna compel their silence noo, and that he'd best tell you and Mr. Gage all he ken."

My respect for Anne Wolcott increased tenfold.

"Did Mery agree?"

Bree urged me to turn back around as she pulled the brush through my hair again. My scalp smarted where she battled a tangle. "No' that I heard, but he sounded chastened."

I bit my lower lip, considering this new information. I'd hoped I might be able to appeal to Anne to help arrange a way to speak openly with Mery away from the prying eyes and ears at Roscarrock House. It sounded like she would be amenable. But there was one more factor to consider.

"Did they seem . . . ?" I broke off, uncertain how to tactfully voice my query.

Bree knew what I meant. "Nay," she stated with a conviction I found both reassuring and surprising. "'Tis obvious they care for each other. But they're no' lovers."

I nodded, trusting her judgment. After all, she was as insightful in her own way as I was. I'd realized that almost the moment I'd met her, and her intuitions had proven invaluable enough times since then for me to trust her discernment now.

"If I asked you to deliver a message to Mrs. Wolcott, would you do it? I know it's outside the realm of your duties. But I don't trust any of the Roscarrock servants, and Anderley . . ."

Bree's expression grew tight.

I sighed. "Well, frankly, I don't know what's come over him. Have you spoken with him?"

She shook her head.

"There must be some sort of explanation," I insisted, trying to convince myself as much as Bree. "Some reason he's distanced himself." Some reason he was treating us all rather shabbily. It was simply too drastic a change in character.

I watched as Bree set down the hairbrush and began plating my hair to be formed into loops. I'd hoped she might have some sort of insight about him as well. Something I'd missed. But perhaps she was too close to the problem.

Regardless, I couldn't bear to see Bree looking so unhappy. I was certain Gage knew more than he was saying, and I vowed I would press him about it the moment I had a chance.

With that intention in mind, as soon as I'd finished dressing, I dashed off a note for Anne and passed it into Bree's safekeeping to be delivered. Then I hastened to find my husband. He was already waiting with his father near the stables, presumably anxious for us all to be off to question Mr. Cuttance. As such, I had to stifle my questions about Gage's valet once again.

I pulled my riding gloves onto my hands and mounted my strawberry roan Figg. The rain had ceased, but the sky overhead was still choked with clouds as we set off toward Port Isaac. The road was riddled with puddles, and I knew within minutes the train of my sage green riding habit would be splattered with mud, but still I longed to urge Figg into a trot. Anything to alleviate some of the tension that seemed to have taken up permanent residence in my frame. However, Lord Gage kept our pace rigidly to a walk—for our safety as well as the horses—on the pockmarked lane.

Our first destination was the Golden Lion, for the last time we'd spoken with the preventive officer turned local constable he'd been emerging from the tavern. We also needed to verify Mery's alibi, or at least verify approximately what time he'd arrived and departed the previous evening. However, it appeared Mr. Cuttance had already caught wind of Branok's deception, for the expression on his face when we encountered him around a bend in the road could be described as nothing short of thunderous.

"Out of my way, Gage," he snarled at my father-in-law. "I'm

goin' to flay the Killigrews alive, and Mery, too. You'll not stop me."

"Why would we stop you?" Lord Gage drawled in retort, reining in his steed so that he blocked the center of the road.

Cuttance seemed momentarily taken aback by this response.

"Though might I suggest arresting them instead." Lord Gage's eyes sharpened. "Unless that's the problem?"

Gage drew his chestnut gelding Titus up next to his father. "Hmm. Yes. I suppose he'd also have to detain himself for dereliction of duty."

Cuttance's face flushed red. "Is that your game, then? Ye intend to blame this entire farce on me?"

"No," Lord Gage replied in a clipped voice. "But you're either part of the conspiracy or wholly incompetent."

The constable spluttered in outrage, seemingly unable to form full sentences, and I feared for a moment that he was about to have an apoplexy. "Now, see here . . . How dare . . . ! I'll have you . . ."

"We found your latest bribe," Gage informed him.

He broke off, his eyes bulging in the face of both Gages' calm implacableness. "I don't know what you're talkin' about," he replied much too late to be believed.

"Of course you do," Lord Gage said. "It's the same place my grandfather used to hide bribes for your father. The hollowed-out log inland of Lobber Point." He turned to his son. "You would think in the last forty-odd years they might have chosen a more honorable course, or at least a different hiding spot, but then the Cuttances were never known for their cleverness."

"Clever enough to catch *you* red-handed," Cuttance snapped back.

But my father-in-law refused to be riled. "As a child of eleven. Hardly a challenge."

"I wonder what his superiors will say when they learn he's

been taking bribes in exchange for turning a blind eye to the smuggling that's still going on," Gage posited.

"Misled the jury at the coroner's inquest as well," his father replied, maintaining the same blithe tone as his son.

I hovered behind them, observing the exchange as I would a theater production. Although I'd known Gage had conducted inquiries alongside and on behalf of his father for years before we'd met, I'd rarely seen them at work together, and only under strained circumstances. Now I felt like I was being given a glimpse into what their collaborations had been like during the early years, before Gage had refused to conform to his father's every wish, causing their initial rift.

Cuttance, on the other hand, was not enjoying himself so much.

"I did not mislead anyone," he snarled. "I believed Branok was dead. Nay one could survive a fall from that cliff! How was I to know they lied?"

Lord Gage's voice dripped with scorn. "By verifying there was even a body."

Cuttance fumed, grinding out his words. "I trusted Dr. Wolcott."

"Who wed Branok's niece's daughter."

The preventive officer made no response to this, and I couldn't help but feel the tiniest twinge of empathy for the man. Had Branok truly fallen from that cliff, his body would have been in a horrific state. While in his capacity as constable, he should have done his duty and verified the corpse's identity and the extent of its injuries to the best of his ability, but he should have also been able to trust the attending physician not to lie about its very *existence*.

If Cuttance was telling the truth . . . And I had little doubt he was. The man was no skilled actor. Then he had every reason to be furious. Branok and his relatives had not only duped but humiliated him, and possibly cost him at least one of his positions. The local magistrate would have to learn the truth sooner or later, and when he did, it was liable Cuttance would be disciplined in some manner.

"As for the smuggling," Cuttance growled, "just because I take the man's blunt doesn't mean I'm actually lookin' the other way, now, does it?"

"Without Branok the wiser?" Lord Gage asked doubtfully.

"Aye!" He puffed up his rounded stomach like an affronted robin. "Let's just say, not all of his relations are rogues."

Titus's head bobbed slightly, and Gage lowered his hand to rub his flank, calming him. "Then you know about the shipment they expect soon."

I straightened, wondering when he'd learned this bit of intelligence.

Cuttance glowered at him. "The *two* shipments they expect? Aye."

Gage nodded in assent. Clearly, he'd been testing him.

"If you know about that, how is it that you didn't know Branok had feigned his death?" Lord Gage challenged. "Or perhaps you did and decided instead to take revenge."

"Then I would be an even bigger fool than ye take me for," Cuttance replied, his horse dancing to the side. "Had I known Branok was alive, I woulda dragged 'is sorry carcass before the magistrate."

"Or tossed him over a cliff, in truth," Gage suggested. "Lost to the sea."

Cuttance eyed him with a disfavor that softened to begrudging admittance. "Aye. Maybe." His gaze darted back to Lord Gage. "But I certainly wouldn't 'ave left 'is corpse to be found now."

There was an undeniable logic to his thinking, for Branok being found dead after Cuttance had unwittingly abetted

Branok's feigned death and burial was the worst thing that could have happened for the constable. If he'd been able to apprehend him, it would not have entirely mitigated his disgrace, but he might have at least saved his position. Or if Branok had simply disappeared, and there was no body to be found, then it would have been his word against those who had already lied. That is, if any of Branok's relatives had even raised an objection.

However, my father-in-law wasn't about to take him at his word. "Where were you yesterday afternoon between four and six o'clock?"

The leaves still clinging to the trees overhead clattered together as a sudden gust of wind swooped down the road. It splattered us with water, but none of the men moved. Cuttance plainly didn't appreciate having the tables turned to have such a question asked of him, and judging from Lord Gage's rigid posture he had no intention of backing down until he had an answer. However, Cuttance's old dapple gray appeared to have had more than enough of the tense silence, for he grunted, tugging at his owner's reins.

The constable sighed, reluctantly giving way. "I was meetin' with Anthony Knill."

I struggled to mask my surprise, for this was not what I'd expected to hear.

"He's your informant." Gage's words were more statement than question, but Cuttance answered him regardless.

"Aye. Though, truth be told, I suspect he gets most of his information from his wife."

He was probably right. As Bevil and Joan's daughter, Morgan was bound to learn more than her dissenter husband about the goings-on at Roscarrock House, but I would never have pegged her as an informant. Unless she didn't know her husband was sharing what she told him with the parish constable.

If she did, then she kept her allegiances and duplicities well hidden.

"I thought Mr. Knill wasn't supposed to return from the market at St. Austell until today?" Lord Gage asked. At least, that was what Morgan had told us some days past.

Cuttance grunted. "Then he returned early. Ask 'im yourself." He urged his horse forward, forcing Gage and his father either to let him pass or confront him more directly. This time they opted to comply. After all, they'd gotten answers to their questions. Answers satisfactory enough to convince me that it was unlikely Cuttance was our killer.

We watched a moment as the preventive officer rode off in the direction we'd come, his horse kicking up an abominable amount of mud.

"Do we carry on to the Golden Lion or return to Roscarrock?" Gage asked.

"Perhaps we should visit the Knills," I suggested.

"No," Lord Gage asserted, his eyes still fastened on the back of the departing constable. "It's doubtful the proprietor at the Golden Lion will be able to tell us anything concrete about Mery's alleged alibi, and the Knills can wait. I want to be there when Cuttance questions my relatives."

I couldn't argue with his reasoning, and I had to admit I was also curious to see how Mery and the Killigrews reacted to Cuttance's queries. However, when he turned to ride after the constable at a faster clip, I restrained Figg to a walk.

"Just a moment," I told Gage.

He drew Titus up beside me. "What is it?" he asked in concern.

"You didn't tell me you'd learned the Roscarrocks were expecting two shipments of contraband."

He turned away even as I scrutinized his countenance. "It

must have slipped my mind. The past few days certainly haven't lacked for distractions."

That was true, and yet I could tell there was more he wasn't telling me. And I had a strong suspicion why.

"Gage, where is Anderley?" When he kept his gaze directed resolutely ahead, I narrowed my eyes. "Why is he never about when we need him? And why have you been so tolerant of his abhorrent behavior?"

"Kiera . . ." he began on a breath that landed somewhere between exasperated and exhausted. "I would tell you if I—"

"No!" I cut him off, keeping my voice low so as not to alert his father riding ahead of us. "Do not give me that line. Bree and I have already been imagining the worst, and should something happen, we need to know whether he can still be trusted."

"Of course he can."

The look I gave him made it clear there was no *of course* about it. "Have you given him some sort of task like you did in Ireland? To blend in and . . . infiltrate."

A flash of irritation tightened his features, but then he relented, perhaps recognizing I would no longer believe his denials. "I asked Anderley to try to insinuate himself with the men on the Roscarrock staff who also act as smugglers."

I scowled at him, unhappy to discover my suspicions were correct.

"*And in that effort,*" he continued before I could speak, "I told him to be a bit belligerent and neglectful of us. To make it seem like he's bitter and not a little resentful of his position in our employ, being dragged hither and yon with such a notorious master and mistress."

"Gage!" I gasped in outrage, making Figg's ears twitch.

"He had to play the part, Kiera," he protested. "It's the only way he could worm his way into their confidences. Charm is useless among such men. He had to make them believe his allegiance was mutable, and his skills as an adventurer, as well as his ability to speak French, were for sale."

"Aren't you putting him in terrible danger?"

"Which was why it was essential that his disdain for us be believable! Why we couldn't tell you or Miss McEvoy. Or Father. Your reactions had to be *real*."

I glared at him, unswayed by his appeal. "You should have discussed this with me. With all of us."

"There wasn't time. I didn't realize that the smuggling was truly continuing until the evening of the welcome party, and I knew that if Anderley was to make an impression on the smugglers, it had to be then."

It was difficult to argue. There *had* been little time to confer, though I refused to concede entirely. "You should have told me," I insisted, arching my chin. "I've become rather good at concealing my thoughts in the time since we first met."

"Not that good."

I frowned. "From you, maybe."

He didn't respond, and I elected to turn my attention to more pertinent objections. "You are asking a lot of him."

"No more than he is willing to do. Anderley likes the adventure," he told me and then chuckled. "Believe me. He's placed himself in far more precarious situations in the past."

Except in the past, there hadn't been Bree.

Even now, I could see Bree's worry-stricken face, hear the hurt and uncertainty ringing in her voice as we discussed Anderley. I knew it wasn't right to ask a person to change themselves for another person, but wasn't it fair to expect them to at least consider how their actions might affect them?

Some of my distress on Bree's behalf must have shown, for Gage gentled his voice, seeking to reassure me. "Don't worry, Kiera. Anderley knows how to take care of himself. I wouldn't have allowed him to embark on this undertaking otherwise."

Maybe so, but I was starting to believe he wasn't capable of taking care of Bree, no matter how much he cared for her.

Placing her firmly in mind, I quietly proclaimed, "I have to tell Bree."

His brow furrowed. "Kiera, you could be putting him in greater danger."

"Fiddle-faddle!" I snapped, borrowing one of my maid's phrases. "Bree would no more place him in danger than she would cut off her own arm, and you know it."

He opened his mouth as if to protest further and then closed it, shaking his head.

We rode on in silence for several minutes with nothing but the splash and squelch of the horses' hooves in the puddles and mud and the occasional call of a bird from the hedges bordering the road to accompany us. The breeze had picked up, swooshing down the lane and making me shiver in my woolen riding habit.

Gage moved Titus closer, resting his crop over his thighs. "You're chilled. Here. Take my coat."

"No," I said, holding up my hand to stop him from removing it. "I'm fine. Truly. It's not much farther now."

His gaze met mine as if to be certain. I recognized it as the olive branch he'd intended and did my best to keep my tone civil.

"Has Anderley been able to learn anything else about the shipments?"

"One is from Roscoff, France, hence his usefulness as a French speaker. They plan to anchor offshore outside territorial waters, like I told you."

"And then the Roscarrocks will row out to collect the cargo?" I asked, recalling our earlier discussion.

He nodded. "And the other is on its way to Bristol from the West Indies by way of the Scilly Isles, laden with tobacco and sugar, among other things."

I turned to him in surprise. "That's not something they could have arranged simply by sending someone over on the mail packet to France."

Gage's expression was solemn. "No. There must be a larger stakeholder. Someone with wealth and connections. From what I've learned, it's not uncommon in such ventures."

"Who?"

"I don't know. But even if we did, it's doubtful we'd be able to implicate them. Such a man would be certain to hide behind his lofty name and layers of inscrutability."

"Letting everyone else do the dirty work."

He turned to me; the shade of his eyes was made all the more blue by the cerulean hue of his waistcoat. "They might not even live in Cornwall. So you see the difficulty."

In our uncovering the larger stakeholder, yes. But also in the Roscarrocks extracting themselves from such an arrangement. After all, if the larger stakeholder had put forth much of the capital and reaped the greater benefits with almost no risk to themselves, they were not likely to allow the Roscarrocks to end their agreement so easily.

I wondered if this was something Lord Gage had ever considered. Or was he determined to see his mother's family as the villains no matter the circumstances?

CHAPTER 25

We rejoined Lord Gage at the crossroads where the trail south led to Trelights and the lane north led back to Roscarrock House. He told us that Mr. Cuttance had veered off toward the village, apparently deciding to speak with Dr. Wolcott and actually view the body this time before approaching Mery and the Killigrews. So we carried on to the manor, intent on pressing the occupants for information one more time before the constable arrived to conduct his own interrogations. However, when we arrived, we discovered with surprise that no compulsion was necessary.

One of the grooms informed us that Great-Aunt Amelia was waiting for us in the library, and a footman stood by the door, waiting to direct us to her before I could even pause to make repairs to my appearance. Mindful of the mud clinging to my boots and the hem of my riding habit, I avoided the rugs when I could. I wondered for a moment if we were about to be asked to leave, but then I realized that would be rather an abrupt reversal of her pleas for us to stay the previous evening.

I'd not had much occasion to enter the library and, in all truthfulness, found it to be rather uninviting. With only one small window to let in the sunlight and no hearth, the room was neither bright nor cozy. As usual, several of the walls were lined with bookshelves, though these were far from full. At first glance, one might have assumed this was because the Roscarrocks had not espoused reading, but books were not cheap, and just because a library was well stocked with numerous volumes did not mean they were read. I had strolled through libraries in the grand manor houses of some of the nobility that had contained over a thousand books, suspecting not even a tenth of them had ever been opened. Though, I had to concede, if any of these books were being read, it was probably not in this chamber.

Amelia perched on an oak settee upholstered in goldenrod damask positioned near the window which overlooked the drive, so she must have seen us return. Joan sat beside her knitting, but she set it aside as we joined them.

"Well, here we are," Lord Gage announced as we crowded into the entrance of the room behind him. There was a touch of annoyance in his voice. "And Cuttance will be along soon."

If this was meant to prod them into swift speech, it didn't work. Instead, Amelia gestured toward the sagging sofa opposite. "Have a seat."

We did so somewhat reluctantly, hovering at the edge so as not to sink so deep into its cushions that we could not extricate ourselves gracefully. My husband and his father might have also given some consideration to the mud splattering their lower extremities, but I'd decided the sofa was already beyond redemption.

We waited as Amelia seemed to struggle with herself. Or at

least, to give the appearance of it, for if she'd called us here, she must already know what she intended to say. "I didn't know at first that my brother 'ad faked his death," she finally began. "I didn't know 'til after he was already buried. Then he chose to reveal 'imself to me." Her hands had lifted to clutch something beneath the lace collar of her dress. I suspected it was a cross or a crucifix.

"That must have been quite a fright," I empathized. If I'd learned anything since being here, it was that many of the Cornish still believed in the old superstitions. After all, the plaster next to their windows still bore the traces of witch marks, and their droll tellers still weaved tails of mermaids and giants roaming the land.

"It was," she conceded. "'Til I accepted he was real." Her lips twisted. "Then I wanted to box his ears for pullin' such a trick. For keepin' it from me."

Judging from the crease that had formed in her forehead upon making this last statement, I suspected that was what bothered her most. Not the fact Branok had feigned his death, but that he'd not informed her of his plans.

I didn't look at him, but I felt a pulse of renewed irritation at Gage for not telling me of Anderley's ruse with the smugglers. It was not even close to the level of deception Branok had perpetrated, but it still vexed me. Recalling the anxiety and distress Anderley's behavior had caused me, I could only imagine the grief and pain Amelia had suffered in those days before she learned the truth. It was a wonder she hadn't killed him herself. Unless she had? But I didn't think so. At least, not for this alone.

"Why did he reveal himself?" Lord Gage queried when what I wanted to ask was why he *hadn't*. Undoubtedly, it was the same sort of rubbish about her not having an authentic reaction.

When Amelia didn't answer, instead eyeing him with misgiving, I guessed the truth. "He needed you to write to your nephew."

My father-in-law didn't react beyond the smoldering anger in his voice deepening. "He knew that of any of the members of my mother's family still living, the pleas of her sister were most likely to influence me."

Amelia at least had the grace to flush.

"But I still don't understand why," Gage stated impatiently. "*Why* did he need you to trick my father, trick *all* of us into coming here? What was so urgent that simply inviting us to come for a visit would not do?"

Joan scoffed. "Ye wouldn't 'ave come for a visit."

Amelia laid a quelling hand on her daughter-in-law's arm, but it was too late. We had already seen a glimpse of the animosity that festered beneath her seemingly indifferent façade.

"Perhaps my father would not have wanted to, but Kiera and I were already curious about you," Gage told them. "How could we not be? After all, fifty years is a long time. Things here might have been very different from what Father remembered."

I couldn't tell from Joan's expression whether she believed us or not, but Amelia nodded her head as if she'd suspected this all along.

"Branok didn't want to risk it," she said. Her pale gray eyes shifted to meet her nephew's. "He needed Stephen to come, and he decided feignin' his own death and makin' it look suspicious was 'is best bet."

"But why . . . ?" I began and she held up a quelling hand.

"Because he is . . ." She broke off, swallowing. "He *was* convinced that only Stephen knows where the treasure is hidden."

The room fell silent as we all seemed to struggle to digest this information.

"What treasure?" Lord Gage demanded after a few seconds.

"From the ship that wrecked against the rocks offshore near Rumps Point," Amelia told him, her raspy voice shaking slightly.

"You and Jago were movin' part of it the night he was . . . he was killed, and ye were arrested."

Lord Gage's eyes were wide with incomprehension. "No, we weren't. Those casks and barrels were filled with gin and brandy and silk, and all the usual contraband."

Amelia shook her head. "Not accordin' to Branok."

"I wasn't even here in Cornwall when that ship wrecked," Lord Gage protested firmly. "Though I do remember everyone talking about it."

"'Twasn't then, but later," Amelia insisted. "Ye were shiftin' it from its original hidin' place."

Lord Gage exploded up from his chair, scraping his hand back through his gray hair as he paced toward the door and then back. "No, I don't believe it. We were just boys. They wouldn't have trusted us to transport something so valuable." He came to an abrupt stop. The range of expressions that flitted across his countenance in those brief seconds told me his thoughts were much the same as mine. "Of course they would," he finally muttered in disgust.

Because two young lads were far less likely to be stopped or pursued than a pair of men.

"What was the treasure comprised of?" I asked.

"Gold and jewels and such." Amelia shared a look with Joan. "Branok was one of the few men still alive who knew exactly what, but from what little he revealed, it seems 'twas fairly a king's ransom."

I arched my eyebrows as I sardonically suggested, "The King of Portugal?"

It hadn't escaped my notice that the droll teller's tale about the wrecked ship and its treasure bore marked similarities to their claims. It also explained why the Killigrews had shown such pointed interest in Lord Gage's reaction to the story.

"Nay," Amelia replied, carefully studying her nephew, who

stood stone-faced in the middle of the room. "Though we did 'ope the droll teller's tale would jog your memory."

"And what?" Lord Gage bit out. "I would lead Bevil to the treasure."

"Aye," she answered softly.

Lord Gage was almost purple with rage. His hands clenched into fists at his sides. I couldn't blame him for his fury. I was angry, too, on *all* of our behalves. Though I was also battling the nerves and panic that always constricted my chest when faced with such raw ferocity. It helped that it wasn't directed at me, but it was all I could do to remain seated and keep my focus on the problem at hand.

Gage reached over to grip my hand, evidently sensing my uneasiness. "So that's why we're here? That's the reason for all the subterfuge?" His voice was taut but tempered. "But why didn't you simply try *asking* my father about it?"

"Branok was certain he wouldn't tell us." Amelia's wariness shifted to aggravation, an emotion Joan hadn't even bothered to hide. "And ye wouldn't 'ave, would ye?" she demanded of her nephew.

"No. Because whatever treasure there was—*if* there even was any—was confiscated by the customs officials," Lord Gage retorted. "We never *made* it to our intended destination. Jago was *killed*, you'll recall. And I was beaten, trussed up, and *arrested*."

I flinched at his revelation of these additional details.

"Branok claimed you and Jago set off with a cart and eight casks, and the preventives only seized two," Amelia countered.

Lord Gage scoffed. "Then they lied."

But Amelia persisted as if he'd not spoken. "That before Jago died, he'd indicated that once you'd realized ye were bein' followed, you'd stashed what cargo ye could before they caught up to ye and then ye tried to run."

All of the color seemed to drain from my father-in-law's face, and he staggered back a step. Alarmed, I reached for his hand, guiding him back to the sofa, which he sank down onto with a thud.

"You remember now?" Joan asked, misunderstanding. There was a subtle undertone of snideness in her voice.

"Jago was still alive when they reached him?" he stammered.

"You didn't know?" I replied gently, clasping his cold fingers between mine.

He shook his head, staring blindly at the worn rug. "They . . . the officers . . . they told me he was dead. Maybe there was more, but I . . . I can't recall."

"There was nothing you could have done," I reminded him. Not if he was being beaten and bound.

"I might have fought harder."

It was a feeble notion, but one I knew he would stubbornly hold fast to.

"One eleven-year-old boy against three or four men?" Gage interjected. "They would only have beaten you more severely and possibly killed you, too."

"You . . . you *were* insensible for a time," Amelia admitted. "They let me into your holdin' cell long enough to bind your wounds," she said. "But once ye woke, they wouldn't allow any of us to return. Though Father and his solicitor put enough of the fear of God into the magistrate and the preventives to deter 'em from ever touchin' even a hair on your head again."

I could tell by the look on Lord Gage's face that he had never been told any of this before.

"How long was he insensible?" Gage asked.

"Oh, but a few hours," Amelia replied, feebly attempting to make light of a matter that was far from it.

"Then he might genuinely not remember what happened to the contraband they were transporting," I said, still clutching Lord Gage's hands. "If he suffered a blow to his head—and the fact that he was rendered insensible for a time suggests that he did—he might not recall that night or the events surrounding it clearly. He might quite literally have lost his wits for a time."

I could tell from my father-in-law's frown that he didn't appreciate my efforts to explain his forgetfulness about such a critical event, even fifty years hence.

"If there really is lost treasure," Gage countered doubtfully, "surely they've searched for it. There can't be that many places two boys could have hidden it on that stretch of coast. Especially if they were being pursued by riding officers."

"They 'ave," Amelia said.

"And?"

"They've not found more than a dozen gold coins, and all those washed up on the beach, probably from the original wreck."

"In nearly fifty years searching they've only found a dozen coins?" Gage reiterated, meeting my gaze.

"Aye."

"And Branok is the only one who claims this treasure even truly existed?"

"He's the only Roscarrock from that time still alive." Her brow furrowed. "Or rather he *was*. But my father and my husband—God rest their souls—both knew about it. And I remember the storm. I remember the wrecked ship. And there are a number of Grenvilles still livin' who do as well. A number who saw the treasure." She scowled ferociously. "Though don't be countin' on 'em to tell ye the truth of the matter. Not when they're just as anxious to find it and keep it for themselves."

Joan agreed. "'Tis why Tamsyn . . ." she nearly spat her name ". . . is so determined to stir up trouble." Her eyes narrowed. "The Grenvilles want that treasure for their own, and doubtless, they killed Branok to make sure of it."

Lord Gage's fingers tightened where I still clutched them

and his brow lowered, making it clear what he thought of these accusations. "Seems to me, she's the only one who's been honest with me since I arrived."

"Only 'cause it benefits her," Amelia replied. "'Tisn't out of the goodness of her heart."

Joan shook her head. "You always were blind to her and all of their wiles. 'Tis what came of allowin' ye to associate with 'em so much."

Lord Gage opened his mouth to argue, but Joan wasn't finished.

"What if I told ye 'twas the Grenvilles who betrayed you and Jago that night. 'Twas *them* who informed the preventives of Granfer's plans to move the treasure. They just didn't know it was to be you and Jago to do it."

"What reasons would they have to do so?" Lord Gage argued. "Part of that treasure was theirs?"

"Aye, but not the lion's share." Joan picked up the knitting she'd laid in her lap. "They made a deal with old Cuttance. He and the other preventives could keep the bulk as long as the Grenvilles still got their cut."

"I don't believe it," Lord Gage replied, shaking his head.

"Then you're a fool," Joan said, her needles clacking together loudly.

Amelia reached over to rest a hand on Joan's leg, staying her. "Ye can't blame 'im, Joan," Amelia told her calmly. "Tamsyn may have lost much of her beauty, but she's still an artful woman." She sighed. "I would forswear the entire matter completely, but we cannot let the treasure fall into their 'ands." Her hand tightened into a fist, and she pounded her leg in emphasis. "Not if they killed my brother in order to get it."

"Even if ye did forswear it, Mery wouldn't give up so easily," Joan groused, her eyes still fastened on her clacking needles.

Amelia's expression turned grim. "He's nearly as obsessed as Branok was. He must see it as his legacy."

Joan snorted. "More like fair game and less work for him."

Listening to their exchange, it would be easy to fall prey to these convenient suspicions they'd woven for us. After all, the Roscarrocks' feud with the Grenvilles was common knowledge. Dolly and Imogen had mentioned a young lad—possibly Jago—had been killed several decades ago because of a dispute between the two families. There was also no denying that ostensibly Mery *did* have the most to gain from his grandfather's death. However, their banter had the quality of a stage play. One enacted for our benefit. And I was suddenly quite certain that everything they'd just said had been in a desperate effort to save the Killigrews' skins. It would have been tempting to ignore their accusations entirely, except for the fact there were some grains of truth.

I was glad to hear they weren't persisting in Bevil's allegations that Lord Gage was the culprit, but then again, that didn't mean they wouldn't tell Cuttance or the magistrate something entirely different. Or hold it over his head as a threat if he didn't lead them to this treasure.

In any case, at least now we knew why we'd been lured here. As such, it was time to reassess our situation. A number of Amelia's revelations—the ones that rang true—had plainly rattled Lord Gage, and I was anxious to speak with him privately, but before I could make our excuses, he jumped to his feet.

"I knew we shouldn't have come here. I told you what they were like. I told you they couldn't be trusted." He stormed from the room, forcing Gage and I to hurry after him. I didn't bother to apologize to Amelia or Joan for our hasty departure. They didn't deserve it.

"Father," Gage called after him as he strode through the

adjoining room and out to the inner courtyard. "Father!" he shouted again, grasping his arm.

Lord Gage rounded on him. "I told you something would go wrong. Didn't I? But *you* knew better." His disdainful gaze shifted to me. "Well, now you see."

I did see, but not necessarily what he wanted. I saw that he was not only angry but confused and dazed and hurt. The pain of the past that he'd thought he'd put behind him, the grief for the friend he thought he'd mourned, even the truth he'd believed he'd known about himself and his mother's family—*all* of it had been overset and dredged up inside him, swirling about in a bewildering vortex. So rather than allow his fury to keep me at a distance as it normally would, I stepped into it. I stepped into the vortex and embraced it and embraced him.

At first, he stiffened, clearly not having expected such an action. I was prepared for him to thrust me away or to demand that Gage remove me, and I hugged him tighter, breathing through the terror that bristled across my nerves at being in such close proximity to an irate male. His chest heaved in and out, and his muscles tensed as if for flight. But then he did an equally unexpected thing, though it was exactly what I'd hoped for. His shoulders drooped, his arms raised, and he embraced me back.

Ridiculously, I felt my throat grow tight and my eyes begin to burn. He was nothing like my father, and yet, hugging him was a little bit like hugging my father all the same. And it had been a very long time since I'd been able to do so. Nearly five years.

I had just fully settled into his embrace, feeling the constriction in my chest ease and release, when he loosened his grip, taking a half step back. He didn't disengage completely, keeping a firm grasp on my arms lest I not be steady, but I could sense his discomfort in having shown so much emotion.

Or perhaps it was mistrust instead. Mistrust of the eyes that might be watching us. His gaze lifted to the upper story, scrutinizing the windows. However, the angle of our vantage made it difficult to tell if anyone stood behind the oily glass.

I turned to Gage, expecting him to be studying our surroundings with the same suspicion, but I found instead that his eyes were fastened on me. The tenderness written there warmed me from within.

"Amelia's revelations were quite the shock, weren't they?" Gage ventured, returning to the reason for all of our conflict.

Lord Gage's flinty stare shifted from the edifice to his son.

"You truly didn't know about the treasure, did you? Or the rest?" I murmured gently. There was no need to put the disclosures about Jago's death into words. Not when they'd already caused him enough pain.

His attention dipped to me, and the furrow in his brow softened. "No."

Lord Gage had toyed with the concept of truth often enough in the past that it was difficult to take him at his word, but this time I believed him. His reactions had simply been too raw, too sincere. However, that didn't mean he wasn't still withholding information.

"Is everything that occurred that night hazy, or is there more you haven't shared with us?" I asked. He had already resisted answering a form of this question, but I had suspected that was from a desire to avoid the pain of remembrance. Since that had already been thrust upon him, I hoped he might prove more cooperative.

His gaze darted to the windows above again, and I wondered who he was most concerned might be watching. "Not here."

"Your sitting room, then," I suggested, but he was already shaking his head.

"I need to speak with Tamsyn."

"Now?" Gage replied somewhat incredulously.

His father turned to glare at him, his jaw set. "Yes."

Gage glanced at me. "Then we'll come with you."

His father turned his head, already striding toward the exit to the stables. "No. It's better if I go alone."

"Better for whom?" I challenged.

He stopped, turning to scowl at me.

I still wasn't certain he wasn't using Tamsyn as an excuse to escape our questions, but whether or not that was true, considering the allegations Amelia had just made about the Grenvilles, marching off alone to speak to her seemed the height of folly. Not to mention the fact his perspective seemed to be skewed when it came to the subject of his late friend's cousin. His view of her was clouded by the past and the complex swirl of emotions remembering it all evoked. He would be better served by taking someone with him who could remain objective. Someone the Grenvilles might think twice before harming.

Lord Gage must have been conscious of at least some of these points, though he chose to focus on the most apparent. "I would sooner trust Tamsyn than I would any Roscarrocks."

"Maybe so, but that doesn't make her trustworthy."

His scowl deepened.

"Kiera's right," Gage told him. "At least take one of us with you. If not me, then Kiera. She might be the better choice anyway. She sees the world differently than you or me."

I knew that he meant this as a compliment, but having my differences pointed out always smarted, no matter the source or their intentions. It stemmed from being scorned and derided as unnatural for too much of my life.

However, Lord Gage couldn't argue the truth of this statement, nor how beneficial this fact had proven to be in past inquiries. So he begrudgingly gave his consent, urging us to follow through the arch in the curtain wall and out into the outer courtyard. There, our attention was diverted by the sight of Anderley speaking to a man next to the squat tower which housed the malting floor.

Given their ruse that Anderley was an incalcitrant servant who had been shirking his duties, Gage could hardly pass by without saying something. He drew up short, scuffling the dirt beneath his boot heel. "Anderley," he barked. "A word."

Anderley's dark gaze flicked to us, settling into a deep scowl. One that would have set my stomach churning had I not now known the truth, but I was careful to affix my features into an expression of mild affront and concern. The man standing with him in laborman's garb melted away, but Anderley maintained his belligerent façade, trudging toward his employer.

Gage lowered his voice, turning his head to speak over his shoulder to me. "It might be best if you left this matter to us." His eyes met his father's, seeming to realize he wouldn't be able to force him to join me, that he would have to inform him of Anderley's ploy as well. "We'll send for you when we're ready to depart."

I nodded, backing away, but not before Anderley's gaze caught mine. I could sense distress beneath his insolent stare, though I didn't know if that was due to my presence or something else entirely. It blunted some of the anger I felt at his having lied to Bree, and I found myself wishing I could offer him some sort of reassurance to ease his mind. I turned away before I could give in to the impulse.

CHAPTER 26

Not knowing how long Gage intended to speak with Anderley, I knew I couldn't venture far. But there was *one* matter I could see to.

Passing through the parlor, I spied a maid through the dining room door, straightening the tablecloth. When I asked if she knew where I could find Bree, she directed me to the walled garden.

Crossing the raised terrace, I descended the steps into the rectangular lower garden surrounded by a squared ashlar border. A riot of late-autumn blooms battled with foliage in shades of burning reds and golden yellows, masking Bree's position until I neared the far end, where a small outbuilding stood surrounded by beech and rowan trees. It was a lovely, secluded spot, and I found Bree sitting on one of a pair of benches nestled beneath the bower of trees, a tartan shawl draped around her shoulders as she stared rather forlornly into the distance at the overcast skies.

She turned at the sound of my approach, and her eyes widened as she surged to her feet. "Apologies, m'lady. I didna think you'd be returnin' for some time yet. Did ye send for me?"

"No, no. Sit," I said, perching on the stone bench beside her. "It turned out we didn't have far to search for Mr. Cuttance."

"Aye. He arrived at Dr. Wolcott's just as I was leavin'. What did he say?"

I filled her in on what the constable had told us, and then shared what Great-Aunt Amelia had claimed about the treasure. Bree's pale, freckled cheeks regained some of her color as I spoke, and her eyes sparkled with an interest I almost regretted having to dim. But she needed to hear the truth.

"Have you heard any of the staff speaking about such a treasure?" I asked, trying to ease my way around to the topic I most wished to address.

"No' since the droll teller weaved that tale o' a wrecked ship." She narrowed her eyes. "Was that on purpose?"

I cast her a sardonic look. "Supposedly to jog Lord Gage's memory."

She scoffed. "Seems a rather convoluted way to go aboot it."

"I agree, but then there are quite a number of things about the Roscarrocks I don't understand." Such as, why all the secrecy when plain speaking would achieve better results? I understood they were mistrustful of outsiders, and Lord Gage in particular, but their stubborn furtiveness bordered on imprudence.

"I'll see what I can find oot aboot any treasure or wrecks from those on the staff who'll talk to me." Bree's brow furrowed. "But ye might ask Mr. Gage to have a word wi' Anderley aboot it as well." She grunted. "If he'll listen."

I cleared my throat. "Speaking of Anderley." I turned to peer around at the rest of the garden to make sure we were still alone, and then lowered my voice. "He's pretending. Mr. Gage asked him to ingratiate himself with the men on the Roscarrock staff who also act as smugglers. To gain their trust and . . . insinuate himself into their crew." I wanted to reach out to her in sympathy, but the way in which she'd straightened, her back turning ramrod stiff, I knew she wouldn't welcome it. "I'm sorry. I just found out."

She searched my features, slowly nodding. "Aye, I ken you were just as concerned as I was."

This wasn't strictly true, for I knew how Bree felt about my husband's valet. I knew her emotions toward him were more than lukewarm, even if she had been reticent to give sway to them completely. Just as I had seen how his behavior since the evening of the party had hurt her.

"I suppose his ramshackle behavior was his way o' showin' hoo much he despised ye and hoo little he cared for your, for *any* o' our good opinions," she deduced, preventing me from having to explain it. Resentment glinted in her eyes. "An' let me guess. He and Mr. Gage didna trust us to be skillful enough actresses no' to give him away."

I didn't bother to hide my own still-simmering irritation. "You would be correct."

She crossed her arms. "Weel, then. Perhaps I need to show him just hoo good an actress I can be."

Hearing the biting malice in her voice, I decided I was glad I wasn't Anderley.

"As long as it doesn't risk placing him in greater danger," I cautioned. "After all, I know how much he cares for you, and we don't want him breaking character."

Her nostrils flared in anger, likely wondering as I had how a man who cared for her so much could fail to consider her feelings before agreeing to undertake such an assignment. But then just as swiftly as it sparked, her fury abated, the embers dimmed by her obvious concern.

This time I didn't stop myself from reaching for her hand.

"Gage won't let anything happen to him," I assured her, praying my husband wouldn't make a liar out of me.

She stared down at our joined hands for a moment. "I'm sure Anderley kenned the risks when he agreed to such a task." She looked up at me. "Mr. Gage would no' have forced him to do it. Just as *you* didna force me to take on that task in Argyll when I was poisoned."

My hand squeezed hers in memory of that horrible night, when she'd nearly died.

"My point bein', we ken what risks we shoulder workin' for you and Mr. Gage. We willingly accept them." Her gaze dipped briefly before she forced it to meet mine again. "But that doesna mean it's easy to accept them on another's behalf."

With this, she pushed to her feet and walked away, leaving me to stare after her.

She wasn't wrong, and I knew it. Very well. After all, how many times had I found my fear of the risks Gage undertook greater than those I did? Somehow it was easier to stomach such danger when you yourself decided to face it rather than when a loved one made that choice. I suspected it had to do with the nature of power and control. As human beings, we always wanted to be the ones to exert it, and when it was exerted on us or in spite of us, we resisted.

Bree also wasn't wrong that with every inquiry we investigated, we placed everyone in our household at risk—be they family or staff. While we never hid this potential for danger from our servants—and, in fact, had gained several employees at least partially *because* of it—were we not just a little bit selfish for not giving greater consideration to how our actions affected them all? Yes, they could always find employment with a more mundane household, and we would happily supply them with a reference to do so, but wasn't that merely absolving ourselves of responsibility in another way?

296 · *Anna Lee Huber*

Where was the line between a proper amount of concern and stifling productivity? Particularly considering we didn't take on these murderous inquiries for our own edification, but more often than not to achieve justice for the deceased and safeguard the security of the living.

I pressed a hand to my forehead, recognizing these were not questions that were going to be answered today. Not when there were more pressing matters to contend with. I made my way back toward the house, climbing the steps to the terraced garden and turning toward the side door when I spotted a flash of color out of the corner of my eye. It had come from the direction of the granite-topped gate piers, and I elected to divert my course out of curiosity.

As I drew closer, I could hear voices conferring softly. Female voices. I slowed my steps, curious if I could make out what they were saying. But autumn was not the most conducive season for stealth. Not when over half the trees had already divested themselves of their foliage. Even damp leaves squelched. Their voices abruptly silenced, and there was nothing for it but for me to reveal myself, lest they think I was deliberately spying. One glimpse around the old piers and they would see me anyway.

"Kiera," Dolly exclaimed as I rounded the corner. She pressed a hand to her chest. "Ye gave me a fright."

"My apologies," I murmured, uncertain exactly what I was apologizing for. They were standing just outside the garden, in the open, and there hadn't been time for me to overhear anything before they realized I was near.

My gaze shifted to Morgan. Her ash-blond hair fell over her shoulder in a thick braid, and she clutched an empty basket in her hands.

"Delivering apples?" I guessed. Or at least utilizing it as a pretense.

She didn't flinch from my questioning gaze, though her stoic expression revealed little else.

Instead, Dolly answered for her. "Aye. Mrs. Hicks intends to bake them into pasties." Her voice was just a shade too bright, which only made me even more curious about what they'd been discussing. But if I asked about it, I knew Morgan would prevent Dolly from answering.

So I bided my time, settling on another topic of interest. "Amelia told us about the treasure."

Dolly's pert nose wrinkled in what appeared to be confusion, and even Morgan's brow creased slightly, though I couldn't tell if this was out of annoyance or puzzlement.

"The one Branok was searching for," I explained further. "The reason he lured all of us here under false pretenses."

Dolly's mouth formed into an O as her cousin replied. "We didn't know Branok 'ad faked his death. We were just as shocked as you were."

I searched Morgan's hazel eyes, intrigued to discover they were very similar to Mery's. Not only in shape and color, but in the acuity and guardedness that swam hand in hand in their depths.

"I know," I said, adjusting the drape of the train of my riding habit over my arm. As necessary as they were to preserve one's modesty while riding sidesaddle, they were annoying to manage when not mounted. "But I wondered if either of you had heard about the treasure. After all, nearly fifty years is a long time to keep such a thing secret. Especially when you haven't been plotting all that time to feign your death to trick your estranged nephew into returning."

Dolly appeared slightly stricken by my blunt speech, but Morgan remained unmoved.

"Of course we've heard the rumors," Dolly admitted. "Though the men tend to avoid talkin' about it in our company." She glanced at Morgan either in confirmation or to ensure she wasn't saying anything she shouldn't. "I know they've gone out to search for it from time to time. I suppose whenever someone suggests a new hiding place, or it strikes their fancy. Or rather, Branok's fancy. He's always the instigator."

"When isn't he?" Morgan muttered dryly, bemusing us both given her previous apathy.

After a few moments' silence, Dolly continued. "It's always been obvious there are things they're not sayin', but that's true of just about everythin' in this family." Her sigh was one of resignation but also frustration. "I've never been sure whether they think they're protectin' us, or they don't want to risk our opinions weighing on their conscience."

Morgan didn't try to answer or correct this assertion, perhaps because it was too astute not to simply let it stand.

Dolly shook her head. "I'm afraid I don't know anything more. Though I am sorry for the way this 'as all been handled. You've been nothin' but 'elpful." Her expression turned wary, and I could sense there was more she wished to say, though she didn't seem to know how to voice it. "How *did* Branok die?" she finally settled on.

I remembered then the way she and the others had looked at me the previous evening, knowing I was about to go off and examine Branok's corpse—to touch it and do who knew what else to it. Like most people, her fear and disgust warred with her curiosity. There had been no dissection or autopsy, but as there was no polite way to say this, I was forced to convey it in a different manner and hope she understood.

"He was stabbed in the back. The cause of death would have been obvious even to the untrained eye."

Tears glimmered in her round eyes and her throat worked as she swallowed. "Would . . . would he 'ave suffered?"

"Not for long."

There was no way I could have known this for certain, and from the look on Morgan's face, I could tell she realized this. But it seemed the kindest answer, particularly given Dolly's distress.

"You 'ad a long night and an early mornin', dearest," Morgan crooned to her cousin. "Why don't ye go lie down and 'ave a rest."

Dolly swiped at her cheeks with one hand while she draped the other around her stomach. It rested there for no longer than a second or two, but it was enough to make me believe that her maid Cora's suspicions had been correct. Dolly was expecting another child.

"Perhaps I should," she agreed before excusing herself to make her way back to the house.

I remained behind with Morgan, filtering through the possible implications of this discovery. If there were any.

"Ye lied," Morgan said once Dolly was out of earshot.

I turned to look at her.

"About Branok not sufferin'."

It wasn't a challenge, but a statement, and I answered in the same reserved tone. "Maybe."

She didn't press, but I could tell that her regard for me had just increased.

"Do you know anything else about the treasure?" I asked, taking advantage of it. After all, Morgan was Joan's daughter, and even though she no longer lived here, she had spent the first approximately twenty years of her life at Roscarrock House, and I strongly suspected she still held her mother's confidences.

She turned toward the lane, and I fell in step with her. "Only that Branok was determined to find it even after all this time." She frowned. "The older he grew, the more preoccupied he seemed to become by it."

I pondered this for a moment as our feet sliced through the

overgrown grass. "What about your husband? Was he party to Branok's intentions?"

Morgan waited for me to meet her gaze. "Nay. But ye already know that." She arched her eyebrows, daring me to contradict her. "What ye really want to ask about is my husband returnin' early."

I wasn't surprised she'd deduced this. I even appreciated her blunt speaking. "I understand he returned from St. Austell yesterday afternoon."

She nodded. "He did. Came straight home."

"After a meeting with Mr. Cuttance."

This succeeded in shocking her. Her head whipped around to stare at me, and I was hard-pressed not to feel a sense of satisfaction, though I at least tried not to let it show.

Morgan scowled. "I warned Mr. Knill that man couldn't be trusted. Cuttance would give up 'is own son to save his skin." Her lip curled in disgust. "I presume he needed an alibi."

"Which also provides your husband with one."

"Why would he . . . ?" She broke off, scrutinizing me unhappily, before turning away. "I see. Then I suppose ye want one for me?"

"Do you have one?"

"Not unless my staff and the apple trees count."

"I'm afraid not." Employees' silence could be bought or compelled. And apple trees . . . well, as far as I knew, they'd yet to develop the ability to see or talk.

"Then I'm a suspect." She sounded more disgruntled than troubled by the idea.

"Did you kill Branok?" I asked, deciding to offer her the same courtesy of bluntness.

She halted, turning to glare at me. "Nay."

"Did you have any reason to kill Branok?"

"Of course no—" Some of her affront faded and she answered me honestly. "Aye."

"Because you and your husband were informing Cuttance about Branok's smuggling operations."

Morgan flushed guiltily before arching her chin. "Aye," she stated defiantly. "'Twas the right thing to do."

"Because you're dissenters?"

She scowled again. "Because Branok was reckless and riskin' the lives and livelihoods of everyone on 'is crews." She huffed. "Smugglin' has gone on for far too long along this coast, largely unchecked, save for the incident with your father-in-law and his efforts to destroy the Roscarrock fleet back durin' the Peace of Amiens. But it carries on to this day, to no one's benefit. 'Tis time it was put to an end once and for all."

"*Can* it be stopped?" I asked, and then cut her off when she would have offered me a glib response. "Really and truly stopped?"

Her mouth fell shut, evidently sensing I had a point.

"After all, just because no one around here is benefiting doesn't mean someone *else* isn't."

"Ye think someone else is fundin' the enterprise?" she asked, quickly grasping my implication.

I turned the question back on her. "Is there?"

She didn't answer immediately, instead turning to gaze out over the rain-dampened fields as she turned the matter over in her mind. "Maybe," she eventually murmured, and for a moment I thought she was mocking my response to her query about Branok's suffering. But then she scraped a hand down her face before admitting, "Probably. Though I have no idea who they could be."

I believed her. "Who is in charge of the smuggling ring now that Branok's dead? Mery? Your father?"

I could tell that Morgan was deeply troubled by this question. "Mery inherits everything, but the men don't respect 'im. Which leaves my father as the most likely leader." A deep furrow split her brow. "Unless one of the Grenvilles angles to take over."

"Which Grenville? Gil?"

"Maybe. But with his gammy leg, 'tis more likely to be . . . Tamsyn." She grimaced. "Ye might have noticed she's also more charmin' than Father."

I wasn't as surprised by this notion as perhaps I should have been. I think the realization that Tamsyn was much more than she seemed had been percolating at the back of my brain for some time. It was evident in the way she held herself, in the way others addressed her, in the way the other Grenvilles deferred to her. Some of the Roscarrocks might not like it or her. They might be happy to belittle and scorn her behind her back. But they were aware she was not one to trifle with. She was also far too knowledgeable about everything around her not to play some significant part.

And yes, she was definitely more charming than Bevil. I'd noted his awkwardness on multiple occasions, his lack of sociability. Which, regardless of fairness, played a role in those chosen as leaders and those who were not.

Mery, on the other hand, was made to seem more influential, more menacing than he really was. He might be the heir, but as I'd suspected, he was naught more than a bit player.

"Then why does everyone keep pointing the finger at Mery?" I asked, suspecting that of all the Roscarrocks and Killigrews—past and present—Morgan was the most likely to give me a straight answer.

She turned away, but not before I could read the shame in her eyes. "I think ye can guess why."

Because of the inheritance. Because all of it went to Mery and none to the rest of them. No matter that it was also their home. No matter that they did the majority of the work to keep it running. It was not a noble admission, no matter how unfair it was, so I didn't press her further.

She carried on down the lane, the clouds scuttling across the sky ahead of her. I watched her until she disappeared over a rise and then turned to trudge back toward the house. Gage and his father would undoubtedly be looking for me by now. In truth, I would be lucky if my father-in-law, in his impatience, hadn't insisted they set off without me. And I suddenly wanted very much to hear what Tamsyn Grenville Kellynack had to say for herself.

CHAPTER 27

"Of course your aunt would make such claims about us," Tamsyn declared after giving a derisive laugh. "She couldn't very well point the finger back at her own family," she jeered, settling back in her armchair.

Upon our arrival at her home, I'd been surprised and then intrigued to find her dressed in breeches. Even more surprising, Lord Gage had barely batted an eyelash at it, remarking, "You always did prefer men's attire."

"Because it's far more comfortable," she'd replied breezily, leading us into the chamber that served as her drawing room. "Far more practical as well. Kiera, dear," she addressed me, "I see that I've shocked ye."

"Not shocked me, no. It's just . . . unexpected," I settled on. In truth, I was trying to imagine my father-in-law reacting with such aplomb to *my* appearing in a pair of trousers, let alone receiving visitors in them. I tilted my head, studying the garment where it molded to Tamsyn's thighs. "Though I admit I have wondered what they would feel like."

Time and again, I had contemplated how much more suitable men's clothing was to the act of painting. It was bad enough that I had to contend with the puffed sleeves which were now so in vogue, but my skirts also hampered my movements as I worked on the portraits in my studio. How freeing it would be to wear just a pair of breeches, a chemisette, a linen shirt, and perhaps a waistcoat.

"Then ye should try them," Tamsyn told me. "Gentlemen always make such a fuss at the notion, but find that they're not opposed to the idea once they see the results."

I peered over my shoulder at my husband, curious about his reaction, only to find his eyes fastened on my lower extremities. I arched a single eyebrow, pursing my lips in amusement as his gaze lifted to meet mine. It seemed I had my answer. Though it remained to be seen how much painting I would be getting done if I tried wearing such garments with my husband nearby.

But observing Tamsyn now—holding court in her agreeable, but far from opulent, drawing room, deriding Great-Aunt Amelia—I suspected she wore breeches for a far different reason than mere practicality. For one, they were symbolic. For another, they at least allowed for the illusion that you were conferring with a man. If any of the Grenville males resisted the idea of being led by a woman, perhaps this helped them delude themselves into believing it actually wasn't so.

"What do you mean, pointing the finger back at her own family?" I asked, curious what version of events she had to tell.

"We all know it was Swithun who betrayed us about the treasure."

"Branok's brother?" Gage clarified. "The one who immigrated to Pennsylvania?"

"Aye," Tamsyn confirmed, leaning forward to brace her elbows on her knees. "Why do ye think he suddenly up and immigrated? When we discovered the truth, your granfer 'ad to send 'im far away before we could take revenge."

"But why?" I asked in bewilderment. "Why would Swithun betray his own family?"

"Because he wanted Branok out of the way. That was the deal he made with the preventives. With Branok dead, that would clear the way for Swithun to inherit." She picked up an apple from the table beside her and produced a knife from somewhere on her person to begin slowly peeling the red skin in one long curl. "There are some in the family who would've preferred it that way."

Considering how little Branok was liked, this was not difficult to believe. If his son Casworan had not yet been born, that left a clear path for Swithun to inherit. But if Branok had been the target, that didn't explain how everything had gone so terribly wrong and Jago was killed instead of him. Unless . . .

"Who ordered you and Jago to transport the contraband that night?" I asked my father-in-law.

He looked up at me, having been lost in his own thoughts, and it seemed to take him a moment to grasp the implications of my question. "I . . . I'm not certain I recall. But it was probably either my grandfather or . . . or Uncle Branok." His jaw hardened with anger, but I could also see the hurt and disillusionment glinting in his eyes.

If Branok had discovered his brother Swithun's betrayal, if he'd known the preventives intended to ambush him that night and had sent Jago and his nephew Stephen out instead . . .

"Maybe he thought the authorities would be more lenient to two boys," Gage suggested, but I could tell that even he thought this excuse flimsy at best.

Tamsyn, meanwhile, was eyeing us all avidly as she finished

peeling her apple. She put me in mind of a spider spinning her web, and for that fact and that fact alone, I doubted the veracity of her claims. Though I had to concede her cleverness in accusing someone who rather conveniently lived thousands of miles away and could not defend himself.

Whatever the truth of that night, Tamsyn was undoubtedly seeking to use the situation that now lay before us to her benefit. But while I was leery of her and Gage seemed guarded, Lord Gage appeared to swallow everything she said whole. At least, he gave no indication of mistrust. And that infuriated me, for she was playing on their past friendship and their mutual close connection to Jago to manipulate him. Just as she continued to do with her next statement.

"Bein' too young at the time, I was never privy to the specifics. But it's interestin' to note that Jago was the one they shot," she drawled, rubbing more salt into the wound.

"Yet I was taller," Lord Gage supplied, clearly filling in the gaps in her implications.

"But surely that's just a coincidence," I protested, finding her insinuations to be a step too far. "All of this happened in the dark of night, remember. The preventive officers must have fired their weapons at your fleeing figures, likely still believing one of you to be Branok, and happened to hit Jago."

"And once they realized they'd not gotten Branok, as promised, they took out their anger and frustration on you," Gage supplied, watching his father closely.

"They hadn't gotten the treasure either," I reminded them. "Not much of it, anyway."

"Nay," Tamsyn replied as if it had been a question. "No' unless old Cuttance was better at keepin' secrets than any of us believed."

"What do *you* know about the treasure?" I queried, resisting the urge to scowl at the crossed cutlasses hung over the fireplace behind her. The lack of art hanging in the room was another thing I was struggling not to tally against her. I'd considered the possibility that she or the Grenvilles had been forced to sell such works, but there were no faded marks on the walls to indicate their absence. A house this size should have boasted at least half a dozen portraits and landscapes, but thus far, I'd seen none. And people who eschewed art of even the frugal variety made me suspicious.

"Only that it came from a wrecked ship." Her mouth quirked wryly. "Albeit not from the King of Portugal."

So the droll teller's tale had prodded her memory as well. Though I noticed she hadn't mentioned anything about it to us until now.

"'Twas the talk of this stretch of the coast all that winter. Half the populace must've traveled up to 'elp pick it clean once the worst of the storm had died down. I wanted to go, but my granny forbade it. Made me angrier than a wasp. Ye must remember it," she told Lord Gage.

He shook his head. "I vaguely remember talk of it when I came to visit during Easter holiday."

"That's right. Ye were back home in Devon when that tempest hit." Her eyes took on a faraway cast as if seeing into the past. "'Twas a fierce one. Blew for almost three days straight. Must've been dozens of ships driven into the rocks offshore and wrecked all up and down the coast of Cornwall."

"Were any of the crew saved?" I asked.

"Aye. Several dozen, includin' the captain. Though they were none too 'appy to watch their cargo disappear across the beach and up over the cliffs. For months after, there were preventive officers and soldiers and the like sniffin' all over the area tryin' to locate it."

If that was true, then it was no wonder the Roscarrocks had waited so long before attempting to transport the treasure from wherever they'd originally hid it. I eyed my father-in-law. It also explained why the magistrate had been so hard on Lord Gage when he sentenced him. It hadn't been any ordinary cargo he'd been apprehended with in his possession. Someone had to pay, and sadly it had been him.

I wondered if he was having similar thoughts. Judging from his pained expression, he seemed to be contemplating something of the sort. Or maybe Tamsyn's words were helping him to remember what he believed he'd forgotten. Perhaps the memories were still trapped somewhere in his brain, he just needed a pick, a prod to help unbury them from the rubble of that difficult time and the sediment of all the years since.

"Did you and Jago ever talk about the treasure with his lordship?" I asked Tamsyn while observing my father-in-law's reaction.

He immediately scowled, first at me and then at his old friend when she answered. "All the time. One of our favorite games was to speculate 'ow much treasure there was and where it was hidden. We even searched for it ourselves. Though we rightly suspected our parents and grandparents would've whipped us if they'd known what we were doin'."

"I don't remember any of that," he objected.

She tsked. "*You* were the worst of us. Always makin' plans to scour one site or another. First that abandoned cottage near Pentireglaze, then the barrows near Hayle Bay, and the mine shafts at Doyden Point. Even a pair of sea caves we almost drowned tryin' to swim into."

Lord Gage had shaken his head through all this and now pushed to his feet. "I told you I don't remember!"

Tamsyn glared up at him. "Maybe ye don't want to."

He strode indignantly out of the room, and Gage excused himself to follow.

I hesitated a moment. Perhaps I shouldn't have pried, but

anything and everything seemed to vex the man lately. Not that I blamed him. There was a lot to be vexed about. But it was difficult to grasp what would help him, to know when to push and when to relent.

"He'll remember when he's ready."

I turned to find Tamsyn watching me. Despite the compassion glinting in her eyes, I'd not forgotten my suspicions about her or the way she was attempting to influence my father-in-law. "And if he doesn't?" Either because he couldn't or because there was actually nothing *to* remember.

Her lips curled into a private smile. "I think we both know the answer to that."

What I *knew* was that she meant to imply Lord Gage was hiding something. But I wasn't about to let the woman sow her sly seeds of suspicion in me. I wasn't fertile soil.

Rising from the settee, I thanked her and turned to leave, but her voice stopped me at the threshold. "A word of advice, Mrs. Gage."

It didn't escape my notice that she'd called me Kiera but minutes earlier. "Now, why does it sound like you meant to say 'a word of warning,'" I rejoined.

Tamsyn shrugged one shoulder. "It's your choice how ye choose to interpret it. I merely meant to counsel ye to take a closer look at those nearer to home. After all, Branok wasn't the only one determined to find that treasure. And if he was desperate enough to fake his own death to draw his nephew and his family here, how desperate do ye think the others will be now that Branok's ploy didn't work?"

The hairs along the back of my neck stood on end, but I was determined not to show her she'd unnerved me. "Where were you yesterday between four and six o'clock?" It was a question we'd neglected to ask, and one that needed answering, though I already knew not to trust whatever answer she gave.

She laughed shortly. "*I'm* the least of your troubles. But if ye must know . . ." Her eyes narrowed. "I never left Grenville land."

Her relish of that statement was incongruent with its substance, which made me suspect there was some hidden meaning I didn't yet understand. So I simply turned to go, and then wondered if I was as foolish as Branok had been turning his back on his killer.

Much as I tried not to let Tamsyn's words affect me, I found myself increasingly chary of those around me and questioning whether we should even still be there. No one had raised the suspicion of Lord Gage being the murderer since Bevil's shouted accusations early that morning. Mr. Cuttance hadn't even bothered to question him, though he seemed to be investigating Branok's latest death with far more fervor than he had his previous feigned one. Perhaps it would be best to simply leave the matter in his hands.

But then I would spy Dolly's anxious features or hear Bevil's fractious voice. Suspect or no suspect, his uncle's murder had shaken him. Just as it had shaken Mery, who now hovered at the edges of every gathering rather than disappearing into a decanter of brandy or off on his own pursuits. I'd even learned that upon our return from Dr. Wolcott's he'd slept in his uncle's former bedchamber upstairs rather than repairing to his cottage. Did he fear being caught out alone and unawares, and incapacitated by his own drinking? Or was he worried about being found out? I tried multiple times to draw him off into relative privacy to speak with him as I'd hoped Anne might arrange, but he either resisted or soon after someone else joined us.

Whatever the reason for Mery's reticence and everyone else's interference, I was exasperated. In fact, I was tempted to wash my hands of him and leave him to his fate, whatever it might be. Only the recognition that my lack of sleep was making me ill-tempered kept me from making a remark I would certainly regret.

Rather than endure dinner with the lot of them, I nursed Emma and then rested for an hour before having a tray sent up. I urged Bree to stay, asking her if she'd learned anything since we'd spoken in the garden that morning.

"No' much, m'lady," she replied with a sigh that reminded me she hadn't gotten any more sleep than I had. She sank down on the bench before the dressing table as I directed her to. "Least, no' much that's verifiable or worth repeatin'. There's an awful lot o' rumors aboot the treasure, and most o' those were heard second- or thirdhand, and I suspect they've gotten jumbled in the tellin'."

"Such as?"

She looked up toward the ceiling. "Let's see. One maid told me a witch guards it, and no' one o' the good pellar kind, but a hag who sold a sailor a wind charm wit' oot warning him no' to open all three knots at once."

I nodded, having heard about the pellars from Mery and the wind charms from Dolly. The charms were naught but specially tied knots on a length of rope. Each knot supposedly contained a different type of wind that the witch had captured within. When a sailor released the knot, he would release the charm and summon whatever type of wind was secured within it. Each length of rope contained three knots holding three charms, though they were not to be used all at once or else one risked disaster. So it made sense that the more superstitious locals might believe the tempest had been caused by just such an occurrence.

"And one o' the stable lads claimed it's buried either beneath the altar at St. Endelienta's Church or her shrine," Bree added.

My eyebrows arched as I took a sip of the tea they'd sent up with my dinner. "I see." How exactly this would have been possible for two eleven-year-old boys to do, I didn't know, but perhaps he believed someone else had found it and buried it there after the fact. "Well, what of Cora?" I asked as I set the cup down. "Did she have anything else to say about Mery?"

"Nay." Bree began to worry the lace trim around her collar. "But she did have somethin' to say aboot Anderley."

I lowered my spoon filled with custard before taking a bite. "Anderley?"

"She said he'd been tellin' the others he might stay in Cornwall when you leave. That life here suited him better."

"But you must see, that's all part of his ruse," I reminded her, speaking in a voice that was barely louder than a whisper.

She nodded. "I ken. But I thought it was somethin' she might expect me to report to you."

"And I would report it to Mr. Gage, so we should react accordingly the next time we see him," I grasped. "Yes, you're right." I frowned down at my meal. "This sort of subterfuge becomes complicated rather quickly."

Shaking my head, I pushed my tray aside, deciding I'd had my fill even though I'd eaten less than half of it. I looked at Bree, expecting her to scold me for my lack of appetite, but she was lost in her own thoughts and clearly troubled by them. "What else did Cora have to say?"

She blinked in surprise, and for a moment I could tell she intended to deny that any other remarks had been made, but then her shoulders slumped. "She asked if I proposed to remain in Cornwall wi' him. And then suggested that his failure to share his plans wi' me first might be a sign he was havin' second thoughts aboot me." Her eyes narrowed in fury. "Acted all empathetic, but I could tell it was false. That she'd be only too happy to see me gone and for Anderley to stay."

"I'm sorry, Bree," I told her. "I guess she's shown you her true colors. But remember, Anderley's playing a part. He's not staying. Cora will discover soon enough that she's the one who's been misled."

"Misled, aye," she conceded, though she didn't sound certain of that.

"You . . . don't think Anderley has been misleading you, do you?"

"Nay." She pivoted to straighten the items laid out across the dressing table, muttering to herself as she did. "He's been quite clear on what he wants. I'm the one who's irrationally cautious. But we canna all be impulsive dreamers. *Someone* needs to be logical."

This sounded like an ongoing argument between the pair of them. One in which I wasn't sure I should interfere. Unless . . .

"Are you afraid he'll come to harm? Because, like I promised—"

"Nay," she cut me off. "I'm certain he'll emerge as unscathed as he always thinks he will." She turned to find me studying her in concern. "Ignore me." Her gaze lifted to my head. "Did ye wish me to repair your hair?"

I pressed my hand to my crown uncertainly. "Is it a mess?"

"No' awfully." But I could tell from the tone of her voice that she was being diplomatic.

"You'd best see to it, then." I rose to move to the bench she'd vacated.

She worked quietly as I ruminated on what she'd revealed about her relationship with Anderley. It was true that the valet was more spontaneous and intrepid than she was, but not recklessly so. At least, not usually. For he also possessed a good head on his shoulders and an appreciation for strategy. Meanwhile, Bree was more cautious and considered, but also not to excess. She enjoyed daring and adventure as much as the rest of us, or else she wouldn't be a member of our staff. It sounded to me like they were locked in opposing views over an issue and unable to find common ground. But much as I wanted to offer her advice on this, I knew that now was not the time. Not while she was unlikely to be receptive.

I glanced at my watch where it lay on the dressing table. And not when dinner would soon be ending, and I had a plan I wanted to put into motion.

It had occurred to me while I was supposed to be resting that interrogating everyone individually was not working. Normally, we took this approach because it tended to encourage witnesses and suspects to share more freely, and it allowed us the opportunity to corroborate evidence we'd heard from separate people.

However, in this instance, they were merely pointing the finger at each other or attempting to muddy the waters by dredging up possibly irrelevant history. If we could interview them all at once—first the Roscarrocks and then the wider range of suspects, including the Grenvilles—perhaps we might be able to separate the wheat from the chaff, so to speak. At the very least, once Mery heard how his relatives were directing suspicion toward him, it might convince him to finally share whatever information I felt certain he was guarding.

But before we could confront them, we needed to confer as investigators. If we had any hope of outwitting their ploys, we first had to be certain we each possessed all the known facts and understood their pertinence.

"After you've finished, I want you to notify Mr. Gage and his father that I need to speak with them in his lordship's sitting room," I told Bree. "And I need you to keep a watch for anyone attempting to eavesdrop. Enlist Lembus's help if need be. Lord Gage's imperious valet would undoubtedly relish such an assignment."

The glint in Bree's eyes told me she agreed.

CHAPTER 28

As suspected, my father-in-law did not appreciate being summoned to his own chamber, but he remained silent long enough for me to explain my thinking to him and Gage.

My husband endorsed the idea immediately. "It's about time we set them back on their heels," he declared as he sank deeper into the scalloped-top sofa, turning to stare broodingly into the fireplace.

Both men's grim countenances suggested dinner had not been an enjoyable affair.

"If it will finally bring this hellish debacle to an end, then I'm all for it," Lord Gage agreed before taking another drink of the whiskey he'd poured into a glass from the decanters on his chamber's sideboard.

I'd not bothered to light more than the single candle I'd used to illuminate my way down the darkened corridor to my father-in-law's sitting room, so the fire crackling in the hearth cast long, flickering shadows across the floor and walls, sharply limning their features.

I clasped my hands in my lap, sitting taller. "Then our first step is to review what we know and agree on what it is we still need to find out. Other than the obvious," I added, lest my father-in-law make a sarcastic remark.

"Let's see," Gage began readily. "We know that Bevil, Tristram, Mery, Joan, Amelia, Dr. Wolcott, and Tamsyn were all aware that Branok was still alive. Though that doesn't preclude someone else from having found out like Tamsyn did. We also know that none of them, save Dr. Wolcott, have alibis for the entire time period in which he was murdered."

"We know that Branok was killed sometime between four and six o'clock yesterday afternoon," I contributed. "And that he was stabbed with a fisherman's fillet knife, approximately nine inches in length with no hilt. A common enough blade that any of our suspects might have gotten their hands on, and just as easily could have discarded into the sea or down one of the abandoned mine shafts near Doyden Point."

"But do any of us believe that Aunt Amelia hiked out to Kellan Head, stabbed her brother, and discarded the knife?" Lord Gage protested. "She can barely make it across the length of the drawing room without requiring assistance."

"That's true." It would be quite a feat, but I'd already been fooled by an allegedly infirm older woman once before. "She might have had help."

"From Bevil or Joan?"

"Or one of her grandchildren. Or a member of her staff, for that matter."

Lord Gage rose to pour himself another two fingers of spirits, apparently unconcerned at the moment that the whiskey had likely been smuggled from Ireland. "But what motive could she have? Branok was her brother."

"Maybe so, but he was also, by all reports, a difficult man. One who was not well liked by anyone." I shifted in my seat, anxious to make my point. "He controlled everything. The farm. The home they lived in. The smuggling operation. All the family's wealth belonged to him." I arched my eyebrows in emphasis. "Despite the fact it sounds like Bevil and Tristram and many of the others did most of the work."

"Amelia must know she's nearing death," Gage remarked not unkindly. "Yet what does she have to leave her children and grandchildren? Nothing but the same tedious life, living under the control of her imperious brother and then his rapscallion grandson."

"But Branok himself unwittingly shows her, shows all of them, the way out. He forces them to help him fake his death, all so that he can lure his estranged nephew here to lead him to a long-lost treasure. But the ploy doesn't work. Not only that, but they must realize that Branok doesn't intend to stay dead, and their part of the shameful affair will be revealed with nothing to show for it," I said.

Gage nodded, turning to me. "However, if Branok were to die, in truth, that leaves only Mery in the way of controlling their own fate."

"And Mery is easily overpowered by the others. He's not respected, nor has he ever shown a bit of interest in assuming leadership. He's not likely to resist leaving the entire enterprise in their hands so long as he's given a large enough stipend to continue doing as he pleases." I paused, thinking back over everything I'd learned about that last living Cornish Roscarrock. "Or so they think."

"Even if he doesn't, now that they've killed once, what's to stop them from doing so again?" The sapphire stickpin in Gage's cravat winked in the firelight as his voice dipped forebodingly. "An accident would be easy enough to stage, particularly for a man of Mery's sottish reputation. And while the property might then rightfully belong to Swithun or his heir, as we previously noted, an entire ocean and months if not years of legal wrangling stand in the way of that changing anything."

"If an accident should even prove necessary," I countered, leaning toward him. "When it's far simpler to frame him for his grandfather's murder."

He swayed toward me in return. "And even if that doesn't succeed, it still further tarnishes his credibility."

"Yes, yes, I see your point," Lord Gage interjected, dashing a bit of cold water on our enthusiasm, an act that was perhaps needed. We were discussing murder, after all. He gestured with his glass as he settled again in his chair, crossing one leg over the other. "And Mery's motive is obvious. But what of Tamsyn? She didn't have a reason to kill Branok."

The disbelieving looks Gage and I both fastened on his father must have spoken for themselves, for his lips pursed and his brow furrowed with displeasure. "Yes, I know there was no love lost between them. Between all the Grenvilles and the Roscarrocks," Lord Gage said. "But why would she murder him now?"

"For the treasure," I stated succinctly. After all, he'd heard her allegations against Swithun. It seemed the Grenvilles had just as much claim to the treasure as the Roscarrocks did. It had to have crossed his mind that Tamsyn might try to charm the information about its location out of him, though I could read in his iron stare that he was about to protest. But I wasn't finished. "*And* . . . control of his smuggling operation."

This startled and then angered him. "Tamsyn isn't involved with smuggling."

"Morgan told me that the Grenvilles are a large part of the smuggling crews," I said. "That they've been angling to take over. And now that Branok is gone and Mery is so unpopular, they may have their chance."

"But not Tamsyn," Lord Gage argued. "She despises smuggling."

"Or she wants you to believe she does."

He didn't like hearing that. His face flushed red, and his jaw hardened into granite.

"But isn't her brother Gil the head of the Grenville family?" Gage asked, keeping his eyes on his father.

"Ostensibly. But with his wounded leg . . ." I knew I didn't need to explain.

"I imagine he places great trust in his sister," Gage replied as we both looked to his father for confirmation.

"Implicitly," he bit out.

Neither Gage nor I spoke, giving his father time to acclimate to this information. His expression as he stared down into the amber dregs of his glass was rigid, but I could tell by the way he'd not brushed aside the twist of gray curls that had fallen over his forehead—the same twist Gage sported on his golden head—that he would not continue to deny the truth. He tossed the glass back, swallowing the last finger of whiskey before setting it aside with a sharp clink on the table next to his elbow. "So be it. Tamsyn is a suspect." He glowered at me. "Which means we haven't ruled anyone out other than Dr. Wolcott."

"We also haven't determined the truth about the treasure or who betrayed whom on that long-ago night."

Lord Gage opened his mouth to argue, but Gage cut him off.

"Surely you can see Tamsyn has as much of a reason to lie as your relatives?"

He grunted begrudgingly, his shoulders stiff.

I was about to make them even more tense.

"I know you don't want to talk about it," I began, waiting until his gaze swung to meet mine, "but I also know that you recognize how necessary it is that you do." I hoped reasoning with him would work, even though his steely countenance was far from encouraging. "We need to know everything that happened, everything you remember. Otherwise, we might never be able to untangle this mess."

I glanced at my husband, finding him observing his father with the same intensity he might any suspect. Which meant that contradictorily, he appeared entirely relaxed and indifferent. For the more interest he had in a subject, the less he appeared to care. I'd identified this tactic early in our partnership, but only recently realized he'd learned it from his father.

However, Lord Gage's normal blasé manner and reserve had deserted him in this instance. So I decided to tread carefully. "Do you remember if there were any disagreements between the Roscarrocks and Grenvilles at that time?"

"There were always disagreements," he muttered. "So there was likely some sort of dispute, though I can't recall it." He rubbed his forehead. "Jago and I largely ignored them." As good friends do.

"What of Branok and Swithun?" Gage queried. "Did they argue?"

"They were brothers," Lord Gage retorted with an incredulous look. "Of course."

Ignoring this display of hostility, I slid toward the edge of my seat. "Talk us through that night. You said Branok ordered you and Jago to move some contraband."

He exhaled a long breath. "Yes. I remember that much. I also remember Jago and I thought it was a great honor. It was the first time we'd been asked to undertake such a thing on our own."

My heart squeezed for the innocence of those boys and how soon it would be lost.

"We strapped two of the casks to a pony, and loaded the others into the cart it would pull . . ." He broke off, frowning.

"About eight chests and barrels in total, you said," I prompted.

"Yes. I . . . don't know where they'd come from, but they'd obviously been buried somewhere near Pentire Point. They were crusted with dirt and sand." He rested one hand along the arm of the chair, opening and closing his fingers. "We were to transport it along the coast to Doyden Point. From there, I thought they meant to lower it into one of the mine shafts along Reedy Cliff or secure it in one of the cottages at Port Quin. They'd built false walls in a few of the cellars."

"But you never made it to Doyden Point."

He shook his head slowly, and the look in his eyes told me he was far away in the past on a narrow track along the wild Cornish coast. "We . . . we were just beyond Carnweather Point when we realized we were being followed. We thought it was our fault because we'd been singing."

I turned to meet Gage's eye, seeing he was just as affected as me by this detail. By this reminder of how young and artless they'd been.

"We tried to urge Lutey to move faster, but he was towing such a heavy load. We should have realized sooner that we could never outrun them, but we'd never been given such a task before." His voice was taut with remembered anxiety. "All we knew was that we couldn't let the barrels fall into the preventives' hands. We were coming up on Lundy Hole. It's a collapsed sea cave," he explained, his eyes as wide as saucers. "So we unhooked the cart and pushed it over the edge." He seemed slightly horrified by this admission, but I could understand the logic of their thinking, given the impossible situation they'd been facing.

"There wasn't time to remove the casks from Lutey's flanks. So we jumped on her back and set off around the bay. But we didn't get far before they started shooting. Lutey reared and we both fell. It wasn't until the riding officers were already on us that I realized Jago had been shot . . ."

His voice trailed away, and I knew he was reliving that

moment. It was scored across his features in stark lines made all the harsher by the flickering firelight.

I gripped the cushion beneath me as a few silent tears tracked down my cheek, restraining the urge to sob. But I must have made some sort of sound anyway, for Gage reached over to rest his hand on mine.

"I don't remember anything after that," Lord Gage murmured.

Because he'd been beaten unconscious.

"Do you think the treasure is still there?" Gage asked, allowing me a few moments to collect myself.

"No. It's long gone by now," Lord Gage answered. "Swept out to sea. But even if not, it's impossible to get to."

We would have to take his word on this.

"Do you intend to tell them where it is?"

His father's face slowly hardened. "No." And then he added, "None of them," in case there was any confusion.

This decision was his alone to make, and I would have supported him no matter his choice, but I couldn't help but think this was the wisest course. For all.

I wiped my hands over my face, brushing away the last of the tears gathered at the corners of my eyes, and lowered my gaze to a shadowed corner of the rug, attempting to refocus my thoughts. "I still don't understand why they didn't tell you and Jago what you were transporting. Or why they asked the two of you, of all people, to move the cargo in the first place. Two people transporting a bunch of barrels by cart along the coast in the middle of the night was bound to raise suspicions, no matter your age."

"Perhaps," my father-in-law conceded wearily. "But if Branok had learned of Swithun's betrayal . . ."

"No, she's right," Gage interrupted. "It doesn't make sense." His dark evening coat strained across his broad shoulders as he leaned forward. "If Branok had believed that Swithun had set a trap for him, then he would never have sent the treasure with you and Jago."

I turned to him sharply, grasping the implication. "He would have switched the barrels and sent some sort of decoy with you instead rather than risk the treasure falling into the preventive officers' hands."

Gage's mouth curled derisively. "Yet he's been searching for it obsessively these last fifty years and feigned his own death to lure you here so he could finally locate it?"

We both turned to look at Lord Gage.

His whole face puckered as if he didn't know how to feel. "Then Tamsyn's insinuations that Branok might have known can't be true. And it calls into question Swithun's alleged involvement, too."

I shook my head.

"Though that doesn't mean Joan's claims about the Grenvilles are true either."

"No, it doesn't," I agreed. "It might all have just been a terrible misfortune." One that they'd been blaming each other for for decades.

Yet one they risked happening again and again with their continued smuggling. How many more lives had to be lost before it stopped?

As if in answer to this silent query, someone began pounding frantically on the sitting room door. We all turned to each other in alarm before Gage rose to answer it.

Lembus stood panting on the other side. "You must come. It's Mr. Anderley."

I sprang to my feet as Gage questioned him. "Where is he? What's happened?"

"He's been carried to his chamber." Lembus's face turned pale. "He's been badly beaten."

CHAPTER 29

By the time Gage and I arrived in Anderley's quarters, pushing past the servants clustered outside the door, the valet was trying to rise from his bed while Bree stood over him scolding. Apparently, he'd been unconscious when he'd been discovered in a heap just beyond the doorstep, but now he was awake and refusing to see reason. At least, according to my maid.

"I must speak with Mr. Gage," he protested, barely able to lift his head.

"Stay doon, ye stubborn man," Bree remonstrated. "He'll be here soon."

"No! I must see him now."

"What is it, Anderley?" Gage said. He knelt by the bed as Bree stepped back, his eyes searching his valet's face. "What must you tell me?"

Anderley's lip was split, and his left eye was practically swollen shut, but he managed to roll the other one toward the crowd by the door.

I stepped over to shut it, first ordering the tallest lad, "Fetch Dr. Wolcott."

He nodded, turning to run off.

"I don't need a doctor," Anderley objected.

"You'll see him anyway," I insisted, and I heard Bree inhale a relieved breath. I guessed she'd already put forth the notion and he'd resisted.

"But . . ."

"You'll do what Mrs. Gage says," Gage told him gently but firmly. His jaw was tight with worry and regret. "Who did this to you?"

Anderley lifted his hand to wave this question aside, flinching in pain. "It doesn't matter. I heard them talking. They were discussing their plans."

"Who?"

"The smugglers. The general crew."

Gage glanced toward the door. "Part of the staff here?"

"It doesn't matter who. I'll tell you their names later. What you need to know is that they were discussing kidnapping someone."

I jolted as if I'd been slapped. "Kidnapping?"

Anderley's one good eye lifted to mine. "Yes. They intend to force his lordship to tell them where the treasure is."

Gage turned to look over his shoulder. "Where *is* Father?"

"He didn't follow us," I replied.

Gage began to push to his feet, but then turned back to press a hand lightly to Anderley's shoulder. "Good work."

Anderley swallowed, jerking his head once in reply.

"Do what Mrs. Gage says." Gage paused in the doorway to repeat this command and then swept from the room.

I spared a moment's worry for my father-in-law and then pushed him from my mind, focusing my attention on Anderley.

Gage would take care of his father. He trusted me to see to Anderley.

"Have you examined his wounds?" I asked Bree.

"Those he'd let me," she answered crossly, but I could sense the fear lurking beneath her irritation.

I gestured to the washstand. "Is that clean water?"

"Aye."

Anderley frowned up at me as I knelt beside the bed, but it had little affect, considering how pitiful he looked. "I can see the injuries to your face. But what about the rest of you?"

He continued to glare up at me mulishly. I had little hope of convincing him to cooperate by force. Even injured he still had several stone of muscle on me. Which left coercion as my only option.

"Bree, go and get me a beeswax candle. These tallow ones will never do."

If she suspected me of duplicity, she didn't say anything, but it was a few seconds before I heard the door open and close.

"Now, listen to me, Andrea Landi," I chided, using his Italian birth name. "You have obviously come out on the losing end of some sort of scuffle . . ."

"Only because there were four of them."

I struggled not to flinch at the images this evoked. "You're suffering from multiple cuts and contusions, and you may have internal injuries that are not immediately apparent. So you are going to lie still and compliant and allow me to examine you." I arched a single eyebrow. "And I will try to preserve your modesty."

His lip pursed slightly at this mocking remark.

Then I leaned closer, lowering my voice. "Because Bree cares for you. Though don't ask me why," I scoffed. "Lying to and ignoring her. Not trusting her with the truth."

Anderley flushed as if chastened.

"I know you were only following orders, but honestly! You and Mr. Gage should know better." I scowled at him. "If you hurt her again by dying because you're too stubborn to let us tend your wounds, why I'll . . . I'll give your body to the anatomists to carve up."

As threats went, it wasn't the most convincing. Given my history with anatomists and dissection, he must know I would never actually carry through with it. The glint in his deep brown eye confirmed this. But he did cooperate when I reached out to gently turn his head.

His hair was matted with blood from a blow above his right ear. His shoulder tendons were strained, making me suspect he'd been dragged by them to the place he'd been found. And his torso was a mass of bruises. I strongly suspected he'd broken a rib, but Dr. Wolcott would be better able to tell.

Bree returned as I was drawing the blanket back up over his abdomen, and I heard her swift indrawn breath. The bruising was a ghastly sight, but I didn't think any of the contusions signaled anything life-threatening, though of course, I couldn't be sure. Any injuries to his lower extremities I left for the physician to examine since his vital organs and the bloodstains seemed to be limited to the top half of his clothing.

"Thank you," I told Bree, turning to take the already lit candle from her. I pressed my hand gently to her upper arm as I did so, offering her a consoling smile. She seemed to steady herself in the face of my composure, so I turned back to our patient.

"Anderley, I want you to follow this light with your eyes . . . well, *eye*, without moving your head. Can you do that?"

He complied and I asked him a number of questions testing his cognition, relieved yet again to discover that he didn't appear to be suffering from any injury to his brain, though time would tell. "I look rather like a cyclops, don't I," he attempted to jest as I set the candle on the bedside table.

"Mare like a fachan," Bree retorted with a sniff.

"What's that?"

"A one-eyed Scottish monster," I replied with some amusement. "One armed and one legged as well." Clearly, Bree was not going to relent so easily.

Anderley watched Bree as she bustled about, straightening linens that didn't need straightening.

"They caught you eavesdropping, didn't they?" I asked, wishing I could offer Anderley something for his aches, though I doubted he'd take it, the obstinate man. Brackets of pain radiated from the corners of his eyes and mouth. So I decided the least I could do was try to distract him, and hopefully extract some useful information from him in the process.

Bree paused in her busy work to listen.

"Yes." He began to inhale deeply and then checked himself, stiffening in discomfort. "I should have been more careful, but I knew what they were discussing was important."

"You said some of them are members of the Roscarrock staff," I prompted.

He named a few men, most of them farm laborers or stable hands.

"What of the Grenvilles? Are any of them part of the crew?"

"More than half," he confirmed. His gaze met mine squarely. "And I've heard them mention Tamsyn Kellynack."

This was nothing more than we'd already suspected, but it was good to have it corroborated.

"Did they say when they planned to kidnap his lordship?"

"Not that I heard," he answered ruefully. "Not before I was discovered."

I patted his arm in reassurance before turning to Bree. "You'll stay with him?"

"Aye," she promised. Some of her prickliness seemed to have abated, eased by my conversation with him. She was even able to look at him without frowning, though her eyes were still clouded with concern.

"Don't let him out of your sight," I told her before spearing Anderley with my gaze. "And *you*! Listen to her. And follow Dr. Wolcott's orders when he arrives."

"I'll be as model a patient as Miss McEvoy was," he vowed.

I nearly snorted out loud at this, covering it with a cough. I well remembered how disagreeable she'd been while recovering from being poisoned. Though in her defense, she *had* nearly died.

As Anderley might have if the smugglers had taken it into their heads to kill him. The thought chilled me, and I hurried off to find Gage and his father.

The crowd outside Anderley's room had largely dispersed. But those who weren't standing in the upper corridor of the servants' quarters were now gathered in the passage between the kitchens and the dining room. A few of them scuttled away as I passed, but the bolder ones remained where they were. For good reason, because my husband and his father stood near the windows in the dining room overlooking the garden, debating what was to be done. Loudly.

"I'm not sleeping on a sofa in your bedchamber like some green lad," Lord Gage argued. "I'll not be frightened into behaving like a fool."

"Then we shall move to your chamber," Gage insisted. "All of us. It's larger anyway."

"Don't be ridiculous. Do you even hear yourself?" He crossed his arms, shaking his head. "We'll keep things the way they are, with Lembus sleeping in my dressing room."

"Lembus is hardly a deterrent," Gage practically hissed. "Can the man even shoot a pistol? Without soiling himself, that is."

My eyebrows shot skyward.

"I don't need Lembus to shoot a pistol. I have my own weapon."

"You are being unreasonable," Gage snapped as I moved toward them, lest our audience hear my every word.

"Father," I pleaded softly, hoping my use of this sobriquet would convey my distress. "Please. They beat Anderley quite severely because he uncovered this plot." I turned to Gage to reassure him. "Dr. Wolcott should still examine him, but I don't think he's in any danger."

He exhaled, his shoulders lowering a fraction.

"But that doesn't negate his sacrifice," I informed Lord Gage. "Or lessen the threat to you."

He grunted, pivoting to stare out the window at the moonlit garden. Pale moths flitted among the viburnum bordering the walk. Their white wings showed like flecks of moonlight against the black of the night. I paused to watch them, taking a moment to catch my breath, to resettle my nerves. Much had happened in the space of the last half hour, and we all needed a few seconds to adjust.

Gage was the first to speak, more steadily this time. "I think we must seriously consider leaving at first light. If Anderley can travel."

I turned to look at him. Most of the lights in the room had been extinguished, but I could still make out his strained features. "You think they still intend to go through with their plan?"

"I think we have to assume they will." He turned his head to peer over his shoulder at the doorway leading to the other rooms in the house. "Clearly, whoever is behind this is growing desperate. And I learned long ago never to trust desperate people."

The throbbing tone of his voice sent a chill up my spine. "What about Branok's killer?"

He shook his head sharply. "I'm not about to sacrifice any of our safety . . ." His lips flattened, as his eyes darted toward the servants' quarters, where Anderley lay bruised and battered. "Any more than I already have, for the sake of uncovering his murderer." He glanced upward. "Who likely lives under this very roof."

I nodded in understanding. It seemed we'd been on the cusp of this decision for some time. Hadn't Lord Gage and I made this very determination last night? I turned to my father-in-law, curious about his thoughts, but his expression was maddeningly inscrutable as he continued to stare out into the shadowed garden.

"But we still have to pass one more night here," Gage pronounced solemnly. "Which is why, Father . . ." At this Lord Gage turned to look at him.

"I do not want to take even the slightest chance they'll drag you from your bed—pistol or no." He exhaled, scraping a hand back through his hair. "If Anderley had not been injured, I would have set him to watch alongside Lembus. I would set in watch myself, but then that leaves Kiera and Emma vulnerable. You apprehend our dilemma."

"Then perhaps we should repair to the Grenvilles," Lord Gage suggested.

Frustration flickered over his son's features. "Except they are also part of this."

"That might be exactly what they *want* us to do," I contributed quietly.

"And Anderley can't be moved. At least not until Dr. Wolcott examines him."

"Tamsyn would never hurt me," Lord Gage insisted calmly, turning back to the window.

"You don't *know* that."

"No, but my instincts are telling me so."

"Your instincts? Is that what you're calling it now?" Gage sneered, his patience clearly frayed to the breaking point.

My eyes widened and cheeks flushed.

Lord Gage turned to glare at his son. "The decision is mine," he stated before striding off.

Gage unleashed a string of curses, his fists tightening as if he wished to hit something. When I withdrew half a step, he looked up at me, instantly contrite. "Apologies."

I offered him a commiserating smile. "He's frightened," I reminded him.

Knowing that, it made sense that he would want to retreat somewhere safe. Or at least somewhere he used to feel safe— long ago. Perhaps not Grenville House specifically, but with Tamsyn.

I nodded after his father. "Go. I'll wait for the doctor."

He reached for my hand, squeezing it as he pressed a kiss to my brow. Then he hurried after his father.

I sidled over to the window, lifting my hand to the worn and faded frame, suddenly anxious to be anywhere but inside these walls. Was that what Lord Gage had been feeling? Was that why he'd so stubbornly refused to listen to reason? The sensation of the house pressing down on me, of foreboding trembling beneath my breastbone, was almost enough to make me run. But I'd lived with this feeling—or something akin to it—for nearly three years during my marriage to Sir Anthony, never knowing when the next blow would fall, but certain it would eventually come. I told myself I could tolerate one night.

The sound of raised voices drew my attention toward the parlor and the entry hall beyond, and I moved to see if it was Dr. Wolcott. He met me in the doorway, his black medical bag in hand.

"Thank you for coming so quickly," I said before becoming momentarily distracted by the sight of his wife Anne, still standing in the entry hall. I was surprised she had come with him, but less surprised when Mery stepped forward, speaking with her in a hushed voice. Their hands gestured broadly, but I couldn't hear what they said.

Dr. Wolcott followed the direction of my gaze before prodding me insistently. "The patient?"

"Yes!" I exclaimed, falling in step with him. "My husband's valet, Mr. Anderley. He's been beaten rather terribly, though I don't believe any of the injuries are life-threatening. However, I would prefer that you examine him."

He paused to look at me just before entering the kitchens. "Of course." A thousand questions seemed to flicker through his pale eyes, but having spent numerous hours last night standing over a corpse with him, I'd become good enough at reading him now to recognize what was chief among them.

"Yes, I trust you. Or else I wouldn't have sent for you."

He bowed his head in mutual regard. "I will do everything I can," he vowed before disappearing into the servants' quarters.

I spared a moment to wonder whether he normally treated the staff. After all, in places like London and larger towns, physicians were often reserved for the gentry and aristocracy, while surgeons and apothecaries saw to the rest of the population. However, in a place as remote as this stretch of Cornwall, I wondered if such distinctions were so strictly maintained. Either way, I was grateful to Dr. Wolcott for examining Anderley.

I'd not received a response from Anne about the note I'd asked Bree to deliver to her earlier that day, so I went in search of her. Admittedly, I was also curious what she and Mery had been discussing so intently. But I couldn't find either of them. They weren't in the entry hall, the parlor, the library, or the drawing room where Amelia, Joan, and Dolly were gathered. I considered searching the rooms I'd yet to explore, but an infant's wail from above made me turn my steps toward the stairs.

I'd nursed her earlier than usual that evening, but had hoped she'd still sleep through much of the night. That was apparently not the case.

"I was just aboot to send for ye," Mrs. Mackay told me as she bounced Emma lightly in her arms. "I think the wee lass is enterin' another spurt o' growth."

This was a wearying thought, but then I reminded myself it would not last long. A few weeks at most. And after, Emma might sleep through the entire night in truth.

I swiftly informed Mrs. Mackay of Anderley's injuries as I settled Emma. The nurse uttered multiple exclamations of outrage. "Is there anything I can do?" she asked.

"Will you look in on Bree and see if she needs anything? She'll be tending to him overnight."

"Aye," she readily agreed. "And I'll lock the nursery door when ye go, just to be sure. We dinna want *any* o' us taken by surprise."

I stared after her as she shut the door and then down at my daughter. Should we be concerned they might turn their kidnapping plans toward another of us? I supposed it wasn't outside the realm of possibility.

After all, men like my husband and his father might not flinch at threats made to themselves, but if I or Emma were ever placed in danger, I knew they would do just about anything to protect us. The surest way to ensure their compliance was through us.

This thought sent another tremor of foreboding through my heart, one Emma sensed, for she began to fuss. I hushed her and then forced myself to take several deep, even breaths. First, I would feed her, then I could think of what to do next.

Emma ate quickly, and I had just stood up to cross the room toward the door as I burped her, intending to lock it in precaution, when the door suddenly burst open. I backed up several steps, clasping my daughter close to my chest as I stared wide-eyed at the intruder.

A lock of blue-black hair fell over Mery's forehead, covering part of his eyes, but what I could see reflected in them was frantic and almost wild. "I-I'm sorry to barge in like this, but I need ye to come with me. Now."

When I merely stood there blinking at him, pressed back against the cradle with my body turned slightly away to shield Emma from his sight, he took a step closer.

"Please, I know this sounds strange, but ye *must* come with me. Before it's too late." He darted a glance over his shoulder. "They'll be here soon."

"Who?" I gasped, beginning to edge to the side, but Mery's gaze followed me. "We know about the kidnapping plot against Lord Gage," I warned, wishing I'd disturbed Emma's feeding and locked the door earlier when I could. Though how long would that have deterred a man like Mery? As owner of this house, he likely possessed a set of keys to every door. No, I should have grabbed my reticule with my percussion pistol tucked inside instead. "So his lordship and my husband are watching," I bluffed. "They'll be here any moment."

"Nay, they won't. They're in the garden." He crossed toward me in three angry strides. This close, I could see that his jaw was shadowed with dark stubble. I fumbled around on the top of the clothespress behind me, searching with my free hand for something I might use as a weapon. I came away with a hairbrush, which I brandished before me. He batted it aside.

"Listen to me!" he begged. "They're comin' for her."

"For her?" I repeated inanely, my gaze dropping to my daughter. Horror flooded me. "For Emma?"

CHAPTER 30

Mery gripped my upper arm. "Aye! Branok knew how much Stephen adored 'er. And when he didn't lead us to the treasure as Branok hoped, he ordered us to kidnap the babe and force 'im to. But I . . ." His hand shook as he raised it to his head, tugging his hair. "I couldn't let 'im do that. Kidnap a child?! It's . . . it's—"

He was stammering now, so I cut him off, beginning to understand. "So you killed him."

"'Twas the only way to stop 'im!" His eyes pleaded with me to understand. "And with 'im dead, I thought the others would see reason. That they'd realize 'twas madness! But they decided to carry on with it." He shook me. "Don't ye see?" he demanded. "They're comin' now!"

My heart surged into my throat. I could barely speak as I allowed him to tow me toward the door. "Where are we going?"

"To the Wolcotts'. Anne is waitin' with their carriage."

But we only made it two steps from the door before we

spotted the hulking shadows of two men standing at the opposite end of the back corridor moving in our direction. Fear shot through me as we all stumbled to a stop. Then they began to charge down the passage toward us faster.

"Go!" Mery ordered, pushing me toward the front stairs. "I'll stall them."

I didn't pause to think what this might mean for him. How they might retaliate for him interfering. After all, they'd beaten Anderley unconscious simply for eavesdropping. My only thought was of reaching the Wolcotts' carriage or, barring that, of hiding somewhere on the estate until Gage could find us.

I dashed down the stairs and out the front door. Those men coming down the corridor had probably come through the courtyard and ascended the back staircase, and I didn't want to risk there being more men waiting there. I stumbled on the uneven paving stones and then righted myself as I turned down the path toward the lane. But as I passed through the gap in the line of hedges, a pair of hands grabbed me.

I shouted in protest, trying to pull free, but of all the ways Gage and my brother Trevor had taught me to defend myself, none of them had involved my holding a baby. Emma began to wail just as a second set of hands seized me from the other side, and a bag of some sort was pulled over my head, plunging me into darkness.

"Quit that," one of the men ordered gruffly, squeezing my shoulder painfully. "Or we'll take the babe from ye."

His threat was akin to a bucket of icy water being dumped over my head. There could be no more effective deterrent. I stilled, clutching Emma tighter, though she continued to howl. I wanted to do the same.

"Hush her," the man demanded. "Or we'll hush her for ye."

I began to bounce her, making shushing sounds, but without being able to see her, I didn't know how well it was working.

The arms pulled me to the right, away from the house. Unless I'd gotten myself turned around in the struggle. Dirt crunched beneath our feet for a short time and then we moved onto the springier texture of grass. It was difficult to keep my feet beneath me, and I would have certainly faltered if their hands hadn't roughly hauled me about.

I heard the jingle of a harness and the distinctive shuffle of horses' hooves. My first thought was that they were leading me to a carriage which would carry me God knew where. My mind screamed at me to resist, to fight back, but the very real threat that they might take Emma kept me compliant. They drew me to a halt, conferring softly. One of the steeds suddenly snorted, telling me how close I was standing next to it. That's when I realized they intended for me to ride horseback.

Panic shot through me. How was I supposed to keep my seat with a bag over my head? As such, I resisted at first when they told me to lift my left foot. When I didn't move fast enough for their liking, they jostled me from behind. "Do it!"

I raised my foot and soon found myself propelled upward by several pairs of hands—one below my foot, another around my waist, and a third under my armpits. It was terrifying and disorienting, for I couldn't see where I was going, and I had no control over where I would land. It was an awkward process, but somehow they managed to propel me into the saddle, though my skirt had hitched up on one side, getting caught under me and allowing cool air to wash over my leg.

One of the smugglers was mounted behind me, so at least they didn't expect me to maintain my seat alone. However, when the wind blew his scent toward me, I almost wished they had. Even through the coarse cloth over my head, I could smell the stench of fish and sweat.

Emma settled once the horse began to move, the steady rhythm of its gait lulling her. For this I was grateful, because I was fighting to keep my wits about me as it was. I couldn't tell where we were going or who we were with. The ground was far beneath my feet, and I was terrified of dropping Emma.

How soon would Gage and his father realize we were gone? Mrs. Mackay must have returned to the nursery by now. And what of Anne waiting for us in their carriage? Surely she would raise the alarm.

And what about Mery? I spared a moment to say a prayer for him. He had tried to help. If only I'd listened sooner. But then, how could I have known he was an ally? He'd been acting strangely all day, but I hadn't known that was because he was watching over us, frightened of what his relatives would do, rather than intent on harming us.

Given the urgency of the moment, I hadn't fully appreciated his confession. That he'd killed his grandfather, not for his inheritance, but because he feared what lengths the man would go to in order to find this treasure he was so obsessed with. Mery had not said the thought out loud, but I had seen the fear in his eyes. If his grandfather would not balk at kidnapping a child to get what he wanted, then what else was he capable of?

I inhaled a ragged breath. And now the Killigrews had carried through with their patriarch's plans. So the question remained. What else were they capable of?

I closed my eyes, trying to breathe through the icy fear flooding my veins. At least with them shut I could pretend the bag wasn't over my head. That I was merely resting my eyes as I rocked Emma to sleep.

How long and how far we traveled, I didn't know. The men with us were largely silent, and besides the clomp of the horses' hooves, the insects sighing in the weeds, and the occasional rumble of the sea, the night was quiet. Between my dread and my disorientation, it had been difficult to gauge time and distance. At some point, I sensed a change in the demeanor of the men. They had relaxed, even calling to each other jocularly from time to time. I decided this did not bode well for me and Emma.

Soon after, we stopped, and the hands that had awkwardly lifted me into the saddle lifted me out of it while I gripped Emma tightly. I was marched into a building. I could tell that much because the air and the quality of sound changed, and the texture of the ground beneath my feet altered. After being guided through a series of turns I was abruptly stopped. The bag was yanked from my head and I was pushed inside a dimly lit room before the door was slammed shut behind me.

I stumbled, righting myself, and then turned around to study the sturdy, wooden door before inspecting the rest of the chamber. It was a narrow butler's pantry. The walls were lined with shelves and cupboards on which china, porcelain, and silver was arranged. A cabinet to my left held silverware. I pulled each drawer open in quick succession only to discover they'd removed all the knives and forks. A single candle burned on the small table where the butler must have sat to shine the silver. A pallet of blankets and pillows filled much of the floor. I supposed I should be grateful they'd given us even that small comfort.

My knees suddenly gave out and I sank down on the bedding, giving way to the spate of tears that had been threatening since we were first captured. Emma blessedly continued to slumber, her sweet face in gentle repose, but I set her down carefully among the blankets lest my shaking wake her. I allowed myself to weep for perhaps five or ten minutes, letting the terror roiling inside me to rise up and engulf me. Then I inhaled a deep, shaking breath, set my shoulders, and told myself, *that was that*.

I would not give in to fear. I would not give in to despair. I would keep my head about me, and I would find a way out of this mess.

My husband and father-in-law would come. We were not

without allies. Surely our abductors could be reasoned with. Especially once they discovered the truth about the treasure.

We would find a way out of this.

I kept repeating this to myself as I laid down beside Emma, leaving the candle burning. My thoughts waffled between that and the words of the third Psalm until I fell asleep.

Without a window, I could not tell what time of day it was, but I could sense it was still early when a knock sounded on the door. A few seconds later—long enough for me to cover myself, I supposed, if I had been tending Emma—I heard the click of the lock and then the door opened. I scowled up at the man standing there, hoping he wasn't about to try to make me wear a bag over my head again. The fellow certainly wasn't known for his good looks, not with his bulbous nose and the jagged scar bisecting his right cheek. However, he didn't react to my anger, but simply ordered me to "come" before turning his back on me.

It took me a moment to rise, for my body was stiff from the midnight ride and sleeping on the floor. I shook out my merino skirts and cradled Emma close. Tendrils of my hair trailed down my back, brushing my spine as I followed him from the room, but I ignored them. My untidy hair was the least of my concerns.

Turnip Nose led me down one corridor and then another while two other men trailed behind us, I supposed in case I tried to run. I glanced about me, looking for anything familiar, but if I'd been in this house before, it hadn't been this part of it. The walls were mostly bare and the floor runner worn. The doors on either side were closed until we reached what appeared to be the morning room at the far end. It was flooded with a pale wash of sunlight from the windows facing the sea to the north. It couldn't have been more than a quarter of an hour since sunrise, but I blinked at the sudden brightness. As such, it took me a few moments to realize I wasn't alone, and precisely who I faced.

Tamsyn stood near a sideboard adjacent to the hearth, pouring a drop of something into her teacup. I suspected it was brandy. This time she was wearing a violet dress. Meanwhile, Amelia and Joan perched side by side on a serpentine front sofa—how apropos—situated before the windows. I couldn't help but note how refreshed they all looked. They certainly hadn't spent the night on the floor, locked in a butler's pantry.

"Oh, my," Amelia breathed at the sight of me. She turned to Tamsyn. "Surely, we can at least offer 'er the services of a maid."

"No, thank you," I bit out, unwilling to accept even a hint of charity from these women. Not after they'd kidnapped me and my daughter. Let them be forced to look at me and see what they'd done.

"Well, at least 'ave a seat and a cup of tea, Mrs. Gage," Joan instructed me. "I should hate to see ye faint from lack of sustenance."

I was fairly certain she didn't care either way, but she made a valid point. In any case, if I was to attempt to reason with these women, then I needed to at least make an effort to be peaceable. Even so, I opted for the chair farthest from them.

Tamsyn took it upon herself to pour my tea, adding a splash of whatever she'd added to her tea to mine as well. Definitely brandy, I decided, as I took a fortifying sip.

"I tried to warn ye," Tamsyn murmured as if chiding a child for pricking themselves with a thorn when they tried to pick a rose. "It's your fault ye didn't listen."

"I thought it was merely advice," I taunted, throwing her words back at her.

She aimed an arch look over her shoulder at me.

Emma had fallen asleep again after I'd nursed her about an hour earlier, and I silently compelled her to remain so. The last thing I wanted was her waking and offering her smiles and adorable babbles to these wretched women. Yes, it might have helped us plead our case, but they didn't deserve a drop of her unwitting affection.

"I do apologize, my dear," Amelia said in her raspy voice. "We didn't want to 'ave to resort to this, but we need the money from that treasure." She shook her head. "If Stephen simply hadn't been so *stubborn*." She pounded her fist in her lap. "But that is a fault of all Roscarrock males. Grenvilles, too," she added with a glance at Tamsyn. "'Tis their fault we're in this mess. And it's up to us to fix it."

"By kidnapping an infant and her mother?" I demanded incredulously.

She waved this aside. "You're merely a means to an end, my dear. As long as Stephen cooperates, you'll come to no harm."

My temper flared, but I tamped it down, knowing I had to remain civil. "And I suppose by cooperate, you mean as long as he tells you where the treasure is. But why do you need it so badly?"

"Because both of our estates are mortgaged to the hilt," Tamsyn explained, earning a scowl from Joan. "Branok and my granfer and father kept throwin' good money after bad, attemptin' to recoup their losses rather than makin' sound investments."

"And that's all Stephen's fault," Joan griped.

But Tamsyn shook her head. "Nay. It'd already begun before that. Of course, it didn't help that the Royal Navy—with Stephen's guidance—captured and sank so many of our ships during the Peace of Amiens in '02. But 'twas only a matter of time before they would've been forced to look for financial backing from someone wealthier." Tamsyn finally selected a chair, dropping neatly into it. "They would've been better off cuttin' their losses and puttin' an end to their smugglin'."

"Branok would never 'ave done that," Amelia countered. "And your granfer and father neither. Even though 'tis no longer profitable. 'Roscarrocks and Grenvilles 'ave been smugglers for hundreds of years, and we'll remain smugglers for hundreds more,'" she pitched her voice low to assert, obviously repeating something one of those men had said.

"Then I gather this stakeholder is threatening to take your land," I deduced, attempting to bring them back to the point.

"If we can't pay our debts, aye," Tamsyn replied.

"And you hope the treasure will cover them?"

"And some."

I shifted Emma in my arms, turning to frown at the hearth.

"'Tis obvious ye don't approve, my dear," Amelia said. "But ye must see we had no choice. Not if we don't want to lose our land and the homes we've owned for generations."

"I don't think that's why she's frownin'," Tamsyn cautioned, and I turned to meet her too-perceptive gaze. "You know somethin', don't ye?"

I didn't answer, hoping she wouldn't guess. But I should have known better.

She sank back in her chair, her lips curling into a furtive smile. "You know where the treasure is."

Amelia and Joan both eyed me avidly.

"You're right," Joan said, her gaze flicking down to Emma in a not-so-subtle threat before returning to my face. "Tell us."

"Please do, so we can put an end to all this unpleasantness," Amelia coaxed.

"You're not going to like it," I told them, accepting there was no use pretending.

"Why?" Joan demanded.

I locked eyes with Tamsyn. "Because he and Jago pushed it down Lundy Hole when they realized they weren't going to be able to escape the preventive officers."

What followed was stunned silence from all three women. Which, I admit, I took great pleasure in.

Tamsyn was the one to speak first. "Bleddy hell!"

Joan turned to glare at her, and I decided to take the opportunity to sow a little discord.

I arched a single eyebrow at Tamsyn. "Preventive officers *you* claimed Swithun sent to apprehend Branok."

However, this failed to rile her or the Killigrew women. "That's just somethin' I said to keep you distracted and chasin' your tails," Tamsyn replied with only half of her attention. The rest was clearly directed to the problem of the treasure.

I sat stiffly, stung by the remark. One look at Amelia and Joan told me their claims about the Grenvilles betraying the Roscarrocks had been a similar ploy.

"Maybe Stephen lied," Joan suggested. "I wouldn't put it past 'im."

"Except it rings true," Tamsyn countered. "I've even wondered myself. After all, Jago was shot just east of there. Makes sense they would've dumped the treasure rather than let it fall into the 'ands of the preventives. And what better place when they 'ad little time to do so than Lundy Hole."

Amelia's hand shook where she stabbed the cushion with her finger. "We need to be certain."

"Aye," Joan agreed. "Maybe some of it's still there."

"But that's madness!" I exclaimed, causing Emma to snuffle in her sleep.

"Maybe so, but the alternative isn't to be borne," Joan shot back.

Tamsyn nodded, pushing to her feet. "I'll send a note to Roscarrock House, orderin' Stephen and his son to meet us there. The next low tide is due just after ten. That'll be the time to go in."

I stared wide-eyed after her and then toward the other

women. This was worse than I'd imagined. I'd thought the truth would make them see reason, that they'd let Emma and me go. Now I wished I'd never said anything at all.

My gaze lifted to the windows and the garden outside, and beyond that the cliffs and the sea. Now that I knew I was at Grenville House, maybe I could make a run for it. I might not be able to reach Trelights and the Wolcotts, but perhaps I could find my way to Auntie Pasca's. Surely, she would help me.

However, my hopes were dashed by Tamsyn's next orders to her men. "Lock 'em back in the butler's pantry."

CHAPTER 31

Turnip Nose came to fetch me again shortly before mid-morning, but this time I was ready for him. I had fashioned a makeshift sling out of one of the blankets to strap Emma to my body, so I could have both hands free. It also served as a useful place for me to stash the largest serving ladle I could find. In terms of weapons, it was far from threatening, but in a pinch, I hoped it would serve well enough as a type of cudgel.

Emma, fortunately, was in a fine mood, especially after they brought me a clean linen for her bottom. She seemed to find it all a grand adventure, looking up at the shelves and rolling about on the floor, exploring this new space. Even now, she offered Turnip Nose a slobbery grin.

One corner of his lips appeared to curl involuntarily before he seemed to recall himself. He thrust a brown woolen cloak at me, and I accepted it gratefully. The journey here during the night had been cold without any outer garment, and the wind on the cliffs today was certain to be biting.

We set off toward the coast by a roundabout route, I suspected to prevent an ambush. I was bustled along near the middle of the group, which included Tamsyn, Joan, Bevil, and Tristram, as well as a dozen or more men with whom I wasn't familiar, though several of them had undoubtedly been part of my escort to Grenville House the previous night. Most surprisingly, Great-Aunt Amelia accompanied us. I had expected her to remain behind, but she hobbled along behind me with the aid of two of the men. In truth, I wasn't certain how much she walked and how much they carried, but none of them complained.

The sky overhead was streaked with mares' tail clouds and washed with the palest shades of blue. Squill and thrift wildflowers dotted the edges of the path along with gorse and wild fennel. As we neared the sea, the crash of the waves against the rocky shore increased, as did the number of fulmars and gulls soaring overhead on the currents.

Curiously, a red-billed chough also seemed to be following us. He would flit ahead, landing on an old fencepost or a pile of rocks, issuing his distinctive call. *Chee-ow. Chee-ow.* Emma squealed, looking about every time she heard it, and I began to believe the blue-black bird was playing with her.

I remembered the legend Lord Gage had told us about the chough. How some Cornish believed King Arthur had turned himself into the bird until such a time when he was needed. If it were true, I couldn't think of a better time than now.

I heard the booming echo of the tide thundering into Lundy Hole before I saw it. Lord Gage had described it as a sea cave whose roof had collapsed, and that was exactly what we saw. An arch of stone was all that remained, its craggy shingled roof looking like it would fall in at any moment. Through the arch, one could see the rise and fall of the turquoise sea beyond.

There was no obvious way into the cave, other than to jump—a dangerous feat, considering the slope of the rocky sides and the shallow appearance of the water below—or to approach it from the sea. Even that would prove dangerous. Anyone with a healthy sense of reason must grasp that the treasure was long gone, carried out on the tide or buried by rubble. There was no sign of the cart or the barrels the boys had used to transport it.

Yet when I glanced at Joan and Tamsyn, they still seemed set on this course. Only Amelia appeared to harbor any doubts.

"This is madness," I whispered as she stood beside me.

She continued to peer over the side, her widened eyes acknowledging the folly, even if her mouth did not. Then she inhaled a ragged breath deep into her lungs. "Father always said the treasure was unlucky. That it might even be cursed." Her gaze lifted to meet mine. "He believed the best thing was to leave it where it lay. And that Stephen should be kept as far away from it as possible. 'Tis why he never asked him to return. For his own safety."

"Yet you did," I reminded her.

"Aye." She turned to stare into the hole again. "Because I 'ad no choice. 'Tis the only way to save us."

I didn't believe in curses. At least, I didn't want to. But I did believe in the power of greed. And perhaps that's what Lord Gage's grandfather had meant, after all. That as long as Stephen was near the treasure, he would never be safe from men determined to find it.

Amelia, Joan, and Tamsyn might be trying to save their families' homes and lands, but that did not absolve them of their actions. There were other things they could try, other steps they could take. They needn't resort to deception, brutality, kidnapping, and potential manslaughter!

Someone gave a shout, and we all turned toward the coast path. As we watched, about a dozen people crested the rise moving toward us. I recognized Gage and his father immediately, and my heart surged in my chest as I hugged Emma close. Words crowded at the back of my throat as I fought the urge to yell at them to flee. To not come any closer. They wouldn't be able to hear me, and who knew how my captors would react.

As they drew nearer, I began to recognize some of the other members of the group, including our faithful staff: Bree, Mrs. Mackay, Anderley—whose left eye was still swollen shut—and even Lembus and our coachman. Dr. Wolcott was also there, along with Morgan and her husband, Dolly, and Imogen. I searched their faces for Mery, but neither he nor Anne were among them. I prayed the reason for that was not death or serious injury. Anne was nearing her confinement, I reminded myself, and such a trek would have been arduous for her. Perhaps Mery was merely keeping guard over her. But the sinking feeling in my stomach persisted.

In terms of appearance, their motley crew was far from intimidating, at least physically. Emotionally, it was a different story. Wife glared at husband. Daughter scowled at father and mother. And cousins appeared angry enough to spit.

I felt a surge of gratitude that they'd come to fight for us—for me and Emma. But it remained to be seen whether their opponents would be swayed.

Gage and his father were stopped a short distance away. They were not to be allowed to come too close, but even at such a distance, I felt the warmth and reassurance of my husband's gaze bolstering me. I nodded once to let him know we were well and then turned to Lord Gage to do the same.

My father-in-law looked like he'd passed a sleepless night. His face was pale and haggard, and the collar of his blue frock coat sat askew beneath his dark greatcoat. The guilt he felt for landing us in this predicament was obvious, and that made the fear and anxiety that had been roiling around inside me turn to cold fury.

For too long, he had carried guilt over what had happened near this spot almost fifty years ago. Guilt that should never have been his to carry. Not when there were older and wiser men who should have looked after him and Jago. It was *they* who should have been transporting the treasure. *They* who should have suffered the consequences of an ambush. Instead, they'd let the penalties fall on those who were weaker and more vulnerable.

And they were *still* doing so. Rather than finding another way to remedy their family's problems, they were once again leaning on the vulnerable to extract them from their folly, heedless of the consequences.

"Nanna, Mother," Morgan spoke first, her voice sharp. "That is enough. Let them go!"

"Listen to her, Tristram," Dolly added. "Don't make this worse than it already is."

"And then what?" Joan challenged. "We'll lose our homes and our lands." She gestured to the gathering at large. "We all will."

"There has to be another way," Imogen pleaded.

"Nay," Tamsyn proclaimed, stepping forward. "Not 'til we've exhausted this avenue."

Lord Gage's eyes narrowed to slits.

"Is this where you and Jago dumped the treasure?" she demanded of him. "Or did your daughter-in-law lie to us? She's quite clever. I wouldn't put it past her."

I was relieved to see some of Lord Gage's spirit revived as he poured venom into his gaze. "Yes. That's where we dumped it."

She scrutinized him a moment longer before lifting her hand in some silent signal. "Just to be sure."

My arms were suddenly seized by two of the men and I was jerked backward to the precipice of the hole, Emma still strapped to my chest.

"Wait! No!" I cried, my heart racing in panic. I could feel the dirt falling away from the back of my heels as I strained to keep my purchase on the earth. "Please, don't!" I begged, grasping hold of their meaty arms in return, trying desperately to prevent them from releasing me.

Emma began to wail, but I was beyond any ability to comfort her. Not when I was trying to save our lives.

I heard other shouts and voices raised in protest, but Tamsyn spoke over them all with chilling indifference. "Tell me again. Where is the treasure?"

"It's here," Lord Gage repeated. "It's here, damn you! Don't hurt them. Don't hurt them."

My breath sawed in and out of me so loudly that it and Emma's keening cries threatened to drown out all else, even Tamsyn's response.

She must have issued another silent command, for the men yanked me forward almost as quickly as they'd pulled me back. I fell to my knees several feet from the pit, one hand pressed to the solid earth and the other wrapped around Emma as I struggled to catch my breath. I felt a sob gather at the back of my throat, but I refused to give it voice. Not now. Not for Tamsyn!

Once I had myself more in hand, I pushed to my feet, feeling a gentle pressure against my elbow. When I looked up to see it was Great-Aunt Amelia trying to help me rise, I shook her off with a spiteful look. One that clearly startled her, but what had she expected? Gratitude? She'd chosen to throw her lot in with Tamsyn. As such, Tamsyn's actions were as much Amelia's fault as her own.

"It's long gone by now," Lord Gage was saying, his entire body vibrating with rage as he tried to make Tamsyn understand. "Washed out to sea."

My gaze shifted to Gage, who appeared as if he'd aged ten years in the last minute. I couldn't nod or smile to console him this time. I could only hope my and Emma's presence was enough.

I pressed kisses to Emma's brow, trying to comfort her as best I could as I searched the faces around me while Tamsyn and Lord Gage continued to argue. Tamsyn's actions had plainly shocked many of them. Those standing in solidarity with Gage and his father, for certain, but also some of Tamsyn's own party. Amelia was shaken, but Joan appeared more displeased. Perhaps she'd thought she would be the one in control, not Tamsyn. Turnip Nose and another two or three men also looked unhappy, though that didn't mean they could be persuaded to take our side.

"Nonetheless, we're goin' to be certain," Tamsyn proclaimed, her gaze shifting to my husband. "And your son is goin' to help."

"Have you gone balmy?" Lord Gage exclaimed. "It's gone!"

But Tamsyn ignored him, issuing instructions to some of her men.

"I won't let you do this!" he shouted.

Tamsyn turned back to him imperiously. "Then perhaps your daughter-in-law and granddaughter . . ." She raised her hand again, but I already knew what that meant, and I dodged the men's grasps before swinging my arm backward to strike one of them.

"I'll go," Gage told her.

I glared at the men when Tamsyn must have signaled to them to stop, promising retribution. Then I turned back to my husband, watching as he was pushed in the direction he'd come by Bevil and a trio of Grenvilles.

"There now," Tamsyn practically crooned. "At least your son is reasonable."

Anderley began to follow, but both Bree and Mrs. Mackay protested, perhaps reminding him that in his condition he would be more of a hindrance than a help. Lord Gage began to argue that he should go, but Tamsyn prevented it. So when Dr. Wolcott and Morgan's husband Anthony separated from the group instead and trotted after the men, I presumed they were headed for a path that would lead down to the beach below.

A few seconds later, Tristram brushed past me, following them as well. Dolly reached out to grab his arm, and though he only spared her a fleeting glance, it was enough to give me hope that Gage might have another ally. At least, I liked the odds of four-on-four better than the alternative. Maybe Bevil would even be convinced by his son and son-in-law to switch sides.

Silence descended as we waited to discover what would happen next. Wind riffled through my hair, now almost entirely divested of its pins, and buffeted the grasses clinging to the cliff top. It carried with it the smell of rain, and turning my head to the left, I could see clouds gathering to the west. This added another level of urgency to Gage's and the other men's efforts below. That and the tide, which would soon be shifting. If a storm out to sea stirred up the waves and currents, this could complicate matters considerably.

I bounced Emma and swayed, pivoting as I did so, ostensibly to comfort her and lull her to sleep, but it also allowed me to study our surroundings once again. I noted that Tamsyn's men appeared to be standing relatively at their ease, with feet propped on rocks or murmuring with one another. Only the man I'd struck after he'd tried to grab me a second time paid me the least bit of notice. His thick, dark brows had lowered as if in affront.

Tamsyn had chosen her men well, for they were all tall and strapping, but they were far from attentive or disciplined. I supposed such was the lot when one was commanding a band of smugglers. However, this factor might work to our advantage.

There was perhaps twenty or thirty feet separating me from my father-in-law. If I could manage to reach them, I trusted that he and some of the others carried pistols. They would not have come here unarmed.

Of course, Tamsyn's men probably also carried guns. But the Killigrew and the Roscarrock descendants among Tamsyn's crew must surely protest the possibility of Dolly, Morgan, and Imogen being shot, turning the tide against her. Amelia had sunk down on a rock, seeming to already be regretting her affiliation with the Grenvilles, and Joan looked no happier.

I bided my time, waltzing with Emma's sleeping form, her warm body a comforting weight against my heart and the sweet scent of her golden curls filling my nostrils. I nudged the handle of the silver ladle closer to the top of the sling to make it easier to extract if and when I should need it.

"There they are," one of the men announced some time later. He pointed toward the bottom of the hole, and a number of Tamsyn's crew crowded closer, including the woman herself.

A few of the men, with Gage at their lead, were picking their way over the rocks and through the arch. They had removed their coats and waistcoats, and some of them had discarded their boots. At points, the water in the sea cave was shallow enough for them to walk with it swirling around their calves. At other spots it surged up over their waists, and at others they were forced to swim.

The cave was deep. They had to traverse several hundred feet to reach the point where the cart carrying the treasure would have tumbled over the edge to strike the rocks below, and with each step, with each stroke, they were forced to fight the current and the tidal surge. It was a tiring endeavor, and the longer they were at it, the greater the risk of fatigue became. Eventually, their muscles would simply give out.

I knew Gage was healthy. I knew he was strong. Our months at his father's estate in Warwickshire had made him even more so. I could only pray that he was strong enough to endure this. Strong and savvy.

As we watched, several more men came into view, including Tristram and Bevil. Tristram appeared to be faring well enough, but Bevil was obviously struggling. I willed him to turn back. He was too old for such an undertaking, but he stubbornly persisted to follow the others.

I couldn't see Dr. Wolcott or Morgan's husband, and I surmised that they'd elected to hang back. Probably a wise decision under the circumstances. They might be able to help those who had become too exhausted to make their way back out of the cave completely and prevent them from being swept out to sea.

More and more of Tamsyn's men began to creep up to the hole, peering over the side to see what had their compatriots so enraptured. They groaned and grunted and cheered, jesting with each other as if they were watching some sort of sporting match as the men below struggled toward their goal. I peered back at Lord Gage and the others still standing at a distance. They could see nothing of what was going on below, and the agony writ across their faces was plain.

A quick survey of the people around me told me now was the time to make my move toward the others, but I hesitated. If I backed away, I wouldn't be able to see what was happening to Gage. I wouldn't know if he needed help. Not that I could do anything to offer it. But the torment of not knowing might be worse.

I looked up to find the chough watching me from his perch on a stunted rowan tree nearby. His beady black eyes were knowing, almost as if he understood my distress. *What should I do?* I found myself silently asking him as much as myself.

Then a shout went up, drawing my attention back to the bottom of the cave. The men were nearing the base, but there was trouble. One of Tamsyn's men had slipped, injuring himself, and the others had stopped to look at him. Even from a height of perhaps fifty or sixty feet, I could see the blood in the water. It bloomed around the man in a steadily growing cloud.

However, Tamsyn was indifferent. "Keep moving!" she ordered the others.

Gage tipped his head to look up at her, his wet hair tangled around his features. I could see how much effort it took to move and even to catch his breath. This was an impossible mission!

But Tamsyn would not relent. "Go!"

The man who had paused to assist the injured fellow began surging forward again, gesturing threateningly to Gage. My hands clenched into fists as my husband turned and resumed his struggle toward the spot where the treasure would have fallen. I swept my gaze over the length of the cave, seeing that the third Grenville smuggler was perched on a ledge some fifty feet behind the others. Bevil was struggling at one of the deepest parts of the cave, and Tristram was speaking to him from a shallower point in between darting glances at the man on the ledge. And all the while the cave echoed with the boom of the incoming tide whenever a larger wave struck the arch.

If Gage was to have any chance of turning the tide in their favor it would be soon, while he was facing just one opponent rather than multiple. But if those around me seized me and threatened to throw me and Emma over the edge again, any gains he'd made would be in vain. For I knew Gage would do anything they asked to keep us safe. Now was my chance.

I began to slowly back away from the hole—one step, two steps, and then a third. But as I swiveled to continue walking calmly but swiftly away, the man with the dark brows reached for me. I was ready for him. And so was the chough.

As he grasped my left arm, I pulled the ladle from Emma's swaddle and swung out, aiming for his temple. It connected with a crack, and he released his hold, stumbling backward, just as the chough dived for his head. I didn't wait to see what happened, but turned and ran, even as shouts and screams lifted skyward behind me.

I didn't stop until Lord Gage grasped hold of me and pushed me behind him into Mrs. Mackay's and Bree's arms, before turning to shield me with his body. Then I could see over his shoulder what had caused all of the commotion.

The man I'd struck had apparently collapsed into the people directly behind him, propelling them and himself over the edge of the hole. Another two individuals dangled over the edge, only their hands and wrists visible as they struggled to pull themselves back up. I realized, with a shock, that one of them was Tamsyn. But my chief concern was for Gage. He'd been almost directly below those people when they'd fallen.

"No," I gasped, imagining their bodies crashing down on him. "No!"

CHAPTER 32

It was a solemn afternoon and evening, one I was certain none of us would ever forget. But all I had to do was look up at Gage's beloved face to recall it could have been so much worse. At least, for me.

I burrowed closer to his side where we sat on the sofa in the drawing room at Roscarrock House, and he tightened the arm he'd draped around me in response. Dolly and Tristram, Anne and Dr. Wolcott, and Morgan and Anthony Knill were seated in similar poses. Mery leaned his head back against the cushion of his chair, his feet propped up on a footstool and his broken arm cradled before him. He, too, was sporting an impressive black eye, though not as swollen as Anderley's.

I had spied Gage's valet in the covered portion of the courtyard just a short time ago, rain drumming the ground a few feet away. Bree was administering some sort of liniment to his facial injuries. I'd intended to ask how they both fared, but once I'd seen the look on Anderley's face and the intent in his eyes, one

Bree seemed to echo, I retreated to the house, giving them their privacy.

Emma was sleeping upstairs—none the worse for our misadventure—with Mrs. Mackay watching over her. Not that there was any more concern for her safety. Not when Tamsyn and half of her crew had fallen to their deaths or drowned in Lundy Hole, along with Bevil.

Gage had managed to avoid their plummeting bodies, but I suspected he would be haunted by the event for a long time. Especially since his initial fear had been that one of them was mine with Emma still strapped to my chest. Once he'd realized that I was still safely above and that no more bodies were about to rain down on him, he'd fought his way past the Grenville closest to him back toward the entrance to the cave.

The man who had been injured, bleeding into the water, had long since slid beneath the waves, and Tristram had clubbed the third man over the back of the head with a loose rock when he moved to attack Gage, redeeming himself in the end. Then the pair began to struggle their way out of the cave, trying to help Bevil between them. But the tide had begun to come in, and the swells from the incoming storm grew larger. It had taken all of their considerable strength just to reach the mouth of the arch. There, Anthony Knill and Tom Wolcott had pulled them to safety. However, Bevil was lost, driven under by an incoming wave and then pulled out to sea by the wicked current.

Those on the cliffs had given up all their fight to either apprehend us or reach the treasure in the face of such tragedy. The remaining Grenvilles had trumped down to the beach to search for their dead, while Joan and Amelia had silently followed us back to Roscarrock House, supported by their daughters and granddaughters.

I had fallen onto Gage with a great spectacle of sobbing once he reached the cliff top again, too overcome from residual fear and lack of sleep. We dropped to our knees, holding each other for some time, until I finally released him long enough so that he could kiss and embrace our daughter. Mrs. Mackay had thankfully taken charge of her after I'd frightened her with my frantic cries for Gage's safety, and I apologized to Emma then, just so relieved we were all alive.

Joan and Amelia had not been so lucky.

Bevil's death, and perhaps their own remorse over the entire affair, seemed to have broken them. They'd taken to their beds, where Imogen now took her turn tending them. Having seen Amelia's haggard appearance and heard her wheezing breaths, I suspected she wouldn't be long for this earth now. Her heart was simply giving out.

As for Tamsyn, I presumed the Grenvilles were mourning her, even if no one here was. No one except for perhaps my father-in-law.

He stood gazing broodingly out the windows into the stormy twilight much as he'd done the evening of our arrival at Roscarrock House. I could not read his thoughts. They were closed to me. But I knew that love did not die easily, and he had loved Tamsyn. Even more so because she was all that was left of his friend Jago. Her cold betrayal might have broken that, but it had been too sudden to destroy it completely.

We were all largely silent, deriving comfort merely from each other's presence as we were each lost in our own thoughts, grappling with pain and suffering and grief. So when Mery suddenly cleared his throat and pushed himself more upright in his chair, I think we were all surprised.

"Perhaps now is not the time. But if not now, when?" He grimaced remorsefully. "I owe all of ye an apology. I've not acted as I should for a long time." His brow furrowed in shame. "I blamed Granfer, but I'm the one who chose to shuck all responsibility.

That stops now." He arched his chin. "Though I'll need your support, Tristram."

His cousin met his gaze levelly.

"Last I recall, you 'ad a lot of ideas for 'ow we could manage our money better. I'd like to hear them, and I promise to listen to your counsel better than Granfer ever did your father."

Tristram appeared to straighten at this pronouncement.

"I'll also need ye to take over the reins should the coroner's inquest decide my killin' Granfer wasn't justified." Mery's firm voice faltered. "I . . . I have to take responsibility for that, too. Anne told me to confide in Sebastian and Kiera." His gaze locked with hers. "And I should've listened to 'er. Had I, things might've all turned out very differently."

"Maybe," Tristram said. "But maybe not." His expression was grim. "They were determined."

Branok, that is. And Tamsyn, who we'd since learned had been part of the scheme from the beginning. The exact nature of their relationship and what he'd promised her to convince her to take part was not clear. It might never be. But her telling Lord Gage that she'd seen Branok walking along the cliffs was all part of their ploy, hoping that while he searched for Branok, he might also finally lead them to the treasure.

It had all been expertly played. Even Tamsyn's decision to understate the matter by telling us she'd only recognized Branok from a distance. The doubt she'd allowed to fester had ultimately made it all the more believable to Lord Gage. Particularly with Bevil baiting him and the others sowing their own seeds to drive him out wandering.

When Branok had turned up dead, their suspicion had initially fastened on Lord Gage, but it had rather swiftly shifted to Mery. Which was why one of their conspirators had always been underfoot when we tried to speak with him.

In any case, the affair was over. The treasure was well and truly lost, and the smuggling ring was broken. Whether Mery and Tristram would be able to save Roscarrock House from Branok's silent stakeholder remained to be seen, but I intended to encourage Lord Gage to help them. To finally heal the rift that had existed in their family once and for all. Something told me it wouldn't be difficult to convince him.

We had all already given our statements to the local magistrate, who had taken it upon himself to visit Roscarrock House personally when he'd learned what had happened, and that such an august person as Lord Gage was involved. There was also the lapse in Mr. Cuttance's previous judgment to consider. Neither my husband nor his father believed the coroner's inquest would return a verdict other than justifiable homicide considering the victim proposed to kidnap a nobleman's infant granddaughter, but there were no guarantees.

Imogen appeared in the doorway then, her face etched with lines of sadness.

"Is it my turn to relieve you?" Morgan asked, sitting forward.

"Not yet." Imogen's gaze swung to me. "She's askin' for Kiera. And his lordship," she added as she turned to him.

I stiffened, uncertain I wanted to speak to Amelia. Not after everything that had happened. But if she meant to apologize and ask for my forgiveness, then I knew I should give her the chance. Especially since we'd be leaving in the morning, and I would possibly never see her again.

"Do you want me to go with you?" Gage asked as I began to rise.

I pressed my hand to his chest, urging him to stay. "I'll be fine with your father."

He nodded, letting me go.

Lord Gage met me by the door, offering me his arm. There were deep shadows in his eyes, and I knew this interview was not going to be any easier for him than it was for me. I hoped that whatever Amelia had to tell us wouldn't make matters worse.

Imogen had left Amelia's bedchamber door ajar, and we entered after rapping. It was dark inside, with just a single brace of candles lit. She lay back in her bed, her gray hair fanned out over her pillow. I thought for a moment she'd fallen asleep while waiting for us, but then she opened her eyes.

Her hand lifted toward me, and I slowly stepped forward to accept it. She didn't rush to speak, but merely stared up at me for a few moments, her fingers lightly clutching mine. "I owe ye an apology. All of ye," she added as she looked at her nephew. Her voice shook so much, it was difficult to make out her words. "I never thought . . ." She shut her eyes against the painful thought and swallowed. "I was wrong," she tried again in a steadier voice. Her pale gray eyes glittered with unshed tears. "I know my sayin' so doesn't take it away, but it's all I 'ave."

I nodded, letting her know I understood, extending her the grace to accept her apology even though part of me still resisted. In time, I would be glad I'd done so.

"That, and the truth about your granfer," she told Lord Gage, who still stood stiffly by the door. "Should've told ye before, but ye weren't ready to hear it, now, were ye?"

She'd already told me how her father had believed the treasure was cursed and was intent on keeping his grandson away from it, but that wasn't all she had to say.

"I know it's not what ye want to hear, but your granfer bought you that commission to protect ye. When the magistrate decided to make an example of ye, because of the treasure, because of the rampant smuggling. Because preventive officers had killed a *boy* . . ." She broke off, breathing hard. "He knew that ye couldn't remain 'ere. 'Twasn't safe. Not that your father would've allowed it anyway. And if your granfer simply paid the fine, then ye would return to your father, and he would make your life a misery."

I could tell by the expression on Lord Gage's face that he knew this to be true. He'd admitted how unhappy his life had been at Liftondown, how useless his father had deemed him.

"So the best solution, the only solution, was to give ye a productive occupation far from here. The Royal Navy seemed like it would suit ye. And so it did. Ye became a fine man," she declared. "But when ye were young, your granfer could see what was comin'. Ye were a restless, impish boy, who already had more charm than ye had a right to. And ye were growin' into a 'andsome, restless man who would only get 'imself into greater trouble. Your granfer did the best by ye he could, and that meant gettin' ye away from here and your home in Devon." Her eyes glinted with approval. "He was right proud of the man ye became. A man ye never would've been had ye stayed."

With this last pronouncement, her head seemed to sink deeper into the pillow. "He loved ye, my boy. More than you'll ever know."

Lord Gage's features were stark in the candlelight, and his eyes glinted with an emotion he could not hide. I didn't know if these words would heal him fully, but they were certainly a start.

"Now," Amelia pronounced on an exhale. "I must rest."

We took that as our cue to be dismissed, and I reached for my father-in-law's arm, cradling it close to my side in what comfort I could offer as we left the chamber.

The world was shrouded in mist the following morning when we departed Roscarrock House, preventing me from having one last glimpse of the sea. But after the previous day's misadventure, I wasn't certain I wanted to. I rode on horseback alongside Gage while his father, Emma, and our staff filled the two carriages rattling over the roads behind us. I'd feared that

Emma might suffer from nightmares after the terrors we'd experienced, but her sleep had seemed to be as sweet and dreamless as always. Mrs. Mackay had assured me she was too young to remember anything, and that was a blessing.

Instead, it had been Gage and I who had endured a restless night, trading turns comforting each other when we woke bathed in sweat. As such, the cool mist against my skin was bracing, helping to wash away the film of fatigue from my mind. For a moment as the fog thickened, I was reminded of my midnight ride with a coarse sack pulled over my head. My muscles responded with lingering fear, but then the haze thinned, revealing the sign at the crossroads leading to Trelights and beyond.

A single red-billed chough perched at the top, watching us with its beady, knowing eyes. There was no way to tell if it was the same bird that had helped me at Lundy Hole, but I chose to believe it was.

"Thank you, sire," I murmured, touching the brim of my sugar-loaf hat.

He gave one low chortle and then took flight.

I turned to find Gage looking at me in question.

"In case he's King Arthur," I explained, choosing for once not to elaborate. Let him believe it was mere whimsy. There were simply some mysteries that were not meant to be explained.

A truth it would have served me well to remember when, with the turn of the new year, we went home to Edinburgh. Work was being completed on the dower house at Bevington Park in preparation for our return the following summer. Meanwhile, we rejoined my family and our friends in Scotland and resumed projects too long set aside for other pursuits. Had I but known that the art which for so long had proven my solace could one day turn deadly, a great calamity might have been avoided.

HISTORICAL NOTE

As with all my novels, I love to weave interesting historical events, facts, and figures with fictional elements. *A Deceptive Composition* is no different.

A large part of the novel is set at Roscarrock House, which is based in part on Roscarrock House Farm near Port Isaac in Cornwall. Many of the external details of the house and the landscape surrounding it are taken from reality, but some of the internal construction has been altered to suit my purposes. Most of the coves, points, and villages, as well as St. Endelienta's Church, are also actual sites in the corresponding area.

The strange grouping of trees at Liftondown that Kiera notes is rather famous to those native to the area, or who frequently travel there. They can be seen from the A30 motorway, and for many they indicate that they're on the doorstep of Cornwall. This copse of trees probably did not exist in 1832, but I couldn't resist utilizing it, nonetheless.

Smuggling is rather notoriously linked with Cornwall, and

for good reason, though smuggling, in fact, occurred all over the British Isles. By 1832, most free trading had been suppressed by the creation of a new preventive force and by changes to the laws that levied heavier penalties on the act and no longer made it as profitable. The smuggling that did continue was usually done by sending agents to France or elsewhere to purchase contraband and hire ships to sail the goods to the edge of territorial waters, where the goods were either sunk in tubs to be retrieved later or were transferred to smaller fishing boats, which would carry the illicit cargo to shore. Most local smugglers did not become wealthy, but it rather supplemented their low incomes as fishermen, miners, and farmers.

One of the most famous smugglers was John Carter, the "King of Prussia," who operated out of Prussia Cove near Mount's Bay with his brothers. Despite their chosen occupation, they had reputations for being upright, honest men, and they did, indeed, ban coarse talk from their ships.

Wrecking is another practice which is infamously connected to Cornwall, though it also happened all over Britain. While it's true that the Cornish had a reputation for being able to pick a wreck clean with precision and speed, they also risked their lives regularly to save the crew members of floundering ships. The notion that they purposely lured ships to their doom on razor-sharp rocks is more legend than reality. If it ever happened at all, the instances were very few.

One noteworthy wreck occurred on January 19, 1526. A great ship of the King of Portugal called the *St. Andrew* was driven ashore by a tempest near Gunwalloe. It was rumored to have treasure aboard—all or most of which promptly disappeared. This wreck and the wrangling between the Portuguese, the English government, and the local landowners over who had rights to the treasure inspired the tale weaved by my droll teller, which was my creation.

Droll tellers were much like traveling minstrels, wandering through Cornwall sharing folklore and ballads. Cornish folklore is a rich and absorbing subject. I mention just a few of the more famous myths and tales, as well as their beliefs in wind charms and various other rituals. Witch marks were not exclusive to Cornwall but can be found in old buildings all over Britain.

The red-billed chough native to Cornwall is a fascinating bird. It's easy to see where the notion that King Arthur chose to take the form of one came from. They are beautiful and canny creatures. Mischievous, too.

John Opie was a self-taught artist from Cornwall known as "the Cornish Wonder." He painted mostly portraits and was highly sought after in the late-eighteenth and early-nineteenth century. He was, indeed, lauded by none other than Sir Joshua Reynolds as "a Caravaggio and Velásquez in one." High praise, indeed.

Edward Trelawny is a fascinating figure. Sailor, author, adventurer, friend to Lord Byron and Percy Bysshe Shelley. The list of amusing anecdotes about his life is long, though there is also great debate about how many of them are actually true. But given the fact that he was from Cornwall and that he took part in the War of Greek Independence where Gage possibly could have met him, I couldn't resist including him even in a limited capacity.

One final note about my inclusion of the Cornish specialty stargazy pie. While this is a real dish—one that is said to have originated in Mousehole to commemorate fisherman Tom Bawcock's heroic actions in saving the village from starvation sometime in the sixteenth century—it is not known when precisely the pie came into being. The earliest recorded mention of the recipe that I could locate was printed in a magazine in the 1920s. As such, stargazy pie might not have existed in 1832, but it also feasibly could have. So I decided to serve it up at the Roscarrocks' party.

ACKNOWLEDGMENTS

Two thousand twenty-three was a stressful year for me, and because of it, I had to rely even more on the people whom I consider my support team than I usually do. I literally would not have made it through the year without them. I'm so incredibly grateful to each and every one of them!

My husband, Shanon, who kept the house running and our daughters fed, and who repeatedly picked me up off the floor and out of whatever puddle of anxiety and frustration and despair I'd dissolved into.

My daughters, whose love and laughter light up my life and make me want to keep going and doing my best.

My parents, whose love and support mean the world.

My agent, Kevan Lyon, who always has my back and an ear to listen.

My editor, Michelle Vega, who almost seems to know how to finish my sentences at this point. I'm so thankful the Lady Darby series continues to be shepherded in her hands.

The editorial team at Berkley, who always do such stellar work.

My cousin Jackie Musser, whose understanding and advice is invaluable.

All my friends and family for their unending support, with special shout-outs to my brothers, my sister, my sisters-in-law, my cousin Kim, my Mom's Group; and in particular, my mom BFFs—Anita, Jessica, Lauren, and Karen—for listening to me grumble and feeding my soul with chocolate and hugs.

And last but not least, a hearty thank-you to my readers, whose love and support, whether relayed in person, posted to social media, or sent in a private message, helps keep me going.

Photo by Shanon Aycock

Anna Lee Huber is the award-winning and *USA Today* best-selling author of the Lady Darby Mysteries, the Verity Kent Mysteries, and the historical fiction title *Sisters of Fortune: A Novel of the Titanic*. She is a summa cum laude graduate of Lipscomb University in Nashville, Tennessee, where she majored in music and minored in psychology. She currently resides in Indiana with her family and is hard at work on her next novel.

VISIT ANNA LEE HUBER ONLINE

AnnaLeeHuber.com

Ready to find
your next great read?

Let us help.

Visit prh.com/nextread